THE
BOOK
EATERS

The Book Eaters

SUNYI DEAN

HARPER
Voyager

Harper*Voyager*
An imprint of HarperCollins*Publishers* Ltd
1 London Bridge Street
London SE1 9GF

www.harpercollins.co.uk

HarperCollins*Publishers*
1st Floor, Watermarque Building, Ringsend Road
Dublin 4, Ireland

First published by HarperCollins*Publishers* Ltd 2022
1

A catalogue record for this book is
available from the British Library

ISBN: 978-0-00-847944-2 (HB)
ISBN: 978-0-00-847945-9 (TPB)

This novel is entirely a work of fiction.
The names, characters and incidents portrayed in it are
the work of the author's imagination. Any resemblance to
actual persons, living or dead, events or localities is
entirely coincidental.

Printed and bound in the UK using 100% renewable electricity
at CPI Group (UK) Ltd

This book is produced from independently certified FSC™ paper to ensure
responsible forest management.

For more information visit: www.harpercollins.co.uk/green

For my mother,
who has been a force of nature her entire life;
and for my dear friend John O'Toole,
who is something of a Jarrow.

ACT 1
DUSK

1

DEVON BY DAY

PRESENT DAY

We have just begun to navigate a strange region; we must expect to encounter strange adventures, strange perils.

—Arthur Machen, *The Terror*

These days, Devon only bought three things from the shops: books, booze, and Sensitive Care skin cream. The books she ate, the booze kept her sane, and the lotion was for Cai, her son. He suffered occasionally from eczema, especially in winter.

There were no books in this convenience store, only rows of garish magazines. Not to her taste, and anyway she had enough books to eat at home. Her gaze skipped across the soft porn, power tools, and home living publications down to the lowest strata, where children's magazines glowed pink and yellow.

Devon ran short, ragged nails across the covers. She thought about buying one for Cai, because he seemed to like reading that kind of thing at the moment, and decided against it. After tonight, his preferences might change.

She walked to the end of the aisle, linoleum squishing beneath her heeled boots, and set her basket at the checkout. Four bottles of vodka and a tub of skin cream.

The cashier looked at the basket, then back at her. "D'you have ID?"

"Pardon?"

"Do you, have, any ID?" he repeated, slowly, as if to someone hard of hearing.

She stared. "I'm twenty-nine, for Christ's sake." And looked every year of it, too.

He shrugged, crossed his arms. Waiting. Wasn't much more than a kid himself, at most eighteen or nineteen, working in the family shop and likely trying to follow all the rules.

Understandable, but she couldn't oblige him. Devon didn't have any ID. No birth certificate, no passport, no driver's license; nothing. Officially, she didn't exist.

"Forget it." Devon shoved the basket at him, bottles clinking. "I'll get a drink somewhere else."

She stalked out, annoyed and flustered. Hordes of teenagers bought booze from other corner shops all the time. It was a daily occurrence around here. That someone would choose to card *her*, so clearly an adult, was ridiculous.

Only after she'd crossed the badly lit street did she realize that she'd left without buying the skin cream. It was a small failure, forgetting the lotion, but she failed Cai so constantly in so many different, myriad ways that even this tiny mistake was sufficient to wring her insides with fresh anger.

She considered going back for it, then checked her watch. The time was pushing 8 P.M. Already in danger of running late.

Besides, eczema was nothing compared to his hunger. Much more important to feed him.

Newcastle-upon-Tyne was a pretty enough city, if a little rowdy for Devon's liking. This time of year, the sun set at 4 P.M. and the sky was already fully dark, the lamps abuzz. The lack of ambient light suited her mood. Compulsively, she checked her phone with its short list of contacts. No texts. No calls.

She slunk past a row of decrepit terraces. Passersby drifted up and down the pavement. A tight knot of people huddled outside one of the houses, drinking and smoking. Music leaked through curtainless windows. Devon took a left off the main street to avoid the crowds.

There were so many things to remember when she was out and around humans. Feigning cold was one of them. Thinking of it, she drew her coat tight around her, as if bothered by the chill. Walking with sound was another. She scuffed her feet with deliberate heaviness, grinding gravel and dust beneath her heels. Big boots helped with the plodding tread, made her clunky and stompy like a toddler in adult wellies.

Her vision in darkness was another awkward one. Having to remember to squint, and to pick her way across a detritus-littered pavement that she could see with perfect clarity; having to feign a fear she never felt, but which should have ruled her. Solitary human women walked with caution in the night.

In short, Devon had always to act like prey, and not like the predator she had become.

She picked up the pace, keen to get home. The flat she rented (cash only, no questions) occupied a squalid space above a tire shop. In the daytime it was noisy, reeked of oil, and filled with the conversation of customers. The evenings were quieter, if no less foul-smelling.

Down the alley, up the stairs to the back entrance. There was no street-facing door, but that was a good thing. Meant she could come and go by dark side alleys, unwatched by curious eyes—and so could her visitors, when she had them. Privacy was essential.

Devon fished out a set of keys, hanging around her neck on a lanyard. The cord was entangled with a brass compass on a steel chain. She shook the lanyard free, slotted the key in, and wrestled briefly with the lock before stepping inside.

Since neither she nor her son required light, the flat sat in perpetual dark. It saved on the energy meter and reminded her a little of home, back when home had been welcoming: the cool unlit calm of Fairweather Manor, with its shade-tinted hallways and shadow-layered libraries.

She was expecting human company, though, and switched on all the lights. Cheap bulbs flickered into anemic existence. The flat contained only a claustrophobic living space, a small kitchenette with fold-out table, a bathroom veering off to the left, and a locked bedroom to her right where her son spent much of every day. She dropped her bag by the door, hung her coat on a hook, and clunked across to his room.

"Cai? Are you awake?"

Silence, then the faintest of shuffles from within.

"No lotion, sorry," she said. "They were out. I'll get some tomorrow, aye?"

The shuffling stopped.

Always, she was tempted to go in and offer comfort of some kind. By the three-week mark, starvation would have ravaged him to thinness, his suffering spiraling into unbearable agony as his body began to produce toxins. The madness already gnawed his mind, incurable except through his next feed, and even after feeding, the craving would remain ever-present. He would either sit in a corner, huddled up and unresponsive, or else attack her in a frothing rage.

Impossible to know which reaction she'd get and so, fingers shaking, she checked and double-checked the bolts instead of going in. One on the top and one on the bottom, both solid things she'd installed herself, and one regular lock that required a key. The room had no window, courtesy of its awkward layout in relation to the shop; no additional security needed there. For once.

Someone knocked at the entrance to her flat. She jumped, felt chagrined, then checked her watch. Ten past eight; bang on time. Just as well she'd not gone back for the lotion.

Devon went to let in her guest. He had a name, but she would not allow herself to think it. Better to consider only his role, his profession: the local vicar. He needed to be no more and no less.

The vicar waited anxiously on her doorstep, wearing a black-and-mustard coat that might have been fashionable forty years ago. He had kind eyes, a quiet demeanor, and impressive patience with his quarrelsome congregation. Not touchy-feely with kids and no severe personal problems that she could find after two weeks of intense stalking. Everyone had small vices and little problems, always, but that was a given, and she could cope with the small stuff. They were only human, after all.

"Thanks for coming." Devon hunched herself smaller. Be uneasy, be reluctant, and above all, be vulnerable. The sure-fire act that suckered them every time. "I didn't think you would."

"Not at all!" He offered a smile. "As I told you on Sunday, it's no trouble."

Devon said nothing, looking sheepish and fiddling with the compass around her neck. She'd done this conversation or some variation of it so many times, tried all kinds of lines, and found it was better to let them take the initiative. Probably she should have put on something more feminine to look even more unthreatening, but she despised dresses.

"May I come in?" he ventured, and she feigned embarrassment for her rudeness, stepping aside.

His gaze snagged on the dilapidated interior. Devon couldn't blame him. She gave the usual, awkward apologies for the state of the flat while he gave the usual demurring reassurances.

That ritual completed, she said, "My son is in a bad way. I spoke to him earlier, and he didn't answer. You may not have much luck, I'm afraid."

The vicar nodded, lips pursed with concern. "If you are happy for me to try, I will see if I can speak to him."

Devon clenched her teeth to hold back a contemptuous laugh. As if talking could solve problems like this. Wasn't the vicar's fault, she'd been the one to say that Cai had depression, but hysteria crept up on her nonetheless.

The vicar was still awaiting a response. She managed a tight nod, hoping he'd read her emotions for the right kind of conflicted, and led him to the locked door.

"You lock your son in his room?" He sounded shocked, and she could feel the weight of his judgment as she undid each bolt. No doubt he thought she had something to do with Cai's present mental state.

If only he knew.

"It's complicated." Devon turned the key and paused, aware her heart was racing. "I need to ask you something."

"What is it?" The vicar was wary, his senses alert to a danger that his eyes could not perceive.

Didn't matter. He'd been lost the moment he stepped inside.

She met his gaze. "Are you a good person?" The question that consumed her, every time. Every victim. "Are you kind?"

He frowned, considering his words. Trying to understand what reassurance she sought, not that he had a cat's chance in hell of guessing. Still, his hesitation was its own reassurance. The bad ones lied, quick and smooth—or worse, brushed it aside, sometimes with humor. Only those with a conscience would stop and evaluate her question.

"None of us are truly good," the vicar said, at last. He put a hand on her shoulder, so gently, so kindly, and she almost threw up on the spot. "All we can do is live by the light we are given."

"Some of us don't have any light," Devon said. "How are we supposed to live, then?"

He blinked. "I—"

Devon caught his wrist, wrenched the door open, and shoved him in. The vicar wasn't frail but Devon was far stronger than she looked and had the element of surprise. He stumbled forward, startled and gasping, into the darkness of Cai's room. Devon yanked the door shut and held it hard.

"I'm so sorry," she said through the keyhole. "I'm just doing the best I can."

The vicar didn't answer. He was already shouting and thrashing.

Really, it was pointless to apologize. Victims didn't want your sorry-so-sorrys when you were hurting them, they wanted you to stop. Devon couldn't oblige, though, and apologies were all she had these days. Apologies, and booze.

The noise of the vicar's muffled struggling trickled away in a minute or less. She could never decide which was worse: the wailing, or the silence. Maybe they were equally bad. After a moment of dithering, she let go of the doorknob. No point locking up. Cai wouldn't be dangerous, not anymore, and better to make sure he could leave his room if he wished.

The flat oppressed, mildewed walls crushing her spirit to flatness. After so many days of ravenous hunger, her son would need to sleep off his feed. In the meantime, she wanted a drink and there was no vodka in the house.

No, wait. She still had a half bottle of whiskey, left behind by the previous person she'd brought to her home. Devon didn't like whiskey, but right now she liked being sober even less. A couple minutes of rifling through the cabinets turned up the errant alcohol.

Bottle in hand, Devon locked herself in the tiny, dingy bathroom and drank into oblivion.

✳ ✳ ✳ ✳ ✳

2

A PRINCESS OF THE MAGIC LINE

TWENTY-TWO YEARS AGO

She was a princess of the magic line. The gods had sent their shadows to her christening.

—Lord Dunsany, *The King of Elfland's Daughter*

Devon was eight years old when she met her first human, though she did not realize what he was at the time. Or rather, she did not realize what *she* was.

Growing up, there had only been the Six Families, scattered across different regions of Britain. Devon's family was the Fairweathers, whose North Yorkshire estate was wedged between low-lying hills and wild moorland. Uncle Aike was the patriarch of their manor because he was the wisest, even though he was not the oldest. Under him were a succession of other aunts and uncles ranging from barely adult to discreetly ancient.

And under *them* were the seven Fairweather children, of whom all except Devon were boys. There were very few women around, for girl-children were rare among the Families. The uncles outnumbered the aunts, just as the brothers outnumbered their sister, and no brides were in residence at the time. Devon's own mother was an unremembered face, having long since moved on to another marriage contract.

"You're the only princess in our little castle," Uncle Aike would say with a wink. Tall and gray-haired, he enjoyed folding his lanky frame into comfortable chairs and drinking copious quantities of inktea. "You get to be Princess Devon. Just like in the fairy tales, eh?" He would make a little flourish with his hands, a smile crinkling up the corners of his mouth.

And Devon would laugh, put on a crown made from braided daisies, and run around the yard in her tattered lace dress shouting *I'm a princess!* Sometimes, she tried to play with the aunts, because if she were a princess then they ought to be queens. But always, the older women withdrew from her with anxious glances, rarely leaving their own bedrooms. Devon eventually decided they were boring and left them alone.

The house itself was a ten-bedroom building, three stories high. It might have been quite ordinary for manors of that type if not for the haphazard collection of parapets, extensions, tile roofs, and Gothic flourishes. ("Courtesy of your great-uncle Bolton," Uncle Aike had said once. "Architecture was his, ah, treasured pastime.")

Beneath the ground, more levels sprawled with delightfully twisted passageways. Devon knew every nook and corner, from the dark sublevel halls to the sun-filled music rooms of the upper floors.

And the libraries. Like the other Families, the Fairweathers had libraries with a flavor all their own: vintage books stitched from carefully aged leather— the darker, the better—with textured, embossed covers. When opened, the brown-edged pages flaked in soft, dry puffs, smelling faintly of March rain. One bite and Devon's bookteeth could sink straight through those covers and chewy strings of binding, tongue alive with the acidic tang of ink-tinged paper.

"Biblichor," Uncle Aike liked to say, rolling the word in his mouth. "That is a word that means *the smell of very old books*. We love biblichor, here. And other old things."

"Everything in the house is old," Devon giggled. Like the paintings in the downstairs dining room; four hundred years old, apparently. "I think *you're* very old!"

Uncle Aike always laughed, was never offended. "Maybe I am, princess, but you'll never make it to my age with that tongue of yours!"

That tongue of yours. Lots of people commented on Devon's tongue. She stuck it out, sometimes, inspecting it in the mirror. There was nothing special about her tongue that she could ever see.

The land they lived on stretched vast to the eyes of a child. Rocky hills couched moorland, full of hollows and peat bogs. In summer, when the moors bloomed purple with heather, Devon chased rabbits and grouse birds. Twice she found otters, whose little fangs looked like her own growing bookteeth. In winter, the grass dried up and crisped with frost. She built snowmen with her brothers and they ran together, ever barefoot, through the hillocks and valley forests.

And then, one January morning, eight-year-old Devon went out on her own in search of snow buntings and red fox vixens. She had heard the foxes barking in the night and hoped to catch a glimpse of one scampering across the snow, like flame racing across paper.

She'd hardly gone three hundred yards, crossing into the small wood behind the house, when an unfamiliar noise snagged her attention. Someone was crashing through the trees and snow with loud, clumsy steps. No one at Fairweather Manor walked so heavily and Devon, intrigued, went to investigate.

A man she didn't recognize slogged and huffed through freshly fallen snow. He was of indeterminate Adult Age, with dark hair and warm brown skin, his chin fully bearded. A curling black moustache framed his nose. Weirdly, he wore heavy boots, long trousers, funny knitted things on his hands, and bizarre puffed clothes that buttoned up to his chin. Another knitted thing sat on his head.

It took her a moment to recognize his gear as gloves, coat, and hat. They were things she knew from stories but had never seen on a real person. He looked so different from adults on the estate, who were rather paler and mostly dressed in dusty old suits. She wondered if he might be a knight of the Six Families, but knights usually traveled in pairs, on motorcycles, with a dragon in tow. He had no partner and no dragon and *definitely* no motorcycle.

She circled behind and tapped his shoulder.

"Hi," she said, and snickered when he nearly fell over with shock. How had he not seen her? All that fabric must have muted his senses.

"Holy—!" He checked himself, took a breath. Frost dusted his dark side-burns, and the hems of his trousers were soaked from melted snow. "Where did you come from, little one?"

Devon was utterly delighted. It'd been at least two years since she'd managed to sneak up on anyone. "Are you one of my cousins?" She skipped around him in a circle. "I haven't seen you before. Why aren't you in a car? I thought all the cousins came in cars."

"Cousin? No, I don't think so." For some reason, he kept staring at her bare feet and knees, and her sleeveless linen dress. "Aren't you cold, love?"

She stopped in her tracks, puzzled. "What do you mean?"

She knew about cold from eating all the right books. Cold was what made snow happen, instead of rain, just like in the Snow Queen story.

It was snowing now, light flakes landing on her arms and filling in her footprints. And it felt different from heat: balmy, instead of spikey. But cold was a part of the world and its seasons, a sensation detached from reaction. Not something that you had to do anything about.

"Strong kid," he said, eyebrows raised. "To answer your question, I'm not a cousin. I'm a guest, I suppose."

Now that, Devon understood. "You're very rude, then," she said, hands on hips. "If you really are a guest to the house, you're supposed to tell me who you are and where you're from."

She knew that non-Cousin people existed in the world: humans, who ate animal flesh and dirty plants plucked from the soil. But guest or not, Family or not, everyone had to show what Uncle Aike called *basic courtesy*.

"Is that so?" A tentative smile. "Very well, my apologies. I'm Amarinder Patel, or 'Mani' for short. I'm a journalist from London. Do you know London?"

Devon nodded. Everybody knew London. That was where the Gladstones lived, far down south. They were the biggest, richest, and most powerful of the Families. She'd met some of their visiting cousins once.

"And you are?" Mani's smile stabilized, became more genuine.

"I'm Devon Fairweather of the Six Families," she informed him. "All of this land belongs to Fairweather Manor."

"The Six Families?" he echoed.

Devon gave up being polite. "What's a jerna . . . jernaliss?" If he wasn't going to do the right words, then neither would she.

"Jour-na-list," he said, with slow emphasis. "The investigative kind. That means I do research and go chasing strange stories. Sometimes, the things I discover appear on the telly. Isn't that exciting?"

"What's the telly?"

Another pause, shorter this time. He was learning to hide his surprise. "Devon . . . interesting name, by the way . . . I actually came here in search of your family. There are rumors about a remote clan living in the moors. I was hoping I could write a story—"

"A story? Like, a new one?" Devon was immediately interested. "Can all jour-na-lists write stories?"

"Well—"

"Will you write one just for me?" Questions burst from her in an excited flurry. "Can I eat it when you're done? I've never had a story written for me to eat!"

The smile slid from his face, like melting snow from a roof. "Eat it?"

"Is that how stories are made? I always wondered but Uncle Aike said he'd tell me when I was older. How do you write a story? I can't write a story. Will it be a book when you're finished? Do all stories become books?"

"You can't write?" he said, bewildered.

"Huh? Of course not!" She goggled at him. "How can we write?" If book eaters could write, they wouldn't need other people's books. The uncles had told her that.

Mani let out a slow breath. "I see." He turned up the collar of his coat. "Do you have a mum or dad?" When she looked confused, he added, lips twisting, "Someone who looks after you. A grown-up."

"Oh. D'you mean Uncle Aike?" Devon said, trying not to let her disappointment show. Uncle Aike got all the visitors. "I guess I could take you to him." She knew the stranger wouldn't be wanting to see the aunts, because nobody ever wanted to see the aunts.

"Sure," Mani said darkly. "Let's meet your uncle Aike."

Devon skipped through the snowdrifts, disappointment giving way to self-consolation. So what if the visitor wanted to see Uncle Aike? She'd found him first. Ramsey would be so jealous. Her other brothers, too, but she didn't like them as well as Ramsey; most were much older and very boring and didn't play with her so much. Anyway, she would rub it in Ramsey's face all week. Maybe *two* weeks.

The forest thinned rapidly into rocky hills whose hard edges were softened with frost. The house unfolded into view, giving the illusion of a pop-up children's book, the ancient parapets jutting uncomfortably against failing winter light. A few of Devon's brothers were kicking a ball in the wild, overgrown gardens out front. None of them paid any attention to her except Ramsey, who looked over in pure astonishment. Devon took smug pleasure in his shock.

"No power source, no crops, no adequate clothing for any of the children. House in a state of disrepair, and the grounds look poorly tended. Yet they have modern cars on the drive." Mani was muttering into a small black device with a red flashing light. "Can't help but wonder what they eat. Insular and isolated, either way. Could these folks be the source of those old local legends?" He caught her staring and smiled disarmingly.

"Follow me!" Devon said, and tugged him, strangely reluctant, beneath the yawning archway into the entrance hall beyond.

A once-rich carpet lay tattered and flat over a rough-hewn stone floor. Crystalline light fixtures hung darkly immaculate, barren of candle or bulb. If they'd ever been lit, Devon had never seen it. The rooms they passed contained low couches or polished wooden tables, the chandeliers and lamps also unused. Walls were thickly lined with shelves, unending shelves. The scent of biblichor suffused everything.

She took a sharp left at the end of the hallway and skipped into the drawing room, Mani trailing after. Several of her uncles were gathered around a particularly large oak table, playing a game of bridge and drinking inktea. The moment Devon and her prize visitor walked in, all conversation ceased. Every head swiveled their way.

"Uncle!" Devon said. "I found a guest!"

"So you have." Uncle Aike set down his fan of cards. "Who are you, sir?"

"Amarinder Patel, freelance journalist," Mani said, and extended a hand. "I was looking—"

"This is private property." Uncle Aike rose slowly. When not stooping, he stood over six feet. "You are not allowed to be here. Journalists, in particular, are not welcome."

Devon looked on, bewildered. She had never seen her favorite uncle so unfunny. So lacking in Basic Courtesy.

Mani lowered his hand. "I'm sorry, I would have called in advance, but I wasn't even sure you and your family lived here. There's no listed phone number on the land registry, no names on the electoral register—"

"Quite so." Uncle Aike leaned forward, knuckles pressed to the table. "Did it occur to you, Mr. Patel, that perhaps we have no wish to be contacted? Least of all by a *journalist*. Private citizens are entitled to private lives."

The air seemed to thicken, stifling Devon's questions. Something was happening that she didn't understand, though nobody seemed to be mad at her.

Mani adjusted his glasses. "Very well, I'll see myself out."

But Uncle Aike pointed to an empty seat and said, "Nonsense. Done is done, and you are already here. Take a seat, please." A muscle jumped in his cheek. "This is what you have come for, yes? To find the members of my Family? Well, come and speak to us, and we shall converse like adults."

"I . . ." Mani fidgeted with his small black machine, turning it over and over in his hands. To the perspective of this fully human man, he had entered a dark and somber room lined with crumbling tomes and populated by looming, pale-faced figures in old-fashioned suits. Not a situation for the faint of heart.

But after a moment, his professionalism and rationality won out. Mani edged over and sat down, squashed between Uncle Bury and Uncle Romford.

"Dev, my dear." Uncle Aike did not take his eyes off the journalist. "Go and play, yes? We will be a little while, having a chat with Mr. Patel."

"But . . ." Devon glanced mournfully at the table, where her guest sat rigid. She always had to leave when the grown-ups talked, and it was *never* fair.

Uncle Aike shifted his gaze toward Devon, shoulders and face softening a little. "Tell you what. Take yourself up to my room, little princess, and find one of the special-edition fairy tales. But off the lowest shelf, mind. Nothing naughty, aye?"

"Oh! I will, I will!" Devon scampered out of the room in excitement. Though fairy tales were all she ever ate, some were better than others, and the special ones in her uncle's study tasted exquisite: the crisp gold bindings, ribbon bookmarks, bright illustrations with multihued inks. An explosion of color and sparkles, words dangling and lingering on the palate.

The last thing she heard before darting up the stairs was her uncle saying, "Romford, shut that door, if you please."

She forgot all about them by the time she reached the top of the stairs. Uncle Aike's study occupied a smallish room on the east wing, and it was here she headed.

Devon slipped in soundlessly. These walls held Renaissance paintings and an eclectic selection of instruments, including a Chinese lute, none of which Devon had ever heard her uncle play. Gifts from 'eaters in other countries, back when traveling abroad had been a little easier. Too much paperwork, nowadays.

A desk and some chairs made for a cozy sitting area; a king-sized bed took up much of the remaining floor space. The windows had long since been boarded over on the inside and fitted with yet more shelves. The closest shelf housed multiple copies of various Arthurian legends; those were usually given to her brothers. Full of stories that girls didn't need to know.

Below that was a row of fairy tales. "Beauty and the Beast," "Cinderella," "Sleeping Beauty," and "Snow White." Various others. All stories of girls who sought and found love, or else who fled their homes and found death. She could almost hear him saying, *The lesson is in the story, my dear.* That was the shelf her uncle had specified.

Devon had other ideas.

She dug out the little wooden stool her uncle kept under the bed and dragged it over. She could, if she stood on her toes, just reach the tallest shelf, which was much more exciting.

From this vantage point she couldn't see what books were there, but it didn't matter. All of those books were forbidden, and thus desirable. Even the most diligent of children got tired of the same meal, day in and day out; she couldn't miss the chance to try something different.

Her fingers closed around the edge of a paper-bound spine and Devon pulled the book free, nearly losing her balance. Her uncle would be cross if he found out, and she might have to eat nothing except boring dictionaries for a whole week, but the excitement of something forbidden seemed worth the risk.

She sat on the stool and examined her prize. *Jane Eyre* was stamped across the binding in a perfunctory script. The red leather cover was embossed with an illustration of a young woman surrounded by flowers. The printing date meant that the author was long dead. A shiver ran through her. That words could remain, printed anew and afresh long after the original writer had died, never failed to amaze. Devon flipped it open at random.

15

* * *

Something of vengeance I had tasted for the first time; as aromatic wine it seemed, on swallowing, warm and racy: its after-flavour, metallic and corroding, gave me a sensation as if I had been poisoned.

How delightfully naughty, how ungirlish and un-princess-like! The idea that vengeance might taste like a particularly exciting book was deeply intriguing. This novel, whatever it was, would surely be far more interesting than the usual fairy tale.

She opened her mouth, teeth unsheathing—and halted. A strange urge came over her to not eat the book at all, but simply to pocket it. To read it, in fact, which was possible to do, if a little wrong.

Reading was a shameful thing. *We consume written knowledge,* her aunts and uncles had said so many times. *We consume and store and collect all forms of paper flesh as the Collector created us to do, clothed as we are in the skin of humankind. But we do not read, and we cannot write.*

Which was fine, except that everybody knew the Collector was never coming back. The book eaters would live and die without ever passing on their gathered information to the Collector's unknowable data vaults. She couldn't see the purpose behind their purpose.

Besides, taking a book from the top shelf was already wrong. It would not hurt to be just a little bit wronger.

One sin beget another; the decision was made in an instant. Devon stuffed the book inside her shirt to take it back to her own room, over in the western wing. She picked her way through the loft to the other side of the manor then climbed down, slipping into her room. By the time she'd read a chapter and hidden the stolen copy of *Jane Eyre* under her mattress, nearly an hour had passed.

She re-emerged into the hallway, straightening her dress and trying not to look criminal. The manor was very quiet, even for a wintry afternoon. The aunts were likely sequestered up in their quarters, from which they rarely emerged. The only sounds were the raucous yelling and shouting of her brothers milling outside but even that seemed muted, and more subdued than when she'd brought Mani through.

She jolted upright. The journalist! How had she forgotten about her guest? Devon took the steps two at a time and half sprinted back toward the drawing room.

But her guest was already gone. In fact, the drawing room was empty except for Uncle Aike, who sat by the fireplace with his feet on a stool. He looked up as Devon entered, and waved her over. "Come in, love. Have a seat."

She snuggled into the chair next to her uncle. "Where's the jour-na-list?"

"Mr. Patel is resting, in a room in the cellar." Uncle Aike had the gentlest hands, never snagging or tugging as he finger-combed through Devon's tangles. "Tomorrow morning, knights will come to take him away."

"Away?" She had only met knights once. They'd been serious and scary, not at all nice or funny like her uncle. "Where to?"

"To Ravenscar Manor," he said, after a moment of hesitation. "It is near the coast, many miles from here. The patriarch there has a use for humans."

"Oh," Devon said, crestfallen that another house would get to steal her guest. "I wanted him to stay."

"I'm sorry, princess. I know you did. But I'm afraid Mr. Patel was not a pleasant man. He wished to tell stories about us to other people."

"Stories are good things. Aren't they?"

"Not all stories are good things, no." Uncle Aike kissed the side of her head. "You only have the right books to eat in this house, because we only give you the right stories, appropriate for a little princess. However, some stories are certainly bad, and your poor Mr. Patel would have written very bad stories."

Devon mulled that over. "Does that mean he was a broken writer?"

"Of a sort." He seemed amused by what she'd said. "Yes, that is a good enough description."

"Oh, I see! Are the Ravenscars going to fix him, Uncle?"

"They certainly will, love," said her uncle, gazing into the fire. "They certainly will."

3

DEVON BY NIGHT

PRESENT DAY

But where did the book eaters come from? There is no evidence to suggest they are a mutant strain of evolution at work, and humanity took thousands of years to develop paper-making technology.

The book eaters themselves tell wildly unbelievable legends of the Collector, an extraterrestrial being who created them to look humanoid, and who placed them on Earth for the purpose of gathering knowledge (book eating) and sampling human experiences (mind eating).

But the Collector, so their bizarre story goes, never returned. Hence the 'eaters remain, remnants of an abandoned alien science project.

—Amarinder Patel, *Paper and Flesh: A Secret History*

Devon dreamed of hell, as she often did these days.

Some humans had sexual fantasies in their nightly visions, or nightmares about going to job interviews naked. Her dream was neither, though it had elements of both.

It always began with the ground opening beneath her feet into a broad tunnel streaked with lava. Cartoonish, that. She fell without resistance or surprise and landed on her knees in a subterranean pit worthy of Dante's *Inferno,* a book that she'd once tried to eat but had spat out because it tasted of brimstone and bile. She'd never had much of a palate for classics.

A voice spoke from the blackness, telling her politely that she would suffer for her sins, and she laughed with relief until she cried. A whip cracked comically, landing across her shoulders, and Devon woke abruptly with searing pain in her spine. She was lying on the bathroom floor, head twisted at an angle and neck protesting with a stubborn ache. Her phone, when she checked it, read 12:04 A.M.

Devon uncurled herself and threw up a belly's worth of whiskey into the toilet. Human food was beyond distasteful and gloopy—she had been curious enough to try it a few times—but alcohol went down easier. Especially wine. Lovely, amazing wine.

Poison expelled, Devon crawled over to the sink and pulled herself to standing. A haggard, lined face peered out from the warped bathroom mirror, haunted by tired circles under each eye. That blend of traits and features, courtesy of her convoluted heritage. Chipped nails, chapped lips, and a Nirvana shirt with more creases than seams completed the bedraggled appearance of an accidental Goth after a bad night out.

"I used to be a princess, you know." Her reflection frowned doubtfully. Princesses in the books she'd read were pretty, delicate things: few of them were six-foot-tall murderesses with a penchant for shorn-off hair and leather jackets. Funny, that.

Devon flipped herself the finger and set about brushing her teeth. Both sets of teeth, because her bookteeth needed cleaning, too. When her breath no longer stank of vomit, she went in search of her son.

Cai had moved from his room to the sofa and fallen asleep on the cushions in a tightly curled ball. So small, so painfully thin. Devon didn't have the heart to move him back to his bed. He might wake if she did, and anyway, he hated being cooped up in that cramped space.

Not that she could blame him. The kind of life he lived would be misery for any child. At his age she'd spent more time outside than in. But Devon's childhood hadn't been ruled by a hunger that drove her to scoop out people's brain matter with her tongue, as Cai's was.

If her son were to have any hope of a functional life, he needed Redemption. Not the religious kind but the chemical kind: a Family-manufactured drug developed specifically for mind eaters. When taken regularly, it allowed him to eat paper the way she did.

The trick was getting ahold of some.

Her mobile phone buzzed on the kitchenette counter. She walked over, picked it up, and flipped the shell open.

> CHRIS
> ive found em. said what u told me to say.
> Lets meet and chat? crows nest pub, 8pm tmrw. will u be there??

Devon thumbed the cheap plastic keys.

Only one of the Families, the Ravenscars, had ever produced Redemption. The Ravenscar patriarchs had kept the ingredients and process a tightly kept secret, which allowed them to maintain a position of power and money over the other Families.

All that changed when, a couple years ago, the Ravenscars had abruptly imploded. Some of the patriarch's adult children had tried to break away from their Family, something that Devon could sympathize with *deeply*. A blood-bath fight broke out that ended with dozens dead, including the patriarch himself. Meanwhile, the surviving Ravenscar siblings disappeared, and took their stores of Redemption.

Good for them; not so good for her son. Cai had been raised on Redemption, like most mind eater children. In the aftermath of the Ravenscar coup, access to the drug dried up almost overnight. All remaining doses were with the knights and kept for their adult dragons.

Cai had only three choices for his future: consume humans, starve to death, or get "put down" by the Families.

Devon wasn't going to let her son starve, nor would she let anyone kill him. The Ravenscars were still alive, somewhere, and that meant there was a chance they could help. If she could convince them it was worth their while.

First, though, she had to find them.

For reasons that Devon could not fathom, the Ravenscars were, as far as she could tell, apparently continuing to manufacture Redemption. There was no reason for them to do so, since they did not have mind eaters of their own to feed.

Whatever their motivations, it made Devon's life easier. For the past year, she had traversed the country, trying to track down the Ravenscars through their chemical suppliers.

In the meantime, she fed her son humans to keep him alive.

After months of searching, she'd finally had a reply. One man, an illicit drug dealer, admitted he was still selling quantities of certain compounds to the Ravenscars. He also claimed he could put Devon in touch. If he were telling the truth, this was the breakthrough she'd sought.

A moaning shuffle broke her reverie. The vicar stirred mindlessly in Cai's room.

Reluctantly, she folded the phone shut. Replying could wait until she got back and Cai was awake. He could help her with the typing.

The vicar lay curled on his side on the floor of Cai's room. A tiny trickle of dried blood ran from his ear. He was still alive; he breathed, he blinked, and his heart still beat. Sometimes he grunted. His survival surprised her. Many of Cai's victims did die from shock, or internal cranial bleeding. Having a chunk of one's brains liquefied and sucked out wasn't pleasant.

But in every practical sense, he might as well have died. His memories, personality, and all he had ever been now belonged to her son. Until the next meal, anyway, when much of that would be overwritten afresh.

Devon went through his worn pockets. Vicars didn't tend to have much money, and he was no exception. She plucked out all the ID but otherwise left the wallet intact. He didn't have enough worth stealing. Not compared to the twenty-odd grand she kept in a bag.

He did have a Bible, at least. Devon liked those. She unsheathed her book-teeth and bit through the spine. Worn leather, loving hands, sweat, communion wine. Words flowed across her tongue, psalms merging with commandments, sacred newborns blending with war and desecration. Wafer-thin paper flesh crinkled delicately with every chew.

Used books never had the crispness of new ones, but they each carried a flavor unique to their owners that Devon, like every proper Fairweather, enjoyed discovering. Twelve bites to finish the book. She wiped ink from her chin, belly pleasantly full even as her head buzzed with archaic verses and old prophecies. Eating settled her mood, and her lingering queasiness from the alcohol abated.

Devon stripped the vicar down to his boxers. He'd wet himself; they usually did. From a sack in the closet, she dug out a selection of tattered, dingy clothes she had collected from charity shops. She dressed him in trousers, shirt, and foul-smelling coat. That done, she put the empty Scotch bottle in her bag and slung it on.

"Up you get." Devon slid an arm underneath his shoulders. He weighed about a hundred and eighty pounds, she judged, but book eaters were strong. She supported him with ease, guiding his shuffling form toward the door. Of those who lived, some could walk, some couldn't. He could. So much the better for her.

Devon checked her watch. Timewise, it was almost half past one in the morning. She steered her charge down the stairs, toward the alley exit. The night hung moonless and dark, punctuated at semi-regular intervals by rusted lamps.

"I'm glad you aren't married," she told him softly as they stepped into a puddle of streetlight. "It kills me to pick the married ones. You know? It's not fair on the children. Or the partners."

The vicar didn't answer. He had no more words to give; the pages of him were blank.

Devon skirted the main streets, sticking to alleys and underpopulated areas, crossing through the local unlit park to avoid a busy neighborhood. In the dark and at a distance, they looked like two lovers, out for an evening stroll, or two drunk friends leading each other home.

Disposing of Cai's victims was one of her biggest hurdles. Ethically difficult, because she struggled with the guilt, but also logistically difficult: the grimly practical aspect of hiding bodies. Even when they survived, she could not keep them with her, incontinent and unable to feed themselves. And simply leaving them at a hospital would be suspicious. Medical examinations might bring to light the strangeness of their injuries.

Fortunately for her, human society already had an entire underclass of people who were functionally invisible.

The homeless shelter came into sight as Devon and the vicar drew closer. Much like the people it served, the building had seen better days. Someone had converted a series of shopfronts by knocking through the walls and replacing the glass windows with metal gratings. Concrete steps led up to a triple-locked door. Some shelters had CCTV, which made things awkward. Devon knew from past experience that this one did not.

She settled the vicar on the steps. He slumped sideways. Devon adjusted him to be more comfortable, tilting his head to a better angle. The absolute least she could do. Then she took the now-empty Scotch bottle from her bag and tucked it into the crook of his arm.

All that done, she cast a final glance around. Empty road, spilled-ink sky, no one about. She gave the vicar a tiny salute. He stared with vacant eyes, a soul unknowing and lost.

"Bye," Devon said, and walked away. She didn't look back, irrationally afraid she might turn into a pillar of salt. The Bible she'd eaten was coloring her fears with a religious tint.

In the morning, someone would find the vicar and bring him inside. Just another poor sod on the streets, having a breakdown, having a stroke, something. They'd be suspicious, but unless they gave him an MRI, no one would ever know what he was missing.

The streets around were dead and still, as if the city were holding its collective breath, and she instinctively matched its silence with her own drifting, fluid walk. Eerie tranquility thickened the air.

Something reflective glinted in the streetlight and she halted, flattening into the nearest shuttered doorway. It was deep enough to hide the lines of her body and from this vantage point, she scoured the streets.

Two blocks down, a solitary man stood in the middle of an intersection. A cream suit cut with a 1980s flair draped his bulky frame. No scarf, coat, or gloves, despite the below-freezing temperatures. A tattoo encircled his neck, visible beneath the unbuttoned collar of his shirt.

Another man walked over to meet him, footfalls eerily silent. Navy pinstripe suit, and the same tattoo etched into his skin, that of a hungry serpent eating its own tail.

Devon wrapped her arms around her chest, squeezing herself tight though she wasn't cold. These men were dragons. Not true mythological beasts, but adult mind eaters, so-named for the stylized tattoos coiling around their throats.

The symbol they bore was old as the Families themselves: an ouroboros dragon that ate itself endlessly. Mind eaters destroyed themselves with their own hunger, for the process of feeding consumed them even as it fed them. An ouroboros was the perfect representation of that bleak concept. Even if given Redemption, which enabled mind eaters to feast on books instead, the *desire* for mind eating never went away.

At some point in childhood, a knight must have inked in those tattoos, as they did for all their charges. Knights had been little more than cast-off sons, once, tasked only with limply enforcing peace between Families and escorting brides between houses.

With the advent of Redemption, they acted now as keepers of monsters, holding dragon hunger in check. Or at least, that was how it was supposed to work. In practice, they tended to wield their "tamed" dragons for their own benefit and gain.

She risked another glance. The two men stood facing each other, so close their foreheads almost touched. If they spoke, it must have been quiet, for Devon could hear no words though she listened acutely. The traffic lights cycled from green to red and still the dragons remained, inert and stationary on the empty road.

Once, she'd feared that life as a dragon would be Cai's fate, tattoo and all. She had bigger problems these days. Like worrying whether her son would go insane before he starved, or whether he'd starve before he went insane.

How much Redemption would the knights have left in their stores? Surely their dragons were fast becoming unmanageable. Like her, they desperately needed to find the Ravenscars. Unlike her, they sought Redemption as a means to reclaim social power; Devon only wanted to save Cai.

Her knees ached from crouching so awkwardly, vision obscured by strands of hair that she dared not brush away. Focus, and control. Be present in the moment. If dragons were roaming, then knights would not be far behind, and that meant she needed to leave the city.

She closed her eyes and opened them again, in time to see a large Volkswagen with tinted windows rumble up from the opposite direction. Tense and still, she watched as the car braked at the intersection and opened its doors. The driver wasn't visible. Both dragons climbed inside. The Volkswagen performed an illegal U-turn and drove off, heading back the way it had come.

Devon blew out a long breath and pulled her jacket tight, as if it were armor that could protect her from danger. Easing from the doorway, she ran home with silent steps.

———•———

Cai was awake when she got back, cradling a Game Boy in his lap.

"You're home again," he said, and she suppressed a wince. He spoke with the vicar's inflection, used the same elongated vowels. These little changes threw her every time. Every victim. "Did you say there was skin cream? I'm itchy."

"No, sorry." She kicked off her shoes, feeling embarrassed and guilty. "Lad at the till carded me for vodka and I walked out, like an idiot. I'll get you some soon, I promise." Always making him promises. One day, she'd keep them.

"It's okay," he said, still absorbed by Mario's endless quest. Outwardly, her son looked like any other five-year-old; small, a little scrawny, dark-haired. Her eyes and her features. The exceptionally long tongue, kept coiled in his mouth, gave him a mushy lisp that Devon found endearing.

But no five-year-old Devon had ever met conducted themselves with such certainty, or such adult poise. He was far too intelligent for his age. Of course, most five-year-olds didn't consume the minds of other human beings for sustenance. Made a big difference, that.

Most days, she wasn't sure how much of Cai remained and how much of him was overwritten with another person. Their memories and thoughts and morality, flooding his mind with their own. She dreaded him remembering and dreaded him having no sense of self. Misery lay down either route.

Devon sat next to him. "How are you feeling?" The couch sagged with their combined weight, springs creaking as she tried to find a comfortable recline.

"Better, I think."

"You think?" she echoed, and brushed hair from his forehead with her fingers. It needed cutting again.

Cai squeezed the Game Boy tight. "I'm still hungry."

"Oh."

"Sorry." He flushed.

"No, no. Don't be." Devon put an arm around his shoulders and hugged him so she wouldn't have to look at his face. "You can't help it. Let me worry about these things. You do you." She added, "It'll be reet, aye?" It was something an aunt had said to her once, and she found the phrase oddly comforting to repeat.

Cai nodded dully. His shoulders were thin beneath her fingers, and the bones of his spine pressed into her arm. Starvation diets would do that to a lad.

His hunger was growing as he aged, and this was the third month in a row he'd needed more than one meal within a span of thirty days. Really, he needed to feed much more than that, but Devon couldn't bear to hunt every week, and logistically it was difficult. She walked the thin line between destroying as few lives as possible, and forcing her son to live in perpetual hunger. As it was, most of every month he was too weak to leave his room.

How the specifics of hunger and feeding actually worked, Devon did not know. There could not be *that* many calories in a few mouthfuls of brain matter, yet without feeding, the madness would set in, whittling away at his fragile psyche. Eventually, his weight would also drop, toxins flooding his system, organs slowly failing. Driven always by need and necessity to consume, per the Collector's biological design.

Cai pulled away, evidently fed up with her hug.

She let him go. "I saw dragons on the streets while I was walking back. We'll have to leave soon."

He pouted at the console, saying nothing. Mario had died on a mushroom while they were distracted.

"Sorry. I know how you hate traveling."

"Where is it this time?" He sounded so listless.

"That's my good news of the evening. I'm meeting the Ravenscar contact." She waved the phone. This meeting with Chris first, grab the contact details he offered, then catch the bus out. Tight timing, but doable. "If this goes well, and they can sell me their cure, we might be going to Ireland very soon." Finally. At long last.

His shrug was sullen. "Can I eat before we go? I'm really hungry." Inside his mouth, that long tongue uncurled and re-curled.

"If I see someone suitable," she said, heart aching at his reaction. He'd lost so much hope over the past few months. She shouldn't expect him to hold out for disappointment yet again. "I'll do my best. But I won't have time to stalk anyone properly."

"I'm not fussed." He leaned across and turned the telly on, flicking idly through the channels before settling on an episode of *Red Dwarf*.

Devon sat for a while, watching despite herself. Lister, Cat, and Rimmer were riding horses, embroiled in some kind of Wild Western scenario. Studio laughter crackled at appropriate moments.

"I thought this was a sci-fi show." Devon didn't catch much television, although she'd eaten a few *TV Guide*s on occasion. It was worth absorbing a modicum of pop culture, if she wanted any kind of shot at fitting in with society.

"They're stuck in an artificial simulation," Cai said, eyes on the screen. "Inside Kryten's head. He's the robot guy."

Devon smiled. "Didn't know you were a fan."

"Oh yes," he said, with an intonation that perfectly mirrored that of the vicar, and a hint of genuine excitement. "When *Red Dwarf* first came out, there was nothing else like it on the telly. Groundbreaking show."

Her smile died, annoyed with herself for walking into such an obvious emotional trap. *Red Dwarf* had first aired fourteen years ago. Long before her son had been conceived or born. The vicar, though, would have been around to see it.

A sour feeling brewed in her belly. One thing at a time, she told herself. Focus on what you can control.

"Hey." She touched his shoulder. "Can you text something for me?" The eternal frustration of not being able to write, even electronically.

"Another text? Do I *have* to?"

"Do you want to find the Ravenscars or not?" she said, waspish, then regretted her sharp tone. He was tired and hungry and exhausted, same as her. She said, more gently, "I know you don't remember what it was like to be on Redemption, but everything will be better when we get that drug again."

"That's what you *always* say," he said, aggrieved. "None of these people ever know anything."

"This one is a dealer, in illegal chemical compounds, who used to do business with the Ravenscar Family," Devon reminded him. She'd explained before; the feedings sometimes confused his memories. "We've been tracking him down since Doncaster, remember? He says he can put me in contact with the Ravenscar twins."

"Okay, okay." He plucked the phone out of her hands. Under her direction, he tapped out *Yes, let's meet. I'll bring cash* and hit Send.

"Thank you." She went to brush Cai's forehead with a kiss; he flinched away. "I'm going to go out this morning and grab you that skin cream, and also our bus tickets. Just in case we have to bail later."

"What about your vigil?" he said. "It's nearly Christmas."

A hollow pain formed in her chest. "I'll hold the vigil if I can. But I have a lot to do first, like getting some more sleep. Too much stalking this week."

"More like too much vodka," he retorted, but he was grinning, and ducked good-naturedly when she swatted at him with a pillow. "I think you need a shower first, 'cause you smell like booze."

"Thanks, kid. Kinda reek yourself, you know."

He stuck his tongue out at her. A momentous bit of effort given it was tubular and eight inches long.

Devon laughed, glad to see something of a child still lingered in him. She threw the pillow at his head and went to take an icy shower.

4

A KNIGHT'S TALE

SEVENTEEN YEARS AGO

"What do you fear, lady?" he asked.
"A cage," she said. "To stay behind bars, until use and old age accept
them, and all chance of doing great deeds is gone beyond recall or desire."
—J. R. R. Tolkien, *The Return of the King*

The whispers were everywhere: *babies made from science.*

The Six Families struggled with fertility. Few girls were born, and those who were born could only carry two children before early menopause set in. Sometimes three, at a stretch.

Out in the wider world, human scientists had begun trying to cure infertility in their own kind, and that excited the Families very much, in case that knowledge could be adapted to book eater women, too.

Devon wasn't supposed to know things like that, since she was still only twelve years old and kept apart from adult business. But Devon also liked to listen at doors and was very good at sneaking around, so she found out anyway.

She told Ramsey all about it while they were playing on the parapets of Fairweather Manor, climbing the sloped tiling as they had so many dozens of times. A mother-bride was arriving that afternoon, after many long years of no new marriages at Fairweather Manor, and they both wanted to catch sight of the procession.

"You're being daft. Devon the Daft," Ramsey said, bracing against the roof. He was always doing that with her name: assigning her a singsong title to go with it. Devon the Distracted. Devon the Dizzy. Or today, Devon the Daft. "Whoever heard of such a stupid thing? Babies born in a test tube? Have you *seen* those things?" He held up a thumb and finger, illustrating the size of a test tube.

"They don't grow *inside* the tube, stupid head," Devon said, edging along the gutter. "They just use the test tubes to help. Like a magical baby-potion." She was guessing, didn't want to admit ignorance.

He laughed. "If you say so!" Ramsey clambered atop the east wing chimney, its flues long since sealed off. "Sounds made-up to me."

"It's not made-up!" Devon perched next to him, fully exasperated by his arrogance. "Everyone's talking about it, and if it works for the humans, then one day, it'll work for us. And if it works for us, then we won't need the knights anymore to arrange all the marriages."

The aunts discussed that a lot, in their private quarters. *No more knights. No more dragons. Women marrying who they please.* And other things that Devon didn't really understand, although she could sense the cautious hope in their words.

Ramsey wasn't listening. "Ey, look! There they are!" He grabbed her arm and pointed.

Devon squinted. A loose knot of vehicles approached in the distance, winding through the moors on the potholed roads toward their manor. The bride was arriving.

Women did not leave home except for marriages, and sometimes parties. Even within the manor, the aunts never seemed to do anything except manage the household or do other tasks that Uncle Aike referred to as *women's work*. And since the Fairweathers had been too poor to afford a wedding during Devon's twelve years of life, this arriving mother-bride would be the first non-Fairweather woman she had ever met.

The procession drew up in a glistening limo, painted the color of chalk.

"It'd have been a horse, back in the day," Ramsey said with a confidence that came from being three years older. "A big white horse with a saddle and . . ." He gestured vaguely. "All that. You know."

"Do you think she could be one of our mothers?" Devon had never seen so much as a picture of her own mother, only heard the name Amberly Blackwood murmured in passing gossip.

"Don't be silly," Ramsey said. "Our mothers have been and gone, all of them. Nobody gets married to the same house more than once."

He was right. She felt chagrined for forgetting.

On the front drive below, the limo door opened with electronic grace and the newest mother-bride of Fairweather Manor stepped daintily from her metal chariot. Pale hair had been teased into a formal style, more suited to a woman twice her age—for she was young, around twenty-two. A white frilled tunic threatened to drown slender shoulders in fabric, and the blue skirt, overwhelmed with embroidery, seemed to weigh more than she did.

"You can tell she's a Gladstone, with that hair," Ramsey said, chin jutted out. "She isn't proper Old Country stock, like us."

Devon rolled her eyes. Ramsey had developed a zealous pride in their heritage lately, even though neither of them had ever been to Romania.

To her mind, Romania, or *the Old Country*, as their elders referred to it, was embroidered dresses on special occasions; it was singing "Star Carol" at Christmas, while one of her brothers ran around them wearing a goat mask; it was offering gifts to the Fate Fairies when new children were born; it was Midsomer parties and harvest celebrations even though they didn't farm or care about solstice; it was strange flower rituals to welcome in the rainy English spring.

But Old Country stock, as Ramsey meant it now, was also dark hair and dark eyes; towering height, strong legs, and broad shoulders. Those traits persevered even as the ethnic heritages of the book eaters had diverged and interwoven over the decades. The palette of their skin tones had broadened, but the Fairweathers remained stocky and looming, strong of build—and nothing like the pale, frail, five-foot-nothing Gladstone girl who had just arrived.

"I think she's sort of beautiful," Devon said, a little dreamy. "She looks like a fairy-tale princess. A proper one."

"Eh. Girl's all right, I guess." Ramsey shaded his eyes. "Hey now, look at them knights! That's a sight to see."

Below, a cavalcade of men in dark gray suits and sunglasses followed the procession at a distance, all ten of them riding pristine motorbikes.

"Maybe you could be one, someday," she suggested, because he always seemed enamored of them.

Ramsey shook his head. "I'd rather be a patriarch of a manor. Money and a house and telling folk what to do." He grinned to himself and Devon rolled her eyes. He was far too daft and cocky.

The knights coasted to a stop in perfect semicircle formation. Some carried an additional rider: brawny men dressed in formal suits. All of them wore full motorcycle helmets, with the visors down. Nothing of their faces or necks could be seen, the grotesque tattoos hidden from sight.

"Dragons," Devon said, uneasy.

"Dragons!" Ramsey straightened up. "I wish we could see one up close."

"It'd eat your brain with its giant needle tongue." Devon stuck her tongue out at him to demonstrate.

He swatted her away. "Don't be a dolt. Devon the Dolt. That's what the Redemption is for. The knights feed them little pills and they don't get hungry for brains."

"Not true," she retorted. "The pills help them not to starve, but they still get hungry and still *want* to eat your brains."

"Can't do it with their helmets on," he said, dismissive.

Down below, the mother-bride cast a glance over her shoulder at the entourage behind her. For a fraction of a second, something like unease settled on her features as her gaze skipped across the dragons' helmeted visages. Then she turned to face forward again, wearing her polite smile.

Aunts and uncles came out in greeting, Uncle Aike foremost among them. At his shoulder followed Uncle Imber, a quiet and tidy man in his mid-thirties. The designated husband.

"You must be Faerdre Gladstone." Even from this distance, Uncle Aike's voice carried. He swept the mother-bride into a hug and pecked each of her cheeks, taking care not to crush the expensive dress. "Allow me to introduce you to Imber."

Devon looked down at her own clothes: a faded linen dress, the lacy sleeves ripped to shreds and the hems too short to cover her nettle-stung ankles. No shoes or socks. Her dresses suffered badly from days spent clambering across the moors, but girls of the Family did not wear shorts and trousers, so that was that.

She looked back at the tidy, well-dressed figure far below. "Do you think you'll ever put in a bid for a wedding?" She couldn't imagine herself as a bride. Easier to imagine Ramsey as someone's husband.

Her brother waved a dismissive hand. "Who wants a wedding? Babies are lame." He laughed. "I'd like a girlfriend someday. Guess it'd have to be a human one."

"That would be nice," Devon said, without thinking.

He shot her a frown. "Girls don't have girlfriends, stupid."

"Some girls do," she said, because she'd read about lesbians in books she wasn't supposed to touch. Like *The Well of Loneliness,* which she'd found in Aunt Beulah's side table once.

"Just like some babies can live in test tubes?" he said, scoffing. "Oh hey, everyone's already gone inside. We should go down, too. They'll be starting the party soon."

"Sounds boring," she said. His dismissiveness stung, made her want to be contrary for the sake of it. "I can't bear to eat 'Rapunzel' for the thousandth time." That much was true.

"We've all eaten those stories a thousand times, and that's good for us," Ramsey said in lecturing tones. "If you eat the same books all the time, your brain will stay fast for longer because it isn't new. But if you eat lots of different books then your brain will run slower."

"What rubbish," she said, trying not to sound uneasy. "I think you're the one making things up, not me!"

"I am not, and it isn't rubbish! It's true, completely true. Uncle Oban ate loads of different books when he was young and filled up his brain with words. Now his head is all full-up with words so he can't hardly move or talk."

Uncle Oban was odd, she had to admit. Ask him a question and it would take him more than half a minute to come up with an answer, his gray eyes staring off into the distance. And walking from his bedroom to the drawing room was a laborious affair, undertaken only twice daily, his steps slow and ponderous.

"Well . . . I still don't care," Devon said, "and I have a better idea than sitting around." She lowered herself off the chimney flues and edged across the tiles, heading for the south side of the manor.

"Hey!" A soft scrabble along the rooftop, followed by a swear word he shouldn't have known, and Ramsey clunked after her. "Where are you going?"

"I want to get into the south library, while everyone is busy meeting the mother-bride." Strands of her dark hair tangled in the breeze. "Are you coming or not?"

"What do you want with the south-side library? That's where the knights leave . . ." He trailed off, eyes widening.

"Where the knights leave their dragons," Devon finished, scooting carefully along the roof's ridge board. "We should have a look at them. I've never seen one up close."

"Are you off your rocker? We can't do that!"

"It's just a look," she said, scornful. "I thought you wanted to see one close up!"

"Well, yeah, I did, but c'mon, they're *dragons*!"

"Oh, don't be such a baby! You're the one who said they're safe because the knights have them trained up," she said, liking her own idea more by the minute. "The party is boring and I've eaten all those books before. Let's have a look at these dragons."

Devon swung her feet over the roof gutter and braced against the downspout to lower toward the window below.

It was against the rules, but she wasn't frightened. Book eater girls were special and rare and didn't get into much trouble. Whenever Devon got into trouble, Uncle Aike never did anything worse than make her eat pages out of a dictionary.

"This is stupid!" Ramsey called down, sounding aggrieved.

"Shut up!" she hissed, and alighted on the wide sill, pressed up against a glass window.

She was immediately disappointed. Rows of oak shelves stood sullen and overladen with books. No one was inside, and there were no dragons to gawk at. Devon frowned, scrutinizing the room carefully.

Ramsey landed on the sill next to her. "Devon the Dumb. Look, the dragons aren't even here. Can we go to the party now?"

"They must be here, the knights always leave them here." She pointed. "One of those back rooms, maybe? We should go in and see."

"I don't think that's a good idea," he said uneasily. "We can't just *go in* and wander around."

"Why not? Are you scared of dragons?" She wriggled her fingers underneath the loose-fitting window. "Or are you only brave when they wear their helmets?"

"I'm not scared, helmets or no," he hissed. "I just think we could get in trouble—"

"So go downstairs and sit in the hall like a good little scaredy-cat. I'll sneak in all by my dumb self without your help." Devon wrenched the window open.

The act threw her off-balance. She pinwheeled backward, teetering on the ledge.

Ramsey grabbed her shirt with a steadying hand. "You wouldn't last five minutes without me."

"I only slipped 'cause you were talking at me." She squashed her too-tall frame through the partially open window.

The south-side library did not get much sunlight. So much the better for preserving the books. The books sat in shadow, carefully dusted and the shelves in pristine condition. Instead of the usual Fairweather preference for dark leather bindings, the cache in here varied enormously: old to new, hardback and paperback, all in different sizes and designs.

Ramsey squeezed in through the window and came to stand next to her. "Five minutes, and then we're leaving," he whispered.

"Shush! If they're in here, they'll hear you."

At least three other rooms led off from this one, fitted with yet more shelves. The farthest room was sealed away from sight behind a shut door, which immediately drew her interest.

"Let's try that postern first." She drifted over the tattered carpets around the L-shaped bend, weaving between cases to reach the farthest end of the library.

"You have really terrible ideas," he muttered. "I bet they're not even in here." His cockiness was evaporating rapidly, to her amusement.

"One way to find out," she said, twisting the brass knob. "And calm down, won't you? I only want to peek."

The door opened soundlessly, just enough for them to squint through the crack.

This side room within was lined with ancient shelves, the wood fractured and dark from years of over-lacquering. Tomes older than the house crowded the space, as did stacks of parchment and vellum written in languages she did not know but could learn from eating if she wished.

But Devon barely registered those forbidden treasures. At the far end of the room stood two men in suits, facing the wall with heads bowed, necks marked with ouroboros serpents in thickly inked tattoos. No helmets. Hands at sides, curled into fists.

Chests rose and fell very slightly with breath, but they otherwise did not move or stir.

"We should go," Ramsey said, in the smallest voice she'd ever heard from him.

Stubbornness welled in her. They'd already come this far. Devon opened her mouth to say *just a second*. But the words wouldn't come out. Sudden uncertainty bubbled in her belly, spurred by the supernatural stillness of the two figures in the room. She had never met any adults who were so *frozen*.

As if sensing her hesitation, the dragons turned around in eerie sync, movements sinuous and fluid.

Bloodshot eyes in pallid faces, nostrils flaring, hands twitching. Full of nervous energy when before they'd been so still, so silent. They strode forward and she did not know whether they were attacking, greeting, or simply curious.

Nor did she care to distinguish. Devon yelped and slammed the door shut, backing away. Suddenly, nosing through off-limits libraries did not seem like such a good idea after all.

"Window," she managed. "Back to the window!"

"Too far, the hall is closer!" Ramsey yanked her around the central shelves toward the south-side library's main entrance.

Behind them, the dragons emerged from the side room, taking diverging paths to circle around the shelves. Picking up the pace as they hunted, wolflike.

Devon and Ramsey skirted another freestanding tower of old books, tumbling over each other in a blind panic to escape—

And crashed straight into a knight.

Ramsey rebounded off the broad chest, landing on his backside and pulling

Devon with him reflexively. She fell atop her brother, tipping her head up to goggle at the man framed in their library's main doorway.

The knight peered down, pale eyes gleaming from a clean-shaven face. He was tall and heavyset, wearing a black suit so stiffly pressed it planed like carved granite. The marks on his collar indicated high rank.

"Hello," Devon said stupidly. She knew this man, though they'd never met: Knight Commander Kingsey Davenport. *Everyone* knew of this man.

The two dragons darted into view, alert and ever silent. They paused on seeing a knight.

"Obedire, dracones." Kingsey drew a languid gesture in the air. "Detain eos."

Both men flowed forward in a blink, one apiece for each child. Devon yelped as enormous hands closed around her biceps, pulling her up and still. Her feet didn't quite touch the floor. Up close, the dragon smelled of sour sweat and over-starched cotton. His palms sweated against her skin.

All she could think about was that tongue, unhindered by a helmet. How well did dragons obey their knights? She was no longer sure of anything.

Ramsey, also held captive, met her frightened gaze with his frantic one.

"I was told this library would be off-limits to children." The commander looked them up and down. "How did you get into this room?"

"It was her idea." Ramsey had the audacity to shoot her a dirty glare, as if he hadn't agreed to everything. "We came in through the window and—"

Devon returned his glare. "I just wanted to look at them. I was only looking. And my brother *chose* to come along." She couldn't believe he would make it all about her. The utter coward.

"Only a look," the commander mused. "You are both very lucky that I came back in to check on the dragons, or you would have found this door bolted from the outside. I can't say for certain what might have happened then." He rolled broad shoulders. "Redemption takes away the need to feed, but it does not take away the *desire* to feed. They still hunger for you, for anyone, to feed on. When it has been years and years since they've fed, as it has for these two, then the craving is strong."

"We won't do it again." Ramsey sounded almost squeaky. "Will we, Dev?"

"Promise," she managed.

"Correct. You will not." Kingsey gestured again. "Obedire, dracones. Desisto. Quiesco."

The dragons let go. Devon landed on her backside with a thump, Ramsey on his knees with a wince.

"Boys of your age have enormous energy and curiosity," the commander said, "but breaking into forbidden areas shows extremely concerning tendencies. I think it is urgent that I speak to your patriarch and bring you back with us when the wedding is over. A lad like you needs the discipline of knighthood."

"You're . . . taking me to be a knight?" The color was paling out of Ramsey's cheeks.

"It was just a mistake," Devon said in a small voice. "We didn't mean any harm—"

"*Rules exist for a reason,*" Kingsey said. "Our rules hold the Families together, keep us safe, and keep order among our kind. Without strict adherence, we risk unraveling. You might view today's mishap as a small infraction, but I think your behavior speaks to willful disobedience and criminal ingenuity, of the kind that often proves socially problematic." He added, "And I think your patriarch will agree with me."

A series of expressions contorted Ramsey's face, each one leaving him paler and more shaken. He opened his mouth and shut it again.

Shock robbed Devon of her earlier annoyance, leaving her hollow and gutted. She folded over, arms clasped around her middle. They'd only wanted a book or two, a meal different and exciting, fun and outside of the usual fairy tales. Yet the day had somehow spiraled from one tiny mistake into a catastrophe and now, if Ramsey were carted off to be a knight—

"What about her?" Ramsey said, tight and low. "It was her idea, her stupid plan, but you're only dragging me off?"

"I didn't mean for this to happen!" she protested. "I never wanted you to—"

"We don't punish girls," the commander said, sounding almost regretful. "But I will say this, young lady. When you break Family rules, understand that those you love will bear the brunt of it, even if you yourself do not. Today, your brother has lost his freedom. Tomorrow it may be one of your children, or one of your uncles and aunts, who takes the fall for your actions. For the sake of those around you, stick with the books you are fed and keep to the boundaries you are given." He rapped her forehead with hard knuckles. "Do you understand?"

She knelt at his feet, cowed by shame.

"Good." He clicked his fingers, as if they were dogs. Or dragons. "Let's have a word with your patriarch."

5

THE HAZEL EYES OF HESTER

PRESENT DAY

Regardless of their origins, I believe that 'eaters have been with us for cen-
turies at a minimum. I am reminded of the myth of vetalas in India, de-
scribed as "evil spirits." They are classed as a kind of early vampire myth, yet
unlike the pishachas (another creature from Sanskrit legend) the vetalas are
not bloodsuckers. Instead, they are more like causers of mayhem, lurking in
darkness, and known for their vast knowledge and deep insight.

Sound familiar? For me, this myth overlaps heavily with what we know
of book eaters.

—Amarinder Patel, *Paper and Flesh: A Secret History*

A sense of unease settled across Devon's shoulders as she ducked into the Crow's
Nest Pub.

She paused in the entryway, trying to suss out the source of her anxiety. Hot
air blasted her cheeks and neck, negating the pleasant outside chill as the glass
door closed softly behind. A tattered wall poster suggested ten helpful ways
to spot cancer; it seemed out of place for a pub. Could 'eaters even get cancer?
One of many things Devon didn't know about her own kind. Girls weren't told
things unless they needed to know.

She craned her head, peering into the main area: high ceilings, plastic
chandeliers, wooden floors shot through with cracks, and streetlights blinking
through leaded windows. Flaking tinsel draped the walls and a plastic tree
lurched in the corner, hung with Poundland baubles. Most people wore bright
colors and cringeworthy Christmas tops, in stark contrast to Devon's own all-
black uniform of jacket, boots, trousers, and shirt.

Aside from the tawdry atmosphere, nothing seemed wrong or out of the ordinary. Yet she couldn't shake that sense of tense watchfulness, an itch between
the shoulder blades that wouldn't quite go away.

Ridiculous. No time for paranoia; she had a job to get on with.

Devon stepped through and pushed her way to the bar. People bustled
around each other, noisy and cheerful. Tomorrow, the pub would be closed

for Christmas Day; tonight, it was open with extended hours to accommodate every alcohol-related need.

She stepped up to the bar, flagged down a barman. "Pint of Guinness, please. Go easy on the head."

"As you like." He pulled the lever, filling a glass. "On your own tonight, then?"

"No." She forced a polite smile and tried not to resent his wholly unnecessary small talk. "I'm waiting on a friend."

"Thought you might be." He handed her the brimming glass and a napkin. "Got any special plans for Christmas?"

The idle question stung.

"Yes," she said, a little sharp. "Later tonight, I'll be holding a vigil for someone I lost ten years ago." The compass weighed like a lodestone.

The barman left her alone after that. Devon paid with a good tip and avoided any further eye contact. She took a long sip from her drink while she waited for Chris, or whatever his real name was.

And waited.

And waited some more.

People brushed past. Laughter rose and fell around her. By eight twenty, she was most of the way through her drink. Devon checked her phone. Nothing. No cancelation, no excuses, they'd simply ghosted. Either Chris-the-illicit-chemical-supplier had gotten cold feet, or he was running late. Neither was a scenario she had time for.

Frustration washed through her frame, amplifying the tiredness, and she leaned against the bar top. If this was a bust . . . Her sanity and patience were a thin veneer these days. Sixteen months of dragging Cai all across England had felt like sixteen years. Exhausting, repetitive, bleak. So many dead ends.

She was finding people, sure. The Ravenscars had sourced equipment and chemical components from a variety of shady human organizations. There were plenty of people to chase up. But such folk were skittish. Many had refused to meet with her or deal with her. Others claimed they no longer supplied that Family.

Chris was the third person to admit he actually had dealt with the Ravenscars, citing one Killock Ravenscar by name. He was also the first to agree to tell her more information—for a price. If he showed up, anyway.

"Pardon, but do you have the time?"

Devon looked over her shoulder. And then looked down—at a much smaller woman. Bright hazel eyes peered up through a pair of rectangular glasses.

Barely over five feet, with rounded shoulders and stocky build. She was somewhere between twenty-five and thirty-five. Her wool coat smelled of expensive cigarettes and her leather handbag was exquisitely made. Devon didn't know a lot about fashion, but she did know a fair amount about leather, having eaten it all through her childhood.

"Eight twenty-five, assuming my watch is accurate."

"Oh." Hazel-Eyes deflated. "That's even later than I thought." Her accent was erratic, a mix of Scottish and Geordie. Border counties, likely enough. Not uncommon in these parts.

"Were you waiting on someone?" Devon twisted toward her.

"A Christmas Eve date, sort of. I think she's stood me up. We were supposed to meet at half past seven." Hazel-Eyes had what Devon thought of as hair-colored hair: a muddy salad of dusty brown and dirty blond. Beneath the expensive coat, the rest of her was that same kind of mishmash, from the brown-green irises and patchwork skirt to the asymmetrical blouse.

"Mine's stood me up, too," Devon said. "Unless they're just late."

Hazel-Eyes squinted at her skeptically. "Do you really think that?"

"No, I guess not." Devon drained the last of her Guinness. "I don't have much luck with people." True on so many levels.

"I think you just haven't met the right person." Hazel-Eyes climbed onto the bar stool. Her feet didn't touch the floor when she sat, unlike Devon's. "Or else you don't give anyone a chance."

"Little of column A, and a little of column B." Devon crumpled a napkin in her palm. She was thinking about how Cai flicked his tongue when he was hungry. "So, um. What's your name? If we're both stuck here, waiting."

"Hester. Like that poor woman in Hawthorne's book, *The Scarlet Letter*? Terribly pretentious, I know." Her grin was self-deprecating.

"Ah, that's not so bad, it's a pretty enough name. Try being a woman called Devon."

Hester snorted. "All right, you win. Let me guess, that's where you were conceived?"

"Nah, Family tradition," Devon said. "A lot of us have location names." Then she added, with rare recklessness, "It was also my grandmother's name, I'm told. She had it worse—her surname was Davenport."

"She was a—oh, I see. Devon Davenport. Ouch." A light, easy laugh. Belonging to someone with a light, easy conscience, no doubt. "Where are you from, anyway? You don't sound like a Geordie."

"Um." The question hit hard, bringing Devon back to reality. Her past was problematic and her goal was to meet Chris, and keep Cai fed. How was this nonsense chat furthering either goal? She needed to end the encounter.

"I'm guessing Derby," Hester said, crossing and uncrossing her legs. Her shoes were either brand-new, or meticulously polished. "Devon from Derby. Am I close?"

But Devon was hungry, too, in her own way. She craved company from someone her own age, who was pleasant and affable and not just another hapless old man. What was another hour of time, in the end? It would keep the disappointment of her failed meeting at bay, at least.

"Hey, are you all right? Was it something I said?"

"Sorry, it's just this pub. All these Christmas lights give me a headache." Devon pushed away her empty glass. "Would you mind if we got out of here and went somewhere quieter? It's so noisy, I can hardly hear you and—"

Hester hopped off the stool and straightened her odd blouse. "I know just the place, and it's only a short walk."

Devon forced a grin, trying to enjoy the moment. What else was there, after all? Chris wasn't coming.

They squeezed out of the crowd, half tumbling to the street. Darkness softened civilization's hard neon edges, and the sudden lack of bodies created a vacuum of calm.

"Do you do this a lot?" Devon wished she could take off her stuffy jacket. "Get stood up on a date and pick someone else, I mean."

"Is this a date?"

"Doesn't have to be." Careful, she told herself. Not too eager, not too desperate. "Where are we going?"

Hester steered them down a couple of blocks and bought a fresh set of drinks from a quayside pub. They must have looked an odd pair, Devon in her heeled boots and severe, dark clothes; Hester, short and pastel and fluttering. But Newcastle had its share of odd folk and no one commented.

Drinks bought, they sat outside in the beer garden despite the chill, people-watching and talking about nothing in particular. Hester chatted easily about books, films, the weather, and various other things like they'd been friends for years—a trait that Devon, who had gone without friends for most of her life, found very odd. And having little she wanted to say about herself, she simply listened as much as she could.

Maybe this was what it felt like to be human and normal, if such a thing as "normal" existed, even among humans. Was this a life she would have wanted?

So impossible to judge. The world was a series of fenced-off fields, each patch of grass categorically greener than its neighbors.

When Devon had been young, she'd wanted to sometimes read books and sometimes eat books, rather than always eating them, but the main thing was choosing her own books, deciding how to shape and immerse herself.

That basic desire hadn't changed with age. She craved, still, a sense that she had options, that her life wasn't an inevitable series of events. Everything in her childhood had been prearranged, her personality and outlook sculpted to fit into the Fairweather narrative. The Families' narrative.

"Either you're the best listener I've ever met, or you're very mysterious and trying to stay silent," Hester said, after her own chatter had drifted to a standstill.

"I think you've confused mysterious for boring. There's nothing to know, honestly." Nothing that would interest a human woman, anyway.

"Oh yeah? I bet I can guess." Hester sat up, leaning forward. "Let's see. I bet . . . I bet your parents are divorced, and that's why you're so aloof." She grinned, sipping her bourbon and Coke.

"More separated than divorced." Devon wondered if her mother still cared about a small girl abandoned to Fairweather Manor. She added defensively, "I'm not *that* aloof. We're talking, aren't we?"

"Separated is basically divorced," Hester said, but that wasn't right or true. Divorce was a choice; forcible separation wasn't. Amberly Blackwood hadn't been given any choices. "And you are the dictionary definition of *aloof*."

"Well—"

"Wait, I'm still guessing!" A bright laugh. "I think your family is fusty and rules-bound, very old-fashioned, and you've been married before but didn't like it. Am I right?"

Something uneasy stirred in Devon's chest. Was it her imagination, or did Hester's gaze suddenly sharpen?

She feigned amusement. "Uh-huh. Sounds like you're projecting, there."

"Maybe I am." Hester blushed, washing away Devon's brief flare of suspicion. "Fine, last guess. I'm going to get something right. I think . . . I think you are a secret bookworm. You've got that pensive look to you. Do you read much?"

"Er." Across thirty years of life, Devon had eaten close to thirty thousand books, and read at least three thousand. "Fair bit of reading, I guess."

It was more information than she could access simultaneously, and her mental sifting grew slower every year in steady little increments. Just like Ramsey had warned, when they were younger.

"I thought so," Hester said, tipping her glass back. "I bet you read everything."

"Nah. Not a literary kind of person. I like thrillers and crime." She shrugged. "Trashier the better. Fun books. *Moreish* books. Leave all that posh lit-fic to the old fuddy-duddy types." Like her uncle. "Want another drink? I'll pick up this round."

"Just Coke this time," Hester said. "When you're my size, you hit your limits faster."

Devon dipped inside to queue up. Her phone buzzed while she was ordering and she flipped it open to check her texts.

Changed me mind. Keep ur money. Sry.

She snapped the clamshell shut and folded it away, too tired and disappointed to even be angry. There were still leads she could chase, a handful of names left on her mental list to check up on.

In the meantime, best if she could find someone safeish for Cai to feed on before they left town. Someone happy, innocent, sweet.

Someone like Hester.

The thought sank through her like a brick in water. In truth, Devon didn't like the idea of feeding women to Cai, and had so far managed to avoid it. It felt worse, somehow, which she knew was irrational. A life was a life, and all that.

Except it wasn't all equal, not to Devon. Drag out Hardin's lifeboat ethics scenario and suddenly you found that there were all sorts of criteria for who to save, and who to drown. Perhaps it was book eater upbringing, whispering to her that women were valuable and less disposable; or possibly it was just a shade too easy to sympathize with someone of the same gender. Whatever the reason, Devon wanted to spare women from her son.

But here and now, strapped for time and options, she found herself considering the choice without recoiling. Cai was hungry, she needed out of Newcastle, this stranger had landed in her lap like a gift-wrapped present. On Christmas Eve, no less. It made sense, if she could manage to woman up and do it.

Suddenly, Devon felt very sober despite the rounds of Guinness. Her son was patiently waiting at home. Guilt swarmed her for having forgotten about him, even for a couple of hours. And elsewhere in the city, knights were circling. No time for weakness.

She collected her drinks and walked back to the table, smiling but laser focused.

When they were halfway through their pints, Devon leaned across the table and said above the din of chatter, "Wanna come back to mine?"

"That depends," Hester said, into her ear. "Is this going to be one of those bi-curious hookups where you wake up tomorrow and decide you like men better, after all?"

Devon considered her answers and settled on honesty. "I don't have a good answer for that. I just like you." And she did, though not the way Hester would have wanted.

"You'll do," Hester said in her dry way.

Devon laughed and hoped it didn't sound hysterical. *You'll do* was a phrase she had sometimes said to herself, when eyeing up potential victims. Mentally, she echoed the phrase back: *You'll do . . . for Cai.* One last meal to lift him out of hunger before hitting the road again.

They finished their drinks and left the bar together, though not before Devon stopped to pick up a bottle of vodka for the road. She would need a drink after tonight's debacle, for certain.

"Is your house far?"

"Just a flat, not a house, and no. Above the tire shop—down that way." She gestured vaguely. "You'll like it." Such a lie.

Hester touched her arm. "Aren't you cold? Do you want to go back for your coat?" and Devon realized she'd forgotten, in her haze of alcohol, to keep her jacket on.

"I'm from the north," she said, like that was a sensible answer in this sub-freezing weather. "I grew up on the moors, it gets very cold out there."

"Really? The moors? How romantic!" Hester shivered into her fur-lined coat. "Next you'll be telling me you grew up in a manor, like something out of *Wuthering Heights.*"

A twang of alarm rang through Devon's head, a sense that the comment was yet again too close to home, but she was tipsy and couldn't not laugh. Besides, what was she afraid of? Hester was human.

Ten minutes later she veered down the alley toward the entrance of the little flat. They walked up the steps in odd silence, Hester waiting while Devon unlocked the door. Both women entered the tiny, dingy flat with its cracked paint and shabby, last-legs furniture.

The door to Cai's room was flung wide and he was visible from the living room, sitting on his bed with a magazine open on his lap. He lifted his head and said, "I thought you didn't like bringing women back."

Hester stopped in her tracks. "You have a child?"

Devon took advantage of the distraction to lock her front door with quiet movements. "Sorry. This is my son, Cai. He's very direct." She found herself oddly grateful that the other woman didn't comment on her son's lisp. Cai was sensitive about it.

"Has he been on his own this whole time?" Hester said. "Where's your babysitter?"

"He doesn't need a babysitter," Devon said, because it was true. A boy with the accumulated minds of twenty-five adults was perfectly capable of looking after himself for a few hours.

"I'm fine on my own." Cai put his magazine down on the mattress and slipped off the bed. He crossed the threshold into the living room, drifting soundlessly on the thin carpet. His arms were smeared with the skin cream that she'd bought him that morning.

Hester tensed, seeming to hold her breath. She twisted the strap of her purse.

"Feel free to have a seat." Devon brushed past her son, heading for the bathroom.

There were few places to hide away in the cramped flat; every room was visible from the living space. But the bathroom had a door, at least. Devon could shut it behind her and not have to face what Cai was doing, not have to *watch* someone die. "Just . . . make yourself at home."

"Oh, there's no need." That purse strap wound tighter and tighter. "Listen, I like you, but I don't think I'll stay very . . ."

She trailed off, looking again at the boy who approached her. They were a strange and haunting pair: a pale waif of a lad, hunger burning beneath his skin like fever; and petite, hazel-eyed Hester, lips pinched with alarm.

Devon turned around, one hand on the bathroom door. "Can I ask you something? Are you a good person? Are you kind?"

Hester blinked, dragging her gaze from boy to woman. "Come again?"

"It doesn't matter." Cai spoke unexpectedly. "None of us are good. Only God can forgive."

That fucking vicar. Tangled anger knotted her chest.

"I seriously doubt God can do anything," Devon said, tight-lipped. "But if you're satisfied, then fine." She shut the door hard.

44

A muffled shout from the other room. Followed by a growling noise, and Hester yelping. Then that hideous silence that congealed like stagnant blood.

Devon didn't feel anything, and never did in the moment when they were being consumed. Afterward would be bad. She slouched over to the sink and ran the tap to splash her face. Cold water to help sober her up.

Christ, what was she thinking, bringing back a young, attractive woman? How was she going to get rid of the body? It'd be far too suspicious to dump someone like Hester at the homeless shelter, especially given she'd left the vicar there yesterday. The towel scraped her face dry. It was old and tattered, like Devon felt.

Soft laughter came from the living room.

Devon froze, hands and face still damp. Someone spoke; Hester's voice. And Cai said something in reply with his soft lisp.

A curious thrill ran across the back of her neck. A thousand possibilities blossomed and she didn't know what to hope for, what to reject. With dreamy slowness, Devon turned off the tap, hung up the towel, and pushed the door open.

Cai perched on the couch, the magazine he had been reading earlier open in his lap. He was tearing strips from it and putting them into his mouth with eyes wide. Hester sat next to him, watching critically with an approving smile as he scarfed pieces of paper.

Both of them looked up at Devon's entrance.

Shock rolled over Devon, shot through with a pain of irrational jealousy. She'd never sat and eaten anything with Cai because he couldn't eat books and *how was he eating a book* with this woman, this girl she'd met on a night out in Newcastle—

"Devon Fairweather, I presume? The infamous princess who murdered her husband." Hazel eyes glinted. "Such an honor to finally meet you."

Devon stared. "Who the bloody hell are you?"

"I represent Killock Ravenscar." Hester touched the corner of her mouth with the tip of her tongue. "Why don't you have a seat? I think it's time we had a frank conversation. You know—woman to woman."

6

THE PRINCESS BRIDE

ELEVEN YEARS AGO

*Everyone had told her, since she became a princess-in-training, that she was
very likely the most beautiful woman in the world. Now she was going to be
the richest and the most powerful as well.*

*Don't expect too much from life, Buttercup told herself as she rode along.
Learn to be satisfied with what you have.*

—William Goldman, *The Princess Bride*

Some years after Faerdre's wedding and the botched library venture, an
eighteen-year-old Devon was again awaiting the arrival of a chalk-colored limo.
Only this time, the limousine was here for her, and the wedding was going to
be her own.

The adults of Fairweather Manor came to see her off. Even the aunts, ever
reclusive, always so withdrawn from her as she grew, made an appearance. A
girl leaving home for her first wedding was a big event and worth marking.
Little Chester, the son whom Faerdre had left behind, gave a happy wave. He
was nearly five now.

Devon squeezed each member of her Family in tight hugs, too overwhelmed
to be tearful. She would not be coming home for four years if the wedding
went well and a child was conceived. Everyone shook hands and hugged. Some
kissed her and wished her luck.

Aunt Beulah was the oldest of the aunts, pushing into her seventies, and
the last to say good-bye. She tugged Devon down to her own stooped level and
whispered in a heavy Yorkshire accent, "Be strong, love, and don't let 'em see y'
cry. It'll be all reet in the end."

"Y—yes, I'm sure," Devon said, a little startled, and gave her an awkward
hug before turning to go. An odd comment. She had no plans to cry, let alone
allow others to watch her shed tears.

The limo waited in the driveway, flanked by knights and their dragons on
idle motorbikes. Knights not only arranged the marriages, as a neutral non-
Family faction, but enforced the agreements and provided a secure escort.

She didn't even have to pack. Her bags were already in the trunk and Uncle Aike was already sitting inside, waiting with a patient smile. Devon glanced back, unnerved to find the old aunt still staring at her.

"Don't worry about a thing, princess," he said as she scooted inside. "Your dear aunt Beulah is rather a killjoy, these days. Eats a bit too much women's fiction, you know how it is."

"I'm not worried," she told him, rallying a smile and giving him a peck on the cheek. "I'm very lucky."

She was indeed lucky. Other people, like her brother Ramsey, had to labor and strive to stand out among his peers, had to endure training and hardship among the knights. Still others—most humans, in fact—lived lives without purpose or direction. Many were crushed by poverty and circumstance. Their women were volatile, disorderly, disadvantaged.

But book eater women were rare and special, having a secure place in society that they were comfortable in. Therefore, she too was rare and special without having to do anything other than exist, and the role she took was one that suited her station.

In short, she had lived a charmed life in a beautiful home, kept safe and happy from a twisted world beyond the manor boundaries. That much she could verify not only from her uncles and the things her brothers said but from the books she'd stolen to read: full of drama, heartbreak, hideous crime, darkness, stress. All of that she had been spared. Jane Eyre living in poverty, embroiled in her tempestuous affairs? *That* would never be Devon.

And here, now, wearing a net of sapphires in her hair and a green debut dress that laced tight across the bodice, Devon clicked on the expensive seat belt in her expensive limousine. She was clothed in wealth and radiant with luck. Though not royalty in a strictly technical sense, she was certainly a princess in all the ways that counted.

Live quietly. Obey the rules. Please the Family. Do all that, and life would be good. Life *was* good.

"Have you heard from Ramsey?" she said, rubbing a thumb along the edge of her seat belt strap. "During his last call, he said he hoped he could come and see me off."

Poor Ramsey, who'd borne the brunt of Devon's last foolish mistake.

"As far as I know, your brother is well, but too busy with his studies for a visit," Uncle Aike said with his usual absentmindedness. "Perhaps for your next wedding, my dear."

Don't be disappointed, Devon told herself. Her brother was a knight and had responsibilities now. She was lucky he still called her at all, after the trouble she'd gotten him into.

It'd taken four years, in fact, before Ramsey had been willing to answer her calls—four hard years of him being miserable under the knights, while she sat at home cooking in a soup of her own shame.

The worst of Ramsey's training had tapered off, and he had settled into a role of his own now. Things would never be the same, but at least something existed between them. She was grateful for the communication, however guarded and irregular it might be.

They drove mostly on the motorway or through small country roads. As was custom, the driver took a path that involved as few towns as possible. She found herself wishing vainly that they could go through a city. Obviously, human society was inferior to what the book eaters conducted among themselves, but she was a little tiny bit curious about it, nonetheless. It was hard not to be.

At one small village, a young couple walked side by side. The lady wore jeans, she noted. Many of the women out here wore men's clothing; very few wore the kind of long dresses that Devon had grown accustomed to throughout her life.

As they paused on a street corner, the woman said something that made the man laugh; he took her hand. Devon remembered holding hands with her brothers when she was a child, but that was entirely different to the couple outside.

"What's he like?" She hadn't voiced that question in the six months since being told of the engagement.

"Your husband, you mean?" Uncle Aike was discreetly eating a volume of Shelley's poetry. "Competent, wealthy, intelligent. You will be quite happy in that house, I am sure."

Was my mother happy? Living with you, in Fairweather Manor? Devon folded her hands into a small knot and imagined saying those words aloud. And Uncle Aike, who was not really her uncle at all and should have been called her father, would say *Absolutely, my dear!* with complete earnestness.

Devon turned her face back to the window, drinking in the scenery. If she knew what her uncle was going to say, then really, what was the point of asking? It would just be an exercise in validation. She wasn't the kind of girl who demanded pointless validation.

Onward they drove, hills rolling back into fields until at last, they came to Winterfield Manor, somewhere on the outskirts of Birmingham. Devon wasn't sure of the exact location. What mattered was the house itself, coming into view as the driveway gates peeled back: elegant and Tudor in design, black timber striping the white walls like an urban zebra.

No tumbling parapets or haphazard extensions. The Winterfields had their house in order.

Immaculate lawns fanned around the driveway, the grass and hedges cut with diamond precision. Devon laughed as their limo circled around a four-tiered fountain big enough for her procession of accompanying knights to swim in, and caught her breath when she saw the Winterfield brothers waiting on a row of proud horses. Fairweather Manor didn't have any horses.

Uncle Aike leaned over. "Such creatures are extraordinarily expensive to keep, and our manor has been in financial decline for a few decades. But that will change, princess, and it will change because of you. The Winterfields have paid a handsome dowry."

And Devon smiled, proud of what she was worth.

Luton Winterfield rode out to meet them, disembarking from his horse as Devon stepped out of her limousine.

Her new husband had the face of a man who wasn't quite as handsome as he wished to be and resented everyone else for that failing. His age was hard to determine; older than thirty, less than forty. Either his nose was too small, or his chin was too big, depending on your point of view. The graying of his once-fairish hair did nothing to soften a hard-lined jaw or define those too-soft features.

Lucky, Devon reminded herself. She was lucky to be wedded with someone from a wealthy house, who would be honest in his contractual terms and look after their child well. So what if she didn't care for how he looked? He would grow on her. Really, it didn't matter at all; looks were arbitrary, shallow, skin-deep things.

Luton tilted his head back with an appraising frown. "You're absurdly tall."

Incredible how much three simple words could diminish you. Devon shrank into herself, confidence rocked. Tall was good—wasn't it?

Uncle Aike snorted. "Luton, my lad. What a character you are."

The other men laughed and Devon did, too, if a trifle uncertainly. She was a grown woman now and could take a joke.

A slender, gray-haired aunt came forward and offered Devon a handshake. "So wonderful to meet you, my lovely. I'm Luton's sister, Gailey, and I am here at your disposal."

"Thank you. That's very kind." Devon grasped her hand, trying not to let her shock show. She was so used to older women avoiding her in Fairweather Manor. Were the Winterfields just friendlier? Or was it that she was a woman now, grown-up and getting married, that made her welcome in their world? Both possibilities filled her with warmth.

The hours that followed were a whirlwind of activity. The knights disappeared, leaving their dragons loitering forlornly in a cellar somewhere. Uncle Aike and Luton went upstairs with some other men to discuss "that damned IVF business." The men were always talking about fertility treatments these days—mostly whether it would work for book eater biology, how to test it, who to test it on, how to acquire equipment.

Devon, meanwhile, descended into a writhing party, of which she was the beating heart. Gailey stayed at her side, steering her through handshake after kiss after curtsy. They met so many people she'd lost count by the time they reached the first set of stairs. Faerdre's wedding at Fairweather Manor had been much smaller, but then the Fairweathers had a smaller house with fewer people.

The manor was as beautiful inside as it was without, arrayed in marble and mahogany with an army of cream carpets and thickly upholstered furniture. The Winterfield libraries favored modern hardbacks, mostly literary and contemporary fiction in a variety of languages. They passed shelf after shelf of intriguing novels, wafting the scent of glossy coating and crisp white pages.

No dark nooks filled with old, leather codices; no voluminous, gloomy tomes; no lingering smell of biblichor. When Devon paused in front of a shelf, Gailey murmured that there would be time for eating in a moment and pushed her, still in her tightly laced dress and pinned-up hair, toward the Winterfield banqueting hall.

The room took her breath away. Four vast mahogany tables were arranged in a square, each one piled high with books. Old tomes, crisp new novels, and thick codices were arranged artfully on stands and stacked into little towers. A quartet of young men played music, of an orchestral variety Devon had never heard before. Her ears rang with delightful noise, and she inhaled the instrumental scent of archaic wood and slightly worn brass.

In the center of the room, so big it leaned over every table, stood an artistic representation of the Tree of Knowledge. Metal and glass fused into a semblance of bark to form a glossy, solid trunk. Branches spread high above the tables, far taller than her and touching the ceiling. Instead of leaves, it sported clusters of printed pages shaped carefully into origami apples. The sheer amount of effort gone into its construction was stunning.

"Come have a seat," Gailey said, above the chatter and laughter. "Eat well! You have a long night ahead."

Devon barely heard. She was too busy breathing in the glittering lights and spice-laden scents, her head full of music and her body thrumming with adrenaline. But she let the older woman steer her to a seat, fumbling for a chair with eyes still wide.

The Winterfields liked their meals styled into faux-human food: roast "meat" made of sculpted paper; pages dyed in a multitude of colors and shaped into delicate fake fruit. A new way of eating, at least to her. She thought about plucking an apple off the tree but didn't quite have the courage.

Alcohol was everywhere. Devon had never tried alcohol before; in her Family, they only drank inktea or water. She almost choked on the wine, with her first mouthful. It wasn't good, exactly, and didn't have the heaviness of inktea, but it was very drinkable. She sipped again. And a third time. It tasted, she thought, like a well-crafted romance novel. Complex, sweet, and a little stinging.

"My god, I'd forgotten how *fun* a good wedding can be!"

Devon swiveled to her left to see Faerdre's beaming face. At some point, between people coming and going and a heady mix of books, wine, and music, the other woman had taken the next seat along. Faerdre had left Fairweather Manor only a couple years ago, and yet it seemed a lifetime since they'd seen each other.

"Hi," Devon said, then kicked herself mentally for sounding like a little girl. She tried to summon something intelligent to say, brain traitorously going blank. "So, um, I'm—"

"You're very tipsy, I should think!" Faerdre fluttered eyelashes that were lumpy with too-thick mascara. "It's good to be tipsy at your own wedding. I was for both of mine!" She put a hand on Devon's skirt-draped thigh. The long, chipped nails were over-painted, color smeared on the cuticles.

"Right." Devon blushed. "I mean, thanks." She drank more wine, conscious of the other woman's warm palm pressed to her leg through the thin fabric.

"Relax. Have fun!" Faerdre brushed a friendly kiss across Devon's cheek. "Look at you, going all red!" She leaned away to grab a plate of "salad": shredded pages of *Midsummer Night's Dream* that were dyed different shades of green, the words barely readable.

Despite the other woman having lived in Fairweather Estate, Devon barely knew her. The aunts had kept Faerdre secluded in the north wing of the manor, and the baby seemed to take up such an inordinate amount of Faerdre's time.

Besides, Devon didn't have the faintest idea how to make conversation with another woman. She still didn't know, even now. Faerdre's appearance left her awkward and stammering. So much for that tongue of hers.

"The Winterfields always throw the best parties, so don't feel too bad about your house. I've seen worse." Faerdre picked up strips of her book-salad, dipping it in her wine with delightful scandalousness. "You can go to these, too, once you've finished with the babies. No more babies for me! I get to drift around, having fun." Her expression turned wistful, and her lower lip quivered briefly. "How's my son doing? He was such awful trouble, terrible sleeper, much worse than my first. But I do think of him fondly."

"Chester's very happy," Devon said, hoping it was true. She didn't see the lad much. He'd cried for weeks after Faerdre had first departed, but he'd got over it. Surely that meant he was all right now.

"Oh, good," Faerdre muttered into her wine. "Lovely. I'm very glad to hear it." She tipped back her glass in a long swallow.

"Can I ask a question?" Devon scooted a little closer, until their shoulders were touching. "Did you mind it?"

"Mind?" Faerdre licked a splatter of green dye off her palm. "What do you mean?" Wine flecks dotted her cheek.

"Everything. Getting married, having the babies."

The former mother-bride sat silent for a long moment, running the tip of her forefinger over her thumbnail. "Well, there's not anything else, is there? Can't live with humans, so it's this or nothing." She took a long drink, then another. "It's only a few years and a couple of babies and then you go on with your life. Live like a queen once you've paid your dues." She brightened. "I don't think I mind. Why do you ask? Do you mind?"

Someone made an inane toast in the background and several people cheered before returning to their quieter revelry.

"No, of course not," Devon said reflexively. Faerdre was right, it was this life or nothing. They could not be knights or human; could only be book eater women, and all that entailed.

And then, feeling awkwardly self-conscious about her answer, she added, "We're very lucky." It seemed important to say that.

"Oh, sure, yes! We have the luckiest of lives!" Faerdre topped up both their glasses with a giggle. "To luck! Cheers, darling."

They both collapsed into laughter. Devon tried to remember what was so funny and decided it was the wine itself.

"God. I'm going to miss these parties," Faerdre said, in between bouts of giggling. "Won't be many more, you know. They say there's only six brides left, in the whole of Britain."

"Huh?" The drink must have been clouding their conversation; Devon felt she was missing a piece of something important.

"Huh yourself," Faerdre said, swirling her glass. "We're rare and getting rarer. Don't you know that?"

"Sure. Everyone knows that." Devon didn't know that. Women were rare among the book eaters, yes, but nobody had ever told her they were getting even *more* rare.

"Only six left," Faerdre repeated. "Won't be many more weddings to go to, unless we can make that science stuff work. That's what my last husband said anyway."

"Science stuff?" Devon echoed, blinking through a haze of alcohol. "Is that the . . . test tube baby thing?"

"Uh-huh. Children born from science. We'll have them soon. Ten years from now." Faerdre started laughing, a little too loudly. "And what will the knights do then, when we can choose our own husbands? What will the dragons do when no knights take them in, and teach them to control their urges? Poor little knights! Poor little dragons!"

Several people were glancing their way, and a few of the knights were staring at Faerdre very hard.

With perfect timing, Gailey appeared at her elbow and said softly, "Time for you to come with me, my lovely."

"Bye now! I'll see you another time." Faerdre winked, blew a kiss, then slumped over the table with head in hands.

"Isn't the party still going?" Devon said, but allowed Gailey to help her up from the table and start leaving the dining hall. "Won't there be a ceremony?" She remembered that in Fairweather Manor, Faerdre had undergone an exchange of contractual marriage vows, while they'd all stood in respectful silence.

"That's not the Winterfield custom, my lovely," Gailey said. They slipped unheralded from the dining hall and set foot on a flight of stairs. "We enjoy a good party, but do not stand on ceremony."

"Then where are we going?" Devon leaned hard on the handrail, head spinning with drink.

"Only a little farther, just down this hall. Mind your step on that threshold. My, you've had a bit to drink, haven't you? I suppose you're not used to it."

"Well—"

"Here we are." Gailey drew them to a pair of doors, the wood elegantly painted. "You have a good evening, my lovely. I'll come and see you in the morning."

A small suite of rooms spread out before Devon, comprised of soft blue walls with delicate floral paper. A bedroom with adjoining four-piece bathroom stood to her left, and a large L-shaped living area curved away to her right.

Luton Winterfield sat on the couch, with a bottle of brandy and two glasses on the table in front of him. A tray filled with folded origami pieces sat next to it. He looked her up and down as she stood in the doorway, a man at least twice her age and old enough to be her father.

"Heels, at your height? Really?" He shook his head, pouring brandy into two glasses. "Sit down and don't flinch, darling. I was only teasing."

Devon debated taking off her heels, couldn't think of a way to do so gracefully. She wobbled over next to him and sat with stiff formality. The origami pieces, on closer inspection, were actually pages from books, each one folded into an intricate little swan.

"Relax," he said, handing her a drink. "It'll be fun." He was smiling, so she must have been doing all right.

Devon took the drink and picked up a paper swan. Her tongue tingled from the first bite, starbursts cascading across her vision.

> *Behold, you are*
> *beautiful, my love;*
> *behold, you are*
> *Beautiful;*
> *your*
> *eyes are doves.*

"What was . . . ?" She would have slumped back if not for Luton offering a steadying hand. "Is that Song of Solomon?" The Bible, but never as she'd eaten it before.

"Words have an effect on us, and so do certain chemical substances." His smile turned slow and ferocious. "Lace a printed page with a little bit of the right stuff and you'll get quite the combination of experiences."

The room was rushing past her. "I feel like I'm flying . . . No, swimming."

"That's why we call them swans." He put another to her lips.

> *How beautiful*
> *you are, my darling!*

Oh, how beautiful! Your
eyes are
doves.

Her head was a hurricane of doves. Luton made pleasant if inane conversation, and she did her best to keep up, answering his biting jokes with her own banter despite the whirlwind inside her mind.

"That tongue of yours," he said at one point, though she couldn't recall what she'd said. "Your uncle warned me."

"Rude!" She stuck her tongue out, like she had as a child, and he nipped it with his teeth. Devon flushed.

A few clumsy kisses later and he started undoing the laces of her old-fashioned bodice, before pulling back to reach for the brandy, saying, "I think you need a top-up."

By her third drink—she'd also had several cups of wine at supper—most of her clothes were piled on the floor in a heap, including the problematic heels.

He draped an arm across her shoulders. "You look cold."

"I'm lucky," she announced. "Also, a princess."

Somehow, they ended up in the bedroom. Alcohol-induced exhaustion clouded her skull. She must have fallen backward on the bed because suddenly she was looking at the ceiling: ornate wooden crossbeams, reddish, protruding; the ribs of a giant creature, viewed internally.

Perhaps she had been swallowed by a whale like Jonah the prophet, Devon thought, trying to remember where she'd heard that story, and then Luton was rolling her over.

She tried to lift her head, voice muffled by embroidered pillowcases and sheets of Egyptian cotton.

"Just relax." He pushed her head back down. "Good girl." His voice was a river, drifting away, and carried her along with it.

7

A TASTE OF REDEMPTION

PRESENT DAY

Of mind eaters, there is even more evidence throughout history. Mesopotamia and Babylonia depict bloodsucking creatures who feast on the young, similar to the Lamashtu, and Lilitu (and Lilitu in turn is interlinked with Lilith, from Hebrew demonology). And that is only the beginning: these legends stretch through every culture and all throughout history.

The details and contexts vary, yet consistent patterns emerge across cultures and time periods to form a single conclusion: we have all of us been prey to these creatures for centuries.

—Amarinder Patel, *Paper and Flesh: A Secret History*

"You've got to ask yourself one question. 'Do I feel lucky?' Well, do ya, punk?"

On the television screen, a scowling Dirty Harry sighted down his gun. The punk didn't feel lucky. They never did. Harry's goodwill went perpetually unappreciated.

Cai appreciated it. Instead of sitting slumped on the couch he bounced from foot to foot as the film played out. He thrummed with energy, mouthing some of the lines to himself.

Devon watched him from the small kitchenette to which she and Hester had adjourned. *Surreal*: adjective. Marked by the intense irrational reality of a dream. This situation was the definition of *surreal*.

"Nice lad. I like him, even if he did try to kill me." Hester leaned against the kitchen counter, sipping water from a chipped mug. "Sorry about all the pretense, by the way. When we got the call from Chris that you were looking for the Ravenscars, and the details of your story . . . Well. Killock wanted to scope you out first, and be sure you weren't some sort of Family trap."

Devon didn't give a flying fuck about Chris just then. "What did you give Cai? Is it—" She couldn't even say it.

"The Redemption drug? Of course." Hester tilted her head as a gunshot echoed from the television screen. "How better else to prove I'm really working with the Ravenscars?"

Devon sat down heavily. As a very young child, Cai had taken Redemption, up until the point the Ravenscars had disappeared overnight—making the drug rarer than hen's teeth. That in turn had triggered a cascade of events in Family politics and Devon's own life, leading her to this room. Sitting across the table from this woman. Everything coming full circle.

"He'll eat books now, the way you do," Hester continued. "No book-teeth, meaning he'll struggle to chew tough covers, but you can feed him printed or written sheets and he'll absorb information from them, instead of brain flesh. He will still be able to write, making him superior to your average book eater, but don't let him eat anything he's written himself; he'll feel rather sick."

"I know. He's taken it before." Devon curled and uncurled her fists. She felt like a prehistoric animal who had been rescued from a tar pit: exhausted from prolonged struggle, unable to believe her luck, and still suspicious that moving too much would make her sink again. "Who are you? Are you a Ravenscar?"

Hester held up both hands. "Guilty as charged. I'm one of Killock's siblings, and I'm here on his behalf to meet with you."

"A Ravenscar in the flesh, then." Devon tried to organize her thoughts, scrutinizing Hester with fresh awareness and a sharper eye. She added, with sarcastic bite, "So you're a princess, like me?"

"Yes, I suppose," came the dry reply.

"Right." Devon considered that. On the television behind them, Dirty Harry fought with his wheel, tires shrieking in a vicious car chase. "Are you really into women, by the way, or was tonight entirely a farce?"

"I could ask you the same question."

Devon decided to change the subject. "Why didn't Killock come down himself?"

"He's our leader," Hester said. "That would be risky."

"So he risks you, instead? A woman?"

"Thanks for the vote of confidence. I can take care of myself."

"I am sure you can," Devon said with apologetic sincerity. "I didn't mean it as an insult, to clarify. But compared to women, the men of our kind are usually . . . How to say."

"Expendable?"

"Your words, not mine."

"I couldn't comment on that. He simply thought it would be more diplomatic to send one woman to meet another, that is all," Hester said. "If you don't mind, can we get down to business?"

"If you like." Devon shifted her weight. "I want to buy enough Redemption that I can leave England. Then I'll find a safe place for both Cai and I to live a free, happy life. Away from the Family." Mostly true, if a little simplified.

"About what I expected, then." Trimmed nails drummed on the counter. "I'll be straight with you and stop dossing around. Killock is currently the leader of our household, and he is willing to give you the drugs that Cai needs. But only if you agree to certain conditions."

"What kind of conditions?"

"You'd have to join the Ravenscar household."

Devon sat back in her chair. "I'm guessing that's a little more complicated than you're making it sound."

"Not at all. Joining, in this case, means living beneath Killock's rule, accepting him as leader, taking his orders, and being reasonably loyal to him." Hester kept rubbing the tips of her fingers against her thumb with nervous energy. "These were the conditions that he agreed with us, his other siblings. As a member of his household, the same rules would apply to you."

In other words, Devon thought, Killock had won his coup and given his siblings a choice between death or obedience. For all they'd run away and supposedly escaped Family culture, the apple hadn't fallen very far from the proverbial tree.

Which rather begged the question, why had the Ravenscar household imploded at all? If Killock had simply wanted a change of leadership, there were ways to do that. He wouldn't have been the first ambitious youth to reach for patriarch.

No, trying to leave the other Families entirely implied a fresh start, yet Devon could see no evidence of anything fresh. She was missing something. Probably a lot of somethings. Currents and eddies of a complicated interfamily feud, all swirling at her ankles, and she was stepping in blind.

Aloud, Devon said, "That doesn't work for me. I already walked away from the book eater patriarchs and Family life once before. I won't live under that system ever again."

Hester's restless hands paused. "He's nothing like the old patriarchs. It's a very different kind of rule."

Devon burst into laughter, almost doubled over.

"Dev?" Cai was on his feet in an instant, looking at her through the narrow kitchenette archway. On the screen behind him, Clint Eastwood stalked purposefully through a building.

"I'm fine." She waved him away. "Just—a funny joke. Watch your film, love."

"Hmph." He lingered for a few seconds before drifting back over to the couch, still shooting her suspicious looks. Sad that he'd heard her laughter so rarely as to find it alarming.

Hester pressed her lips into a line. "I was being serious!"

"Still a joke, though, innit?" Devon took a wheezy breath to calm herself, and got up. "Christ. I need a drink."

"Pour me one, if you would." Hester moved to sit at the table, legs crossed and one foot jigging.

Devon glowered, but politely dug out the vodka that she'd bought earlier and poked around for a couple of tumblers. Never a simple solution in sight, she thought sourly. Everyone always wanted something you didn't expect.

The smell of cheap alcohol clogged up the space between them, adding a thick layer of sourness to the semipermanent stench of car grease from the tire shop below.

"I want life-changing drugs for my son, and I'm willing to pay for them." Devon slid across a vodka-filled tumbler. "I *don't* want to come and live with another lot of people who are essentially the Family all over again, much less stick my foot in where it's not wanted with your pseudo-patriarch."

"Then I guess we both go away empty-handed." Hester scraped something undesirable off the side of her cup and sipped carefully. "Personally, I don't see the problem. Is it such a bad offer?"

From the living area, Cai was still watching them. No doubt he was inhaling every word, as always.

"Is Family life such a bad life?" Devon shot back, pleased to see the other woman wince. "Wealth, privilege, posh houses. What's not to love, eh?"

"It won't be like that." Her expression was complex and unreadable. "It will never be like what it was." A statement as vague as her intentions.

"If you say so." Devon coughed on vodka fumes. "Why would he *want* me in his household, anyway? Some risky runaway with a load of baggage and a lot of knightly enemies?"

"He respects you. What you've done, what you've been through. Your commitment to survival," Hester said, and Devon wondered how much of that statement was true, and how much was the other woman's own invention. "Listen, you don't have to make decisions straightaway. I am simply inviting you to come with me to meet my brother. If you don't like it, you do not have to agree to anything."

"That so? What happens if we wander up there, decide we don't like it, and try to leave again? Surely your brother would think us a risk? What's to stop me running back to the Families someday and spilling everything?"

Cai said, from his seat on the sofa, "We don't have any other options, and Killock must know that. He's the only person in this country who can give me Redemption, so we *have* to deal with him, and on his terms. Or I'll starve out here."

Both women looked over.

"Let's not get pessimistic," Devon said. All too conscious of the other woman listening and watching. "We don't have to think about that yet—"

"We *do* have to think about it now." Cai draped his elbows over the back of the couch. "One a day keeps the eating away. That's what they used to say when I took Redemption at the old house. If I don't have another dose tomorrow, I'll need someone to feed on very soon. And the knights are closing in. That's what *you* told me earlier."

Devon hesitated. He was right, but the problem was that none of this stuff with joining the Ravenscars or getting ensnared in their internal feuds fit in with her carefully laid plans. She couldn't explain that to Cai, though, because she hadn't told him the full truth of what was going on. For his own protection.

She looked back at the other woman. "Can you give us a moment?"

"Why not. I could do with a cigarette anyway." Hester rose and ghosted past them in a shuffle of fabric, stepping through the front door to the stairwell just outside.

When she was gone, Devon got up and stalked from the kitchenette to the living room, sitting heavily on the coffee table in front of Cai.

"I do want their cure for you. But it's complicated." *Much* more complicated than he knew, she thought tiredly. "This situation we'd be walking into sounds like a right mess. We have to be careful."

Cai pressed Mute on the remote control, silencing his film. "I don't keep all the memories, you know. Or if I do, I can't always summon them up. But sometimes . . ." His mouth twisted. "Sometimes I'll wake up thinking about Mary, decide I should visit her grave, and then remember that I can't because she's not my wife and I never married. She was just the electrician's wife. Do you remember him? Fifth person you brought me."

Actors engaged in a silent mock-battle on the television screen and Devon sat frozen, fingers knotted together. He'd never talked about his eating before. Not like this.

"I've been married fifteen times and signed eight divorce papers," Cai said, with the unflinching directness of a five-year-old. "I have been four different kinds of religious and not religious at all. I've almost died twice and passed twenty-two driving tests. I remember going to war and killing a civilian by accident. Her blood ruined my uniform." He wrinkled that snub nose in absentminded distaste. "I remember the sound a woman makes when you hurt her for the first time. I remember hurting you, through *his* eyes. I remember the sounds you made."

Devon touched her throat, and said nothing. She dared not look at him, in case she saw the echo of her ex-husband in his face.

"I remember those things even though I haven't done them. I suffer those sins without committing them—that's how the vicar would say it. I am not those people and I'm also not me. I can't ever be me, I'm too full of other lives." Cai turned the remote over and over in his hands. "Twenty-five times you've asked *Are you a good person?* You asked them, not me, but now I'm all of those people and the question is mine, twenty-five times over."

"Cai . . ." She had lost control, and this conversation had sailed off in wild directions without her.

"I'm not finished," he said. "The answer is no, I'm not a good person. I can't ever be, even if I eat good people, and especially not if I eat bad ones. The only thing I am is an actual monster. You won't call me that but it's what I am."

"That isn't true. Don't think that."

"Isn't it? Every person I've ever consumed thought I was a monster, in their final moments. They were afraid of me."

"Everyone is a monster to somebody." Devon didn't have to think for this answer; she'd prepared it long ago, in readiness. "But you are not, and never will be, a monster to me."

The worst and best lie she'd ever told him.

"I'm glad," he said, "but it doesn't change how I feel. I'm tired, Dev. I don't want to eat. I don't want to hurt people. Not when there's a cure, *right there,* and we can have it. Does it matter what Killock is asking right now? We'll figure it out. *You'll* figure it out. You always do."

Devon said nothing, only sat next to him with an arm out.

Reluctantly, he let her fold him into a hug. He'd been so clingy as a baby; these days, Cai liked his space. Tough and independent, like her. Also damaged like her. Her heart hurt. The things she had done to him. The things they'd done to each other.

He nestled into her shoulder, a gesture so incredibly rare that her heart melted a little. "If I can't get Redemption, I don't want to keep going on like this. I don't want to keep going on *at all*."

"It won't come to that," she said, alarmed. "We'll get you more Redemption."

"I know," he said, and she squeezed him tighter.

Devon disliked messy confusion, and this was far less neat than her plan of grabbing drugs from the Ravenscars in exchange for cash, and then disappearing to another country. But in the end, did it alter so much? As long as she got to where the Redemption was kept, there were ways she could make this work. Regardless of whatever was going on with Killock Ravenscar or his strange siblings.

Someday very soon, she would have to tell her son the truth about her plans, and who she kept contact with—and in turn, the truth about what she had done during the first eight months of their escape. There was that hole in his memory, and the implant scar on his abdomen that she'd so far explained away as a birthmark.

The thought made her slightly sick. So many secrets. Perhaps—

"Hello?" Hester stuck her head around the door, cigarette trapped between her fingers. "I'm sorry to interrupt, but I think we're about to have company."

ACT 2
MIDNIGHT

8

GIFTS FOR THE CHRIST CHILD

TEN YEARS AGO

In the windowless tomb of a blind mother, in the dead of night, under the feeble rays of a lamp in an alabaster globe, a girl came into the darkness with a wail.

—George MacDonald, *The History of Photogen and Nycteris*

Devon thought she must be dying. Every contraction brought worse agony and she didn't understand how this could possibly go on and on, yet it did.

A handful of Winterfield women flitted around as she screamed into her pillows from pain, then cried from the shame of screaming. Writhing and moaning was for weak women—wasn't it? Not strong, young, six-foot-tall book eater brides. Birth was supposed to be her whole raison d'être, after all.

Six hours into labor and Luton came by, barking disgruntled orders for someone to "give that girl something before she makes us deaf."

"She can't help it," Gailey said, hand on Devon's head. "The infant is back-to-back."

"What?" Devon gasped.

"What?" Luton echoed. "Do we need external intervention? Surgery, or ah . . ."

"It's not a problem," Gailey assured him. "Just a long and painful labor."

That sounded like an enormous fucking problem to Devon, but she didn't have enough air left over to complain.

Luton did, however. "Long? You mean this will be hours? Then give her a sodding injection, for God's sakes! If I have to sit through another minute of this howling I will lose my bloody sanity. It's supposed to be Christmas Eve, I want some peace."

The women objected with hissing, angry statements she couldn't hear. Pain was part of book eater tradition; trauma made it more difficult for mother and child to bond, which in turn made it easier for mother and child to be separated.

But Luton's will won out, as did his desire for a quiet Christmas Eve. A pinprick Devon barely even felt, stabbing into her thigh. He watched with narrowed eyes and fingers in his ears, this man who was supposedly her husband. She resented him for treating her with such indifference, and also simultaneously wanted to collapse at his feet to sob with gratitude.

Sleepiness took hold as the diamorphine kicked in. Pain still prevailed but more distantly, the echo of something she hated instead of agony she was immersed in.

"It'll wear off." Gailey seemed to be speaking from the other end of a very long, echoing tunnel.

"Then give it to her again when it does. Some of us have work to do!" He left with footsteps that seemed to reverberate. His voice had an echo, too. Everything was humming. Devon felt like a quivering string.

The rest of the birth slipped through gaps in her memory. She could index her brain for any sentence in every book she'd ever eaten, but thinking back on those remaining hours summoned up only fragments of sensation and flashes of garbled conversation. The diamorphine made her sick to her stomach; it also seemed to swallow the minutes, skipping erratically through the hours.

Without warning, the pain ceased abruptly. No more contractions, no more pushing. She gazed at the ceiling above her bed, stunned to be alive and seething with betrayal because fairy tales had never described birth. Women buzzed around her, talking about cords and cutting and the baby—

The baby. She struggled to sit up. "Let me see him!"

"Not a him," said Gailey, and passed her the child. "You have a healthy little girl, my lovely."

"A . . . girl?"

"Merry Christmas, love. Your own little Christ child."

And Devon reached out with sweat-slick arms.

She stared, awestruck, at the writhing form with a red, crumpled face. The tiny fists and swollen cheeks.

Nothing externally had changed. The galaxy still spun in vast unknowing indifference, and the uncaring world still flowed past beyond the confines of her bedroom. But here in that moment, the axes of Devon's personal universe tilted and she was left teetering, off-balance to the core of her being.

The baby wailed, sounding like a stepped-on frog.

"She'll be hungry. You should nurse, my lovely. Be good for you both." Gailey came over, helping Devon sit up straight, to undo her top and position the scrabbling infant while the aunts gasped and fluttered. *A girl! A girl! Such incredibly good fortune!*

Silence fell as the tiny thing latched, eyes drifting closed. Stillness pooled like blood and still Devon sat, stunned and terrified to move in case her universe tilted again. The aunts were already cleaning up: wiping blood off her legs, changing the sheets around her as best they could. Someone carried the placenta away.

"Your milk will be black, when it comes in," Gailey said. "Don't be alarmed by that. All perfectly normal."

Devon just nodded, too overwhelmed to speak. Perfectly normal? How could anything be normal ever again? Her life had been a series of twisted fairy tales in which she had imagined herself the princess, but this, here, living and breathing and snuffling in her arms, had more truth than all of her swallowed stories combined.

She was her daughter's whole world, a realization both humbling and empowering. Devon had never been anybody's world before—had never been anything at all, in fact, except the sum of paper flesh she'd consumed without thought.

"Can I name her?" She spoke the question to no one in particular, too dazed to remember what the protocol was.

"No need," Gailey said, stuffing bloodied sheets into a laundry basket. "Luton has already chosen 'Salem,' should the child be a girl."

Salem Winterfield. The syllables mushed in her mouth like rotting paper. It made her think of witch trials and women being burned, and seemed such a heated nomen when stuck to chilly old Winterfield.

"I don't like that." She peered down at her daughter's soft, chubby face. "It doesn't suit her at all."

"Don't be daft, it's a perfectly lovely name! Here, support her head better— that's right."

Devon was too tired to argue. Too battered and still bleeding, with a naked infant curled on her naked chest. She found "Salem" was sticking in her mind, whether she wished it to or not. As if her daughter had been tarred irrevocably.

A knock at the door, distracting her attention. Luton had arrived. He was bleary-eyed, yawning, still in a dressing gown, and Devon realized with surprise that it was half past four in the morning. She'd completely lost track of time.

"The tongue," Luton said, scrubbing at his face with the heels of his hands. "Has anyone checked?" He didn't approach, likely put off by the bloody mess all over the bed.

For a brief, exhausted moment, Devon stupidly thought they all meant her own tongue—*that tongue of yours!*—and couldn't fathom why that would be worth mentioning.

"Baby's fine, no proboscis," another aunt said. "She's a girl in any case, Luton."

"Girls can still be mind eaters. It happens, albeit rarely," he said. "But I agree, she looks fine in this instance."

He drew Gailey aside, after that, and spoke in low tones, saying something about registrars and doctors. Practicalities that needed taking care of. Gailey pursed her lips, nodding at appropriate points.

Devon hugged her daughter close, both annoyed at Luton's questions and relieved at their answers. A healthy girl. Yet a part of her was angry it should even matter. A mind eater girl would not be marriage material, and that was all Luton thought about.

She looked down at the snuffling lump in her arms, swamped with an unsettling mix of dread and pride. *There's only six brides left in the whole of Britain,* Faerdre had said. Did that make her daughter the seventh bride-to-be? The thought was anxiety-inducing for a multitude of reasons.

Luton came over to Devon's bed, gaze still averted from the blood. "You did well, Ms. Fairweather. I'm glad to hear the child is a girl, and healthy. I hope you will forgive me for returning to sleep, but the hour is unsociable, and I have a full schedule tomorrow."

"Yes, of course," Devon said, fumbling for polite words. Didn't he feel it—the power, the trauma, the awe? Why hadn't the axis of *his* universe tilted, as hers had?

She debated thanking him for intervening with medication, then decided against it and bent over her daughter instead. Luton had only helped because her pain had been inconvenient to him, and now that her mind was clear of drugs and agony Devon seized on that fact with sharp cynicism. He didn't deserve her gratitude for what was merely basic courtesy.

After he left, the baby was taken away by aunts to be weighed, cleaned, and dressed. One of the aunts helped Devon to the bath, dousing her bathwater in an army of luxury products before leaving her in peace.

The revelation struck Devon with the force of a speeding train as she sat, exhausted in a porcelain tub, naked and alone and clothed in bubbles: she could not give Salem away.

There was nowhere else to take this sentiment, no plan or specific goal. It was simply a truth that she felt and would not deny. Salem was hers, clunky name and all. No one had the right to separate them.

Devon stepped out of the bath, dripping suds on the floor, and wrapped herself in a bathrobe. She limped back into the freshly changed bedroom and slithered between the covers, whispering her thanks as one of the aunts laid Salem next to her.

"Sleep," Gailey said, tucking the covers around them both. "We'll have someone stay with you, these first few nights. No need to worry about rolling on the child in your sleep."

"Can I raise her?" Devon asked. Salem's tiny hands curled around her adult fingers, grasping tight; they held each other fast. "I can stay here longer. I don't mind."

Gailey squeezed the pillows roughly, plumping them up. "That's not how it works."

"Why not? Why can't it be?"

"Oh, my lovely." Gailey put a hand on Devon's head, as if she were a dog. "Listen to me, and carefully. No one gets more than three years to nurse the child, and after that all women must go on to their next wedding. Marriages are carefully negotiated, to limit inbreeding."

"I know," Devon said, then realized she was holding the baby too tightly when Salem started to cry. "I know the terms of my contract, I understand our struggles with fertility," she said, calmer. "But I thought—"

"No," said Gailey. Seeing Devon's expression, her own softened a little. "All mother-brides experience this. It is completely normal, and we have all been through it. Including me."

"You've done this?" It shouldn't have surprised her, because of course all women who could have children had done so. All the same, Devon struggled to picture Gailey as young, wedded, pregnant, and nursing. Specifically, she couldn't fathom how someone could go through this same experience yet still advocate for it, as other Family women seemed to.

"Naturally, dear." Gailey folded her hands one atop the other. "As I was saying, we all struggle with the leaving. Your mother probably struggled. But in the blink of an eye your baby will be grown up and getting wedded. Soon enough, she'll have children of her own. When she does, think of how happy you'll be to have scions in another house, a lineage of your flesh. Is that not a beautiful thing?"

Devon had no fucking idea what to say to that.

"Trust the process," Gailey went on with a tired expression. "After three years, you'll be dying to get away from the babe. I certainly was." She quavered a little; the other aunts looked at each other, saying nothing.

"What? No, I won't!" Did they think she was stupid? Easily distracted, easily put off? "I want to stay with her!"

The older woman frowned, face pulled into severe lines. "Why don't we put a plan in place? Scheduled time away from your daughter. Some mother-brides do that. Helps to not bond so much."

"Time away?" Devon struggled to keep the panic out of her voice. "We don't need any time apart!"

"We'll talk about that another time. Get some rest for now, my lovely." Gailey was already retreating from the room with slumped shoulders, toward her own quarters.

In fairness to the woman, she was probably exhausted, too. It'd been a long labor for everyone. Devon was willing to forgive that, and tired enough to take the advice about sleeping. She drifted off, Salem curled in the crook of her arm.

But Devon was rather less forgiving when Gailey came back some ten hours later, a calculating look in her eye.

"You're showing all the warning signs of an over-bonded mother," Gailey told her. "This may seem harsh, but I think you should agree to an early intervention."

"That's ridiculous. I'm agreeing to no such thing!"

Gailey waved the other aunts over. Three women held her down while another pried Salem out of her fingers. Devon was two days post birth, still bleeding, unable to stop them or put up any resistance beyond shrieking.

"Enjoy yourself," said one of the older women. "Relax and get some rest."

"Fuck you!" Her words bounced limply off their retreating backs, landing no true blows.

Devon lay in bed for the next few hours, too angry to cry, consumed with shame and failure. Follow the rules, toe the line, live the good life; that's what she had been taught all her life. But Devon didn't want a good life. She wanted her daughter, no more and no less. The knight commander's promise all those years ago that bad things only happened to those who broke rules felt like a hollow echo. She'd been good, she'd obeyed, yet Salem was still being taken away.

It was unfair. And something in her, a rebelliousness long dormant and buried by the shock of Ramsey's punishment, stirred in her chest.

When she felt stronger, she got out of bed and flung the books and cups of inktea that they brought. Salem, lovely Salem, was every bit as fierce. Those piercing wails could be heard across the house. Devon paused in her destruction to kneel by her locked door, listening with anguished satisfaction until at last her daughter was grudgingly brought back.

"I didn't agree," she said, voice cracked, but Gailey only shook her head.

They came back the next day, to do it again. As before, two women tried to hold down a swearing, spitting Devon.

She was stronger today. Fought like a badger and shrieked like a banshee until her throat was raw.

They had almost finished disentangling Salem from Devon's grasp when Luton strode into the room, face red and tie crooked.

"The hell are you doing?" He scowled at a hyperventilating Devon, who took advantage of the distraction to snatch her child back. Salem nuzzled frantically and Devon almost tore her dress trying to pull her top down to nurse the child.

Gailey puffed up. "This is women's business."

"On the contrary. This is my house, and therefore, this is also my business." Luton stared her down; his sister cringed back, instantly deflated. "I ask again, what are you doing?"

"Luton, she was showing classic signs of being overly bonded, so I proposed short periods of trial separation. It's a technique that has worked for other brides, in other houses—"

"Well, it clearly isn't working here! My God, I can't take a piss without having to listen to an infant wailing or a girl crying!"

Devon wanted to snarl that she hadn't cried a tear, not since the birth. Shrieking with rage was entirely different. Instead, she locked her jaw shut. However selfish his motives, Luton was at least de facto on her side.

"If we remain firm, it will prevent a host of problems for everyone in the long run."

"Problems?" Luton looked at Devon, who cradled a nursing Salem close. "Right now, the girl is happy, the baby is happy. Which means I do not have a headache. Where is the problem? Why distress them?"

"My concern is when they need to be separated—"

"When we need to separate them, we will do so," he said, a wrinkle of irritation between his brows. "I see no value in preemptively causing upset. If Devon is uncooperative, we can hardly apply for a wet nurse, and then the baby will starve! Do what is needed to make mother and child happy for now. You *can* manage that much, can't you?"

Gailey swallowed, face darkening. She exchanged glances with the other aunts.

"Glad that's agreed." Luton strode back out.

Devon curled around her daughter and watched him go, heart turning to a ball of spikes inside her chest even as she broke into a sweat from sheer relief. Three years was enough to change their minds, and she would do exactly that.

No one was taking Salem away from her.

9

THE TEN FIFTEEN TO EDINBURGH

PRESENT DAY

In previous eras, mind eaters were mostly killed at birth. That changed in the 1920s, when the patriarch of the Ravenscar Manor took it upon himself to create a "cure" for one of his sons, who had been born a mind eater. Whether he did so out of love, or out of a practical realization that there was power and money to be had from such a venture, is a matter of speculation.

All we know is that, some twenty-five years later, he eventually succeeded in creating a prototype of the drug we now call Redemption. And the Six Families were changed forever.

—Amarinder Patel, Paper and Flesh: A Secret History

In the alley below Devon's flat, a lone dragon walked up the detritus-strewn pavement. Crossing from one end of the alley to the other.

Devon dropped to a crouch behind the railing of her flat steps. "They're learning my methods. The knights must have gone straight to check the shelters this time."

"Shelters?" Hester crouched at her side, a still-smoldering cigarette between her fingers.

"Where I leave Cai's victims. Humans mostly ignore their impoverished, so almost no one tips off the police."

"True. They're as cruel as we are, in their own way." Hester held up a compact mirror, angling it to see around the railing of the steps. "He's gone. For now."

"A little close for comfort." Devon checked her watch; 9:50 P.M. The mobile phone was burning a figurative hole in her pocket. If she was going to flee to the Ravenscars tonight, then she needed to let *him* know. Aloud, she said, "Did you drive down here? Is there a car we can take?"

"Sadly, no. A friend drove me to the city limits a couple days ago, and dropped me off."

"Huh, curious choice. Why not hang around?"

"In case this was a Family trap and the city was full of knights." Hester added reluctantly, "And I didn't realize we'd be leaving under such duress like this."

"Fair enough. I guess we're taking the train, then."

"Train?"

"With you. To see Killock Ravenscar."

"I see." Hester stubbed out her vanilla cigarette on the filthy brickwork and flicked it off the side. "Not that I'm complaining, but why the change of heart? I thought you didn't trust me."

"It's not my decision, is it? Cai needs your cure. I can't deny that. If I want a shot at giving him a free and happy life, then I need Redemption, and a path to safety." Devon stalked back into the flat. "I'll start packing."

"What's happening?" Cai said. "Are we still leaving?"

"Yes." She grabbed her suitcase by the wall and took it to the bedroom. "Grab your Game Boy, please. No, put it in my messenger bag; there won't be room in the case." On top of the clothes, she squashed down the handful of old fairy-tale books she still owned: *The History of Photogen and Nycteris*; *The King of Elfland's Daughter*; *Princess Furball*.

"All right." He unzipped the messenger bag and tucked his console inside. Important things stayed in there, like their twenty-odd grand in cash, an emergency book to snack on, and her mobile. And now the Game Boy, which gave his life continuity. Something about the same levels, the same challenges held his attention despite all those disparate feeds he consumed.

"Can I help?" Hester said, still hovering near the front door.

"Thanks, but I'm already done." Devon slammed the suitcase shut on her meager possessions. "I need the toilet before we leave." She also needed a phone call before they left.

"We're in rather a hurry!"

"Right, and I'll be quick." Devon escaped into the bathroom before any other objections could be raised.

She sat on the seat—because she did need to go—and dug out her mobile phone from her coat pocket. Her list of Recently Called only had four contacts in it. She selected a particular number and pressed the Call button.

At times like these, Devon intensely disliked her inability to write or even text. If not for that, she'd be able to text discreetly, instead of having to do these awkward calls where she might be overheard.

Three rings, followed by the stillness that came from someone picking up but not speaking.

Because it wasn't safe to talk, Devon pressed the asterisk key in rapid succession. On her end, the phone was perfectly silent, but for her listener, they would hear the sound of a key dial arranged into longer and shorter beeps as she converted the phrase *Change of plan sit tight for more info* into a string of Morse code:

-.-. .... .- .--.—.. /—.-. / .—. .-. .-. / .... .-/-.—. .... .-/ .-.—-. /——-.. / .-. .-.—-.-.

She waited a tense few seconds, receiver to her ear, for a series of return beeps to ping down the line.

Roger that.

"Are you done yet?" Hester called through the door.

Devon covered the mobile's mic with her thumb. "Keep your shirt on."

Not enough time to get in touch with her other contact. She'd just have to go with Hester for now, and get in contact later. Devon hit the flush, yanked up her jeans, then closed the mobile and washed her hands before stepping out.

"I'm ready." Hard enough to keep her coded conversations secret from Cai, and now she'd have to avoid Hester, too. She felt the start of a stress headache in her temples.

They slipped down the stairs in a tight group of three, Hester leading the way with Devon following, her small suitcase and messenger bag slung across one shoulder. Cai stuck close to her side as they left without a backward glance. All homes looked the same when abandoned.

"We're tight for time." Hester had one hand stuffed into her purse, and Devon wondered what weapon she had hidden in there. "Give me a shout if something catches your eye."

The night they walked beneath was not the night Devon had stepped into a couple of hours before. Sobriety drew sharp the lines of every building and the temperature had dropped colder. The sidewalks were slowly thinning of people. Somewhere distant, clusters of revelers shouted and cheered on the eve of Christmas.

Cai tugged his lip anxiously. "What happens if we meet a dragon or a knight on the way to the train station?"

Hester shortened her purse strap so that the bag was close against her body. "Then we run and hope to shake them in the station crowds."

St. Mary's Cathedral came into view as they segued from St. James Boulevard onto Neville Street, its solitary bell tower thrown tall against a dark winter sky. They were not far from the train station, only two blocks away on the other side of the road.

"This would have been easier and less dangerous if we'd left sooner," Devon said, scanning the crowd with narrowed eyes. "I could have met you hours ago, if you'd wanted."

"I had no idea it was so urgent!" The other woman's glasses were misting up from her own breath as she spoke. "Besides, you're the one who dossed about in a pub for an hour."

"Well, you weren't exactly in a hurry to—" Devon began, the words dying in her throat.

Two men were standing on the wide courtyard steps that led up to St. Mary's Cathedral, their backs toward her. The first man was a dragon, rendered faceless by his helmet. The second man had the same dark hair as Devon, the same slant to his shoulders but a little older and taller and broader. Wearing a pressed suit with his hair combed back neatly. He half turned and she caught sight of a lapel pin, shaped like a tiny silver tree, which pierced his collar and nailed it in place.

Ramsey Fairweather, now a Family knight. Her brother and friend; her enemy and hunter. The second man was one she'd also met and knew to name: Ealand, a friend of Ramsey's. Also a knight.

She wasn't surprised to see them. This was the encounter that she'd been expecting, even waiting for. The knights were nothing if not reliable and predictable.

Still, this particular timing was inconvenient as all hell.

Hester slowed her pace. "What's wrong?"

"Knights ahead, ten o'clock," Devon said.

"Stay calm." Hester swiveled to the right, toward the road. Completely cool and unfazed; she was a veteran at this. "Let's cross the street, see if we can pass them by."

"They'll see us," Cai whispered. "If they look this way—"

"Keep your head down, and don't panic." Devon took her own advice, a curious kind of excitement stealing over. After so many days of drab repetition, she was almost relieved to have something happen.

They closed the distance to the station with rapid steps, crossing a road nearly devoid of traffic. Devon keeping her head down and Hester keeping her collar up. For a moment, it seemed they might slip past simply by crossing the street, when a taxi pulled up to the nearby curb.

A group of drunken young men spilled out. One of them tripped over the curb and pinwheeled like a clown while the rest broke into loud, horsey laughter.

Ramsey turned automatically at the noise and saw them at once. His form stiffened and the dragon at his side swiveled around in a sharp, jerking motion, as if someone had pulled an invisible string to whip him tautly in their direction. Ealand followed his gaze, eyes widening.

"Fuck," said Cai.

"Watch your bloody mouth." Devon caught him by the wrist and started running. Chilly night air slapped her face from the speed of her jaunt. Hester also broke into a run, keeping pace.

The sidewalk had grown slick with ice as the temperature had continued dropping through the evening, and her cheap boots skidded on gum-scabbed pavements, too clunky for efficient running. Devon kicked them off in a fury, to the astonishment of the taxi passengers, and ran barefoot on the cold ground. Hester swore and almost tripped over the discarded boots.

"But you get to swear!" Cai ran free and light in his too-small shoes and she couldn't remember the last time she'd seen him move so fluidly. They'd fled cities before, once with human police circling and once with knights on their tail, but she'd had to carry him both times. "How come I have to watch my mouth?"

It took Devon a full two seconds to parse what he was on about. "What?!" she said, shoving him beneath the arches of the station entrance. "For Chrissakes, I'm a grown-up. Swearing is my privilege!"

"Departures board." Hester pointed. "Find out what platform we're on! We need the next train to Edinburgh."

"Well, I'm twenty-five grown-ups, so I can say bad words twenty-five times more than you," Cai said.

"You're a grown-up when I bloody well say you are, not a moment sooner!" Devon said, fuming. Why did children always have to talk back at the worst times? "Hes, don't bother with the board, it's platform six."

"Are you sure—"

"I've eaten the train schedule. Let's go."

The situation fractured into a series of moments.

Four men detached from the shadows of the station, all closing in a tight circle. Two were knights in suits, two were dragons—dark tendrils of ink marking their necks.

The taller of the knights pointed straight at Hester, calling out above the station noise, "A Ravenscar!"

Hester pulled a revolver from her purse and headshot all four men with stunning accuracy. Screams and gasps. The remaining passersby fled or ducked for cover.

Knightly bodies disintegrated as they fell, flesh growing brittle and pale, ink layers peeling away to sheaves of paper that fluttered through the station. Each hit the floor as a pile of paper-stuffed suits.

"Awesome!" Cai broke into a grin; Devon was speechless.

Ramsey Fairweather burst through the station entrance, accompanied by another knight and a lone dragon. He saw the crumbling forms of his colleagues and hesitated, caught off guard.

Hester whirled and shot him. He ducked smoothly behind the closest pillar, the other knight ducking with him. The dragon stood uncertainly out in the open, half crouched and scowling.

"Shit," Hester snarled.

The gun was empty, Devon realized. A five-shooter only.

From the safety of his covered position, Ramsey called out, "Obedire, dracone!"

The lone dragon snarled, peeling away from cover, and sprinted forward.

Devon picked up her carry-all and flung it straight at him. It was a good throw, making a perfect arc through the air despite its awkward shape. The dragon didn't dodge in time. He toppled from the weight of a hefty bag to his face. Clothes and books scattered on the concrete as the zipper burst.

"Hold tight," Devon said, and slipped an arm around each of her companions' waists.

She bounded through the station with six-foot strides, no longer caring about looking inhuman. Nothing was going to be more conspicuous than the other woman opening fire in a public place. Right now, they simply needed to get away.

"That knight is chasing us," Hester shouted into her ear, while Cai said, "Dev, I think we'll miss the train!"

"Shup up, both of you!"

Pedestrians were meant to go up the stairs and over the footbridge to reach the other platform. That would take too long. Companions held fast, Devon coiled her strength and *leaped* the gap between train platforms.

She landed cleanly on the gravel that lay between both sets of tracks, rebounding up and over to platform six—accompanied by the noise of Hester's swearing and Cai's laughter.

Devon pelted through the waiting room past a scattering of shocked travelers, out the other side, and then straight onto the last Christmas Eve train to Edinburgh. Right as the conductor blew his whistle.

10

THE PRINCESS RETURNS
TO ELFLAND

SEVEN YEARS AGO

She rose at once, and now Earth had lost on her the grip that it only has on
material things, and a thing of dreams and fancy and fable and phantasy,
she drifted from the room.

—Lord Dunsany, *The King of Elfland's Daughter*

Salem wanted shells for her third birthday. She had never been to the sea and wasn't allowed to go, but had fallen in love with the idea of waves upon beaches. Devon sought an audience with Luton in the evening, knocking politely on his study door.

"Shells? Where did she get such ridiculous ideas from?" said Luton. "The girl is barely eating books."

"She's eaten 'The Little Mermaid.'" Devon cringed at his expression. "Isn't that okay? It's a classic, I grew up eating it. And I saw it on your shelves, so I thought—"

"You should have checked with me first," he said sourly. "Still, I suppose there's no harm. I'll see if I can get her some shells. Anything else she wants?" For all his grumbling, Luton remained indulgent of Salem, a fact that seemed to surprise him as much as it did Devon.

"No. You've given me a lot as it is. I'm grateful."

She was lucky. Other mother-brides had to give up their children. But over the months Luton had listened to Devon's arguments, had seen the strong bond between herself and Salem, and agreed to give special consideration, providing Devon lived with them and did not take the girl back to Fairweather Manor. Sometimes, the rules could be bent.

Behave, be good, toe the line, follow the rules, and the patriarchs would be good to you. In the end, that had proved true after all, to Devon's chastisement. She should have trusted that wisdom sooner. After all, it was Family traditions that had gifted her Salem, a child she might not have otherwise had, and the girl was a truly wonderful thing.

"Grateful," he echoed, and a funny expression crossed his face, as if he'd swallowed a bug by mistake.

She thanked him and left. Shells for Salem, lovely little dark-haired Salem who found butterflies funny and hadn't met a tree she couldn't climb and loved to go riding with Devon, tiny though she was.

Taking the steps two at a time, Devon ran down the stairs and out into the garden populated by acacia trees and Spanish rosebushes, where her daughter was tossing pebbles into an ancient fountain.

"Mum!" Salem held her arms out and Devon scooped her up with a smile. Her daughter was a mirror of herself: same wide-shouldered build and aquiline features and dark hair. Luton had contributed nothing more than a technicality.

Strangely, she had never missed having a mother till becoming one herself. With both arms around her daughter's back Devon could, if she closed her eyes, imagine a young Amberly Blackwood from long ago, picking her up in the same way. But even then, the only face she could picture on such a figure was her own, albeit older. It was so hard to imagine a thing you had never seen.

From the other end of the garden, Gailey and the rest of the aunts watched with a scowl. They'd welcomed Devon among them when she had been pregnant, but after Luton's change of heart, they no longer spoke to her. If she so much as glanced their way, they drew back.

Not that Devon really cared. She had woods and streams and frost-laden gardens to explore with her child, sometimes on foot and sometimes on horseback, with Salem carefully bundled on the saddle with her. Let the old bats enjoy their self-inflicted isolation, stuck in their fusty quarters for most of the day. Devon set off into the cultivated orchards of Winterfield Manor, holding Salem's small hand.

Luton was true to his word, arranging for a box of shells to be bought and delivered to Winterfield Manor. Devon inspected them carefully the evening before the party, then packaged the lot in pastel gift paper.

Salem turned three on Christmas Day, the ground dry and crisp with a sprinkling of frost. Devon spent the morning hanging bunting in the main dining room, and even took the time to put on a forest-green chiffon dress. She had never cared much for dresses but Salem loved pretty fabric, both wearing it and seeing it. The things you did for a child's happiness.

Birthday parties had never really been "big" at Fairweather Manor, but the Winterfields liked celebrations. The garden was filled with people, sitting and talking or wandering about. Luton even took time from his work schedule to come outside, smartly dressed but looking ill at ease.

"Thank you for coming," she said, slouching down because he hated looking short next to her. "Lemmie will be glad to see you."

Luton swirled a cup of inktea and didn't answer. He'd never used her nickname for their daughter.

Salem zigzagged through chairs before circling back around, eyes bright with joy.

"There you are, Lemmie. I have a present for you." Devon held out the paper-wrapped bundle.

"From both of us," Luton said quickly. As if it had been his idea and not hers, but she let it slide. He had bought them, after all.

Salem snatched the package and poked a hole in the thin, crinkling paper, crowing with delight. "Shells!"

"Lots of shells." Devon drew the girl into her lap and helped to unwrap the rest. "We can make a necklace with some of them, if you want."

Salem picked up the biggest shell and put it to her ear, smiling. "Sea!"

Other adults came forward, along with the handful of older Winterfield children. Salem did well out of her birthday. She was plied with small gifts, mostly the usual children's picture boards that she'd recently started eating as her bookteeth came in.

A package of toy teacups had also arrived, courtesy of Fairweather House. Devon twinged with embarrassment on seeing the address label; she'd hardly had contact with home in her three years here. But Salem took so much of her time and energy, not to mention the constant tiny tug-of-wars with Luton. She couldn't call them, since Uncle Aike did not keep a connected landline.

"Ms. Fairweather."

Devon jumped, startled to find Gailey standing in proximity. "What is it?"

"Mr. Winterfield would like to see you. Come with me, please." Gailey's expression was flat and dour.

"Luton? But he was just here." Devon swiveled her head, surprised to find her husband had apparently left. "Can't this wait? It's the middle of her party."

"Won't take a moment," Gailey said stiffly. "You'll be returning very soon."

"Fine, if I must." Devon kissed the girl's hair. "Go play, Lemmie. I'll be right back."

Salem didn't look up as they left. She was too busy arranging shells in a neat row by size, squinting in the winter sunlight.

"This way," Gailey said, as if Devon didn't know the layout of Winterfield

Manor by heart after all this time. Perhaps, as with so many things about Gailey, she simply operated on autopilot, speaking words and making gestures that had become as reflexive as breathing.

Devon, following dutifully, resolved to never become such a robotic old woman. She took the stairs two at a time, impatient to get the visit over with, and turned on the landing toward Luton's study.

"No—your quarters," Gailey said. Her hands were twitching. "He wants to see you in there."

"What's this about?" Devon was struck with a sudden urge to flee back to the winter garden, where her daughter waited.

"Devon, please don't argue with me today." Gailey sounded tired. "I have things to do and other places to be and . . . it won't take long."

"Fine, suit yourself." She stalked off down the hallway toward her own room.

Luton Winterfield was waiting when she got there, sitting in the miniature living area that Devon shared with her daughter. He'd taken off his smart jacket and thrown it across the couch arm. A newspaper spread its heavily inked pages across his lap. Oddly, he was reading it, rather than eating it; a rare sight.

"Hello?" She spoke her greeting like a general sending a scout into hostile territory.

"Took your time." Luton flipped a page of his newspaper. "There's a cup on the side table, right next to you. Drink it, please." He wasn't actually reading, just running his fingers over the pages with agitated energy. Fiddling with it.

She looked to her left, inspecting the mug. "What's this for?"

"It's just tea, for God's sakes." He hadn't spoken to her so sharply in over a year. "Drink it and sit, won't you? I cannot abide argumentative women."

And Devon couldn't abide rude men. But she was only twenty-two, felt she owed him for giving her Salem, and didn't want to cause an argument. Every single day was fraught with tiny conflicts between herself and the members of this sodding Family. Pitching a battle might align him against her.

She picked up the cup and drank. Bitterness made her gag.

"What's in this?" It wasn't *just* tea, like he'd claimed. The taste of ink couldn't compensate for whatever had been put into the cup.

"Go wait in the bedroom," he said. "We'll speak shortly." When she didn't budge, he said with visible annoyance, "I will explain everything. I just require a moment to compose myself."

She didn't yet know how much of a coward he was, or she'd have been more suspicious. Devon went to the adjoining room and sat on the bed as directed.

The minutes stretched by, and Luton didn't appear. She could hear the newspaper rustling, the shuffle as he occasionally moved around; that was it. He was waiting, as she was.

Drowsiness set in, weighing her bones like liquid mercury. Something was very wrong and she stood up, determined to . . . what? She couldn't remember what needed doing. Salem was in the garden and something was wrong.

The ground came up to meet her as she crumpled to the floor. The last thing she remembered before dipping into blackness was the sound of footsteps approaching and the touch of chilly fingers thumbing her eyelids.

A confusion of movement, lights, and voices; people around her. Sleep that wasn't sleeping, and dreams that weren't dreams. She was a princess in a cave, a dragon roaring all around, but it was only a car engine. Countryside flickered by like a cheap animated show. More hands, more moving; a scent she recognized.

Then darkness, and softness.

Devon woke sometime late at night with a splitting headache, a roiling stomach, and a terrible feeling of loss. She scrubbed her eyes, battling queasiness.

This wasn't her bedroom. Or rather, it was her bedroom—but in Fairweather Manor, not Winterfield Manor. And the scent she'd caught was of heather and wet moors, rolling steeply outside her window.

Still dressed in green chiffon, she slowly turned over. Two men were in the room, both of whom she recognized. Uncle Aike sat in a chair with legs crossed, holding a half-eaten book on a plate. The title was something in Japanese, a language she'd never eaten before and so could not read.

At his side stood Ramsey Fairweather. She almost didn't recognize him; more than ten years had passed since they'd physically met. He looked older, as one would expect, hair cut short from unruly boyish tumble into a military buzz. His features, always a trifle sharp and narrow in boyhood, reminded her now of a hatchet blade.

"It's you," she said. Her head throbbed.

"Hello, Dev. Been a few years, eh?" Ramsey toyed with a silver pin on his lapel. "I should call you Devon the Dame, now that you're grown."

The old nickname habit filled her with a rush of warmth. "I missed you."

"Still sentimental," he said. Deflecting, as always. "How's married life?"

Married. Marriage. Luton. *Salem.*

She sat bolt upright. "Where's my daughter?"

Aike bit a corner off his Japanese book, speaking for the first time. "At Winterfield Manor, where she belongs." His bookteeth were unsheathed for eating, distorting his words. "And you've returned home, at the close of your contract. Where you belong." Under his breath, he added in Japanese, "*Eshajōri*. As they say."

Even then, she didn't understand. "No, that isn't right, I get to stay with Salem because Luton and I reached an agreement—"

"Let me be direct," her uncle said between mouthfuls. "Your husband lied, princess."

"Lied?" She sounded small and pathetic, even to herself. Devon looked to Ramsey for confirmation, or reassurance.

Her brother stifled a yawn and examined his nails.

"There is no special agreement," her uncle said. "Five hundred years of 'eater traditions do not get overturned on the whims of one pampered girl." A long-suffering sigh. "Still, I wish he had not done so, since he has only made things harder in the end, but what happens under another house's roof is their affair. I suppose he thought it would be the easiest way of pacifying you. For what it's worth, I am sorry, my dear."

"You don't understand. It's her birthday and I said I'd be right back!" She looked pleadingly at her brother. "Won't you take me back? Why aren't you saying anything?"

"Don't be so dramatic." Ramsey sounded . . . annoyed.

"Your child is weaned and three years of age." Uncle Aike wiped ink-stained fingers on a napkin, transferring his now-empty plate to a side table. "The contract is over, princess. Do you understand?"

Something in her was cracking, little spiderweb fractures that spread and spread. If she breathed too deeply, she'd fall to pieces. Oddly, the thing she couldn't stop thinking about was Gailey's pitying looks and incessant yet subdued anger. Not directed at her, but for her. How unkind she had been to the other woman.

Devon the Deceived, she thought inanely. A stupid girl who was easily tricked.

"Princess," Uncle Aike said again, recalling her attention.

"I want to see Salem, just one more time," she said, knowing it was ridiculous to voice such a desire. "The least you can bloody do is let me say good-bye!"

"That tongue of yours, eh?" Uncle Aike dabbed his lips. "Lower your tone, please."

Devon bit the inside of her cheek, marveling how someone she had once loved so much could become someone she hated so unreservedly. It struck her as a terrible, petrifying irony that the book eaters thought of themselves as Families and yet did not value family at all. Daughters were commodities; sons, totally expendable.

And children—

She had to get out of here. She had to rescue Salem.

Devon launched out of bed, almost tripping over the chiffon dress she'd put on this morning for Salem's sake, everything for Salem, she would run back to Salem and fuck everything else.

"Dev, stop!" Ramsey sprinted after.

Devon wrenched the door open and stormed down the hallway, crashing into startled uncles and nearly running into an eight-year-old child. Faerdre's little boy, left here by his mother, and Devon couldn't remember his name after four sodding years in Winterfield Manor. She charged past him in a haze of fury.

Floor-to-ceiling shelves were looming, dusty guardians, the books gleaming like endless rows of teeth in wooden mouths. Instead of going down the main stairs she whirled through the first-floor drawing room, knocking over tables and chairs as she went, in a bid to make the chase difficult. Ramsey, not far behind her, tripped on something and swore. No one told *him* off for using bad words.

There was another passage down through the back stairwell and it'd be easier to lose her brother on that route. When had the house become such a cramped, twisting maze? Such a fearful and gloomy place?

"Stop, for fuck's sake!" Ramsey caught up to her at last as they both tore out into the front hallway, his fingers catching a fistful of tulle fabric. "What are you doing?"

"Going back to Winterfield!" She yanked her sleeve out of his grip, spun round, and crashed straight into Uncle Aike, who had taken the other set of stairs while she had detoured through the house, until he'd come out in front of her.

Devon backed away, hemmed in between the two men. "Get out of my way!" She was alarmed to see Family members gathering in the shadows, watchful and sad. One of the aunts shook her head mournfully.

Uncle Aike held up his hands. "Princess—"

She spat; he recoiled. "I'm not your princess. Princesses are bullshit. Your fairy tales are bullshit. Stop treating me like a child and use my *name*!"

"Devon," Uncle Aike said warningly, in that do-not-argue-with-me tone that no longer frightened her, because the only thing that frightened her anymore was losing her daughter.

"Piss on the manor," she said. "I hate this shitting house and I hate these books and the wedding you made me have and I'm just trapped here with a bunch of—"

"Devon—"

"—*bloody fucking monsters!*"

Uncle Aike uncurled from his habitual stoop, drawing up to his full height. "Young lady—"

She snatched up a vase from a side table and threw it at his head. He ducked sideways, astonished, stumbling against Ramsey, who staggered back from the unexpected weight. Ceramic shattered against the wall behind them.

She darted around both men and through the foyer and out of the house and across the driveway. Heading south toward the woods, toward Birmingham, where Salem waited to be rescued, shouts and cries ringing out behind her.

Devon ran.

11

RAMSEY AT THE CHARGE!

PRESENT DAY

When the game is going against you, stay calm—and cheat.
—George MacDonald Fraser, *Flashman at the Charge*

Ramsey looked at Ealand, the latter frozen with indecision. "Get the dragon and get out of here, both of you!" He shot to his feet.

The center of the train station had become a swirling maelstrom of ink-sodden paper, courtesy of the corpses Devon's "friend" had left behind. Passersby were screaming and security—or the police, or both—would be here any moment.

"Wait!" Ealand sounded panicked. "What about Kingsey's orders—"

"Fuck Kingsey, get out before the humans arrest you!" Ramsey called over one shoulder, sprinting after his sister's fast-disappearing form. "I'll be in touch!"

This whole situation was so typical of Devon. Even when they were children, she would charge ahead into the woods, into ravines, over cliff edges and up sheer walls, never thinking of what awaited. Never giving thought to whether a tree branch might snap beneath her feet, whether gutters and pipes—not made for climbing—could hold her weight, or just whether whatever-the-fuck-she-was-doing was a good idea, full stop. She didn't bloody think.

And it had always fallen to him, this job of chasing her down, of bailing her out or rescuing her sorry arse when she got into trouble. She would have disagreed with his assessment and spun her selfishness as a choice on his part. *So, stay at home, then.* Would have argued that she'd never forced him to participate in their escapades. *I never asked you to come with me, dummy.* But she thought that way because she lacked responsibility and insight.

Ramsey lacked neither. It was the responsibility of men to rescue women from themselves, and men of the Families did not shy from duty. Duty bade he run after her.

He just wished she didn't run quite so fast.

Shops, faces, and peeling-paint walls flew by as he bounded and sprinted in her footsteps. He stormed through it all, aggrieved by the chaos and sloppiness.

Wasn't *all* Devon's fault, if he were being honest. In fact, his commander—Kingsey—bore the lion's share of the blame. If Ramsey had been in charge, they'd have hung back, followed at a distance. They should have tried to find out *why* Devon was traveling with a Ravenscar, and where she was going, rather than leaping to accost the woman.

But Kingsey hadn't been around to lead the men himself, nor had he left any specific instructions other than *intercept any Ravenscars you find* even though that was clearly a stupid course of action. The only Ravenscar who knew anything worthwhile was Killock himself, and capturing one of his useless siblings would only have risked scaring the bugger off.

Too late now. The most senior knights had panicked, acted reflexively to follow Kingsey's tentative orders, and got shot for their trouble. Now their quarry was spooked, the humans had noticed them, disaster and mess everywhere. They'd be lucky if Killock didn't go into hiding after this.

Ahead, Ramsey caught a glimpse of Devon's tall form as she flung herself and her two companions aboard the 10:15; saw, as he forced his legs to pump a faster speed, how the doors to their carriage slammed shut. Engine beginning to gather momentum.

Helluva jump, from here to the train. He went for it anyway; was out of options, otherwise. Carriages pulled away from the station and he leaped in a great, muscle-tearing bound. Fifteen feet near enough and it *worked*.

He landed, hands clamping on to the external handrails that bracketed the doors. Feet scrabbling for purchase on the hanging step, sweat breaking out across his skin.

The 10:15 to Edinburgh departed from Newcastle Station into the darkness of a Northumbrian winter night, gathering to a pace that even a knight would have found impossible to match. 'Eaters were fast, but not that fast.

A few seconds to breathe while his heart slowed to a reasonable beat. Feet braced firm, Ramsey wrenched the doors partway open. Half squeezed, half stumbled inside, panting from exertion. Relieved to have salvaged something from this mess.

The last carriage was not meant for passengers. A staff-only compartment with machinery, lockers, and a broken snacks trolley. The one occupant—a lone middle-aged ticket collector—shot to his feet, pale with shock. Humans always had a kind of nervous energy that reminded Ramsey of chickens.

The ticket collector fluttered at him. "Sir! Passengers are not supposed—"

Ramsey swung a hard punch to the temples.

The man dropped.

"Nothing personal, mate." He bent over the unconscious figure and scavenged himself a new identity.

Knight, begone. Ramsey shed his appearance as a snake sheds its skin, tossing aside his own clothes to don the conductor's kit. A black uniform jacket, buttons intricately rough. Didn't fit well, though. He was both leaner and broader than the man whose clothes he'd taken. Fabric pulled tight across his back. Seams pinched his shoulders.

Small considerations. He pushed them aside, kept dressing. The transmitter under his shirt pressed its hard edges against his ribs as he changed. His secret weapon against Dev, for keeping her in check. He patted it fondly.

Flat cap next, pulled low across the forehead. Changed the shape of his face. He liked that. The jaunty angle made him look harmless. The trousers and shoes he left alone. His own dark slacks and leather brogues would do.

The ticket machine came last, slung over one shoulder. The heavy metal weight of it felt good. Could pretend he had a gun, like lads in films. Like that Ravenscar bitch.

A red scarf hung from a peg. He plucked that off, wound it around his neck. It hid his mouth, made him look stockier. Hopefully enough that Hester wouldn't recognize him, if she saw him again.

Disguise complete, he hoisted the semi-naked ticket collector under the armpits and tossed the man, still unconscious, through the half-open carriage exit.

The soft body tumbled and rolled, soon out of sight along the disappearing length of track. Perhaps the man had survived, or perhaps not. It didn't matter. What *did* matter is that he would not wake up on the train at an inconvenient time and cause problems.

Ramsey checked for the emergency hunting knife strapped to the inside of his leg, and relocated it—still sheathed, of course—to an inside jacket pocket.

Time to find Devon.

He paused at the entrance of the connecting passageway before entering the next carriage, first to listen and then to look. Minimal chatter, and nothing of his quarry. Several people tried to show him tickets or buy new ones. Ramsey told them the machine was broken and they left him alone.

The next carriage and the one after that were the same: thickly populated with tired, sweaty humans trying to make it home before the start of their pointless holiday. Also notably empty of his sister and her companions. The smell of so many people in close quarters made him glad for the scarf he wore. At least no one tried to buy a ticket.

Six minutes after boarding, Ramsey located his sister.

He caught the sound of a child laughing while out in a connecting passage-way, mixing with the low, unfeminine pitch of Devon's voice. Alert and wary, he paused by the exit of the fourth carriage. Listened at the loosely shuttered door of the fifth carriage.

"Don't get too comfortable, we're not home and dry yet." A lilting, northern-sounding voice; must be the Ravenscar woman who'd killed his men with such efficacy. "Wish I'd brought more bullets. Just in case, and all that."

Ramsey listened, intrigued. He'd always fancied owning a pistol, done a bit of target practice for fun once or twice. The paperwork required for them was awkward, though, as it would be for any regular book eater.

"You're a ridiculously good shot." Devon, unmistakably her voice. "Four clean kills in a handful of seconds, all moving targets. Where did you get the gun?"

He'd heard enough. Had to move quick. Ramsey took out the transmitter, holding it in one hand with his thumb on the button; would look like a walkie-talkie to the casual observer. The ticket-collecting machine he held in the other hand. Trigger finger ready, he opened the shuttered door with an elbow and shuffled in.

All three of his quarry sat on the floor of the connecting passage between carriages, and all three looked up sharply as he entered.

Hester Ravenscar—he recognized her at once, had studied the files and Family photographs to death—was nondescript, having neither a beautiful face nor an interesting figure. Dressed like a recovering hippie. If he hadn't already seen how deadly she was, he would have dismissed her entirely. The boy, Cai, was also visually uninteresting. Small, slight, dark-haired. Nothing to indicate the true monstrous nature beneath.

Devon, though, looked like a poster child for Dykes on Bikes: tall and rangy, hacked-off hair, all-black clothes and far too much leather. Slouched against the wall like some delinquent city youth. A far cry from the lace-skirted girl in braids he recalled from long ago.

His sister blanched with shock as he walked in. Disguises didn't mean much at their level of familiarity. Her gaze dropped to the transmitter held firmly in his fist and her jaw tightened.

"Evening, ladies," Ramsey said, still half-buried in the winter scarf. Hat pulled low, almost to the eyebrows; comical, under other circumstances. "I'm afraid we don't allow passengers to sit on the floor in this part of the train. Mind if I move you along to the carriage?"

91

✳ ✳ ✳ ✳

"You two go get seats," Devon said, climbing to her feet. "I'll buy us tickets and catch up in a second. Did you say we were heading to Edinburgh?"

"Edinburgh, yes," said Hester, after a pregnant pause, and Ramsey could sense the tension rolling off her. Reluctant to share information, he guessed.

But she moved off quickly enough with Cai at her heels. Probably keen to avoid further questions.

When the connecting door shut after them, Ramsey said calmly, "If I were actually hunting you, you'd be finished. You've ten seconds to give me an explanation for that massacre back there."

"How did you even get—" she began, then wisely checked herself for once, swallowing the question. "Your men attacked us first. What was I supposed to do? Grab her gun? I might as well admit I'm a traitor and working for the Families!" She looked guiltily over one shoulder, as if the Ravenscar woman might burst through, crying vengeance.

"None of that, ta. A simple heads-up about what you were doing, where you were going, and who you were with would have been nice." Ramsey wasn't going to blame his superior in front of her. "At the moment we have an entire squad dead, and fuck knows what will happen to the two people I left behind."

"Again, what was I supposed to do?" she bit back. Her gaze kept going toward the transmitter. "Here's a thought—don't come running after us next time! I didn't know she had a sodding gun, in any case!"

"Has she told you who she is?" Sweat made his palms slick but he kept a firm grip on the transmitter, and a cool six feet away from Devon. Couldn't be too sure she wouldn't try something. "Or what she wants from you?"

"Obviously," Devon said, clearly annoyed. "She's a Ravenscar and is taking me straight to Killock. Like you wanted. Isn't that the whole point of me dragging Cai through this hell?"

"It is, yes." He fiddled with the ticket machine. Stupid thing. Hard to work one-handed but he didn't dare remove his thumb from the transmitter. "Where is she taking you? Is Edinburgh your final destination, and what's been agreed?"

"Somewhere in Scotland, that's all I know. Fairly sure Edinburgh isn't the final destination, only a place to change over." Leather-clad arms crossed. "They're offering me Redemption but I must agree to live under Ravenscar rules. It's complicated."

"Interesting," he mused. "Still, it doesn't matter what they're asking for, because you won't be hanging around or living with them long term, no? This all ends once we find Killock." He finally got the stupid machine to spit out two tickets, and proffered them carefully across the distance between them. "How long till the next stop? What even *is* the next stop?"

"Eighteen minutes till we arrive at Berwick-on-Tweed." She snatched the tickets from his grasp. "Don't you eat train schedules for your local area?"

"Aren't you a sarcastic cow." Ramsey had better things to fill his brain with than train schedules; that was *her* job. "Here's what we do. Five minutes from now, I'll be pulling the emergency stop and turning off the lights, if I can access them. When that happens, convince this Hester Ravenscar that knights must have made it on board, and that the three of you should disembark early."

"You want us to abandon the train?" she said, incredulous. "What will *you* be doing?"

"Making your lie into truth, naturally. Me, my knife, and a carriage of shrieking innocents will give you all the panicked stampeding needed to fuel this story of knightly pursuit."

"Christ, Ramsey! How many people are you planning to kill?"

"None, you dolt. Only frighten them enough to get a few running and screaming up and down this train." Like fucking chickens, he thought. With him as the fox.

"But why?" she hissed. "What's the point of all that theater?"

"The point is the disruption itself," he said sweetly. "You may not trust me at present—"

"No shit!"

"—but I'm invested in your success, at least for this moment in time. So ruin Miss Ravenscar's plan, keep her off-balance. Still get to their secret location, but on our terms, not hers. In short, stay alive, Devon, and stay smart. Remember: Killock didn't send this sister of his because he thought she was incompetent. This cow killed four trained men tonight without blinking. Don't let her keep any edge on you."

Devon surprised him by sucking in her cheeks and saying, "Fine. Then we might as well go the extra mile, make it particularly convincing. Send a knight or two out to scout for us, give us bogeymen to hide from and dodge."

He nodded again. "Not a bad idea. We'll track your phone and send a knight to intercept the pair of you along the road, if I can get one out in time. Have a little car chase, or something." Ramsey ran his tongue over his teeth. "But keep this one alive, please. I'm tired of cleaning up bodies, and knights are not infinitely expendable." Quite the opposite, these days.

"I can't promise that—"

"Just do your best." Ramsey flicked her forehead, like he had when they were children; she scowled. "Don't get any funny ideas about running off with these people and their magic pills, aye? Because I will always catch you when you run. Always. Remember that."

She curled her fists, said nothing.

"Go," he said, waving the transmitter, "before I change my mind on this entire venture and blow your son into next Thursday." The one security he held against her: the ability to end Cai's life from a distance, at the press of a button. "And remember that I'm not the only one with a transmitter."

"Of course I remember, and I was already going." Devon whirled away from him and back toward the carriage. Tickets still clutched to her chest.

"Make it convincing," he called after her. "You have a lot riding on this."

She didn't look back, but he caught the flinch of her shoulders and was satisfied.

Ramsey watched her leave, then drew out his knife. Eyed the carriages he'd come through, remembering the smell of them. Anticipating their noisy, tiring chaos, the claustrophobic way they'd crash around him.

Get on with things, he told himself, and tightened his grip around the hilt.

12

THE PRINCESS AND THE GOBLINS

EIGHT YEARS AGO

It was foolish indeed—thus to run farther and farther from all who could help her, as if she had been seeking a fit spot for the goblin creature to eat her in at his leisure; but that is the way fear serves us: it always sides with the thing we are afraid of.

—George MacDonald, *The Princess and the Goblins*

Pursuit wasn't immediate. For the first half hour Devon fled blindly through the tangled trees, both elated and unnerved to hear nothing but silence. Before long, she was cut and bruised from stumbles in the woods, and very lost. No going back, though. She pushed onward through snow-encrusted trees and mulchy, half-frozen earth and came up against a tall barbed-wire fence.

The edge of Fairweather Manor.

The land beyond was unknown to her.

No going back. Devon flung herself against the fencing, toes and fingers easily finding purchase. Up, and over. She landed in an awkward roll on the other side and set off in the snow toward where she thought Birmingham was. A big city, surrounded by roads, only a couple of hours' drive. Finding the Winterfields' home would surely be a matter of ease.

The Families were not on her side. This realization struck Devon like a bell-ringer with a gong mallet, shaking her all the way through even as her lungs burned and her feet pounded the underbrush, nose full of the scent of ever-greens and fresh snow. The Families were her blood relations, people she loved and had been loved by; her entire world. They were now her Great Enemy.

In fact, they always had been. However loving her childhood, her flesh was still theirs, her goods for the selling. Like pigs or chickens raised for the slaughter, she had developed affection for her keepers, and they for her. But that did not stop her from being consumed; pig farmers still chewed their bacon with enjoyment. Affection only made cruelty rueful.

In the distance behind her trilled a soft, high whistle.

Pursuit. Her skin broke into goose bumps and Devon ran harder. She hadn't done much running about since Salem's birth but desperation lent her strength. Evasion should still be possible if she could get somewhere with people, where the knights might be shy to accost.

Except she feared dashing across the moorland, out in the open with knights streaming toward her on motorcycles, dragons clinging to their backs. Here, at least, she could lose them for chunks of time, hide her tracks and her noise in the tangle of frosted woodland.

Closer to a town, and she might have made it. As it was, less than two hours after leaving the manor she had knights fanning out on all sides, barely fifty meters away, and Ramsey among them. She couldn't see him but she'd heard him shouting, knew his voice too well.

Other figures darted with furtive strides, all of them black-clad and wearing ubiquitous motorcycle helmets. A snapshot flashed through her brain as she ran: Luton, bending over a newborn Salem. *The tongue. Has anyone checked?*

Dragons lived at the periphery of her world as voiceless apparitions. She knew them to be the twisted, crazed children who sported proboscises instead of bookteeth; who hungered for minds instead of books like a kind of watered-down zombie; who lived in a knight-run facility somewhere near Oxford because they could not be trusted to resist their own hunger, even with Redemption to hand. She knew, too, that they were now wielded by knights to *troubleshoot Family problems,* as an uncle had once put it.

Devon, it seemed, was now a Family problem. One they had no compunction about solving in violent or lethal ways should she step out of line. If a dragon caught her, he'd unfurl a hideous mosquito tongue and stick it down her ear, a gross parody of intimacy, and suck her life, memories, entire psyche away in less than a minute.

Ramsey called out something in Latin. The high-pitched whistle sounded again. And fear like Devon had never known before riddled her body with sudden weakness. She zigzagged in a blind panic, too breathless to even scream.

"Girl! Stop!" The closest dragon had a voice like a bullhorn, and he wore no helmet. Veins ran dark beneath his abnormally pale face, the skin pallid from lack of sunlight. So much for voiceless, faceless, or mindless.

Fear lent fire to her feet. She didn't stop, choosing instead to sprint across a dry brook and up a crumbling bank. Devon ducked beneath a set of low-hanging branches and crashed straight into a living nightmare: another mind eater, who had somehow circled in front and now flung himself at her.

They both fell to the ground, struggling. He was even taller than she and more thickly built. Dark eyes bulged, the pupils mere pinpricks. He tried to hold her down, spittle flying from parted lips.

Lips. Hiding a proboscis tongue.

Revulsion surged into strength and she headbutted him, hard. He howled like a wounded wolf, blood splattering from his nose. Devon shoved him to the side, rolled to her feet—and lost the breath from her lungs as two more dragons barreled her over.

Outnumbered three to one, Devon punched, clawed, kicked with a fierceness that surprised and exhilarated her. She'd tussled with her brothers as a child but not for years and never like this. Fear melted away, freeing her limbs and tightening her reflexes.

It wasn't enough. One moment she was ripping someone's hair out by the fistfuls while kicking another person in the shins. The next moment she was somehow down on the ground, the first man kneeling on her chest with his hands around her neck while a second grabbed her legs and a third pinned her wrists.

She never even saw the knights arrive, didn't notice them filtering through the trees or hear Ramsey shouting *Locum tenentem!* to the dragons.

A snapping sound, like an oversized rubber band, followed by a pinch in her chest. A sky's worth of lightning bolts flooded Devon's body. Pain crackled through her muscles. It felt like strings of acid winding through her flesh.

The longest five seconds of her life before the Taser burst finally ended. Her mouth was full of blood; she'd bitten her tongue. None of her limbs worked and wooziness crept into her skull. Someone gave a sharp whistle, and the dragons withdrew, making grumpy huffing noises.

"I'm sorry, Dev." Ramsey came to stand over her, Taser gun still pointed her way. "But you have to learn, and this is your lesson. If you run, we will always catch you. *I* will always catch you."

Devon stared up at him, crucified by a mix of emotions. She should have been getting up to flee but lethargy weighed her bones, and her body cringed in remembered agony. Was a Taser supposed to hurt so much? Or was this a particular agony that only book eaters felt?

"Back in the day, they had ways of dealing with girls like this," said a green-eyed knight, stepping into her field of vision. "Fit girls with ankle tags and all sorts. Maybe your sister needs one of those, huh?"

"Nah. She won't do it again." Ramsey nudged her with his toe. "Will you, Dev?"

She tried to speak, couldn't. Tried to spit, couldn't do that either. Breathing was a challenge. Knights filtered through the trees around her, soundless and eerie. No, not soundless—she was losing sound, and sight. Dizziness encroached, bringing blackness with it.

———•———

She woke the next morning and lay in bed, feeling sick. Someone had finally changed her out of the silly party frock and into an aunt's prim nightdress, the collar itchy around her neck with unnecessary lace.

A part of her wanted to get up, try again, run for the hills a second time. Her body refused to budge; she was weak from not eating, and from too much running. Weak, too, with fear and trauma. Dragons were a terrifying thing.

To her shame, she still hadn't moved several hours later when Aike came by, carrying a selection of books on a platter.

"I hear you have not eaten since returning to us from the Winterfields' yesterday," he said. "Can I persuade you to take some sustenance?" He wasn't calling her princess, at least. And she would never again call him uncle, either.

Devon remained curled in her bed and staring straight ahead, ignoring the proffered food. She did not want to eat anything he had handled.

Aike set the platter down untouched. "I am sorry about the hunt, but you left us little choice."

Devon found it hard to care about his apology. "What happens now? Will you put a tag round my ankle? Track me like a wild animal?"

He blinked. "A tag round . . . oh good Lord, no one has done that in years! In any case, it was only ever knights who resorted to such barbaric practices. You are still a daughter of this house—"

"Your daughter. Just bloody say it, I'm *your* daughter!"

"—and will be treated as such." He wouldn't say it, only looked at her tight-lipped and brow furled: the great fortress she could not crack.

"Bastard," she whispered.

"As for what happens, we leave you to consider your actions, and your options," said Aike with skin-crawling gentleness. "You have one more marriage contract to fulfill, and one more child to offer up."

"I don't want to get married again." The idea of a second wedding made her bile rise. Once, it had given her goose bumps of excitement.

"Devon." He interlaced his fingers, looked vexed. "You do not have a choice, none of us do. The survival of our species depends on every 'eater playing their part. Do you understand how few fertile women remain of our kind? How difficult it is to negotiate marriages that not only benefit the Six Families, but prevent too much inbreeding?"

A spark of fire flared in her chest. "Easy for you to say! It's not your body and your child who gets taken away!"

"You would do no different in my place." His calm assurance was steeped in an arrogance so thick she could only be dumbfounded at the assertion. "If it's any consolation, it will not be like this forever. When we start rolling out the IVF treatments, we will no longer need the knights to arrange and enforce marriages. The next generation of girls, your daughter included, will find things a little easier."

Someone knocked before she could attempt to formulate an answer.

Aike twisted in his seat. "Ah, yes. Speaking of your daughter, I have arranged a guest to come and visit."

Devon had barely enough time to sit up straight before Luton Winterfield walked in, unaccompanied aside from his formidable manners and well-pressed suit.

"You!" Devon struggled to keep her face straight and her reeling emotions under control. She was torn between demanding he return her daughter, begging him for correspondence, and trying to rip out his throat; indecision snarled up the words in her chest.

"I'll see myself out." Aike sketched a swift bow and left.

Luton looked at her very carefully, as if they had only met for the first time and he wished to memorize her features. "I suppose you hate me?"

There was nothing to say to that. She gave his question the silent contempt it deserved.

"I am sorry about this business with Salem," Luton said, as if they were discussing real estate; but then, he was a surveyor, out in the human world. "If it's any consolation, the first child is the hardest. Or so I'm told. The next will be easier."

"I don't want it to be easier," she said, finding her voice again. "I want to raise my daughter!" They all loved apologizing, she thought bitterly. She'd had three apologies today, still counting. Didn't stop anyone behaving abominably.

"I am well aware of what you want." Luton held out a hefty pendant on a steel chain, produced from the depths of a pocket. "I brought you something. Take it if you wish. Or leave it, if you don't."

The pendant spun, catching the light. A thick, circular disc with embossed carvings on the outside.

Pride fought against curiosity; curiosity won. Devon snatched it off him.

Her nail found a catch. A locket? She flicked it open. Not a pendant or a locket at all, but a compass, and a beautiful one. The needle wavered uncertainly. On the inside of the lid, someone had fitted a picture of Salem. It must have been recent, perhaps a couple months before her third birthday. She was sitting out in the gardens that Devon knew so well, smiling and adorable. Sunlight caught the elfin features.

"The exterior pattern is the Winterfield coat of arms. Though we have some differences in personality, you have performed your duties well and provided my estate with a healthy daughter of whom I am very fond." He cleared his throat. "I am told you are struggling with the transition home, in part due to my handling, and I thought it might be appropriate to provide you with a memento. To make things easier."

Devon snicked the compass shut, fingers curled tightly around it. "You took away my child, and want me to be grateful because you've given me a trinket in exchange? Fuck you. You're not forgiven."

His eyebrows rose. "Is that so? Well, if you do not want the compass—"

"I didn't say that." Devon made a deliberate show of dropping it into her nightshirt pocket. "Someday I'm going to come back, hang it round your neck, and walk off with my daughter."

"That is pure fantasy, and won't happen," he said with a certainty that burned her to the marrow. "Here is what *will* happen. I am going to tell Salem about you, and keep your memory alive."

"What are you—"

"I am going to tell Salem about you," he repeated. "I'll give her pictures of you, since she misses you very badly right now. And I will tell her that her mother will come back to see her one day, but only if her mother loves her enough. For her tenth birthday, perhaps; you'll be well out of your next marriage by then." He waved a finger. "Behave and play your part, Devon, and you will make that rendezvous with Salem. But if you back out of your second marriage and cause trouble, I will be forced to tell your daughter that you do not love her and do not wish to see her."

"You're lying!" A desperate kind of terror seized Devon's joints, eroding her earlier fury and courage. "Just like you were lying before!"

"Believe what you like. I came here to do you a favor, not field your paranoid accusations." Luton got up and walked out.

She shrieked curse words after him, aware of how feral she sounded.

No one took any notice. Outside her room, someone drew the bolts to lock the door in place. Voices murmured as her guards exchanged places. Everything locked down, closing down. Her pitiful escape attempt had ended. No drawn-out fight or even a last stand; simply hunted, bagged, and dragged back.

She was becoming the wrong kind of princess, the sort that fell in with goblins and got locked away in towers.

Shame crept through her veins and grief hit like a mind eater's punch. How stupid she had been, to think anyone would listen. How naïve they must think her, an idiot girl believing whatever lie the patriarchs offered up. Her threat to Luton was an empty thing carrying no weight, which she could not enforce.

Devon the Daft. Devon the Dolt. Devon the Deceived.

The stitches that held her life together were collapsing into dust. The Families were strong, entrenched, practiced; she was nothing, head full of their carefully selected books and empty of practical knowledge.

Dull realization grew around her like choking vines. The only way out was to behave. Every time she defied the Family, someone else paid the price. She still didn't win by following rules, but at least she lost less badly.

Be passive, be good, bear the next child, get a modicum of freedom. And even if they did not allow her to visit Salem, she would still have more freedom after her marriages were completed and some of the duties settled on her shoulders were lifted.

That meant she would not see Salem this year, or the next, or even the next. Awful, almost beyond enduring.

But the alternative was worse: to act too boldly, inviting more restrictions. To run the risk that Luton would make good with his promise and convince Salem that Devon did not wish to see her. If Devon ever wished to see her daughter at all, she would bear the misery, the heartache, the impatience of her need.

She curled up on the floor, hands locked around the compass, and willed herself to breathe.

13

IN THE COMPANY OF WOLVES

PRESENT DAY

But curing mind eaters of their hunger did nothing to solve the fertility problems that have plagued this species. For that problem, the book eaters did what they have always done best: encourage human technology to advance from the shadows, and then borrow from it.

The basics of IVF they mastered long ago. Easy to do when one can learn human medical science just by having a hearty "lunch" of textbooks. But the great difficulty in using such technology lies in adapting it to tricksy 'eater biology, and putting it into practice safely.

And what kind of world will it be, I wonder, when book eaters can freely have children? A terrible question for the future.

—Amarinder Patel, *Paper and Flesh: A Secret History*

"Go!" Devon half shoved, half barreled Hester and Cai toward the nearest train exit.

She'd gotten back to the carriage where Cai and Hester were seated and had just enough time to say *I think I've seen knights on the train* when the engine had ground to a halt. The lights had failed almost straightaway. Shortly after, Ramsey had gone to work with his knife, rousing fear and horror in human passengers—who in turn had fled blindly through the now pitch-black carriages, crying murder and seeking help.

With all his antics, Devon had encountered no difficulty in convincing Hester and her son that the knights had gotten aboard their train, or that all three of them should abandon the journey.

They staggered out, along with a spill of other people, into a frosty Northumbrian night amidst the sprawling, empty, wild fields. From behind them on the train, several people were screaming. The sky above hung malignant: clouded over and moonless, perfectly atmospheric.

Hester stumbled, falling against Devon's shoulder. They steadied each other and kept running through the tall, half-frozen grass. Trying to put distance between themselves and the beleaguered 10:15 train.

They'd gone perhaps two hundred meters when Hester exclaimed, "Wait!" and jerked to a stop. "My handbag is missing. I don't have it on me!"

Devon twisted round. "What's so important about a handbag?"

"Is that rhetorical?" Hester had already swiveled away to squint across the three hundred meters of wild fields. The train was barely visible from the gentle swell of the land. "My wallet and mobile phone and my gun were in there. And the bag itself cost four hundred quid, though I suppose that doesn't matter." Her aggrieved tone suggested that it did, in fact, matter. "The biggest loss is the gun. It was an heirloom."

"Do you want us to try to go back?" Devon said, looking uneasily at the train. Ramsey, she knew, would not take kindly to seeing them return.

"No. Not worth the risk." Her hands clenched briefly, then uncurled. "Still. I had pencils in there. My sketchbook, too."

"Sketchbook?" Devon said, nonplussed. She'd never heard of a book eater drawing, though it was technically possible. They just weren't creative in that way, as a species. "Were they *your* drawings? Was it important stuff?"

Hester gave a deprecatory laugh. "No, I guess not." She scraped up her loose hair, wild from running, and tied it back with savage efficiency. "Let's just go. Before I change my mind."

"About that," Cai said. "Where exactly are we headed?"

"The closest town, which is probably Alnwick." Hester plucked at her mud-speckled skirts. "Get there, get transport, and nip across the border into Scotland proper."

"I think what he meant was, where's our endpoint?" Devon said. "Which bit of Scotland are we going to?"

"That's not safe for you to know yet." Hester started trudging away.

Devon exchanged glances with Cai. He shrugged.

The three of them straggled through the scratchy nettles and overgrown fields, the musky scent of soggy earth and tangled weeds clogging up Devon's nostrils. She sneezed twice. No snow out here, just chilly and damp.

After another half kilometer, they reached a two-lane road that wound like a curving ribbon of black ice. Devon peered down each direction, flexing her still-bare toes on the slickly frozen road. "No people or pursuit, but also no cars or houses."

Hester squinted at a road sign. "Looks like this is A1086. If we have any sense at all, we should be steering clear of the town and walking to the next place along."

"The next town?" Cai wilted. "But I'm tired now. Do we *have* to walk all night?"

"He's right," Devon said. "We need sleep, all of us. I've been up for more than a day, and not eaten nearly enough for a long trek."

She was indeed bone-tired, but beyond that, Devon also wanted time to observe this woman, and to learn more about what might await them at the Ravenscar household. The only concrete assurance they'd been offered was a single dose of Redemption while the rest was a blank unknown. It was well and good for Ramsey to not give a damn for whatever lay in store, but it wasn't his neck on the line.

"It shouldn't take all night to get there," Hester said, plucking at a loose thread on her sleeve.

"What do you mean, *shouldn't*? How far are we going?"

"I'm not supposed to tell you where we're going until we're there." Uncertainty made her seem smaller. "It isn't safe."

"Oh, for heaven's sake. Listen, you're used to caution. I understand that. But we have to work together right now. How far are we going? Will you tell me that? Not where, just how far?"

"About eighty miles," said the other woman guardedly.

Devon ran a hand over her face. "And you think *eighty miles* won't take all night?"

"Well, obviously it would if we walked it, but it's a short drive in a car! Someone was supposed to meet us in Edinburgh, once we got there." She grimaced. "I'd ring them to check in but my phone was in that sodding bag."

"We're nowhere near Edinburgh, nor is Edinburgh necessarily safe for us anymore. In the here and now, we are very much without a car. Which makes eighty miles one hell of a walk."

"Do you have a better idea?" the other woman said, exasperated. "I suppose you think we should bed down here and camp outside!"

"Not outdoors. Indoors." Cai pointed, his ragged sleeves billowing in a sharp winter wind. "There's a bed-and-breakfast down the road. We could go there? Then find another way to travel in the morning."

Both women looked at him.

Devon said, "Have you been here before?"

"Sort of. The lawyer stayed once, for a walking holiday in the moors. He traveled loads in these parts."

Hester raised an eyebrow. "The lawyer?"

"B and B sounds good." Devon didn't feel like explaining *the lawyer* or any of Cai's other half-remembered victims. "Let's go. I want to get off my feet."

Hester threw up her hands. "I don't have any money, my wallet was in that purse—"

"I've got a few quid."

"A few? How much is that?"

"Enough to cover us." Devon reckoned twenty grand could cover most B and B stays.

"All right! I give up. The two of you are so determined to stop, so we'll stop. Where do we go from here?"

"I know where it is," Cai said. "Not far. I won't miss it."

They set off again, this time through the half-frozen grass and following the line of the fence. Devon walked alongside Hester, while up ahead, Cai navigated terrain that only a dead man inside his skull remembered. They'd know soon enough if his stolen memories were still accurate.

"I'm glad you're not a Family trap," Hester said, face obscured by curling hair. "It was a possibility that crossed my mind."

"The night's still young," Devon said with a lightness that belied her own internal cringing.

Hester didn't laugh. "Killock, my brother, had a theory that you were both a setup. That Cai wasn't really your child—"

"He's mine."

"—and the whole thing was a ploy for the Families to access Redemption." She flushed. "Anyway, it feels silly, now, to say that. Five minutes around the pair of you and that bond is clear as day. And he's got your features."

"He carries the look better," Devon said wryly. "Can I ask something? A coup I understand, young men are ambitious and like to be patriarchs. But what did your siblings gain by running off to *hide* in the wilderness? You're not selling Redemption anymore or making any money, which must be tough. Maybe I'm missing something, but I don't understand why Killock didn't just . . . stay put, and you lot with him. The other Families wouldn't have really cared about a change of power in your manor."

"I'm afraid Killock will have to explain that to you in person. It's extremely complicated and delicate."

"I guess," Devon said, annoyed and frustrated. Every time she thought their conversation was going somewhere, she hit walls.

"It'll make sense when he does, I promise." The Ravenscar woman stepped over a patch of frozen mud, gaze on the uneven ground in front of her. She said, almost as an afterthought, "You're not at all what I was expecting."

"Aye," Devon said, "and what were you expecting?"

"Another me, I suppose."

Before Devon could get her head around that cryptic answer, Cai turned around and called over his shoulder, "I think I see it! That place, just ahead."

They all halted to have a good look. Alndyke Farm sprawled just off the road, only a few hundred meters from the small row of houses. A stone cottage crouched beneath its heavy tile roof like a squat gray turtle-god of darkness. But it was prettily maintained: quiet and clean, with a hint of that British faux quaintness that such places traded in.

The hour was closing in on midnight by the time Devon stalked up the gravel path with crunching footsteps, Cai at her side and Hester trailing a little behind. The entrance wasn't locked and the lights were still on, but no one was at the desk. Unsurprising, given the hour.

The owner, a small-framed woman called Nadiya, was not pleased to be woken. She was even less pleased to see a gaggle of battered, unkempt people demanding a room. Devon's bare feet got a shocked side-eye.

But she had no good reason to turn them out, especially when Devon paid double for the hassle. Money had a way of curing human resentment.

Twenty minutes later and a hundred quid poorer, the three of them were piling wearily into a cottage across the courtyard. The room held two double beds, freshly made up and decorated in a pastiche of rustic life that Devon found baffling. Alndyke was already an actual farm. Why pretend to be a fantasy one?

"Who's sleeping where?" Devon said, even as Cai flung himself onto one of the beds. "Hey, take those shoes off!"

"In a minute." He melted into the pillow with a groan.

"I can take the couch if you want the other bed," Hester offered. "You look like you need the rest."

"Don't be daft. I'll bunk with Cai. I've done it often enough. I'm calling dibs on the shower, though." She ducked into the bathroom.

"Don't take too long!" Hester called from outside. "There's only one toilet, you know!"

Devon rolled her eyes, then stripped off and ducked under the fall of icy water. Just long enough to rinse the grime from her hair and skin. Her feet were foul, but there was nothing to scrub with except a single bar of dried-out soap that crumbled into gritty chunks when she picked it up. So much for a scrub.

She toweled off and climbed back into her dirty clothes with reluctance. Well, she'd worn worse.

Clean-ish, or at least clean-er, Devon stepped from the bathroom, to the relief of a frantic Hester, who promptly took her place and shut the door with pointed force.

Cai lay curled on the bed, fast asleep. His shoes were still on. She pried them off and tucked him in, tattered clothes and all. The boy reeked of sweat and dirt. He'd need a shower, too. Patches of eczema marred the joint between foot and ankle, and also the crooks of his elbows. She wondered if taking Redemption again would help or worsen his skin. Decided it didn't matter.

Careful, so carefully as to not wake him, Devon tugged up the edge of his shirt, revealing the smooth scar on his abdomen. Barely an inch across, little more than a silver line of skin. No flashing lights or uncomfortable lumps he'd ever complained about; no outward sign of the tiny, surgically implanted device embedded in his peritoneal cavity.

Lying to him was wrong, but it seemed too heavy and strange for a five-year-old who already carried the sins of other people and many victims on his shoulders. He had enough to worry about.

Sometimes she wondered if the device was really there, or had somehow deactivated. It seemed so improbable as a concept. But reality always reasserted itself. Devon had seen the surgery done, watched the stitches put in afterward; her son carried death with him, at all times, and did not know it.

And if she ever faltered, she only needed to think about Ramsey. *Go, before I change my mind and blow your son into next Thursday.* Every time he threatened Cai's life—as he had tonight, and no doubt would again—she swallowed down the boiling stew of her overcooked rage and tried to play polite. He could end her son with the flick of a button.

Scuffling sounds came from the bathroom. Devon dropped the edge of Cai's shirt and repositioned herself less suspiciously, just in time for Hester to emerge. In the space of ten minutes, the other woman had tamed her hair and uncreased her clothes. An impressive skill.

"You left this on the sink, by the way." Hester held out the compass.

"Oh!" Devon snatched it back with lightning speed. Careless, so careless. Christ, she really was tired. "Thanks," she added lamely.

"No problem." The Ravenscar woman sat on the other bed, the gap narrow enough their knees knocked, and began brushing out wet curls of hair with her fingers. "Nice trinket. Family heirloom?"

"Memento of my daughter."

Hester paused, mid-finger-comb. ". . . Oh. I'm sorry, I wouldn't have picked it up if—"

"It's fine." Devon opened the compass to display it. "Have a look if you want." Everyone should see her daughter.

"She's lovely," Hester said, subdued.

"Of course. All little children are beautiful." Devon snapped the compass shut and wound the chain around her palm. "Adults, not so much. We've done too many things in our lives to be beautiful."

An uncomfortable beat of silence, and then Hester gestured at the mini fridge. "Do you want a drink?" Her laugh sounded anxious. "Pretty sure they have wine in that thing."

"Aye, I'd like that."

Hester got up, dug through the mini fridge, and pulled out a bottle of cheap white. "Can I ask you something? Were you happy as a child? Growing up in your Family."

"Yes." Devon didn't have to think about her answer. "I was really happy. I had freedom, or thought I did. Maybe it would be better to say, I truly enjoyed doing the things I was allowed to do. I know everything was twisted and perverse by the end, but I still wish I could have given Cai some of that joy."

Moors. Heather. Foxes. Otters. Sunshine and snow, barefoot in a thunderstorm. All those things existed and had been hers, yet she had managed only to pass on a legacy of pain.

"Makes sense." Hester filled a couple of B and B mugs, since there were no glasses. "I would have liked to have met happy-Devon, I think."

"Your own life isn't exactly spun sugar, either."

"I've hardly talked about myself." Hester set down the bottle, picked up the cups.

"It's what you don't say."

"You're too observant for your own good, then." Hester sat beside her this time, almost shoulder to shoulder, a mug in each hand. Her proximity was a pleasant solidity. "Here, take one."

"Thanks." The ceramic handle sweated condensation against her palm. "So, um. Do you have kids?"

"No. Never had children."

"What, really?" Devon raised an eyebrow; the other woman was her age, and a book eater. So—"How'd you avoid that one?"

"Random chance." Hester took a long drink, finishing most of her mug in one go. "All healthy Family women suffer from premature ovarian failure as a default. In my case, that failure came in childhood, instead of in my late twenties."

Devon didn't trust herself to answer. She was afraid to open her mouth and end up saying *How lucky are you?* when that wasn't actually fair; she didn't know enough about Hester's life to judge whether infertility was lucky or not. She had no right to project that kind of assumption on someone else.

"Anyway, I feel so silly. I should have known you've had more than one child," the Ravenscar woman was saying. "Where is she, your daughter?"

"Birmingham. I haven't seen her in seven years."

"I'm so sorry, that must be hard," Hester said, low. She drained the last of her wine. "I hope you don't mind me saying, but there's a strange comfort in knowing that you miss your girl. I don't remember my mother very well, but I like the idea that she is missing me, somewhere."

"Me too," Devon admitted. The response felt inadequate. Thousands of books eaten and she still lacked the language to say anything about her own matriarch. How did one give shape to absence? Fill a black hole with light?

As a child, she'd imagined what it might be like to meet her mother. As a young bride, pregnant and glowing, that hypothetical scenario had expanded into a fully-fledged fantasy, one where Devon could envision reuniting with Amberly, the pair of them bonding over their shared experiences.

These days, she didn't like to think of it at all. She wasn't ready for the experience of encountering her mother in the flesh; she would never be ready. Just as well it was unlikely to ever happen.

When the silence grew too strong, Devon broke it down by saying, "Are you close to Killock—do you know him well?"

"Sort of?" Hester yawned into her palm. "I suppose I know him as well as anyone. He was a gentle boy and a good brother, when we were growing up."

"Would you not describe him that way now?" Devon said, feeling her way cautiously.

"Not really, no. I wish he listened more." Hester looked tired, or perhaps it was just the wine. Either way, her eyes were drifting closed, small form slumping. "Sometimes he frightens me."

"What do you mean?"

No answer.

She looked down. Hester had passed out, her head still on Devon's shoulder.

"Never mind," she said. Feeling oddly protective, she eased the Ravenscar woman to the nearby bed and plucked the wine-stained cup from her lethargic fingers, stashing it on the side table.

"I think," Devon said, "that I'm not going to like your brother very much."

Hester slept on, breathing deep.

Time to complete her yearly vigil for Salem.

She went to stand by the window, head pressed against the window frame, and flicked the compass open. The faded picture of a three-year-old girl peeked out.

The vigil was never anything except painful, and this year was particularly excruciating. Somewhere to the south, her daughter would be rising in a few hours, with a birthday party and pretty celebrations to mark turning ten years of age.

Ten years old. The birthday Devon was supposed to be turning up for, according to Luton's agreement. And she would be absent, having abandoned one child to save another.

No doubt Salem's father would relish the moment, she thought with bitterness. But none of Devon's choices had included the possibility of an ideal solution, and the conditions required for her to keep that promise would have meant giving up Cai for dead, or worse.

This was the best she could do. Her daughter would have to wait.

"I'm so sorry, but I can't see you after all," she whispered to the darkness, breath frosting on the unglazed windows. "I'll come back for you when I can." She squeezed the disc until the ridges dug red lines into her fingers. "Happy birthday, Salem."

Stillness entwined with her weariness, a particular kind of exhaustion that seemed years and years deep. Unwilling to disturb Cai or to invade Hester's personal space, Devon left her companions to their beds. She crammed her tall frame onto the faux-rustic sofa and fell asleep.

14

THE PRINCESS AND THE OGRE

SIX YEARS AGO

*The princess was all alone again. To make matters worse, her father prom-
ised her hand in marriage to an ogre, who had agreed to give the king fifty
wagons of silver in return.*

*The princess was horrified when she heard what her father had done,
and begged him to change his mind. But her father was determined to carry
out his bargain.*

—Charlotte Huck, *Princess Furball*

There was a kind of peace in surrender.

Though it shamed her, a part of Devon embraced the relief of simply giving
up. The only path back to her daughter was also the path of least resistance and
so, seven months after her failed escape, Devon did not fight when the Fairweather aunts came to prepare her for a second wedding.

"Breathe in, love," Aunt Beulah said, fingers against her rib cage. "The
marrying doesn't last forever. Stay strong, and stand tall."

Devon sucked in and stood straighter. It was the same heavily embroidered
Romanian dress that she'd first been gifted more than four years ago, only now
it was tight across the bosom and hips, and they had to fight with the fabric a
little. These things were to be expected. She was older and had birthed a child.
Her daughter. No, don't think of Salem.

Strong hands pulled the laces taut and Devon imagined that she was allowing her heart to be laced into her body. Keep it together. Another marriage,
another child, then she'd be able to petition to see them.

Inwardly, she was already making arguments. She could ask Faerdre for advice, if she ever saw the other bride again. Did Faerdre want to see her children?
Did she care? She'd seemed bleak at Devon's wedding, on reflection.

They were princesses, of a kind, and this was how princesses lived: safe in
towers, married to men who competed for them, one way or another. Even in
the happiest fairy tales, princesses did not usually have much choice. They were
prizes to be won or given away and there was no other context in which she
could understand her life.

On a too-hot July afternoon, Devon left her childhood home for the second time. Her departure went unheralded on this occasion, the aunts hiding in their rooms, the uncles steadfastly ignoring her. Maybe there was no longer any need for the pretense, or else they were just genuinely embarrassed. Either way, Devon was grateful. A Family sendoff for her second unwanted marriage would have felt cruel beyond bearing.

Instead, she was bundled into a much smaller limousine with a pair of knights for her entourage—one of whom was Ramsey himself.

The last time she'd seen her brother, he'd been standing over her in a wintry forest, weapon pointed at her head.

"After you," Ramsey said, and even smiled. Sort of.

Devon shuddered, and got into the vehicle.

She ended up squashed between Ramsey and another knight named Paulton. Aike sat across from them. A single dragon loomed in the next seat, soft hands tucked between large knees and unknowable face hidden by a motorcycle helmet.

"Told you I'd make it for your second wedding," Ramsey said, and laughed like he'd delivered a joke. "How've you been?"

Devon pressed her lips together and stared at the floor. She could not bear to make friendly conversation.

The drive from Yorkshire to the Norfolk Coast took considerably longer than the drive from Yorkshire to Birmingham. Lulled by the motion of the vehicle, and disinterested in the landscape outside, she dozed off for real—only to be shaken awake what seemed like moments later by Ramsey saying, "We're almost there."

Devon nodded, remembered that she hated him now, and looked out of the window to avoid his gaze. Her brother stifled a yawn.

Easterbrook Manor was like no other house that Devon would ever again visit. She sat in subdued silence as they drove over a well-paved road through the Family grounds, stunned by the gardens, working orchard, small organic farm, and a bizarre series of moving structures that Ramsey informed her were windmills.

"Windmills?" she said, curiosity briefly overpowering her hatred. "For electricity?"

"Yep. Electricity is sellable. The Easterbrooks have successfully leased much of their land to human businesses."

Seasonal fruit pickers moved through the fields, working and caring for them. Tractors pottered in methodical rows. The workers were poorly dressed, and many seemed tired.

"I thought we weren't supposed to interact with humans," Devon said. "And why are most of them women? I would have thought women wouldn't want such jobs."

"Better field labor than brothel labor," said Paulton. A muscle jumped in his cheek.

"Brothel?" Unease coiled in Devon's belly. She understood the idea of brothels from her scattered reading, but what that had to do with Family, she didn't grasp.

"Aye, it's a roulette of bad choices," Paulton said. "Farmhand if you're lucky. Brothel if you're not. Organ harvesters if you're too old for either. It's a grim business."

"Interaction is fine, integration isn't," Ramsey said, ignoring his colleague's interjection. "The Easterbrooks don't integrate with humans. No humans are employed inside the actual house. In fact, most of these people aren't employed at all, strictly speaking, because they're in this country illegally and are just grateful for whatever pay they can get." He rolled down the window, hanging an elbow out. "It's a good racket. Aside from a couple techies, most of the Easterbrook boys are stewards and landlords—"

Paulton snorted. "That's one word for it."

"—who take enough of a cut from the farms and energy mills to keep the house going," Ramsey went on, giving him a hard glare. "And in turn, that means they spend less time among the local population than lads in other houses. Your last husband, in comparison, had to be very careful to stay out of close human contact in his job."

"It's dirty money. Made with suffering. I can't believe the patriarchs allow it, honestly." Paulton looked aggrieved. "*My* house, the Gladstones, don't do anything of that sort."

The air inside the limousine seemed to be growing thicker and warmer.

"Eh, come on, it's only humans," Ramsey said, sounding annoyed. "Not like they're trafficking in other book eaters."

Trafficking: transitive or intransitive verb. The word had a number of definitions but none of them made sense in the context her brothers were using. What was so bad about transporting people? Wasn't that what trains and cars did?

"Don't be obtuse," Paulton said. "Sure, they're only humans, but have you seen those hellholes they keep the girls in? I wouldn't put a dragon in one of those!"

Ramsey started laughing. "Since when were you such a fucking softie?"

"Enough, Paulton," Aike said. "And Ramsey, act your age and station, for heaven's sake."

"Act my age?" Ramsey still sounded amused. "How about you mind your own business and keep your mouth shut, you decrepit old fuck? Knights don't take orders from you." His easy contempt startled Devon. It startled Aike, too; his hands fluttered, and he blinked owlishly. "Besides, Paul and I are only joking around. Aren't we, lad?" Ramsey jostled the other man's shoulder.

Paulton pulled a face, muttered something unintelligible. Aike, to Devon's astonishment, said nothing at all.

Gravel crunched as the car ground to a stop.

Aike opened the door, still silent, and ducked elegantly from the car.

Devon dragged herself out and stood to stiff attention. Princesses behaved politely, always, and this was her role. She didn't have Ramsey's freedom to be rude to their uncle/father.

Easterbrook Manor was old-fashioned, kept in its original Tudor design, but the interior was painfully modern and bright. Lights flooded the entry hall and everything from the internal doors to the chandeliers seemed to be set with glass. Quartz chips refracted in sparkles from the red-marble floor.

White shelves discreetly filled the alcoves, the books upon them arranged by color and size to create an undulating rainbow of spines. A crisp bibliosmia scent of freshly printed paper, with a faint undercurrent of petroleum. Devon wrinkled her nose. Modern books had good stories, but she hated the oily taste of glossy pages.

Celebrations were already underway. A handful of people drifted past, laughing and drinking from flutes that refracted yet more light. All in formal dress and all wearing jewelry. Sparkles and shine everywhere. Devon put a hand to her head, overwhelmed by the glittering.

"There you are, Aike." Matley Easterbrook came down the main stairwell with casual confidence, two other men at his heels. All three of them in pale suits.

Matley was younger than Luton, though still older than Devon; taller than Luton, though still shorter than Devon. Sepia skin and dark, tightly curled hair spoke to their Mediterranean heritage.

Book eaters often had complex and convoluted ethnicities. The different households across different continents had long ago blended with lineages, bolstering failing lines on all sides.

Only delaying the inevitable, she thought. Increasingly, there were just fewer book eater families to merge with, and those who survived in other countries were harder and harder to access. Passports, immigration, paperwork, visas, and all that official stuff made cross-continental marriage almost impossible to arrange in modern times.

"Always a pleasure." Aike had recovered his poise. He wore a wide, toothy smile that he reserved only for other men of the Families, and had never shared with her. "I am pleased to introduce you to Devon."

Every eye fell on her, and she stiffened under the onslaught of attention.

"Hullo, kid." Matley was difficult to look at; that pearl-colored suit turned him into a blazing beacon in their over-lit house. "Good lord, you're a tall one, aren't you?" He gave her shoulder a squeeze, gripping much too hard.

Devon steeled herself into not flinching. Showing weakness to this man would invite derision, she felt. Luton had been cold and indifferent; Matley, she suspected, might be actively unpleasant. The kind of man, in fact, who trafficked humans without a whisper of remorse.

When he got no response, Matley wheeled away and said, "These are two of my brothers, Wight and Jarrow."

"Congratulations on your wedding, cousin." Wight picked a cuticle on his nails. His real attention was on the party happening in the reception room.

"Congratulations, cousin," Jarrow echoed awkwardly. He looked even younger than her, and she was only twenty-three. "Happy returns."

"Thanks." The banality of the exchange grated on her. "Very kind."

Matley swept his arm to one side. "Wight, please escort the knights to the barracks where they can check in their dragon. Jarrow, if you'd be so good as to escort our bride to the celebrations." He offered a twisting smile to Aike. "And cousin, if you'd like to come with me to the office, we can finish discussing the business side of things."

Ramsey and Paulton left with Wight, dragon trailing after them. Aike disappeared with Matley, none of them so much as glancing her way.

Devon stood in a daze, feeling as if nothing about the day were real or tangible. Get through the wedding, she reminded herself. One day at a time. Wedding, marriage, child—then Salem. Eventually. There was nothing else she could do.

"If you'll follow me, Ms. Fairweather." Jarrow's strong Norfolk accent clagged her ears. "We've a party on for you."

"I'm looking forward to it," she said, almost truthfully. At least the party would be a distraction, with plenty of alcohol. Devon thought she understood Faerdre a little better these days. The other woman's smile, so cheerful at the time, seemed brittle and forced on reflection.

As they approached the reception room, a pair of young men pushed past in a rush, carrying stained glasses. One of them shoved the dining room door wide and as it swung back, the figure of Luton Winterfield was briefly visible, laughing and joking.

Devon froze in place. Cold sick built up in her stomach and threatened to rise in her throat. How dare he come here, be here, torment her again, see her like this when he had her daughter, beautiful Salem, tucked away in—

"No." Her feet wouldn't move. She could not face Salem's father. Salem's *kidnapper*.

Jarrow paused. "Is something wrong?"

"I changed my mind. I don't want to celebrate. I don't want to be here." Her voice seemed to echo in the waiting room, ricocheting off the stupid glass everything and the too-bright lights.

He tugged at an earlobe. "You don't want to go to the wedding celebration? I thought brides liked the parties."

She was supposed to say something, a chance to recover the facade and pretend everything was fine. Submit. Be passive. Be cowed and give no threat, and earn the chance to see Salem again.

Somehow, she managed to stutter out the words, "They're very noisy. Too many people." Stupid. Like she was a small child, frightened by lightning. Except she *was* afraid, of this Easterbrook boy whose family trafficked in lives, even if they were human; of Matley, cruel and arrogant, whom she would have to marry. If Jarrow took offense to her words, she would be in trouble.

But even as she filled her lungs with breath to say *All right, let's go in now,* Luton half turned to address someone else and Devon's resolve crumbled afresh. She pressed up against the wall where he wouldn't see her. The door slowly drifted shut again, obscuring the room.

Jarrow said, "Was your first husband in there?"

His guess skewered her. She realized too late she was nodding, tried to shake her head instead. The room spun, the lights searing inside her head. Why was everything so sodding bright?

"Sorry. I just need a moment and then I can go in." Lying, lying, lying. Her courage was dropping second by second.

He astonished her by saying, "D'you like video games?"

The question dispersed her mounting distress with its sheer unexpectedness.

"*Video game*: noun," Devon said, struggling to keep her composure as she confusedly rifled through her internal dictionary. "An electronic game in which players control images on a video screen." She frowned. "What does that even mean?"

Jarrow broke into a grin. "You had to eat dictionary pages, too? Glad I wasn't the only rebel child! Which one did they give you?"

"Erm. *Merriam-Webster*." She wondered if she should specify the edition, decided it didn't matter. Her heart rate slowed, the heat inside her chest dying down a little.

"Ah. We eat *Oxford* in this house. But only those of us who ask too many questions, too young." He pointed toward the stairs so recently descended. "Come on, I'll give you a little tour of the house, and introduce you to some games. Might not be your cup of tea, but it's probably better than gnawing on your own nerves, right?"

". . . Right. Sure." Anything to stave off the misery of her own wedding for a few moments. Anything to avoid being reminded of how far she was from Salem, how long it'd been since she'd seen her daughter.

Jarrow led her up two floors, down hallways lined with postmodern art and chandeliers that sprouted from the ceiling every five feet. The carpet squished like mulch under her ballet flats and the air reeked of faux floral scents. Several more hallways later, they fetched up in what was apparently the gaming room.

It was like she'd stepped into a parallel universe.

She stared, dumbfounded, at the large entertainment center that covered one entire wall. It housed an equally large television screen connected to a small gray box trailing wires, one of which ended in a strange, curved device covered in plastic buttons. Devon had never seen anything like it before. Her own manor eschewed *modern nonsense*, as Aike would have phrased it.

"This is my PlayStation," Jarrow said, as if that information were illuminating. He passed her the knobby curved device. "Here, have a controller and take a seat."

She sat on the large red sofa, holding the thing in her palms. "What does it control?" No lights in here except for that which poured from the screens; blissfully dark.

"The game, silly. Hold it like this." He arranged her inflexible fingers into a counterintuitive position.

Devon did her best, the controller sitting awkward in her palms. Fingers at strange angles. "Maybe you'd better take it," she said, handing the thing back to him. "I'm not sure it suits me."

"Just takes practice." Jarrow took the controller off her and pressed buttons on the PlayStation. The screen changed. "You want a beer before we start?" He pronounced "beer" like "bear."

"Um." Devon had never drunk beer, pronounced "bear" or otherwise. "Yes, I'd love one, ta."

"Cool." He disappeared out of her sight, toward a storeroom at the back.

The words TOMB RAIDER appeared on-screen, along with some credits, and an opening sequence. A dark-haired woman in a blue top with a crisp Queen's English accent started speaking to an American man. She appeared to be some kind of spy.

Devon, who had never seen a film or cartoon or television of any kind, let alone a video game, gaped at the screen in spellbound astonishment. It was the closest thing she'd ever seen to real magic.

Jarrow came back, put down two cans of beer, and dropped next to her on the couch. "You ready?" He'd taken off his smart jacket and already seemed happier, more at ease.

"How come only your house gets this stuff?" Devon tipped back her beer. It hit far less hard than wine and, though sour and yeasty like one of Uncle Romford's military fiction novels, went down easily enough. "I love games already and we haven't done anything yet!"

He laughed. "Watch me for a bit, and I'll show you how to play. Only one person can use the controller at a time, so we'll have to take turns."

Devon sipped from her bear. Her beer. She watched him play and listened to his explanations, drinking in the details, fascinated by the technology. This was not how she had expected her day to go. Not that she was complaining.

After the first level, she said, "Can I try again?"

Jarrow ceded her the controller with polite reluctance. Devon "died" in-game almost immediately, laughed out loud, and restarted for another attempt.

The game was simply another medium for stories, much as books were—albeit electronic instead of paper-based. She let herself forget about the wedding, and the Old Country dress that squashed her ribs. Lara Croft's struggles to run, jump, shoot, and solve puzzles became Devon's struggles and that suited her fine, because Lara's problems were far more fun than Devon's own.

A revelation struck her and she hit Pause, thunderbolted by an idea.

"Summat wrong?" Jarrow said.

"She's a princess."

He shot her a quizzical look, one eyebrow raised. "Er . . . kind of? If you take a really loose definition of the word. Lara *is* aristocratic gentry, I suppose, which is pretty similar."

Devon barely heard him. She could only look at the choppy, blue-shirted woman on the screen: a princess who rejected her castle in favor of adventures and muddy boots. Who went treasure-hunting with a gun strapped to her thigh and fought bad guys.

"I don't understand," she said. "Why can't I be a Lara Croft kind of princess? Why am I like . . . this?" The controller sat heavy like a misshapen stone. Her eyes grew hot from a toxic potion of beer and mixed emotions, too many for her to process or name even with the help of a dictionary in her brain.

Jarrow tugged at a curl. "I—"

The door banged open, making both of them jump. Matley Easterbrook walked in, to the sight of Devon sitting startled and drunk; and Jarrow next to her, jacketless and guilty.

"I've been scouring the house!" Matley said, jabbing a finger. "Have you both been here the whole time?"

"It's my bad," Jarrow said quickly. "I asked if she wanted to try a gaming console—"

"For two hours? You had one task, to take her down the hall!"

"The fault is mine," Devon cut in. "We don't have games in Fairweather Manor. My Family is a little old-fashioned about human tech. I was just curious."

Matley shifted his gaze. "Your uncle's having a fit, girl. He thought you'd done a runner. Again. Since apparently you have a history of that kind of thing. But here you are, hiding away with my little brother." He sniggered, so juvenile for a grown man of his age. "Any other bloke, and I'd be questioning your fidelity."

Devon blinked, confused; Jarrow had gone beet red. The context was missing but Matley was either mocking her, or Jarrow, or both.

"Anyway, you're here and not gone walkabout." He crooked a finger, as if she were a dog. "On your feet, love. The night's only getting older."

A buzzing filled her ears and her peripheral vision seemed to fall away; she could only see Matley, framed by long, hard lines and too much light. There would be no drink or drugs to mask this encounter, those small kindnesses Luton had carelessly offered. Her newest husband would be a thing to endure, not experience.

Devon stood up, swept with sudden nausea. "Catch you later," she said over her shoulder, and strode from the games room at Matley's side, held upright by the laces of her dress.

Jarrow gave a tight nod from his place on the couch, ensconced in silence and staring at the controller in his lap.

ACT 3
WITCHING
HOUR

15

RAMSEY AND THE
MOUNTAIN OF LIGHT!

PRESENT DAY

There's a point, you know, where treachery is so complete and unashamed that it becomes statesmanship.
—George MacDonald Fraser, *Flashman and the Mountain of Light*

Ramsey had found the emergency stop easily enough and cut the wiring that controlled the lights. Most were out, the rest on the blink. The 10:15 to Edinburgh became a long stretch of dark, unmoving carriages.

He darted down the aisles, blade in hand and perfectly comfortable in the shadows that obscured human vision. A slice, a nick, a few close shaves. Screams and shrieks. A couple dozen humans bleeding lightly, badly frightened. The ensuing stampede was pure delight.

He'd discovered as a young man that humans, and indeed many 'eaters, had a propensity to take the known for granted. To believe that events or experiences would continuously remain predictable. Ramsey had learned to abuse this assumption. When he broke their expectations spectacularly, it was easy to seize control.

Like tonight, for example. A practical and reasonable thinker would pinpoint that a single man with a knife was hardly a threat to an entire carriage, let alone a whole train. If they tackled him en masse, he'd be done for, even with superior 'eater strength. But by acting unexpectedly, he had upended their faith in events remaining logical.

Rationality always went up in smoke at that stage.

A peek through the window. Devon loping off into the fields, Hester and Cai at her side. Job done, then, no need for excess violence. Better make himself scarce before the "chickens" grew courage. They did outnumber him significantly, even if they had forgotten that.

Ramsey backtracked toward the nearest exit, partially retracing Devon's footsteps. Pushed through screamers and criers. Revolting cowardice, he thought.

Outside, finally. Some humans out here but not as many. Not so packed in.

The air was refreshing and crisp; a break from the meaty smell of crowds. He took a good lungful. Stashed the knife back in its leg holster. Felt good there. Carrying a short blade was gentlemanly.

Something caught his eye, strewn on the trampled ground. Ramsey walked over, nudged it with his foot. A purse. One he recognized; Hester Ravenscar had been carrying something similar. Could be hers.

Expensive leather rubbed slick and dry beneath his hands as he picked it up. Rifled through it gently. Cold metal; aha. He withdrew the pistol, stared at it. A five-shooter. It'd been reloaded. Who kept a gun in their purse? Someone who wanted to conceal it not on their body. Who would leave it behind? Someone in a hurry.

Definitely Hester. Was sure of that, now.

He turned the thing over, examining. Expensive and old. Custom? Yes, but based on a standard revolver. He recognized the emblem burned into the haft, too. Three red stars and a thick red line, sitting above a stylized lion. The motto: *In Defiance*. He grinned. The Ravenscar crest.

Turned the gun over. On the pistol butt, very subtle, were engraved the initials *WR*. Interesting indeed. He guessed—that was too weak a word, he'd have staked *a lot of fucking money* on it—that this gun had once belonged to Weston Ravenscar. Until he'd been violently removed by his own offspring.

Aloud to the world at large, Ramsey said, musing, "Did he give this to Hester, or did she take it from his corpse? Why does *she* have it instead of Killock?" and then listened intently, as if someone might answer.

No one did, of course. The humans on the train were still busy being noisy little brats, only slightly calmer now that their attacker was apparently no longer among them. Someone had found the lights and fixed them, which abated their fear.

"Intriguing, but you are not a question I can pursue at this point," Ramsey informed the gun, then slung the whole bag over one shoulder. He had nothing better to carry it in, and wasn't daft enough to shove a loaded weapon into his waistband.

The train tracks stretched tediously. Best start walking or he'd be here all night. There was a lot to do. Before anything further could happen with his sister or the Ravenscars, Ramsey had business with his own knights to settle first. The gun had given Ramsey ideas.

He set off, heading southwest; not due west, as Devon had.

Realized he was hungry. Been a long evening. He wrested free his emergency book, stored in the same body pouch as the transmitter. Flashman novel, his favorite kind of comfort food. Bit through a corner, pleased by the creamy texture of the pages. Gunfights and sex sizzled on his tongue.

The Six Families did not discriminate by skin color, so neither did Ramsey. Couldn't afford to when their population was barely sustainable. But the inherent racism and bawdiness of these Flashman books had always struck him as flavorful and fascinating all the same.

Self-hate was intrinsic to the entire human race. He'd come to that conclusion after his various dealings with humans. When they could not find enough to dislike in their own selves, human folk went looking for flaws in their neighbors. Delicious, that tendency.

A buzzing against his hip. Ramsey glanced down. The rattlesnake hiss of a mobile phone going off in his pocket. Swallowed a last mouthful of book and pulled out his phone. Pressed the green answer button.

"Ramz?" Ealand sounded stressed, as usual. "Where the hell have you gone? You're all over the news!"

"*We* are all over the news. Thanks to Kingsey." Couldn't keep the tartness out of his voice. "I'm somewhere between Newcastle and Berwick. Where is the commander?"

"Still in Newcastle. He's not best pleased, not pleased at all." Ealand's voice dropped to a semi-whisper. "Says your spy has betrayed us. I think he's dead set on pinning the blame for tonight's disaster on *you*."

"Is he, now." Stay cheerful, Ramsey thought; stay unruffled. Stay in control of the conversation. "That's funny, because *my spy* as he calls her has done nothing of the kind. Devon and Hester Ravenscar are traveling to the Ravenscar hideout. Couldn't ask for a better solution."

A caught breath. "Are you sure?"

"You all saw Hester there. And I spoke to Devon on the train. They got off before Berwick and she'll be in touch shortly. Wants us to send a knight to 'check in' on them, by following her phone signal."

"Well, that changes everything! I'll let Kingsey know—"

"No," Ramsey said. "Say nothing to Kingsey."

A confused silence. "But . . ."

Ramsey altered his tone, sweetened it. "E, you've been a good friend. Trust me or don't on this one, I won't judge, but I haven't got time to explain. Only, I think it's better I deliver the news in person."

"Then what *do* you want me to tell him?"

"That I'll be waiting for him, and all the rest of you, at St. Michael's Church. Just outside Alnwick." Checked his wristwatch, scanned the sky. "ETA three hours."

"Damn, Ramz. When you say waiting for him . . ." A muttered phrase that wasn't audible, followed by, "Fuck it. I'll pass on your message. Can't guarantee how he'll react."

"Cheers, mate." Ramsey hung up, mentally picturing the commander's face as he stuffed the phone away. The sullen, deep lines.

Knightly life had been a shock to child-Ramsey. Training was harsh and the older knights let their youths sort out any aggression or disagreements among themselves, meaning the youngest and smallest suffered the worst. Ramsey, proud and young, had suffered spectacularly.

The first night in Oxford, Kingsey Davenport had taught Ramsey the secret of fear and power by locking him in a room with a live, ravenously hungry dragon, and waiting till it nearly killed Ramsey before giving a command word at the last moment to keep it in check.

Afterward, while Ramsey curled on the floor of his new home and cried like a girl, Kingsey had bent down and said, *You will never have to fear what you have mastered.* The words meant nothing at first. He hadn't understood at the time but had remembered the words all the same.

Every month or so, in between the trainings and beatings and exhausting regimen, Kingsey would repeat the exercise, putting Ramsey back in that room with an unleashed dragon. *Learn to handle your fears.* All the young men went through it. Still dreamed of those encounters.

But he got older and learned to fight and memorized command words. Soon, those sessions did nothing at all to spark fear in Ramsey until, at last, at the age of twenty-four, he got bored and killed the fucking dragon. Broke its head against the wall and screamed at it while it bled to death, because he could.

Afterward, such stillness. The silence shocking. Kingsey coming in, hand landing heavy on Ramsey's shoulder and that gravel-grinding voice saying, *You will never have to fear what you have mastered,* only this time Ramsey had understood it.

Banish fear by dominating what you fear. Simple enough. Amazing he'd not thought of such a self-evident truth on his own. Some things had to be experienced to be understood, though.

As a lad Ramsey had cursed the man for dragging him out of Fairweather

Manor and upending his life. As an adult, he was thankful. Cruel training had hammered strength into his spine, lent a cold speed to his actions. Sharpened his raw edges. Violence, he came to realize, had only happened to him because he had once been the kind of person to deserve it.

These days, he was another kind of person. One who meted violence out instead of suffering it. He would not feel guilty for causing harm any longer. If the people he hurt didn't like being hurt, they should never have been weak in the first place.

So Kingsey had taught him, and so Ramsey had learned.

But Kingsey had forgotten all the things he'd taught others. Become weak, become the kind of person who made mistakes. The kind of person who deserved to be hurt.

At present, Ramsey had some new *thoughts* about that.

———— • ————

A couple hours of walking and he finally washed up in some suburb or another. Wasn't Alnwick, though. Checked his watch, looked around. It was 2 A.M. on Christmas Day; no buses, no taxis. He'd left his motorbike in Newcastle. For the sake of speed, Ramsey decided he'd have to nick a vehicle rather than walk and be late.

The nearest house had a car parked in the garage. Toyota Prius, red, newish; that would do. Only, he needed a key for the car, and that meant breaking into the house to find it.

Front doors were easy to jimmy. He had no trouble. Gripped the handle, wrenched until the internal mechanisms snapped. Wrestled into a family home strewn with toys and Christmas Eve mess. He sniffed at the smell of cold goose, curled a lip at the unwashed flute glasses still pooled with last night's champagne—gone flat, now.

Some Families celebrated Christmas, some didn't. The Fairweathers had, with their usual Romanian customs. The knights hadn't. Ramsey remembered liking the festive fun, but could no longer enjoy the memory of anything Fairweather-related, not anymore.

Told himself to focus, then rifled casually through the kitchen until he found the car keys hanging on a hook. *Got it.* He turned to go.

A small girl was peeking around the corner, wearing unicorn pajamas.

"Morning, little one." No need to alarm or harm the kid, he decided. If she started howling, he could always reassess the situation. "What are you doing out of bed, eh?"

"I heard you come in," she said self-importantly, then added with a suspicion he found extremely admirable, "You don't look like Father Christmas. At *all*."

"I'm one of his elves," he told her. Cheeky on a whim. "Can you keep quiet till I'm gone?"

She did keep quiet, only giggling a little bit when Ramsey walked out of the front door and unlocked the red Toyota Prius. Merry fucking Christmas. He gave the girl a grin and a wave. Then put the car into fifth gear, roaring down the icy roadway with indifferent abandon.

Street signs pointed toward the town he wanted; he followed. Less than forty-five minutes till the rendezvous. Plenty of time. And then his own personal reckoning with Kingsey.

Close. He could sense it. The make-or-break moment of their order; transformation, or disintegration. Could go either way. He was excited by either prospect, satisfied he'd have been a major player regardless.

Without the knights, the Families might have died out, too self-serving and small-minded to arrange fair marriages and keep the lineages from collapsing. They should have all been on their knees with gratitude for the knights ruling and protecting and serving. Instead, the patriarchs spoke of disbanding, and "redundant organizations" in casual tones.

The Family didn't care. Saw the knights as finished, superfluous in the face of fertility treatments. No arranged marriages with reluctant houses meant no need to internally enforce those monetary agreements and keep the lines of succession flowing. No more heavy-handed knight commanders, wielding more power and influence than any non-patriarch was ever supposed to do. And the dragons, long a source of contention the patriarchs could not form a consensus on, could be disposed of entirely.

Not acceptable. Not to Ramsey.

He cared intensely whether the knights survived, found himself appalled by the idea they might be disbanded. The dissolution of their order predicted a kind of dissolution of himself. *Knight* was all that he was, and without that identity or purpose he might disappear into the ether. So he felt, anyway. And he didn't fear that dissolution exactly—he feared almost nothing anymore—but he did object to it.

Fertility treatments on the horizon meant nothing. Marriages would still be fraught, still need arranging. Dragons were still useful in a myriad of ways. He saw no reason those things should change.

But without Redemption, it would be impossible to maintain their power.

And so the quest for Redemption mattered to him, because the knights mattered to him.

Make or break, indeed.

Add to that: the problem of Kingsey. Mentor, commander, father figure, frightful bastard. All good things. Except now he was an incompetent old man, brain bogged down from years of book eating, making decisions too slowly. Fearful, in his old age; mastered by worries, instead of mastering them. The patriarchs ran circles around him.

He thought of tonight's bloodbath. All because Kingsey had feared the situation and striven to control it, an admirable goal, except he'd *lost* control of it, instead. Given it away to a junior officer, rather than staying involved himself, or staying on top of things. That was the clincher and the nuance. Dominate what you feared, sure, but the commander had confused *lashing out blindly* with *taking decisive action*.

Ramsey wouldn't make that mistake. He wouldn't forgive Kingsey for it, either.

———— • ————

In this buzzing mode of sleep-deprived, adrenaline-fueled anticipation, he arrived at last in the market town of Alnwick, carrying no other possessions beyond some cash, a long-distance bomb transmitter, and a purse with its unexpected gun. Bullets jingling in the inner compartment.

A far cry from several days ago when he'd driven to Newcastle with a full squad of knights, a hefty suitcase, and his favorite dragon. On the other hand, he was one step closer to salvaging the future of his order, and likewise his place within it. Ramsey considered the trade-off more than adequate. Sent a mental hat-tip in Devon's direction, for her role in that.

Like so many places in the north, Alnwick was all history and no future. Gardens and castles for tourists, dwindling high streets and rising unemployment for locals. He skirted the town center, parked his car on a quiet road, and got out, leather bag in tow. Left the door open with the keys still in the ignition; someone else would nick the car and cover his fingerprints with their own. He walked the remaining distance to St. Michael's Church.

Seven motorbikes were parked around the church. Men would be waiting inside. His watch read 3 A.M., the witching hour. Oddly appropriate. Ramsey smiled, jaunted through the crumbling gravestones. Enjoyed the atmosphere, enjoyed the cool and quiet place that the whole world became when all the humans had fucked off to bed.

And then he stopped in front of the doors, contemplating. A tiny part of him was still afraid of Kingsey, of facing him down. He could admit it. Just for a moment. Fear was a long-lived, enduring thing. Up until the very last moment, when you mastered it. This was normal.

A deep breath. He ducked into the church.

Seven knights stood in shadow, clustered at the front. One was Ealand, a good friend. The rest were familiar, too: Llanfor, Prescot, Ashby, Wick, Stalham. But Ramsey didn't care about them. Someone had knocked over the podium to create more room. Dramatic moonlight, like a film. Flashman would have approved.

"Merry Christmas, one and all." Ramsey Fairweather walked up the aisle like an abandoned groom, still in the ticket collector's jacket and cap; ill-fitting, too tight. A woman's leather handbag slung from one shoulder. He'd never felt more confident, and more anxious.

"Save the niceties." Kingsey stepped forward with a well-disguised limp, cane scraping and dragging on the echoing floor. "Today has been the ruination of us."

If the knight commander ever wore a color other than black, Ramsey had never seen it. Could not envisage the man as dressed any other way. Head shaved close, smart cap, black gloves and now, with the onset of years, a black cane. That wide-shoulder frame, once so menacing to a much-younger Ramsey, had stooped and caved with the years, the muscular weight of him withering into bony gauntness.

Ramsey made a deferential salute. "Well, you would know, sir. The past year has been a disaster under your leadership."

Uneasy silence. Ealand looked sick, the other knights merely surprised by Ramsey's reckless tendencies.

"Your spy is gone, and the Ravenscar with her. When we could have had them both." Kingsey, so angry and leery. "And you lay the blame at *my* feet?"

"The Ravenscar patriarchs were notoriously careful with their secrets," Ramsey said blandly. "We have no reason to assume they shared their scientific knowledge with a woman, not when Killock is still alive, and there are plenty of other sons in the house. Seizing Hester might have lost us the Ravenscars forever."

The commander hesitated, off-balance. That pissed Ramsey off. Younger-Kingsey would never have shown such weakness. The old man was cracking.

The other knights saw it, exchanged anxious glances. Ramsey could see them adjusting, weighing, considering the situation as it changed. A hint of respect for his brass.

"We don't know the status of the other Ravenscars," Kingsey said at last. "We have no guarantees that any of them are still alive! If we lose that trail, if we cannot track your *sister* to her destination, then we are done and dusted. For all any of us know, Killock could be dead, or Hester living apart from the others—"

"See this?" Ramsey withdrew the embellished pistol. Held it high so they could see the crest, plain in the moonlight. "This gun belonged to Weston Ravenscar. The same one Hester was using at the train station. I got it off Devon"—a slight lie, a simplification of events—"a few hours ago. The surviving Ravenscars are alive and well. Killock, specifically, is alive and well. Keep our cool, follow the trail, and we'll have what we're looking for."

Kingsey glowered and extended a hand. "Let me see that."

"As you like." Ramsey leveled the pistol and fired.

The bullet blew out the back of Kingsey's head. Gore showered the podium and Ramsey took a large step back, revolver sweeping the room. Having a gun was every bit as fun as he'd hoped.

"Christ—"

"Holy shit!"

"Ramsey, what the fuck!"

All of them shouting and talking, hands going to hips where hidden blades were carried. Except Ealand. Surprised yet resigned. Calm, too. Good old E.

Ramsey said, gun still held level, "This operation has been a shitshow from start to finish. Kingsey got four of us killed tonight because of his own irrational fears, and that's four more than we could afford to lose. Bury this bastard, follow my lead, and in *two days* we can have Redemption again. Start producing it within our base, even." Paused, to let them process that. "Gentlemen, we've succeeded in our mission. Two years of work and the restoration of our order is in sight. All that's left is to track Devon's location."

Gestures, frantic glances, hissed communication as seven men wrestled with the power shift proposed to them. Ramsey waited. They would either kill him or follow him.

Kingsey on the floor in front of him. A heap of flesh and crumpled clothes. The veins turning to dust and the skin to parchment as they watched. Finally resembling what he'd been for years: a flimsy thing, made of paper. *You will never have to fear what you have mastered.*

"You know I'll follow." Ealand spoke first, his boots still stained with the commander's dried-out, inky blood. "But did you have to kill him?"

"He was killing our order with his idiocy," Ramsey said, gaze straying to the suit-clothed bundle of papery flesh. "Men leaving in droves. Do we even *have* knights left, down in Oxford?"

More shuffling feet and then Llanfor said, guarded, "Six knights returned to their Families yesterday. Abandoned their posts on the assumption that we're disbanding."

Six yesterday, four today. Ten knights gone in a weekend. Ramsey grimaced. "What's our total remaining?"

Ashby answered this time. "Less than twenty men, including us." He was looking any and everywhere except at the dried-out corpse. "About eight dragons? Kingsey kept putting them down to conserve Redemption . . . sir."

The afterthought of *sir*. But with their ex-commander so recently dead, Ramsey felt it was a good sign. Yes, he had just committed a one-man coup, but he'd done so efficiently and with purpose, armed with evidence and a plan. They clung to his confidence. His competence, as he stepped into a self-created power vacuum.

Promising all around.

"Tough, but we can work with that." Ramsey put a booted foot on Kingsey's papery corpse. Crushed the chest to dust, the once-beating heart to powder. He looked up, smiled. "File out, men. We have a raid to plan, and some prodigal ravens to catch."

16

PRINCE CHARMING
PLAYS *TOMB RAIDER*

SIX YEARS AGO

Knowing nothing of darkness, or stars, or moon, Photogen spent his days in hunting. On a great white horse he swept over the grassy plains, glorying in the sun, fighting the wind, and killing the buffaloes.
—George MacDonald, *The History of Photogen and Nycteris*

Memory was an anchor. It could ground you in a storm, keep you from drifting. But anchors could also weigh you down and keep you from sailing free. Devon's memories of Salem were both, keeping her sane yet also weighing her spirit with heaviness.

She would wake alone each morning and lie in bed for several moments, just breathing. Just thinking about her daughter. Some days, breathing was all you could do.

Matley Easterbrook never stayed the entire night and Devon was grateful for that, because she could not rest with that man in her room. Prey did not relax when predators lurked.

Easterbrook Manor was large and lush and modern, many-roomed and fashionable. It had gardens and fields and a cultivated forest; it had stables with six horses, and hired humans, carefully vetted, to look after them. Somewhere, there was even an indoor swimming pool and a gym.

Devon had no interest in any of it. She hadn't left her quarters since the marriage night two weeks ago, and today would be no different. There was nothing to leave it for. She was only here to endure Matley, pregnancy, childbirth, the loss of her second child.

Today felt particularly lethargic and pointless, for no particular reason she could name. After a while, she crawled out of bed, taking a long shower to scrub the stink of Matley off her skin. She came out of the bathroom ensconced in a heavy towel, only to find that one of the staff had brought her breakfast while she was bathing.

Yet another stack of fairy tales sat on her end table. The books were the modern kind, with that glossy varnish to the pages that Devon found sickly. She walked over, still draped in a towel, and flipped open a page listlessly.

Once upon a time there was a beautiful young princess, whose hair was the color of pure gold. She was frequently lonely and unhappy, for her mother had died when she was a baby, and her father paid little attention to her.

Devon flung the picture book hard. It fluttered rather than flew, landing limply at her feet. She picked it up and ripped the pages out one by one. Scraps of paper floated down.

Think only of Salem, and seeing her again. Don't care about this marriage, don't think, be like Faerdre, switch it off, live for better days. *Live for that tenth birthday.* She repeated that mantra to herself, under her breath, until it was a background hum of determination. Only it was so difficult to do or stick to, when she had nothing but these four walls to occupy her time—

A rap sounded at the door.

Devon jolted, clutching the towel reflexively. "Who is it?"

"Jarrow Easterbrook," said a muffled, somewhat-familiar voice. "We met on your first day here, if you remember. Do you have a minute?"

"I . . ." There was no sense antagonizing the people of this manor. Not if she could manage to pull herself together and be polite for a few moments. "Just a second, please."

She threw on a plain linen dress, toweled off her hair, and went to let him in. "Can I help you with something?"

"Sort of?" He shifted lean weight, jittery as a race dog. "I came to ask if you felt like playing *Tomb Raider*. You know, that game you tried here, on your first day?"

Her brain actually could not grasp what he'd said. "Pardon?"

"I don't mean to offend." He tugged on his hoodie strings. "Only, you seemed to like video games, and the Fairweathers don't have them. Could be a fun thing to do, right? I thought I'd extend the offer if you wanted to come along and play again."

Some princesses climbed out of towers to escape, or were rescued by princes with swords and ropes. Video games were hardly rope to a better life, but *Tomb Raider* still offered a kind of escape, if only in her mind.

"All right," she said. "As long as I'm back by evening." Princesses always had to return from their dances by nightfall—something that had seemed magical as a child, but rang ominous as an adult.

Jarrow's grin lit his face. "Seize the day, eh?"

Devon followed him down a level, and most of the way across the sprawling, many-roomed manor. She hadn't left her room in so many days that just stepping outside made her feel exposed, as if she walked the halls naked, a sensation not helped by the prying eyes and whispering voices of the Easterbrook siblings and staff who they passed in hallways. Jarrow was either indifferent or inured to it.

Her discomfort eased once they reached the games room. The sofa was criminally comfortable, Jarrow had access to an unending supply of beer to drink and graphic novels to eat, and *Tomb Raider* took her far away from her own twisted story. For the first time since being torn from Salem, her spirits lifted a little.

"We could try something two-player," he said, after she died as Lara on yet another difficult level. "You ever played *Crash Bandicoot*? It's brand-new, just out."

Devon shook her head, annoyed he even had to ask. Of course she hadn't tried *Crash Whatever Bandit Cute*. She hadn't tried anything, having lived in a prison of edible fairy tales her whole life. "Can we finish this one first? I don't mind if it is difficult."

"You're the guest." He offered her another beer, which she politely declined because Matley would fume if she showed up drunk. All of Jarrow's awkwardness from earlier had subsided.

"Are you sure it's all right for me to be here?" she said. "Using your game room, I mean."

"It's not mine. Not really." He was eating something called *Watchmen*, ink-heavy and rich-tasting, like all graphic novels. "The consoles, games, all that . . . belongs to Vic."

"Who is Vic?"

Jarrow took another bite from his graphic novel. "Victoria Easterbrook. My older sister." He hesitated, chewing slowly. "That bedroom you're staying in used to be hers, too."

The hair on the back of her neck prickled. "Used to be?"

"She doesn't live here anymore." A muscle in his shoulder twitched. He said, almost as an afterthought, "Vic liked games a lot. We used to play together."

Currents flowed beneath the calm surface of his words and Devon, seeing a thing she could drown in, said nothing. She had her own currents to deal with and didn't have enough headspace to even feel bad about ignoring his.

"Anyway." He finished the graphic novel and picked up the controller, polishing the plastic on his sleeve. "You can come here all you like. Nobody else ever used this place except me and her."

Despite herself, Devon was aware of the room taking on a different texture based on the context he'd given. The wallpaper, for example: elegantly patterned in swooping dragonflies. Vic's choice, surely. Devon couldn't envisage Jarrow having picked it out. The games themselves stood out, too. *Tomb Raider* was definitely one that Devon would also have chosen, had she ever had the option. An adventuring princess would have been catnip for any book eater woman. Victoria might be gone, but her voice still echoed.

The opening music started up, drawing her back into that shared virtual experience and away from the real world. She hardly noticed the passing of hours as they spent the rest of the afternoon and much of the evening in the games room. By some kind of unspoken agreement, neither of them mentioned the Family again, nor Matley.

She was therefore taken by surprise when, at a quarter to seven, Jarrow hit Pause and said, "It's getting late. I think you might need to go pretty soon."

"I know." She stood too fast and knocked the coffee table; empty beer cans wobbled. "Thanks for the invitation."

"No problem," he said warmly. "Come back tomorrow, if you want."

"You don't have to invite me here because you feel sorry for me," she said, suddenly and uneasily defensive. "I'm a bride, and I'm lucky. This might not be the life I expected when I was little, but it's better than a lot of people get."

"I didn't say anything about feeling sorry for anyone," he said, and she couldn't read his expression. "I just get bored playing on my own, that's all. So you're welcome to come break up my boredom."

"Bored?" she said, floored into forgetting her pique. "Of playing games?"

"Anything is boring if it's all you've got." His sweeping gesture took in the small room with its stacks of comics and video games and wire-tangled technology, but she knew he was encompassing more: his Family, hers, all of the Family. Book eater life. "I eat more novels in a year than most humans will read in a lifetime and yes, I'm bloody bored."

"There's worse things than boredom," she said.

His face fell. "I know. I know there are. My sister, she used to say . . ." Jarrow blew a sigh and said, "Never mind. I dunno what I'm talking about. Come back tomorrow, if you want." He waved a hand vaguely. "Only if you want to."

She curled and uncurled her fists. "Why are you being kind to me?"

"I'm not," he said uncomfortably. "You're a guest, I'm a host, and I have games. This is just basic courtesy."

Basic courtesy. Somewhere along the way, she'd stopped being deserving of that, or other people had stopped bothering to give it.

"I'll think about it." Devon slunk out in a rush, feeling confused and tired.

The corridors drifted by in a blur, her thoughts whirling and keeping her distracted. She didn't understand their interactions—either what Jarrow wanted from her, or she from him. In a world dominated by Family ties and nothing else, the concept of friendship baffled her.

Jarrow himself baffled her, full stop. He oozed discontent and she couldn't understand what he had to be discontented about; he was open and easygoing, but also impenetrable and oddly inflexible. He was too much work, and the whole thing was more stress she didn't need.

And yet, that evening, Devon found herself turning over video game levels in her head. She was still thinking about puzzles and strategies when Matley came to see her for their "nightly duty," as he referred to their attempts to conceive. *Tomb Raider* puzzles continued to occupy her brain as she reluctantly peeled off clothes and climbed into bed, staring at the ceiling over Matley's shoulder.

By the time he'd left she'd thought of several solutions to try. Somewhere along the way, she'd come to a decision and cemented into the idea of returning to the games room. Sleep came swiftly after.

In the morning, more fairy tales arrived for breakfast. She disdained the offering and instead took her time showering and got dressed with unhurried slowness before picking her way toward the games room.

Jarrow said nothing about her presence when she arrived. He seemed to have expected her: beers and books waiting, controller primed. Hoodie already on, as if he'd not moved or changed from the day before.

She sat down, picked the controller up, and rested it delicately in her lap. "I've been thinking about that level. We're going about it wrong."

"Cool. Let's have a go, then." He flung himself back on the couch.

The next three weeks were a strange kind of duality between the unpleasant physicality of her nights, followed by the disconnected gaming of her days. Neither of them spoke about Matley, her marriage, Vic, anything; theirs was an alliance in distraction, a unified commitment to head-in-the-sand escapism.

And within that space she could be safe and happy, buried in the worlds of

Lara Croft until *Tomb Raider* wrapped up, after which they moved on to *Final Fantasy*. Another vast digital world in which to get lost.

———— • ————

After the second month of marriage, her cycle did not appear. Devon wasn't sure whether to be relieved for what had stopped or afraid for what came next; the misery of pregnancy, certainly, and all that reality entailed.

She opted, in the end, for resilience. Salem had her heart, and no other child would take that place. Feel nothing, care for nothing, and you could not lose anything or be robbed.

The doctor who came to Easterbrook Manor was a human man. Devon knew this not from the way he looked or walked or anything else he did, but because he could write. In front of her very eyes he produced a clipboard with various forms, and began filling them out. She craned her neck to see the letters he scrawled.

Devon Fairweather. Female. Age 23. The pen wobbled and scratched its way across the paper while she stared. Devon had attempted to write, like all book eaters did when they were young. And like all book eaters, her attempts had devolved into illegible scrawls. Carry on too long and the muscles would cramp from wrist to forearm, black spots appearing in your vision.

If the doctor was aware he performed a miracle, he did not show it. When the writing of forms was completed, he asked her to come closer while they worked their way through a basic physical exam: checking blood pressure, measuring height and weight, listening to her heart.

Devon complied, albeit reluctantly. Her gaze kept drifting back to the clip-boarded paper in his lap, so casually scrawled with written words. It seemed an awful risk to bring a human to the heart of a Family house. Of all people, surely he would be most likely to notice her inhumanness.

He tapped her shoulder to indicate she should move, and she marveled that it felt no different to her own: skin stretched over bone, flesh in the usual places; tiny hairs and tangible lines. They might almost be the same species. Had she ever touched Mani, the journalist-guest from long ago, during his brief venture to Fairweather Manor? Hard to remember after all these years, but Devon felt sure she hadn't.

"Your wife is exceptionally healthy," the doctor said to a hovering Matley. "Even for one of your kind. Very strong, could be stronger if she took a bit more exercise."

Of your kind. He knew what she was. Devon tensed.

"Don't get hysterical," Matley said, observing her expression with a lazy half smile. "John works with the migrants we employ. He is trusted, and discreet." He was sitting on the dresser chair, fiddling with a chunky black mobile.

"But what about the rules?" No fraternizing with humans. No working with them. Devon had absorbed all of that early on.

"What about them? We cannot earn money without taking risks. There is a reason my manor is wealthy while yours languishes on the edge of debt. Besides, your brothers have jobs, don't they? Not much of a different choice. Either we work among humans and hide our nature, or employ a few trusted ones and then don't have to worry about slipping up."

"I see." No point arguing. It wasn't her business, or her manor. "You're right, I'm sure."

The doctor found a vein, pricked her skin, and began his blood draw. The electric fireplace flickered behind him, devoid of any woodsmoke scent.

She tried not to hold her breath. "How long will the results take?" No one at Winterfield had tested her pregnancy like this. They'd simply *waited for nature,* as Gailey had put it.

"A few hours. I'll let you know the results straightaway, of course. Truthfully, though, the blood test is a formality. Librovarian women—"

"Libro-what women?" She'd never heard the term before.

"*Librovarian* is my private medical term for book eaters," John said, removing the needle and fussing with the little vial. Full of her black blood.

"Oh." Such a human thing to do, she thought. Humans were always driven to naming things, describing them above and beyond their function. It would never have occurred to any of her kind to invent a name other than "book eaters," in all its functional, unimaginative glory.

"Women of your kind are biologically very regular," John said. "You are certainly pregnant. It is just a question of how long."

Pregnant. Devon had been expecting him to say that all morning, had been expecting it to happen since being packed off to the Easterbrooks, but hearing it spoken aloud still made her breath come short. The mantra. Remember the mantra, she urged herself. Don't care. Don't think. Shut it all off. Only Salem.

"Is this my last pregnancy?" she said, because she'd heard the rumors, heard that some book eater women could carry three, and that sounded like her idea of hell. "I won't have any more?"

"Again, almost certainly," John said, still scribbling. "We'll confirm after the birth, but your baby-carrying days are at an end."

"Don't suppose you can tell the sex? I've heard that's a thing that can be done, with human technology." Matley crossed and uncrossed his legs. "She's had a girl before, you see, and we're hoping for a repeat performance."

"Mm." John rubbed his nose, leaving a smudge of ink on the skin. "Possible but difficult. You'd need access to a hospital ultrasound, and a qualified technician. I could help you arrange that, but it'd cost a bit. Never a guarantee, either—scans can be wrong."

"Hospital full of humans? No, not worth the risk. We'll take the surprise. It's tradition, in any case."

"I must warn you, if she has already had one girl—"

"Yes, yes, I am aware. Excruciatingly unlikely she'll produce anything other than a boy." A sound went off in his pocket; Matley's mobile, ringing. "Excuse me, I'd best take this call."

He stepped outside, speaking in a low voice.

"I should be gone, too." John clipped up his briefcase and gave her a cursory nod. "Good-bye, Ms. Fairweather. I'll attend to you in the coming months should anything go wrong."

"Thanks." Devon's thoughts were elsewhere already. Thinking of another pregnancy, another labor, another birth. How would she feel, holding another soft bundle of scent, tears, and paper-thin flesh in her hands? She broke out in sweat, unable to picture any child's face but Salem's.

The mantra. Salem. Remember the reasons for enduring.

She took out the compass Luton had given her. A cold, hard, tangible reminder. She sat by the window and traced the lines of her daughter's face, preserved in glass and frozen in time.

17

THE PRINCESS
LETS DOWN HER HAIR

SIX YEARS AGO

And now she grew thoughtful. She must hoard this splendour! What a little ignorance her gaolers had made of her! Life was a mighty bliss, and they had scraped hers to the bare bone! They must not know that she knew.
—George MacDonald, *The History of Photogen and Nycteris*

Devon found her second pregnancy was strangely restful, perhaps because she'd given up entirely. Hope was a thing you lost when simply trying to imagine better days became so exhausting, overwhelming, and depressing a task, that one opted for despair out of sheer weariness. Giving up brought peace.

At Winterfield Manor, Devon had spent much of her pregnancy wandering the grounds aimlessly but happily, always by foot since she'd been barred from riding due to her condition. But Easterbrook lands were riddled with farms and human labor, things that distressed her rather than soothed her. She stayed indoors.

Having little enough to do and few other places to go, she spent a week or so pottering miserably in her room, watching rain clouds pelt the workers and fields alike, before finally venturing down to find Jarrow again.

She entered the games room without knocking and simply said, "I'm here to play," in answer to his puzzled expression.

"Um, hello," Jarrow said, hitting Pause in astonishment, "I mean, sure. But isn't it kind of late?"

"I'm pregnant, if you haven't heard," she said. "I don't have to see Matley in the evening anymore."

"Congratulations, I think," he said, after a minute. "You, um . . ." He scratched his head. "No beer, right? I'm guessing. With the baby and . . . Can I get you some tea? And wanna keep playing *Final Fantasy*?"

Devon nodded.

———•———

The happiest six months of her life were spent in Jarrow's game room, staying up all hours of the night and drinking inktea and being mostly ignored by the rest of the Easterbrook troupe. She had never been more trapped, yet so free.

"It's strange," she told him, on one of their many afternoons lost to the worlds of PlayStation and Nintendo. "When I thought about my future as a little girl, I could never have imagined any of what I'm living right now. And definitely not this." Her gesture took in the games room, encompassing not just consoles but the unconventional friendship they'd struck up.

"None of our kind imagines the future," Jarrow said, stretching out his legs. "We make plans and we predict things, but really, it's too difficult to think about life outside the bounds of what we've already experienced. Which is exactly what the future is: life beyond what we've already experienced."

"Jesus, Jarrow."

"What?"

"Just . . ." She hit the Pause button. "You actually listen when I talk to you. And think about responses and say things that are pointful, and . . . it's weird, that's all."

"Jesus, Dev."

"What?"

"You've a low bar for friendship, that's all."

"If it's such a low bar, then how come most people can't meet it?" She sounded bitter, even to herself.

"I guess most people are kind of shite, then. Shite enough to make bare-minimum Basic Courtesy layabouts like me look good, eh?"

"I suppose." She added, without thinking, "I wish it had been you. I could have done all this so much easier if I had a husband I liked, but instead I have Matley. No offense to your brother."

A very awkward pause and then he laughed an unfunny laugh, a vein pulsing in his temple. Almost a sob.

"Did I say something wrong?"

"It would never have been me, that's all. Sorry."

"Why not? I mean, you're a little young, but it doesn't always have to be the older brothers, does it?"

"No, it doesn't, but they'd never pick me all the same. Not when there's so many others vying for the role."

Games music looped endlessly in the background. *Press Play,* the video screen urged. Neither of them did.

"I don't understand." Even as she said it, an unexpected memory surfaced: Matley on her first night here, leering from the games room doorway.

Any other man, and I'd be questioning your fidelity.

"No one's told you, have they?" Jarrow said. "Suppose I should tell you, before you hear it from someone else. It's common enough as a joke in this house." He set down the console controller and picked up the television one, pressing Mute to silence the volume. "I don't like women."

"What do you mean?" she said, affronted. "You do like me, don't you? We get on."

He groaned, dragging a hand through curled hair. "No, you're not understanding. I don't like any women in the way men are supposed to."

"Oh, do you like men? That's no big concern. Lots of knights and brothers—"

"No, not that either." He plucked invisible dust off the sofa arm. "I'm asexual. I think."

"Um." That was not a word Devon had encountered in her forays into fiction, so she sifted rapidly through her dictionary knowledge. "Which one?"

"Huh?" His turn to be confused.

"The word has four definitions?"

Jarrow snorted, throwing his head back against the couch. "Go on. Give me your four definitions."

"'Lacking sex or functional sex organs.'" She reddened a little.

"That's definitely not the problem." He was laughing, not at all embarrassed.

"'Involving or reproducing by reproductive processes,'" Devon said, with all the dignity she could muster. "That isn't what you mean either, is it? You're not an amoeba or a mushroom."

Jarrow shook his head, still smiling.

"'Not involving, involved with, or relating to sex: devoid of sexuality,'" she said, and this time he was silent. Devon added, "*Merriam-Webster* also specifies, 'Not having sexual feelings toward others. Not experiencing sexual desire or attraction.'"

"That's the one. That's what I am. Uninterested in procreation or people in—in that way men are supposed to be." He finished off his beer, rolling the empty can between his hands. "I've never felt *that way* for a single person, you know. Never tried to pick up human girls, or wanted to get married, or . . . Matley used to say I was a deviant. D'you know he has a porn stash?" Jarrow shook his head. "Most of my brothers do. Just not me."

Deviant: noun. Someone or something that deviates from a norm.

She surprised herself by saying, "I'm a deviant too. For what it's worth."

He looked up, still rolling the beer can. "What d'you mean?"

"I like girls." Devon had never said that to anyone before, not even herself. "I mean. I think I do. But how do you even know, when there aren't any around, to be sure? It's just a feeling, from reading about them in books. And the few that I've met in real life."

Jarrow was quiet for a long moment. "Ah, damn. That must make these marriages very hard on you."

"I don't know any different, do I? It's just my life."

"Just your life." He crushed the empty can to flatness. "Doesn't it bother you? The babies, getting married, all that."

The question unsettled her, an echo of what she'd asked Faerdre, years ago at the first wedding.

Long-lashed Faerdre, pretty and bright and sparkling with her hand on Devon's thigh as she leaned in for a "social" kiss. Long-suffering Faerdre, bored and lonely and drinking far too much wine at someone else's wedding.

She gave him Faerdre's answer, because it seemed fitting. "Well, there's not anything else, is there? Can't live with humans, so it's this or nothing."

"That's not what I asked," he said quietly. "Forget about duty, obligation, whether there's better or worse options. Do you, Devon Fairweather, mind being a bride who gives up her children?" He pointed at her belly. "You're pregnant. For the second time. Are you going to mind, giving up that child?"

"It isn't so bad." She hated him for asking. For caring. She hated everyone else even more for not asking, and not caring. "I'm lucky. I have a privileged life."

"What? *What?*" He turned toward her in a rare moment of expressiveness, eyes wide and nostrils flared. "Dev, you have a daughter! Would you be happy for her to get married like you've done? How are you going to feel when she goes through that, in a dozen years' time? Will you still be saying it wasn't so bad and telling her she's lucky?"

"I . . ." For a brief moment, Devon was struck by a vision of three-year-old Salem, giggling and rolling around in bed while someone pushed her face-first into a pillow and hiked up her skirt.

Stupid, stupid, stupid, because Salem would be much older when she got married, but that still might be her fate, her experience. And why not? It had been Devon's. She had been willing, more or less, but if her daughter was not, what then? The experience would be nightmarish, as Matley was for her. It might be nightmarish even if Salem *was* willing.

"I don't have your choices," she said, resentment leaking into her words. "We don't all get to say no. I haven't got sisters to shoulder the burden. You're asking me this like I have a say and it's cruel, Jarrow, really cruel, because for you these things *are* a choice."

He flinched. "I'm sorry, I didn't—"

"*Of course* I mind. Christ! I miss my daughter all the time. I can't talk about her but I can't stop thinking about her, either. I hate not having options, I hate how we live. Privileged and oppressed, exotic and dull. I try not to think of her getting married." She glared at him. "Does that answer your question?"

Jarrow leaned forward, gripping her hand. "What if I could help you have choices?"

"Such as? I've tried running away before. I don't think I even got five miles."

"You didn't have a plan, or resources," he countered. "Look, come with me to the back room. I want to show you something."

This was a bad idea, but she only had time to kill.

"All right." She followed after, belly filled with tingling.

The games room held a small storage area that he'd outfitted as a kitchenette: a specialist kettle for boiling inktea, cupboards of graphic novels to snack on.

It also held maps. The one Jarrow wrested down to spread open covered the kitchenette table completely and flowed over the edges in an ocean of excess paper.

Devon had never seen a map before in her life and couldn't stop staring. "Is this England? Where are we, on it?"

"It's the United Kingdom, which includes England, and we are here." He pointed. "Norfolk Coast."

She touched the spot he pointed to. "I had no idea our country was so large."

Jarrow burst out laughing.

"What's so bloody funny?"

"Ah, not your fault. Look." He took down another map from the cupboards and spread it atop the first. "That's our country, Dev, compared to the rest of the world."

Green-tinted continents shouldered up from matte blue seas. Swathes of land and vaster swathes of ocean. Landmass after landmass, populated with people, and there at the very top sat an impossibly small island that she barely recognized the shape of, from the first map: her dinky little country.

She'd eaten a fantasy novel once, a lush and alien book full of words that made her dizzy, containing a sketchy map of invented places. At the time it had seemed vast, but it hadn't been nearly as large or detailed as the real-world variety in front of her.

"The world is so big," she said, dumbfounded. "How did I never know?"

"Because they don't teach girls things that matter." Jarrow pushed the maps toward her, across the table. "Get eating. It's the fastest way to learn information and I've got loads of copies." He grinned.

"Pardon?" She must have misheard. "Surely eating maps doesn't work?"

"Yes and no. Paper is paper, up to a point. I've eaten copies already and it's worthwhile. I know a lot of placenames, have a sense of where they are. It helps." He gestured at the graphic novels. "Similar to eating those, yeah? And picture books you had as a child. Mostly the words remain but you still get a feeling for the images. Sort of."

A chance to expand her knowledge into something useful and forbidden. Devon unsheathed her bookteeth and bit through the folded world map. It tasted of air-conditioned factories and slick, slightly bitter ink. The petrochemical coating sat heavy on her tongue, sticking to the insides of her cheeks. She grimaced.

"I brought you some ketchup," he said, taking a squeezy bottle from one of the shelves. "It's a human condiment, but the acidic content works like a charm on glossy coated paper."

No plates in the games room, so Jarrow squeezed ketchup all over the map and rolled it up like a printed tortilla wrap. Devon bit into her map roll.

Words formed in her mind, a long list of places. If she concentrated, she could almost picture them laid out. As if someone had scrubbed away the drawing of the landmasses and left the city and country names unchanged, roughly marking out relative locations.

Only, there were so many. Countries and their capitals stacked up inside her head and the glossy paper made her nauseous. The ketchup tasted like an absurdist comedy, but Jarrow was right; it took the edge right off that plastic coating.

"Lemme show you something," he said when she'd finished. "If you're not too tired of seeing things, that is."

"No." Devon licked ketchup off her thumb. "I don't mind at all." She'd have to remember his trick. There were a *lot* of glossy books in this house.

"I'll show you the different Families." Jarrow unrolled the first map again and stabbed a finger on the map. "This is the Davenports in Powys, Wales." His finger moved upward, sweeping across dotted networks of cities. "Easterbrooks on the Norfolk Coast; that's us." More upward. "Your friendly Fairweathers, up in the Yorkshire moors." Back down to the south. "The Gladstones, in London." Somewhere in the forested middle regions. "The Blackwoods were here, though they've collapsed and dispersed to other houses."

"Huh. My mother was a Blackwood. I wonder where she's living now."

"In the south somewhere, probably. A lot of them folded into the Gladstones." His finger moved back out toward the west-middle areas. "This is Winterfield, in Birmingham. Where your daughter is."

Devon clenched her fists until her nails cut lines into her palms.

"And the Ravenscars are up here, on the north coast. Even more north than your Fairweather Manor." He tapped the map with a nail. "Do you know about them?"

"The ones who make Redemption?"

"That's the ticket. Until the Ravenscars developed that drug, dragons were just killed or managed by their own Families. These days, they're allowed to live, because they've been useful, but no one trusts them to run their own household in case they go rogue and draw human attention. That's where the knights come in. Babysitters for the Families' unwanted dragons, and matchmakers for our weddings."

"What's that have to do with escape?"

"Nothing directly, since you ask! I actually opened this map to show you Ireland. Both Irelands." He dragged a line across the map to the other side of Britain, pointing at a small cluster of islands. "See this? Northern Ireland is in the United Kingdom, but the Republic of Ireland is a whole separate country. With an unguarded border between them."

"I don't understand?"

"*Unguarded border,*" he said impatiently. "Think, Devon. What's the main thing that makes escaping the Families difficult?"

She goggled at him, at a total loss. "They're . . . powerful?"

"Nah, not really, they just pretend they are," he said. "It's the fact that we can't easily leave this bloody island, because none of us have any proper documentation."

"Oh. Of course."

"But we *can* do it if we chain our journey through Northern Ireland," he pressed. "We could take a ferry there without needing passports, since it's part of the United Kingdom. Then drive quietly across the border into the Republic, because they don't have border checkpoints between the two. Boom, out of

Britain." He grinned. "If you want to escape the Families, all you have to do is take a ferry to Northern Ireland."

She said, doubtful, "Aren't there book eaters there?"

"Not anymore! The last of the Irish 'eaters dispersed in the 1940s. Some went abroad to America, never heard from them again. The rest merged their lineage into the Ravenscars and the Winterfields. Both Irelands are free of the Families." He leaned forward, face aglow with excitement. "What do you think? Good idea?"

"I . . ." She put her head in her hands, overwhelmed by all he was suggesting. Overwhelmed they were even discussing this at all. "Stop. Please, stop. I'm glad you care, it means a lot to me. But I can't up and go to this Ireland place. Northern Ireland, whatever. I have a daughter, Jarrow. There is no plan we can concoct that will let me bring her, because she's trapped in Birmingham."

His face fell. "She'll be trapped whether you go or stay."

"But if I stay, I'll get to see her when I'm done having children. I have a meeting, it's all set up on her tenth birthday. If I behave, if I do as I'm told and—"

"Listen to yourself," he said, almost a growl. "The Family have you fooled into thinking life is a fairy tale. There is no happy ending to this story. It is just a con."

"Don't talk to me like I'm bloody stupid." She kept her voice low, her jaw tight, in contrast to his wild gesturing. "If I go with you, I will *definitely* never see Salem again. That's a certainty. She'll be lost to me forever. Staying is my only chance, however slim."

"Oh for god's sakes, Dev, there is no chance at all, right? They are *never* going to let you see your daughter again! When have you ever heard of mothers visiting their biological children? Why the hell would they make an exception for you? Did your mother ever come to visit?" His fists battered the table in sudden fury. "Fucking think about it! *Do any mothers ever visit?*"

She stared at him with eyes wide and lips parted, a child struck dumb. A memory of Uncle Aike lounging in her bedroom, ankles elegantly crossed as he said, so casually, *Five hundred years of 'eater traditions do not get overturned on the whims of one pampered girl.*

"It's bait," he stormed. "They're saying this bullshit to keep you quiet until you're old and tired like the aunts, and don't have the heart to fight anymore. Can't you *see* that?"

"Just shut up!" She clapped her hands over her ears. "I came here to play video games. That's the only escape I'm interested in. The only escape that is possible for me. If you want to leave, you can do that. Go off and don't come back. No children, no responsibilities anchoring you down. But you don't want that, do you? Because this isn't about me or my life, it's about you and your need to . . . to rescue someone!"

Jarrow folded into a chair as if she'd sliced his tendons.

Silence cowered between them.

"I'm sorry," she said, and when that didn't seem enough she added, "If you no longer want me to come here, I'll understand."

"Don't be daft," he said, after a moment. "You're always welcome to play games, or anything else. Always." He reached out and scraped the map off the table, stashing it into a drawer. "And if you ever change your mind, let me know. I'm serious."

What that offer cost him, she couldn't begin to guess. Even in her distress she was grateful.

"I'll think about it," she lied, and turned away from the maps that were too real of an escape, back toward the safe prison of the games room and its promise of digital abandon.

18

THE MANY FACES OF DEVON FAIRWEATHER

PRESENT DAY

The book eater inability to write by longhand in any form, including codes or pictographs, is truly fascinating. They cannot even type electronically! I am reminded of situational mutism (such as that experienced by some autistic individuals or people with anxiety), where someone may have healthy vocal cords and academic knowledge of human language, yet still be unable to communicate verbally.

I believe book eaters experience a similar communication processing barrier. Any action the brain categorizes as written communication becomes psychologically impossible for them to perform. The fact that mind eaters can do it easily must surely, to them, seem a cruel irony.

—Amarinder Patel, *Paper and Flesh: A Secret History*

Devon dreamed again of Hell, with that same sense of absurdist comedy.

Instead of a pit opening up, she found herself riding a train whose destination was Heaven, although no one wanted to take her ticket. Cai sat next to her, Hester in the seat across. Both were keen to see what Heaven looked like. But Devon knew better; Heaven was a lie. They needed to jump off the train into the fields of fiery death outside.

She flung herself from a ghostly train, but her companions did not jump with her, only watched from the doorway with sad faces. Devon crashed into a pit of fire and kept going. She fell through level after level after level of molten heat, deeper and darker and hotter until, finally, she landed on a rustic sofa in a self-catering B and B cottage.

Devon snapped awake, sitting up so fast her head spun. She'd rolled off the sofa in her sleep, hitting the floor with a thump. Her head ached.

Light streamed through the cheap lace curtains, making her squint. Cai wasn't anywhere to be seen, but a pile of his clothes sat outside the bathroom door, which was shut, and the sound of running water came from within.

"Merry Christmas, sleepyhead. You're the last one up." Hester sat on the edge of her bed with legs crossed. Dressed, alert, and looking far less stressed than the night before.

"What," Devon groaned a yawn, "time is it?" Morning sunlight washed out her black clothes to an unhealthy gray. The carpet beneath her face smelled like mothballs.

"Almost eight A.M." Hester gestured at the room's little television, which was turned on with a low volume. "Look, we're famous."

On the flickering screen, a well-coiffed news anchor was speaking.

We have urgent news of a shooting incident in Newcastle Central Station on Christmas Eve, followed by an aggravated series of assaults on the Edinburgh line. No casualties reported, but the police would urgently like to speak to a man and a woman, believed to be traveling together toward Edinburgh. They are also in search of a train conductor, who is accused of attacking passengers before disappearing. More information as it comes in.

Reports say the man is roughly six feet in height, dressed in black, with fair skin and dark hair. The woman is around five feet tall, wearing a patterned blouse and long skirt—

"No casualties, huh?" Devon said, swallowing a second yawn. "Just inexplicable piles of ink-stained paper, moldering on the ground."

She thought of Ramsey, wearing that train conductor uniform. There was only one explanation for how he'd gotten it. She wondered if the *real* train conductor would turn up alive. And what he would have to say about the man who attacked him, if so.

"Being on the news is bad," Hester said. "We might run into trouble if our hosts think that description is awfully familiar. All the more reason to get out of here."

"I'd feel better if I knew exactly what I'm walking into next," Devon said. "How is this going to work? Do I just rock up and introduce myself to your siblings?"

Hester got up and started shaking dried mud from her shoes. "I'll bring you to Killock and you'll have a chat with him. He's very charming."

"Fair enough." Devon thought of Hester's confession from the night before: *Sometimes he frightens me.* "We still need a way of getting there."

"Two steps ahead of you! I've already been down to reception this morning to ask around. Don't look so anxious, we don't match those daft police descriptions on the television! Anyway, no dealerships that she knew of, but—but!—the farm itself has an old hatchback they've been trying to get rid of for several months. I reckon we could take it for a test drive and not come back."

"Or, we can just buy it." Devon raked her fingers through her hair to unknot the tangles. "And we should. If they're not already suspicious of us, they absolutely will be if we steal a vehicle." Attention from Ramsey was one thing. Attention from human police was quite another.

"Buy it?" Hester said, poise rattled. "How much money do you have, precisely?"

The water switched off, thumping noises from Cai clambering around in the bath. He would be out soon.

Devon snagged a nail in her hair. "Tell me where we're going, precisely, and I'll tell you how much money I have, precisely."

Hester flared slim nostrils.

"Even if you take a scenic route to avoid towns, eighty miles isn't exactly *Journey to the Center of the Earth*. We'll be there by this afternoon. What are you afraid of? That I'll betray you before you get me somewhere secure?"

"It's not that simple. Killock insisted on secrecy. He asked me to keep you in the dark as much as possible."

Devon abandoned her hair to its tangles. "Let me get this straight. Everyone has to do what he says and live under his rule, you're sometimes afraid of him, and he's also paranoid. Remind me again how he's supposedly different from the other patriarchs?"

"That's not . . ." Hester picked at a thumbnail, lips pinched.

"Dev?" Cai stuck his head around the door. "I don't have a towel."

"Oh, for heaven's sakes." Devon scooped one off the floor and tossed it at him, trying not to show how rattled she felt. "Take it in with you next time."

He huffed at her and shut the door again, that odd mix of overly competent five-year-old who could manage his own shower but also never remembered to bring in towels or clean clothes.

The sight of him, however, was a sharp reminder of her priorities. She needed these folks to trust her, or Cai would never be okay again, and Devon would never be free of Ramsey. Perhaps she ought to yield, just a little, just this once.

She turned back to a very amused-looking Hester and said, "About twenty grand."

The other woman's smile faltered. "Come again?"

"I took twenty-six thousand, three hundred and seventy pounds from Matley Easterbrook's vault. There was more, but the rest didn't fit in my backpack."

Devon picked up her jacket from the couch, shook it out, and stuffed her arms into the sleeves. "I've got about twenty thousand pounds left, I think. Need to sit and count it out. Plenty for a cheap old car."

"You broke into the Easterbrook vault?!"

"Didn't Killock take his father's accounts?" Devon said, sidestepping the question. "This is no different."

"Killock had years to plan, and all of us helping," Hester said, equally evasive. "You were one woman alone."

"What're we doing this morning?" Cai wandered out of the bathroom looking cleaner than he had in a long while. But also moving a little slower, and the bright energy he'd carried yesterday seemed faded.

"We are about to buy a car," Devon informed him. "Wanna do your starving orphan act? Should knock a bit off the price."

"Not an act," he said mournfully. "I'm really hungry."

A week ago, those words would have twisted her gut. Today, Devon could smile apologetically and say, "Hang in there, love. Just a few more hours." She counted out five hundred pounds in twenty-pound notes and handed them across to Hester. "Here. You and he should be the ones to do the purchase. I don't have shoes and I look dodgy as hell."

"Oh! I mean, sure, if you trust me to—"

"We'll never finish this trip if we don't start trusting each other." She handed the money over in a thick wad.

"Right." Hester took the proffered money and cleared her throat. "Innerleithen."

"Pardon?"

"You wanted to know, right? I'm letting you know." Hester folded the money with deliberate care and tucked it into a pocket. "We are going to Traquair House, on the outskirts of Innerleithen. It's only a couple hours' drive from here."

"Never been there, never heard of it," Devon said, nonplussed. "But I appreciate the trust. Thanks for telling me, even if I don't have a bloody clue where it is."

"Well. Like you said, the success of our journey requires mutual reliance," Hester said, sounding embarrassed. "Informing you of the destination is a small enough gesture."

"You'd have needed to tell me in the next couple of hours anyway." Devon picked up the television remote and unmuted the news channel. "Come grab me when you've got the car, aye? I want to see if there are any updates about us, in the meantime."

"It's a plan." Hester unlocked the door and held her hand out to Cai. "All right, young man. You get to be my accomplice."

Devon sat patiently on the edge of the bed until they'd disappeared, keeping her eyes to the screen. When the door clicked shut after Hester and Cai, she got up, drew the bolt as a precaution, and rang Ramsey on her mobile.

He answered on the first ring. "Tell me this is good news."

"Innerleithen," she said, a little breathless. "We're going to a place called Traquair House in Innerleithen, it's—"

"A town in the border counties. I know it." A pause. "Innerleithen, of all places! Why there, I wonder?"

"How should I know," she said, exasperated. "Maybe it was the first place they could find? Anyway, I need a few days to settle in once we get there."

"Fine. I need a little time myself, to organize things on this end." He sounded serene, cheerful. Almost pleasant, like boy-Ramsey had been during his best moods. "Let's set a date. December 26, at twenty-three hundred hours. Send a confirmation text once you're there and keep your phone if you can; we can track it."

"That's tomorrow evening," she said dazedly, counting up in her head: barely thirty-six hours. "Are you sure?"

"Why the fuck wouldn't I be sure?" he snarled, roused to sudden ire. "It's not a *problem,* is it? You're not on goddamn holiday, Dev."

"No. No, of course not." A brutally tight window, but it would have to do. "It's fine, I was just surprised. Is there anything else?"

"Don't fuck up. Don't try anything stupid. Look out for the knight I'm sending your way. See you in a day and a half." The line went dead.

Devon watched the call disconnect and wondered how Ramsey had fared last night, stranded on that train with his superiors breathing down his neck. How he'd explained the dead bodies and everything else that had gone wrong with the knights' actions. She suspected, with a kind of grudging admiration, that he'd not encountered any trouble. He was a tough person in his own, spiteful little way.

That toughness made him blind, though. Ramsey thought himself so strong and so frightening that no one would dare to get in his way, and thought of her as so desperate and so shaped by circumstance that she wouldn't have a path around his enforced treachery and spiraling plans.

The only intelligence he ever acknowledged was that which mirrored his own, Ramsey believed his strength came from his own cruelty, and so could not recognize such qualities in other people—including her.

So much the better. If Devon wanted to enact her own plans, she simply had to take advantage of Ramsey's blindness.

She cricked her neck, brought up her Recent Contacts, and pressed the Call button again, but this time for a different number: the one she'd called yesterday evening, before leaving the flat with Hester and Cai.

Three rings, followed by cautious silence.

"Nycteris follows the firefly," she said, because there was no need for Morse code at the moment. "It's me."

"Which, like herself, was seeking the way out," came the answer, and Jarrow Easterbrook sighed theatrically. "Still gives me a heart attack every time you ring, you know. I'm losing years off my life over here."

She couldn't help but smile. He never changed, not in the ways that mattered.

"It's good to hear from you." Devon crushed the handset against her ear. "Things are moving, and very quickly. Can you pick me up from Traquair House, in Innerleithen?"

"When are we talking? How quick is quick?"

She grimaced. "Tomorrow, apparently. Although I'm not sure exactly when we're leaving."

"Jesus, Dev! One day's notice? Really?"

"You've had months to prepare," she protested. "Okay, fine, it's not fair, but it's all I've got. Ramsey is going full throttle."

"Fuck me."

"Is that a no?" she said, iced with sudden anxiety.

A rustling noise. Paper being rifled.

"Are you there?" she said. "I don't have much time—"

"It's enough time, I can do it," he said. "Listen. At the juncture where the Leithen Water tributary meets the River Tweed, you will find a trio of riverine islands. Meet me there tomorrow morning."

"A trio of *what* now?" Damn his romanticism, she thought with annoyance. "Can't we just meet in town?"

"Fuck, someone's coming, gotta go." He hung up.

Devon clutched the disconnected receiver, vacillating between relief and anxiety. So much to juggle, so many spinning plates. Focus on the goal, she thought, chest squeezing. Focus on the goals, not the obstacles. On the needs, not the fears.

Two days. Only two days.

Devon stood, scooped up her bag, and went to catch up with her other two companions. The car would be ready by now.

———·———

The inside of the little gray Ford smelled like the outside of a farm. A few miles in, and Devon felt compelled to roll down the window and hang her head out. The balm of snow and woodland soothed her offended nose. In the driver's seat next to her, Hester hummed as she steered them toward a twisting country road. Avoiding the motorway. She'd insisted on driving, since she had shoes and knew where they were going. Fine by Devon.

Haggling had been straightforward enough, and if the farm owners found it odd that Hester paid in cash, they hadn't complained. Likewise, neither Devon nor Hester complained when they charged far more than the car was worth. As with the room last night, money solved a host of quibbles.

As they'd pulled away, she'd glanced in the rearview mirror; the farm owners were staring after them with hands on hips, heads leaned together. Devon had wondered briefly if the pair would end up filing a police tip-off, then decided she didn't really care.

The miles drifted by and Devon leaned her head against the rest, oddly tired despite a good night's sleep. Too much cumulative exhaustion. She was just starting to doze off when Cai's voice jerked her to wakefulness.

"Do you hear that?" He peered through the back passenger window, craning his neck. "Sounds like a motorcycle coming down the road."

Devon sat up, instantly alert. "Where?"

"Which direction?" Hester said. "Are you sure?"

"Ahead of us!" He pointed.

Hester hit the brakes abruptly, throwing all three of them against their seat belts, and stuck her head out of the window to listen.

Devon also peered out. The narrow country road lay empty, couched between grayish-green fields and speckled with sheep. And cutting through that domestic silence was the unmistakable burr of a bike engine. Too far to be seen yet, on that twisting road.

"From the front," she said. "Coming toward us."

Hester revved the car back into motion. "The two of you duck down and he likely will just pass us by. Hurry!"

Cai hunkered down, eyes squeezed shut. The speck blossomed into a lumpy squidge of black, growing bigger as the two vehicles streamed toward each other. The knight was clearly visible on his black bike, ironically helmetless, smart suit obscured by an expensive bomber jacket.

One of Ramsey's knights, out scouting for them. Here to have a flashy car chase, just as she'd requested. His voice floated up from her memory: *Keep this one alive, please. I'm tired of cleaning up the bodies of my men, and knights are not infinitely expendable.*

Fuck that. Every knight she could kill in advance improved her chances of getting out of this mess alive, and even better if it made her look good in Ravenscar eyes.

"What are you doing?" Hester hissed, eyes on the road. "Duck down!"

"No." Devon lunged across and wrenched the wheel to the right, ramming the knight at sixty miles an hour with their little gray Ford.

Bike hit car at a skewed angle with a brassy clang. Hester swore and stomped the brakes. Devon bruised her chest against the tight restraints of the seat belt, guts slamming against her ribs.

The knight cascaded up and over the windshield in a tornado of limbs before landing on the ground near the passenger's side.

A single moment of stunned stillness and then he rolled over, trying to crawl away. Black blood streamed from his nostrils and from a ruined eye socket. One of his legs bent in the wrong direction, and he could only crawl a few inches.

Devon unclipped her seat belt and swung the car door open with all her strength. Door met knightly head with a dull clunk. It was one blow too many. He flopped back to the tarmac, stunned into unconsciousness.

A frustrated shout from Hester as Devon vaulted from the Ford, still barefoot like she had been in the forest all those years ago, running and hunted. For a moment she stood above the prone knight, spasmodic indecision holding her in place. Murder, much like the secondhand clothes she wore, never quite felt comfortable.

But she still remembered all too clearly the fear and horror of that first escape attempt. If the patriarchs had required her death, the knights would have delivered without a backward glance.

Besides, the only good knight was a dead knight.

Necks were hard to break so Devon took the easy option and, prying the knife from his belt, spiked his blade through the fifth left intercostal space. Straight to the heart.

He never regained consciousness. Thirty seconds of stillness, as winter sunlight slowly warmed the frost-limned road and the knight bled out inside his own chest cavity. She stepped back, breathing through her nose.

"At last, we meet the woman who killed Matley Easterbrook." Hester leaned against the car. "I was beginning to wonder when you'd show yourself."

"What about you?" Devon said. "When will *you* show yourself?"

The knight was already decaying, skin grown thin and brittle and pale like parchment as his veins dried up. Lines of inky blood traced uneven patterns across the exposed flesh.

"I won't lose sleep over one dead knight," Hester said, ignoring the question pointedly. "But for the record, I did not appreciate you snatching the wheel. That could have gone diabolically wrong."

"Sorry. Split-second decision. It wasn't fair of me."

"I could have just driven past him. I'm not sure this was worth the fuss."

"We're still an hour from the border. He might have alerted the others."

"You don't think this murder would alert them?"

"Not if they don't find the evidence." Devon picked up the clothes, shaking out the ink-damp mess of paper. "I'll hide the suit and motorbike. They'll notice he's missing eventually, but by then we'll be out of their reach."

Hester duly obliged. Devon dumped an armful of stained fabric into a ditch by the side of the road. Picking up the bike with both hands, she flung it into the hedge. A heavy thing to toss, though fun to watch it go flying.

Cai, meanwhile, observed them from the back with an expression Devon couldn't read. She met his gaze briefly, held it for a few seconds before turning away. He'd seen worse. What was one more murder in his presence?

Inwardly, she was already rehearsing excuses to Ramsey. *I couldn't stop her. She was the one driving, because the Family never let me learn that skill and also because only Hester knew our end location.* Of course, that was assuming he even asked—because he wouldn't have the chance, if she had her way. By the time he thought to suspect anything, Devon planned to be long gone.

The idea that she might never see her brother again gave her a sudden kick of endorphins and she almost smiled.

Hester sank into the driver's side. "I suppose we're lucky Mr. Flying Knight here didn't crack the windshield."

"I'm always lucky," Devon said, clipping in her seat belt. "This is what luck feels like."

"You're bloody weird, you know that? God almighty. Let's just get to Innerleithen." Hester put the car into gear and drove off, leaving the empty road well behind.

None of them looked back.

19

THE EXILE FORMERLY
KNOWN AS PRINCE

FIVE YEARS AGO

The Prince was beside himself and, in his despair, he fell down from the tower. He escaped with his life, but the thorns into which he fell pierced his eyes. Then he wandered quite blind about the forest, ate nothing but roots and berries, and did nothing but weep over the loss of his dearest Rapunzel.
—Hans Christian Andersen, "Rapunzel"

Devon thought she would never love anyone as much as she'd loved Salem. Wounds healed into scars, the skin growing thick and rigid and protective, or so folk said. Along with once bitten, twice shy; time cures all; and other such clichés.

The clichés were wrong.

Devon was wrong.

When the time came, she birthed her second child on the games room couch of Easterbrook Manor, because even after her water broke she opted to keep playing *Final Fantasy* through the early contractions. Only when the pain ramped up too severely for her to hold a controller did she allow Jarrow to run off for help. By then, she was lying on her side and not fit to walk anywhere.

And afterward, when her newborn son lay in her arms and opened his swollen eyes wide, her heart cracked open all over again as if she'd learned nothing at all the first time around.

"A boy," said the closest aunt, and murmurs of disappointment chased the announcement.

A mere three aunts lived at the villa, out of some forty adults. Devon knew none of their names and had exchanged not a word with any of them till now. They'd attended her birth anyway, because that was what women were expected to do for each other.

"A boy! Amazing!" Jarrow had mostly flitted around the edges of the room, kept out of the way by irritated aunts. "How do you feel, Dev?" He sounded twelve, and excited joy rendered his features childish.

"I . . . I feel . . ." Devon looked down at the squirming bundle cradled against her chest as the aunts fussed around her, taking away the placenta and mopping up the mess.

The mantra, she thought. Don't care, don't bond, think only of Salem—

It didn't work. The rehearsed words fell away; she was attached. Again. To another tiny creature who would snuff out her spirit when she lost him to the Families, only this time things were harder because he was a boy—horror!—and might grow up to be something worse than a bride: a knight, or even a husband. Or both. A hurter of women and a hunter of princesses. And still she would adore him, hopelessly; pine for his loss, endlessly.

For here was the thing that no fairy tale would ever admit, but that she understood in that moment: *love was not inherently good.*

Certainly, it could inspire goodness. She didn't argue that. Poets would tell you that love was electricity in your veins that could light a room. That it was a river in your soul to lift you up and carry you away, or a fire inside the heart to keep you warm. Yet electricity could also fry, rivers could drown, and fires could burn; love could be destructive. Punishingly, fatally destructive.

And the other thing, the real bloody clincher of it all, was that the good and the bad didn't get served up equally. If love were a balance of electric lights and electric jolts, two sides of an equally weighted coin, then fair enough. She could deal.

That wasn't how it worked, though. Some love was just the bad, all the time: an endless parade of electrified bones and drowned lungs and hearts that burned to a cinder inside the cage of your chest.

And so she looked down at her son and loved him with the kind of twisted, complex feeling that came from having never wanted him in the first place; she loved him with bitterness, and she loved him with resignation. She loved him though she knew no good could ever come from such a bond.

"Dev?" Jarrow said again, recalling her to the moment.

She burst into tears.

Spooked by the noise, her newborn opened his mouth wide and began to wail. From out of his mouth flopped a tubelike tongue, curling and uncurling weakly.

"Oh, no." The blond aunt covered her mouth with both hands, like a distressed Victorian heroine.

The others peered over, faces immediately paling. A heated discussion broke out between the other two; something about who would have to inform "the men" and how long they should wait.

Vision blurred with tears, Devon found herself trying to tuck her crying son's tongue back into his mouth, as if she could tuck away in him the things other people found awful and hide them out of sight. The tubular tongue curled around her finger like a warm spaghetti strand and he settled at once, soothed by suckling like any other child. She remained immobile, tears evaporating as the aunts argued behind her.

"Shit," Jarrow said. "Matley's going to bloody flip, when he gets back." But he looked worried rather than disgusted, and she was grateful for that.

"Can you blame him? What a waste," said the oldest of the women. "I'd best let the knights know. Another one for their dragon pens. Poor little monster."

"I don't care what Matley or anyone else thinks," Devon said, and was met by shocked faces. "My son is beautiful."

"This child will grow up to consume minds," said one of the women who'd been arguing. "Our concern is not with how he looks, but what he will grow into!"

"I thought we didn't care about humans," Devon snapped. "Why are you bothered if he eats a few? And he hasn't eaten anyone yet. He's only a baby!"

"Eventually, he'll wean off that milk and grow into his hunger," said the first aunt, nostrils flaring. "Dragons do not care what they eat, or who, so long as they do. Your son would eat *you*, given half the chance."

"Redemption—"

"Cures the need, not the want," said the older woman. "He will crave minds all his life no matter how much Redemption you give him. Dragons are never safe, can never be trusted. Only managed."

"He's still beautiful," Devon said. "He's still mine." The baby fussed again, no longer conned by suckling a mere finger, and she eased him to a breast. All the things she learned to do from having Salem. "What is his name? Did Matley pick one?" He didn't latch the way Salem did, and the sensation was odd, but she could get used to it.

"It doesn't get an Easterbrook name."

Devon twisted her neck around to the sight of Matley, who had stalked in silently and now stood behind her. He wore white slacks and a white shirt, painfully searing as ever in that shadowed room.

"It doesn't get an Easterbrook name," he said again, tense strain cording his shoulders and neck. "It'll get whatever the knights give it."

The room descended into awkward stillness and Devon lay rigid, conscious of her bare legs smeared with blood. Of her bare chest and sweat-stained face. Matley's presence had somehow rendered her vulnerability obscene. She felt, absurdly, like a sinful Eve standing before God and realizing her own nakedness for the first time.

Jarrow unzipped his hoodie and draped it over her and the baby, with a muttered "Here, don't want you both to get cold."

"Thanks," she whispered.

The oldest aunt was talking. "Mat, this isn't the time," she said, palms pressed together like a pretend nun. "The girl hasn't had a moment of rest—"

"Isn't the time? For a father to see his son?" Unpleasantness warped his features. "What a waste. Three years I'll have to spend, feeding and clothing this thing, being extorted by the bloody Ravenscars. Only for the knights to take it away at the end and use it as a prop for their own power. What happened to the days where we could *choose* what happened to our own dragons? He should have died in birth."

Devon was speechless with fury.

Matley caught her glare, and narrowed his eyes. "God sakes," he said, "was it so incredibly difficult to squirt out a girl? You managed it for the Winterfields."

"Sex is determined by the man's sperm," Devon retorted, tongue getting the best of her, but so what because it was bloody fucking true. "Don't blame me for your failing."

He slapped her so hard her vision went black for a split second. She fell back against the sofa, arms still clenched around her son. Her ears keened like cutlery had been dropped on a tile floor, not helped by the shrieking aunts in the background.

Matley locked his hands around her throat. Devon should have let go of her son to fight but instead she held the child tighter, alarmed that he might attack the boy instead of her. She was already weak and exhausted from birth and now she couldn't breathe. Tightness and ache radiated from her throat into her chest, her head, the hollow behind her eyes.

Jarrow barreled in despite his shorter stature and lighter frame, shouting something she couldn't hear because her ears still rang.

Matley jerked away to fend off his younger brother and Devon gagged, gasping for air as he released her. The last thing she saw before passing out was the Easterbrook aunts descending in a flock on the two men, trying to pull them apart.

———————— • ————————

Many hours later, Devon woke in her own bed. Her throat felt like someone had fed it through a paper shredder, and the swollen parts of her neck felt hot to the touch. Swallowing had become an act of bravery.

At least Matley was gone. She hated him, possibly more than she loved her children, and could sense that loathing building in herself the way a gale gathered pace into a storm.

She lay for a minute or two and imagined her husband swinging from his expensive chandeliers by one of his own silk ties, only to become annoyed when the fantasy gave her no satisfaction. Hate was losing its emotional edge, becoming a common thing she lived with instead of a treasure she nursed.

Her arm was going numb. Devon looked down to find the boy nestled next to her, fast asleep in the crook of her elbow. He bore no injury; perfect, pristine, unharmed by his father's spurt of anger.

She freed her trapped limb and turned over to catch sight of Jarrow slouched in the bay window of her room, fiddling with a handheld console. The words GAME BOY were printed underneath its tiny green screen. He hadn't yet noticed her small movements, but then she hadn't noticed his till now; he could be so still, when focused on his games.

She tried to say *Hello* but all that came out was a cough. The fire in her throat cranked up a notch.

"You're awake," Jarrow exclaimed, twisting round. "I'll get you a drink!" He disappeared into the bathroom. Somehow he found a cup, filled it from the sink, and brought her water. She drank, and thought she knew how sword-eaters must feel.

When she was done, she pointed to the faint bruises on his face. Needing to know if he was hurt, and how badly, from that tussle with his brother.

"Ah, don't worry about me. I'll live. But listen, I have a better way for us to talk." He dug out a slim booklet and presented it tentatively. "Might be a bit of work to eat it, but on the other hand, your throat will take weeks to heal up. I'd shred it for you if I could, but then you wouldn't learn anything by eating it. Empty calories."

Devon ran a thumb along the booklet. It had no cover in the traditional sense, just printed pages on stiff paper on which a title was printed:

THE MORSE CODE: Learning and Practice
(Revised Edition)

She raised both eyebrows in polite confusion.

"My sister, Vic." He tugged an earlobe, frowning with uneasy remembrance. "She had this interest in Morse code. Also spy thrillers, retro British mystery stuff. We used to send messages when we were kids, mess about playing James Bond. Useful for us."

Understanding dawned. He wanted her to communicate in a way that mimicked writing, without requiring writing. A language of sounds that did not need her voice. Devon smiled, and squeezed his hand.

"Glad you approve." Jarrow brought her a bowl of water and, page by painstaking page, tore each sheet, soaked it to soften, and passed it to her to eat. Not too wet, nor shredded; the information would be inaccessible to her if too much damaged before she could absorb it.

The pamphlet had a sparky flavor, the way she imagined static would taste. Not bitter, simply neutral, slightly metallic though there was no metal in the ink or paper. She ate slowly, pushing through the agony swallowing caused her.

"Trying to write out the dots and dashes doesn't work, by the way; our brains still register that as writing, because they're just stand-ins for the letters," he said. "But tapping works. A kind of cheat."

Devon rolled her eyes. <Fucking Collector and their rules for us> She squinted at her fingertips. <Also tapping hurts finger>

"Oh! That reminds me, nearly forgot." Jarrow reached into a pocket and fished out a thimble, slipping it onto her finger. "Now you can do it more easily, eh?"

The gesture startled her; it was oddly intimate, reminiscent of a groom slipping a ring onto his bride, except she'd never done that. The Families eschewed wedding rings, since their marriages were not intended to last. But it was very fairy-tale-esque all the same. Princesses in books were forever doing things with thimbles.

She caught his palm and tapped, <Thank you>

"Isn't it great? How easy was that? Almost as good as writing!" His grin was the brightest thing she'd seen in years. "You're very welcome, by the way. But slow down a little, I'm rusty with translating Morse in my head."

<Slower. OK> Her next message she regretted, because it stole the smile right off his face. <Where Matley>

". . . ah. Gone on a holiday, or something." He wouldn't meet her eye now. "He'll keep clear of you, if you keep clear of him."

So there was a hard line that even the Easterbrooks wouldn't allow one of their sons to cross. Devon wasn't sure whether to be relieved they placed any limits, or furious that the limit wasn't more reasonable. Both, probably.

<But are you okay>

"I'm fine. We just scuffled a bit."

Devon didn't believe him. Their fight had looked a lot more serious than a plain scuffle. She started to tap that out when he held up a hand to forestall her.

"Hey, listen. I'm glad you woke, because I actually came here to give you this." Jarrow put his Game Boy in her lap. "I hear it gets proper boring, looking after babies. This can keep you occupied while you're doing all that nursing, eh? Doubt you'll get down to the games room much, until your throat heals."

The console rested in her grip, lighter and denser than it looked. <But Game Boy is yours>

"I wanted you to have mine. Because I think of us as real family, not *the* Family. And siblings, you know, give each other stuff."

<Vic was your family too> she tapped, after a moment. <Birth sister and real sister>

He shot her a guarded look, but nodded. "I miss her. She'd have liked you."

<Jarrow. Where is Vic>

"She struggled with the marriages, the children. Like you did. She couldn't accept things, made a fuss." He sighed. "She got on Matley's nerves and he sent her away, in the end. The Families like to do that, when folks cause problems: send them somewhere else to live, where they don't have friends or support networks." His eyes were red, but still dry. "I call her sometimes. It's not the same, though."

<So sorry> Her apology sounded stupid and trite in Morse code. It would have sounded stupid however she conveyed it.

"Vic bought the same lie about keeping her head down and getting to see her kids again. The truth devastated her, when she realized." The electric fire-light illuminated his curls like a halo. "When I told you ages ago that they're not going to let you see your children again, I wasn't trying to frighten you. I was trying to warn you. Women can travel a bit and go to the parties, but no one is going to let former brides anywhere near the manors where they have a scion."

<That was why you wanted me to run away with you> she said, filled with bitter resignation.

"Yeah."

The infant startled awake with a wail. Devon gathered him close to murmur timeless reassurances that she'd learned from books in lieu of a real parent. He fussed a little before settling against her shoulder and she held him close, palm to the back of that small, fuzzy head.

Perhaps she should have been grateful to the knights, because if they did not exist to keep dragons alive, then none would be saved. But she couldn't summon up any gratitude for such grudging care. Did anyone hold the dragon children when they were afraid? Seemed unlikely. Dragons were raised in barracks; that was common knowledge. Beyond that, the specifics eluded her.

She buried her face in the dark curls, seeking comfort in the familiar scent. This boy—taken away. Not even to a life of relative ease and privilege as hers had been, or as Salem's would be, but to an existence that was categorically and unequivocally bad.

In fairy tales, the princesses got everything: true love, happy ending, their children to keep and the monsters or witches or ogres defeated. Life didn't work out like that. No one would write Devon a happy ending, and the universe did not owe her a daughter. The best she could hope for was to keep her son, or else lose both children entirely.

An image filled her head of a ten-year-old Salem, waiting forlornly in the Winterfield courtyard for a mother who would not be arriving. Growing sullener with the years at that betrayal, and the abandonment. A worse alternative: Luton had fed Devon nothing but lies and Salem had already forgotten her mother existed, as Devon had forgotten her own.

It hurt, to think of that. It hurt in places and in ways that she didn't have words for.

But it did not hurt as much as abandoning the boy in her arms to an even worse fate. She had to choose between them, and it was no choice at all. Salem was already lost, through Devon's failure. And her son needed her more.

When he was settled at her breast, she reached across, tapping thimble to wood. <Help me>

Jarrow blinked. "Help you? How? What with?"

<Help me take him to Ireland. Like you offered before>

His mouth opened and closed.

<I know he is dragon and that changes things but if we can steal some Redemption and—>

"Aw, Dev." The bed springs sighed as he shifted his weight. "You have the worst timing, you know that?"

A thump of fear beat in her chest. <What do you mean>

"I'm being sent to live with the Gladstones, too," he said wearily. "The same chalet they exiled Vic to live in, just off the main house." He flushed at her appalled expression. "It could be worse. They were going to send me to the knights, but the knights don't want me because I'm too old to train. Thank *God* for that mercy."

But it was still her fault he was being sent away, she thought, and felt sick. He was being punished for defending her from Matley. As Ramsey had once been punished for following her lead. If only she'd held her tongue, both times.

<You are here to say good-bye> she said, engulfed by sudden rising panic. <The Game Boy is your good-bye present>

"Yes. I'm sorry." His turn for the apologies. "I meant it when I said you could reach out, if you changed your mind, but I can't do what you're asking. I'm leaving today. I shouldn't be here at all, only I couldn't go without checking on you first."

<But why teach me Morse code if you are just leaving anyway>

Someone pounded on the door, calling Jarrow's name; they both jumped.

"Just a minute," he shouted over one shoulder, then turned back to her. "'Cause you can't talk, daft woman! I've asked a couple of the aunts to eat Morse code books, too. They'll be able to understand your requests, and look after you across the next few weeks while that throat heals up, a'right?"

No, she wanted to scream. It wasn't all right. <Will I see you again?>

"Definitely. I promise. Only, it might have to wait until, um, your son has gone to the other dragons." His smile was sad and sickly. "I'll travel and find you. When all this is over."

<That is years from now> she tapped frantically. <I will not see you for ages>

"I know. I'm . . . so sorry, Dev. Really, I am."

Everything was happening too fast. All her doors were closing, her options receding. Even her last resort, dangerous flight with a child in tow, was a life raft withdrawn, leaving her floundering. She was about to be alone in a hostile house with a child she could not keep. Again.

The person outside knocked harder, shouted louder and more impatiently.

"Shit. I have to go." He bent to give her a gentle hug, careful of the baby, and said in her ear, "Listen. If you ever feel like ditching the Families, with or without your kids, then get in touch. I'll help if I can, I swear."

She wanted to tap out, *How? I can't write I can't call* but there was no time. Another Easterbrook brother stuck his head in, saying, "C'mon, mate. We don't have all day."

"Bye," Jarrow said again, and left with the last of Devon's light.

20

HOUSE OF SAINTS

PRESENT DAY

Though I find the Collector story to be wholly absurd, I struggle to conjure a better theory. Aside from the teeth, eaters do look *identical to humans. Yet they cannot interbreed with us and have strange organs, extreme strength, and dark-vision. They also consume either books or minds, processing that information in ways that defy all known biology, and they decompose in a manner suggestive of—dare I say—magic.*

In truth, to the naked eye, they are profoundly a magical species. And if I must choose between believing in the Collector, or believing in magic, *then I am reluctantly inclined to go with the former.*

—Amarinder Patel, *Paper and Flesh: A Secret History*

Their little gray car crested the heather hills of Scotland and began needling its way through winding paths to the valley-town of Innerleithen below. Devon, looking out the window, was mesmerized. Moors undulated for miles toward the north. Snags of cloud tumbled low across a silver-blue sky. Twisted trees populated gnarly slopes, snow blanketing the small stone houses. Wide banks by a sweeping river, dotted with optimistic fishers—even in this weather!—wearing waders. Picture-perfect, like one of those charity shop postcards done to capture British nostalgia.

She rested her head against the cool glass. "Do the residents of this town know?"

"Know what? About the family who moved into a derelict old mansion a couple years ago, did it up a bit, and now have a locally run artisan brewery? Sure, they know."

"Working in the open. Interesting tactic."

"Don't know what you mean," Hester said. "We're law-abiding citizens, aside from a bit of tax dodging and some illicit drug production, but that's nothing compared to the Winterfields and their dodgy law firm, or the Easterbrooks and their human trafficking."

"I can't argue with that."

They drove through a juncture, past a sign that suggested turning left to find St. Rowan's Primary School. Hester steered straight through town, heading for its south end.

"Will I have friends, someday?" Cai said, eyes on the receding school sign. "If I have enough Redemption to live without hunger?"

Devon looked at him in surprise: this small, intense figure, so precociously intelligent and aware for his years. The idea of managing his friendships, helping him to navigate those social situations, seemed overwhelming. More so than killing knights or luring humans home.

Come to think of it, Devon herself had never made friends, just played with her siblings and cousins. How did one *make* friends? Let alone keep them? Mysterious. Then the unbidden thought: maybe she'd find out with Hester. Stupid, that; she wasn't planning to stay.

"I hope you will have friends, wherever you end up," Hester said. "You will always have to guard against your hunger, but you seem safe enough with your mother. I'm confident you can learn to be around others without risk."

"Oh, okay. How long are we staying?" Cai said, sitting up a little straighter. "If Killock likes us and we like him, can we live here forever?"

"Let's take this one step at a time," Devon said. "Make sure Killock *does* like us." She already knew she wouldn't like him: a combination of gut instinct and lifelong experience of Family patriarchs.

The center of Innerleithen peeled away, slushed and salted roads melding back into rolling, snow-slung forests. They crossed the River Tweed over a long, low bridge. Devon could not help but scan its waters for evidence of riverine islands, as Jarrow had specified. Her view wasn't good enough from the car to pick out any such land masses.

A mile or so past the bridge, they approached a vintage-style sign reading TRAQUAIR HOUSE with a white arrow pointing down a smaller road.

"We're here, safe and sound," Hester said. She followed the sign, turning off the main road and onto the grounds of what was, presumably, Traquair itself.

They drove slowly down a long driveway, sculpted with green lawns and shadowed by ancient trees. Off to one side were a collection of smaller buildings, mostly wooden, and what looked like a rather elegant garden of extraordinary size.

Directly ahead sprawled a white building, as big as any Family manor. And more fortified, she thought; iron gates, concrete posts, small windows. A house that had seen conflict. There was a long history of fighting between Scotland and England.

"You don't have much security," Devon observed. "Don't you worry the Families will find you?"

"The Families are barely looking for us. If anything, I think they were relieved when we disappeared. Solved a lot of problems for them." Hester cruised through a pair of iron gates, slowing the Ford to a crawl. "As for the knights—even if they came calling, a few locks on the gates wouldn't help. Not being found is our first and best line of defense."

"I guess so." Devon thought about Hester in the train station, the accuracy of her gun. If the rest of the Ravenscars were similarly fierce, then the knights would have a fight on their hands. "Everything with your clan seems to be complicated. Including you, and your place in it."

"You have no idea." Hester parked up on the gravel, yanking the hand brake. "I'm going to introduce you to Killock today. When we first heard you were looking for us, it was his idea to bring you in and offer sanctuary. However, you will have to convince him you're safe, trustable, and genuine. Are you willing to answer his questions? There are gaps in your story that we're curious about."

"If he wants to know how I escaped the Easterbrooks, then I am willing enough to share," Devon said, watching dust skip through slanted sunbeams. "I'm not ready to talk about my daughter with strangers, though. That's all in the past, anyway."

"I'm sure that will be fine." Hester unclipped her seat belt, took a breath. "Listen. When we go inside, you are going to find out things about me that I have concealed. Please understand that I have never hidden the truth out of maliciousness. I've lied about myself only because Killock asked me to be circumspect. I'm sorry, I know that doesn't make any sense right now, but it will very soon."

The back of Devon's neck was prickling from alarm. "I'm not liking the sound of this."

"We should hurry, they'll know we're here and will be expecting us." Hester got out of the car and walked across the driveway toward the heavy doors.

Devon exchanged a long and troubled look with Cai, who shrugged. They both got out and followed Hester. No going back now.

Entering Traquair House felt strangely familiar to Devon, as if she had been there already and seen it all before. In one sense, she effectively had. The Ravenscars had wrangled their way into an ancient estate home, blending British tradition with 'eater needs. The whole setup was very Family. Whatever the beef with their deceased father, ingrained custom lingered.

The house itself bore a legacy of violence. Iron studs covered a solid oak door, which Devon recognized as a form of reinforcement against invading English soldiers. It was old, and strong enough to withstand a solid ax blow or two. The hallways surprised her: narrow, low-ceilinged, built of whitewashed stone. Not regal or royal, just built for war. A series of servant bells hung above one of the beams, in different sizes and tones.

Someone had set up a small nativity scene on the entry table, a faded Mary kneeling over her wooden infant in his tiny manger. Carved animals clustered around. Wise men loomed awkwardly in a corner, and Joseph stood with blank-faced reserve to one side, his face so worn the features were flat.

A tightness formed in Devon's throat. The story had a resonance that drew her in, that of an outcast mother taking shelter in unlikely places. Devon was no virgin, Hester was no Joseph, and Cai was hardly the next Messiah. Still, the spirit of it spoke to her all the same.

"Hes! Thought I heard you returning." A man emerged from the furthest room, shuffling out to meet them. He was in his sixties and of Asian-Indian descent, thick glasses perched on his nose, and a solid walking cane in one hand. "We were starting to worry when you still hadn't come in. Saw you all over the news this morning."

"Always wanted to be famous," Hester said with a wry smile. "Is Lock around?"

Devon's attention was wholly captured by the man with glasses. Something about him was overwhelmingly familiar, memories clawing at her urgently.

"Killock is up in the drawing room with the others." The newcomer glanced at Devon and she saw the same recognition in his expression, without any of her confusion. "Is this her? The Fairweather woman?"

"It is, but she can't stay to chat," Hester said. "I'm sorry, Mani, but I really need to see Killock first."

Mani. Short for—

"Amarinder Patel, who wrote stories for the telly," Devon blurted out. "You're the journalist who came to Fairweather Manor!"

"Who?" Cai said, confused, while Hester started in shock.

"So I am." Mani seemed unruffled by her outburst, a far cry from the nervy journalist Devon had met as a child. "When there was talk of bringing in *Devon Fairweather* to this house, I did wonder if it would be the same girl I'd met all those years ago, and here you are. Fate is a funny old mistress."

Devon's mouth was open. She shut it. More than twenty years had passed and yet she could see, in the aging lines of his features, a glimpse of the younger reporter he'd once been.

"How do you know each other?" Hester said, bewildered.

"Her Family are the reason why I came to *your* Family," Mani said, gaze not leaving Devon's face. "I stumbled onto Fairweather property many years ago while investigating a news story. Got myself caught by a rather younger Devon, then sent up to Ravenscar Manor. And here I am, still." He offered a bleak smile.

"I'm so sorry," Devon said, awash with mortification. "I had no idea what my uncle was truly like back then, or what he'd do to you."

"You were only a child. I don't carry a grudge. If not you, someone else would have found me." Mani's face was impassive and she could not tell if he truly meant what he said. "At any rate, I am here now, among these . . ." He trailed off, adjusted his glasses, and peered at them both. "Does she know, Hester? Have you told her what you are?"

"Told me what?" Devon said, while Hester answered simultaneously, "No, not yet. Killock's request, to hold back the details."

"What is everyone talking about?" Cai complained.

"Hm." Mani took off his glasses, cleaned them on his shirt, and put them back on. "Best we all go up to the drawing room, I think."

"I agree that would be best," Hester said, sounding strained. "My brother will explain everything clearly."

"Do follow me, if you like." Mani turned and began making his way up the stairs.

Devon bit back a frustrated retort, and followed after.

Mani led them up a curving stone staircase, the hewn steps slick from centuries of use, then along another hall and toward a set of ornate doors from which laughter and conversation leaked out. From this angle, it was impossible to see into the room.

"This way." Mani shuffled through the door, without waiting to see if they followed.

Hester put her hand on Devon's arm. "Be careful of Killock. Watch your step around him." She withdrew her hand and strode after Mani, into the room.

"Wait," Devon said, darting after her, "why do I need—" She stumbled to a halt, just inside. Cai crashed into her from behind.

A kaleidoscope of luxury greeted them. Red carpets, painted crossbeams, and lavish furniture; tables scattered with books. Paintings on every wall, of long-dead human nobility. Marble mantels above a roaring fire. A harpsichord nestled demurely in its own nook, inked all over with flourishes and Latin phrases along its wooden body, while a man whose face she couldn't see played an elegant classical piece across its keys. In the far corner, a granddaughter clock marked the loss of time.

A dozen or so people were gathered in here. All of them were chatting and joking, attention taken up with conversation and board games. Presents, drinks, and party favors littered one of the tables, along with paper Christmas crowns and playing cards. Scented candles burned out the smell of berries and frosted evergreens.

Everyone was eating. They browsed tables of books, peeling away tough covers to eat the softer paper within like diners shelling out lobster; a meal for those who could consume paper, but also had no bookteeth. And the tongues: she could hear them in the soft lisping of their conversation, so reminiscent of Cai. Could see them, glimpsing the coils of flesh in their mouths as they chewed and spoke.

"Mind eaters," Devon said, dumbfounded. "You're *all* mind eaters."

Conversation dropped as the entire room turned in Devon's direction. Cai went rigid.

"Personally," said the man at the harpsichord, his voice loud in the silence, "I have always detested the term *mind eater*. It's rather crude and outdated."

Devon narrowed her eyes. "What term do you prefer, then?"

But it was Hester who answered. "People. We're all just people."

We, she'd said, as if she were one of them. Not *they*. And Devon realized with a jolt that she'd never seen Hester eat a book during their journey.

Not one single time.

"My sister says *people* where I would say *saints*." The man behind the harpsichord stood up at last, no longer hidden behind its varnished frame. Tall but slender, with dark reddish hair in a tight ponytail. Gray slacks, gray turtleneck; gray eyes, too. "Welcome back, Hes."

Devon was still reeling, too many shocks in a row. Every surviving member of the Ravenscar household was a mind eater, Hester included.

But how and why were there so many? Families didn't keep their mind eater children. This was, after all, the entire purpose of the knights: to prevent mind eaters living free and unchecked, with nothing but their own willpower keeping the hunger at bay.

She was conscious of Cai clutching her hand tightly, and squeezed back.

Perhaps the Ravenscars had somehow hidden their mind eater children away, rather than sending them to the knights, like every other Family. Yet that raised its own questions. Where were the book eaters, for instance? Why didn't they have any book eaters *at all* among their number?

"Merry Christmas, Lock," Hester said, giving a deferential curtsy. Aside from a difference of hair color, she and the other Ravenscars shared a strong resemblance. The same lines of jaw, the same broad collarbones. The same long-fingered hands, and slightly snubbed noses. "We've had a difficult journey and I'm absolutely ravenous, but I've brought mother and child in safely."

And Devon, watching her, was struck by another uncomfortable thought. If Hester was a mind eater, where was her tongue? How had she hidden it?

"So I see." Killock Ravenscar swept Devon with his gaze from top to toe. "A Fairweather princess in the flesh, come to join us in lonely exile here." He muttered under his breath, inexplicably in singsong, *"Until the Son of God appears."*

With enormous mental effort, Devon pushed aside the shock she felt and pulled herself together. She stood before that scalpel gaze, acutely conscious of her bare, filthy feet; her torn jeans with the mud-dragged edges; her crumpled blouse that reeked of three days' worth of sweat, and probably alcohol. A long way from the manicured girl who had once stepped from a chalky limousine in a spotless Romanian dress, but that wasn't a bad thing. She was stronger and wiser than her younger self, and strange men no longer frightened her.

"If you're going to tell me that I'm tall," Devon said, "then just don't. I'm aware."

Mani made a choking sound. Hester drew a sharp breath.

But Killock only laughed and held out his hand. "Ms. Fairweather—may I call you Devon? Titles are so formal—please allow me to welcome you to Traquair. *Without* any comments about your height."

"Cheers. I appreciate it." She shook his hand, warm and dry like his sister's. "My son needs to eat before we go anywhere. I came here because I was told he could have Redemption, and never need to feed off humans again."

"Yes . . . your son." Killock shifted his gaze downward. "Hello, young man. What's your name?"

"Cai Devonson." He remained half-hidden behind Devon's back. "I don't get a Family surname because I'm a mind eater, so Devon made one for me."

"Interesting choice. 'Cai' is a knight's name—did you know that? Sir Kay, from Arthurian legend. Though we pronounce it differently these days." Killock stooped to his level. "Pleased to meet you, Real Knight Who Is Not a Family Knight. You look like your mother, if you don't mind me saying."

Cai clutched his Game Boy. "I don't mind."

Killock reached into a pocket, unscrewed a small plastic bottle, and handed him a chewable pill. "The gift of Redemption. From my own supply."

"Thank you!" Cai's face lit up as he snatched the pill from the older man's palm. He hesitated then said, "Is it true? Are you really a house of . . . of . . ."

"A house of saints," Killock said. Again, with the strange choice of word; *saints* was not a term Devon would have thought to reach for. She might love her son, but she didn't revere him as holy.

Hester, meanwhile, stood pensive, hands on hips and gaze on the floor. The warning she'd given earlier to *watch your step* was going off in Devon's head like a siren. Killock was smooth, polite, even charming, and yet every time he spoke it made the back of her neck itch. There was a hidden edge to everything he said or did, a kind of intensity that unbalanced her.

Killock straightened his spine. "Having welcomed you here, I will admit I remain unconvinced that you can be trusted. My experiences with the Families have not been good. We have escaped here to live our own lives and I cannot allow anything to threaten that."

"My experiences with other people, full stop, haven't been good." Devon thought he sounded very much like a traditional patriarch: that lofty turn of phrase, evocative of some Victorian nobleman. "We share a common need and a common enemy. Does that carry any weight for you?"

"It does." He sketched a bow that she found slightly ridiculous. "I will admit, I am curious to hear about the demise of your husband. Aside from you and me, I have never met another exile from the Families."

"If it will put your mind at ease, I'm willing to explain how Matley Easterbrook died, and how I escaped."

"How he died?" Killock said, suddenly shrewd. "Not, how you killed him?" Hester tilted her head.

"Yes, how he died." Be steel, be calm, be focused, Devon told herself. "It's a long explanation. My only request is that Cai remain elsewhere. He doesn't need to hear this."

The Ravenscar siblings exchanged glances. Hester said, "Are you all right with being separated from your son?"

"If I don't answer your question, I'll have far bigger problems," Devon said, "and the things I will talk about may cause him serious distress. He already knows a lot of this, and does not need to hear it repeated."

"I don't want to listen," Cai said, holding up the Game Boy. "I want to play *Mario* while you talk. I don't mind waiting. I wait all the time."

Killock's features settled into contemplative stillness. "As you like. We will find someone to sit with your son. In the meantime, let's adjourn to the library."

21

MONSTER

FIVE YEARS AGO

There is love in me the likes of which you've never seen. There is rage in me the likes of which should never escape. If I am not satisfied in the one, I will indulge the other.

—Mary Shelley, *Frankenstein*

The physical damage cleared up in a couple of weeks but the psychological damage lingered on. The sight of hands, any hands, made Devon's throat tighten, a strange and highly inconvenient trigger that she couldn't seem to shake.

As Jarrow had promised, aunts came by every day to assist her with the newborn. Devon tapped out terse messages, grateful for the communication he'd given her while the tendons of her throat slowly healed.

A few weeks later, after she was able to speak, one of the aunts came to inform Devon that Matley wished to see her.

"He knows where my room is," Devon said, soothing her fussy baby. "Why do I need to go anywhere?"

The aunt just shook her head. "He wishes to see you in the games room."

A chill ran through her. "When?"

"Right now, naturally."

Naturally, Devon thought sourly. She wrapped the baby in a sling, wondering all the while what Matley wanted with Jarrow's private refuge, and followed the aunt to the other side of the house to the games room.

Except it wasn't the games room anymore. A new brass plate was fixed to the wall, etched with the words CONTROL ROOM. The door stood open, lights flickering within.

Devon stepped inside. The stench of cabling, dust, and chrome filled her nose; the air tasted of static. Someone had boarded up the windows. The couch that had been her home across pregnancy and childbirth was missing, as were the shelves, consoles, game boxes, controllers, everything.

A series of thirty-odd television screens had replaced the entertainment center, everything trailing dark wires and jacked into a large console. Each screen displayed a different grainy image of various locations around the estate:

fields, orchards, driveway, dining room, libraries. The hallway outside Devon's room, on the centermost screen, but not her actual quarters.

She was swept with a sense of waste for Vic's lovely games collection, chucked out like trash. She'd never get to know the ending of *Final Fantasy* now; strange how it bothered her to think about. At least the Game Boy had been saved. That was secure in her room, hidden under her bed.

The baby began to fuss in his sling, breaking Devon out of her stupor. She shushed the boy, jigging him up and down.

"There you are. Tardy as ever."

Devon turned around to find Matley Easterbrook emerging from what had once been the little kitchenette. That, too, had been converted; the table stripped out, and the cupboards overflowing with spare electrical gear. No more maps. No more detailed escape plans.

"What is all this?" Devon said, whimpering baby held close against her chest. "Why am I here?"

Matley folded his arms, flickering screens casting patterns across his face. "I suppose you know that your child is destined for the knights."

How well she knew. "What of it?"

"I asked if they'd take the boy earlier," he said with a disgruntled snort. "But they don't want him. Too young to live off anything but milk and apparently it is difficult to dose infants with Redemption. They'd prefer you to nurse as long as you can."

"Why do they have to take him at all?" she said, desperation making her bold. "Maybe I can work, to pay for his Redemption costs? My uncle might be willing to—"

"It's not about the cost," he snapped. "Mind eaters cannot be allowed to live freely without anyone keeping them in check. They revert to their nasty feeding, otherwise." A slight shudder ran through him.

Devon knew that, had already known it was pointless to ask. It still hurt to hear the answers spoken again.

"If you'll let me finish," he went on, "I consider you a risky guest, given your history. One liable to spend the next thirty-six months plotting hotly to run away." Matley pushed past her, coming to stand at the console with its many screens. "I want to preempt any such idiocy on your part by informing you that I've upgraded the security for this manor. *Substantially* upgraded."

He pressed a series of keys. The screens compiled into one single video footage display across their conjoined surfaces: the control room itself, with Devon standing stiffly in the heart of it.

"It's a state-of-the-art electronic in-house security system. I have given you privacy in your room but most of the house is wired and watched, as are the gates to this estate, and I'm the only one who knows the access number to this console. Good luck climbing out of *this* tower, princess."

"Kind of you to think of me." Sarcasm kept her grounded against shock. "I'm flattered to be worth the time."

"This isn't just for you. You're not that special," he retorted with his usual pettiness, and dropped into a swivel chair. "I was going to upgrade the security anyway."

Typical Matley, she thought. Every scrap of satisfaction had to belong to him.

"If you don't need me for anything and there is nothing to do here, then I'm going for a walk." She needed to think. To process.

"One last thing," he said, and held up a thimble. *Her* thimble, the one Jarrow had given her to communicate with. "Still need this?"

"That's mine. Jarrow gave it to me—"

"To communicate with, which you can now do without it." He crushed the thimble flat between forefinger and thumb, and set it down pointedly on the table.

Devon stared at the misshapen disc that had been Jarrow's gift, and squeezed her son tight to her chest.

"You're free to go, by the way," Matley said. "Be aware you'll have an escort every time you leave the house, for the next three years. Think of him as a replacement Jarrow, eh?" He snorted. "Try not to act too suspicious on your walks. He's authorized to neutralize you, if need be."

His words left her cold.

As prophesied, an unfamiliar man was waiting in the hallway as Devon left the control room. He was short but brawny, and sported an enormous plastic earplug. Chewing hard on nicotine gum. A human, and therefore surely less strong than her.

But he was also armed with Taser, blackjack, and walkie-talkie. Likely other weapons, too, that she couldn't see. She remembered all too well how Tasers felt.

"Going for a walk, are we?" Earplug snapped his chewing gum loudly.

"No," Devon said, and retreated to her room.

Earplug followed her all the way to her door but did not come inside, nor object when she drew the bolts. Thank heavens for that at least.

In the privacy of her own quarters, Devon curled up on the window seat to nurse her ever-hungry son, trying to think.

The manor had hardly been a playground before. The Easterbrooks, with their servants and seedy illicit businesses, were fond of security. Matley's upgrades only made that worse and tied everything to him personally—the codes stored in his mind, because he could not write them even if he wished to. He could do this because, like Aike, he was patriarch, a role he'd won through a complex system of votes in which women could not participate.

There was also nothing she could do to change her situation. The system was too big, too vast, everything out of her reach and all obstacles impossible to overcome. If she left, they'd hunt her; if she escaped, her son would starve without Redemption; if she fed him sans drugs, that meant finding human folk for him to eat and then watching him go insane. And all of that was predicated on the assumption she could escape at all, much less survive in human society with a hostile Family on the prowl.

Devon looked at her sleepy, squashed-face little boy, cold wind at her back, and decided that she would enjoy every single day she had with him, until those days ran out. And when they finally came for him, these knights, these men of the Families, wrapped in their own arrogance and wielding cruelty like weapons, she would fight.

It'd be the death of her, but perhaps death was the only ending she had a right to claim, after all her years of cowardice and subservience.

———•———

Time ran away with itself for the next two years. Devon breathed in days and breathed out nights, suffused in the moment. Long orchard walks blended with even longer afternoons spent reading or eating books, all with a baby at her side. She moved through her minutes in a daze, because her life was irrevocably different yet nothing had changed.

She took her son on the walks, carrying him in a woven shawl like Romanian women had done in the past, partly because the Easterbrooks were reluctant to give her even small conveniences like a baby carriage, and partly because she found a wrap more convenient. Earplug trailed wherever she went, or sometimes it was another armed human man, who she thought of as Tallboy.

As she rambled, always accompanied but perpetually lonely, Devon took her time to think of a name, because it bothered her to keep calling her son *the baby*.

She'd never named anyone before. Traditionally, the Families gave their children first names that were always drawn from locations in Britain, a practice that subtly set them apart from human culture while also not requiring any of the creativity that their species often lacked. But since Matley didn't want him, and she no longer liked the Families much, Devon decided to dispense with that custom. She would make the effort to use her imagination, such as it was.

She wavered back and forth on whether her choice ought to have great meaning or significance of some kind. In the end, though, she couldn't be bothered with any pretentiousness and just picked *Cai* because it sounded nice. It was also short, easy to remember, and wasn't a location. Good enough. Then she cobbled together a matronym for his surname. Cai Devonson—why not. It would do.

"Sleep, Cai," she'd whisper, rocking him to sleep at nights after her escorts had gone to bed, and the electronic alarm systems were engaged. "Sleep, little one. Will you dream of me when I'm gone?"

Weeks stretched into months. Spring flourished into summer before fading into autumn. Cai grew like a tumor. And by his second birthday, Devon had begun to fear her son.

Not that she didn't love him; she did. There were endless things she loved about him, like the nautilus whorls of his obsidian hair, and his bright axinite eyes, and the warm tint of his skin, a few shades richer and darker than her own. Next to him, she looked almost ashen. She loved the way he tilted his head sideways at every new object or toy, and the fierce way he laughed, especially when doing something dangerous like jumping from high places.

Her fear came from other things. The way he could cross a room before she'd hardly noticed, even though her own reflexes were superhuman. He spoke early, and his first word was *hungry*. She found that sweet, until he started saying it while looking at her head.

Sometimes, while she was tidying their quarters or eating a book or having a bath, Cai would creep up on her with soft steps and nuzzle at her ear. He liked to flick his tongue clumsily, like a snake.

"Don't do that," she said, a little chilled.

"Hungry!" Cai pouted at her. A baby still, though he wouldn't always be. The craving was already in him.

She decided it was time to ask for Redemption, and Matley reluctantly arranged to have it ordered from the Ravenscars at eye-watering cost. She tried to ignore his seething resentment.

When the first delivery arrived, Devon sat on the edge of her bed and inspected the tiny, chewable pills in their glass jar. Unstamped, unmarked, somewhat crudely made; they crumbled a little too easily when handled, leaving a powdery residue on her skin. They smelled of iron.

There were no alternative options, though. The secret of how the Ravenscars had made their magic cure, or what process had led them to such a discovery, was tightly kept. Different Families had tried to find their own cure but had no success with it. Most didn't know where to start. As ever, the book eaters' limited imaginations did not help them here.

Even with Redemption, Devon couldn't help but wonder whether her son would "snack" on other people if she let him. Whether, in fact, she might wake one night to find his face closing in on hers. Tongue gunning for her ear.

But he cried when she left him to sleep on his own in the cot, and seemed so deeply unhappy in the cage-like crib, that she eventually let him stay in her bed. What else could she do? He was only little. She took to lying awake long after he'd fallen asleep, body tensed in readiness.

———————— • ————————

Season rolled into season. So little time. She tried to enjoy every moment. They went for more walks, playing outdoors when possible.

Matley grudgingly provided more Redemption as Cai weaned himself off milk. Once or twice, he came in to check on them in person. The first time he said nothing, merely eyed Cai for a while before leaving.

The second time he said, unexpectedly, "Does that thing love you, or does it just want to eat you?"

"If Cai ever decides to feed on me, you'll be the first to know," she said sweetly, which was enough to have him backpedaling out of her room. Even for adult book eaters, revulsion of dragons lingered strong. They did not see Matley again for months after that.

Another wan and lonely spring passed by. Devon spent it singing and humming as she trudged after her wandering toddler, ever-amused to hear Earplug huffing behind them. Other children avoided Cai; other adults avoided Devon. That suited her. She found it hard to hide her contempt of them in person.

Her life shrank and narrowed to a succession of lonely, windy days spent under orchard trees or in Easterbrook gardens, out and about in all weathers. Cai's birthday went unremarked by everyone except Devon, who sang him "Happy Birthday" and made him an animal menagerie to play with, by folding paper she tore out of books. He laughed with delight and she almost cried, thinking of Salem's lavish parties. Salem was a prisoner, but a well-treated one, her birthdays as welcome and celebrated as Cai's were not.

Winter thickened into the holiday season. Christmas Eve passed, a big party with presents and lights and laughter. Devon was not invited, nor Cai, which made him sad. He watched from the hallway with a wobbling lip, old enough to understand that their world had shut him out.

"We'll do a proper Christmas when you're older," she promised, leading him away from the rooms where they'd been excluded. An empty promise, but she couldn't bear to see him cry.

"Hungry," he said unhappily, and sniffled at her.

Hungry was something he said a lot, even when he'd had plenty of Redemption. But Devon knew he did not mean food in this instance, nor even the unnatural craving of a mind eater. He hungered for something less tangible yet just as crucial: an antidote to loneliness. He craved, even then, the company and acceptance of other people.

Unfortunately, Devon didn't have any pills for that.

———— • ————

Christmas morning woke her with the sound of hail crashing against the house. And a car engine, revving in the drive. She stumbled out of bed and stood at the window. Matley's car was pulling up. He got out, arguing indistinctly into a mobile phone. And then he looked up, straight from the courtyard below, pointing at her window.

Devon took a step back, alarmed for no reason she could pinpoint. Something in his expression had carried fury, in addition to his more usual loathing. Was today the day they'd come for her son?

Cai sat up in bed and said, quite calmly, "Mummy, I'm very hungry."

She looked at him, tearing her gaze from the window. "I know, love. But we're out of Redemption, so you'll have to wait a little bit. Won't be long, Matley said there'd surely be a shipment today."

Frustratingly, the most recent order of Redemption had been inexplicably delayed by a fortnight, and the last pill from her previous order had been used up yesterday.

"Hungry *now*." Those axinite eyes gleamed dark, his skin paler than normal. The proboscis tongue unfurled slowly from his mouth, then rolled back up.

Devon swallowed. She'd never found her child revolting, not in the slightest—until that moment. A hint of what other book eaters saw in him, and her own reaction shamed her.

"Be patient," she told him, and hoped she sounded cheery. "Anytime now, and Matley will bring you something to eat." She'd never called the man *your father*, ever.

Cai stared at her with far more intensity than any three-year-old should have. His irises darkened to black, pupils and whites seeming to shrink.

Devon began to dress, tossing aside her nightshift for a long linen dress, struggling with the laces as she always did. She had just finished braiding up her hair when someone banged on the door. Probably someone bringing the much-needed Redemption delivery.

"Just a minute!" She went to let them in.

On the other side stood Matley Easterbrook, flanked by Earplug and Tallboy. All three of them carried blackjacks.

"I came to say Merry Christmas, princess." Her husband strode in, followed closely by the two men. "Or maybe I should say *good-bye,* since this is your last day here."

Cai said, pouting and sulky, "Snack? Snack now?"

"What?" She backed away from the three men, keeping her son behind her. "The knights aren't due till the New Year—"

"There's been a change of plan." Matley surged toward her. "The Ravenscars are gone, kaput, finished. No more Redemption."

"Snack," Cai repeated, with increased grumpiness. "Mummy. Mummy, I'm hungry!" He sulked at Matley, who ignored him. "Where snack?"

"Gone?" she said, incredulous. "How the hell can an entire Family manor just disappear? What happened to them?"

Tallboy laughed. Earplug smirked.

Matley glared at them till they fell silent, then turned back to her. "Look, it doesn't matter, right? Not women's business, you wouldn't understand," he added, and she realized from the sharp, embarrassed tone that Matley himself didn't know. "The point is, there won't be any Redemption coming, ever again."

"No more Redemption?" she echoed, horrified. "But—"

"Shut up and listen," he said. "The knights are in chaos, probably disbanding. Nobody needs or wants your brat anymore, and I sure as hell can't feed him, so it's over. Go quietly back to Fairweather Manor, and I won't make you watch while I put this thing down."

Put this thing down. Her lovely, laughing, lonely boy. Like a sick dog. He wouldn't even get to be a dragon: that last, tiny, horrific scrap of *but at least he'll be alive, and cared for* and they couldn't let her have even that.

"Stay away from him." Fury drowned out her fear. "If you won't take care of him, then I will, but I will *not* let you kill him!"

Matley hit her with the blackjack.

Devon staggered sideways. He hit her again and she knocked back against the fireplace, catching a granite corner against the side of her head. White heat shot through her skull.

The other two men walked over and all three of them formed a tight triangle, peering down at her sprawled form and bleeding head.

Devon tried to roll over. Earplug stepped on her shoulder, pinning her flat to the floor.

"Hungry, hungry, hungry!" Cai sounded on the verge of a tantrum, tiny hands curled into tiny fists.

"Stop messing about and tie her up already." Matley bent and picked up a startled Cai by the nape of the neck. "I'll deal with the dragon."

Wrong; they were wrong. These men called her son a dragon but *she* was the only dragon in this room. The fire from her injured skull was nothing compared to the heat that ignited in her chest. Cai wailed and she breathed rage.

"Don't move, aye?" Earplug leaned in close. "You—"

Devon unsheathed her bookteeth and lunged for his throat.

Blood bathed her tongue, sickly and bitter, not sweet like ink. His flesh was a wet, soft, living thing, not the warm dryness of leather or paper; the bones of his neck rolled like marbles in her mouth. Twenty-six years' worth of boiling anger was singing in her veins and, jaw locked tight, Devon *wrenched*.

Earplug's esophagus tore free. So did half the skin on his face. He gurgled and collapsed like a stringless puppet. Blood sprayed her chest in a hot, sticky baptism.

"Holy . . ." Matley said, gasping, his grip on Cai slackening. Tallboy stood at his side, petrified and stunned.

"*Hungry!*" Cai twisted in his father's grasp and clamped his mouth on Matley's ear.

Matley snarled a torrent of curse words but Cai clung on, preternaturally strong for a child of his age.

Devon couldn't see it happen, but she could hear it: a faint snicking as the probiscis tongue shot forward, piercing through Matley's eardrum and into his brain.

The blackjack dropped from rigid fingers, rolling across the floor to bump against Tallboy's feet. Tallboy screamed and did nothing except clasp his blackjack, statuefied with horror.

". . . ungh." Matley crumpled to the ground as if all the tendons in his legs had been simultaneously cut, hands pawing reflexively at the little boy who still clung to his neck. Cai curled around his father's head, eyes half-lidded like a milk-drunk infant. The pawing hands slowed, then stopped, then dropped to the side.

Matley tipped over to slump in the spreading pool of Earplug's blood.

Too much for Tallboy. He shrieked and bolted for the door.

She couldn't let him get away. Devon sprang like a cat. A six-foot, blood-soaked, half-dressed cat. She tackled him with a sideways lunge and they landed together, him sprawled faceup and her atop his chest.

"Monster!" he howled, his fists raining uselessly against her. "Fucking monster!"

"*Yes*," Devon said, and shredded his throat like a cheap paperback novel.

ACT 4
DAWN

22

FATHER, SON, AND HOLY SPIRIT

PRESENT DAY

It isn't fair, and it isn't right. Aren't we people, too? All Families are family. The Collector made us all, each for our purposes, even if we no longer follow those purposes so strictly. We are no more or less deserving of compassion or the right to free lives than the book eaters are. Why should we live under lock and key?

Weston must agree to set us free. Give us the secrets of Redemption, allow us to emancipate the other dragons. The least of what we deserve.

And if he does not agree, then I will do what I must. Whatever it takes.

—Killock Ravenscar, private journal

The Ravenscar siblings stood in the gray winter light of the First Library, with Mani quietly occupying the far corner. All three of them listening in perfect silence.

Devon sat with hands tucked between her knees, gazing out through the windows. Traquair's garden maze filled the window view, dark and overgrown. Even in bright winter sunlight it looked the way her life felt; tangled, full of dead ends.

Into the breathy stillness, Killock said, "And afterward? How did you escape the premises?"

"After Cai ate his father's mind, I found Matley's keys, cleaned out his private safe, and got the hell out." Her gaze wandered, drinking in the room. Shadows played over rows of vintage books on oaken shelves. Darkness soothed the eye, thick carpets cushioned bare feet. The scent of softly aging paper and warm wood encompassed them.

She had missed this kind of house, she thought, and felt chagrined. Years of wanting to get away from the Families and their manors yet here she was, reveling in that environment. Once a princess, always a princess.

"The Easterbrooks didn't give chase?" Mani pulled out a notepad and began scribbling.

"I borrowed the car before any of them knew what was happening," Devon said, sinking back against her too-comfortable chair, "and managed to get to the train station. We caught a train at random, ended up in the south. It took the knights a while to start tracking us down."

Hester had dug out a pad and pencil from the study desk, but unlike Mani, she wasn't taking notes. Devon, glancing across at the expanse of pale paper, was startled to realize the other woman was sketching something; trees and foliage, a hint of hedges. Her view from the window.

"Interesting." Killock coiled and uncoiled his tongue like a serpent. "But consuming a book eater mind is not the same as consuming a human one, due to the vast quantity of information that book eaters can retain. That is an experience that changes us. How did your son cope with such a feed, at such a young age, without enduring severe psychological trauma?"

"He didn't cope. After a few hours Cai was nearly vegetative." Rocking, swaying, gibbering to himself. "I met a woman in the park, with her baby. I saw them and I had this idea . . . you know, because a baby's mind, it's so blank, so small, and . . ."

Devon squeezed her hands together. "No one else was around. I knocked the mother out and gave the baby to Cai. In the state he was in, he didn't object. I'm not sure he even remembers."

And this, even this horror, wasn't the full truth. But she couldn't give anyone else the truth. Not yet.

Hester's voice floated the words, soft and quiet. "What happened to the baby?" She held her pencil perfectly still, poised above the sketch pad.

"Returned it to the mother. The whole thing took about ten minutes and nobody else noticed."

Not strictly what happened—the context had been different—but the basic fact was she'd destroyed that infant before giving it back.

The child would have missed all its developmental milestones, by not showing emotion or personality or making attempts to communicate. All the things Devon had taken such joy in with her own children would never belong to that woman. Ten minutes to ruin a whole chain of lives.

Cai had never called her "Mum" again, not since that day, and Devon hadn't pushed the issue. She understood perfectly. Biologically she was his parent and always would be, but emotionally they had become something closer to partners in crime; mutual abusers locked in codependency.

Either way, *mother* felt like a title she no longer deserved to hear from anyone.

"This was our doing, these events. We were the catalysts," Hester said finally.

"Our decision to leave must have shuttered the knights. Triggered the killings of any living dragon children."

"I am not responsible for the actions of others," Killock said frostily, running a thumb along the line of his jaw. "I'm not really sure what you'd have had me do, Hes."

"Given the other Families the secret of making Redemption, like you promised, for a start. Maybe—"

Killock cleared his throat. His sister flushed and made a show of straightening her blouse. Devon listened to them with faint astonishment. Had the freeing of other mind eaters been the original goal behind Killock's coup? And if so, why hadn't he done as he'd promised? Something had gone wrong there.

"According to what you've told us, you and your son spent what, two years on the run?" Mani said, drawing everyone's attention back to him. "Do the Families care so much for a woman with no fertility, and a child who they cannot feed?"

"Good question." Killock angled himself away from his sister.

"The Families care nothing for me, and the knights at present are mostly defunct." She was acutely aware of walking a knife edge. Too much of the wrong emphasis, and she'd arouse their suspicion—their well-founded fear that, in fact, the knights were seeking the Ravenscars. "The ones who hunt me do so because it's personal. One of the knights is a brother of mine."

"Your brother is a knight?" Hester put her sketch pad on the table and leaned forward in her chair. "The men in the station—"

"You didn't kill him," Devon said, and couldn't help but sound rueful. "More's the pity. He is high up in what remains of the knights. They're acting alone, without the Families' support."

"And the two years?" Killock prompted. "That is a long time in the wilderness, so to speak. Why wait so long to seek us out?"

"I didn't wait, it just took me a long time to actually figure out what had happened to the Ravenscars. You're not easy to track down! Even the Families couldn't find you. And I wasn't exactly well educated on inter-manor politics."

"A minefield, that," Mani murmured, pen still scratching.

"Living hard, learning to kill for your son, frantically hunting down any sign of our chemical suppliers, all while running from an old enemy." Killock traced an idle pattern on the arm of his chair, his nail catching on loose threads. "That is a lot to endure, Devon of Fairweather Manor. Someone else might well have abandoned their child and taken the chance to seize their own freedom."

"I don't need freedom for myself. Only for Cai." She hadn't forgotten Salem, but this wasn't the time or place to discuss her daughter. "If I can make his life better, then I'll be happy."

"Optimistic, though I can't fault you that." He leaned back in the chair, which creaked with strain. "Anything else you wish to share of your adventures, Devon? That is an invitation, to be clear, and not a demand."

Anything else? Well. She could tell them about the relief that alcohol brought as the months had dragged on; about the guilt-ridden dreams, and the compass with Salem's picture that weighed heavier than chains. About all those nights standing over her son's sleeping form as she thought about smothering him, then stopping herself. About the discarded victims she'd carried, one by one by one to a slew of homeless shelters over the months.

But if Devon talked about any of that, then she'd have to talk about how you really could get used to anything, with enough time and motivation; how her crimes swiftly dwindled from horrific and extraordinary to a facet of her everyday reality.

She had worked out at some point that this was how the Easterbrooks conducted their trafficking without breaking a sweat; how the patriarchs overlooked the suffering and servitude of the mother-brides they destroyed; how humans could continue to exist in an infrastructure of misery. Trauma became routine, and cruelty mundane. Just life, innit.

Likewise, her obscenely selfish love had become a guiding light. She no longer cared for anyone but her kids, and Jarrow. Herself she had concern for, but only as a means of helping Cai. For love, she would wield Ramsey Knight like a weapon to cut herself free from the Families and not look back. As long as it preserved her son.

None of that was anything Killock needed to know, however.

"Only one thing to add," Devon said, because she didn't want to leave the silence hanging. "We share the same sin and the same anger. I would bet my left arm that you will never, in your lifetime, meet anyone else who understands what you've been through as well as Cai and I will understand. We may not be born under the same roof, but we are family of a kind. Don't you think?"

Hester touched her throat.

"I never said what we had been through," Killock answered in silky tones. "Are you so sure we have that much in common?"

"I can put two and two together," Devon said. "I'm guessing the Ravenscars have been keeping their mind eater children in defiance of the Families' customs, because there are a lot of you here. Likewise, there are no book eaters in this household." She slouched against the overstuffed armchair. "I'm also guessing the 'coup' was more of a civil war. Mind eater Ravenscars versus the book eater Ravenscars, that kind of thing. It sounds like you wanted to free other mind eaters? By giving away Redemption?" Her gaze flicked briefly to Hester. "Which your patriarch refused to do."

"Bang on the money." Killock smiled. "Allow me to give some context, if I may. After my predecessors developed Redemption, the patriarchs stopped killing my kind at birth. They decided our lives were worth the hassle. We can write, after all—an increasingly important ability in a modern world that requires paperwork and literacy. And we can steal identities at a pinch, if needed. The only question was how to balance our usefulness against our inherent danger to others."

"They did not trust us to live unsupervised," Hester said, crossing and uncrossing her ankles with tense energy. "The hunger would always be a temptation, even when we can subsist on books as you do now. Hundreds of years of fear isn't easily overturned, I suppose. The knights already existed to arrange and chaperone marriages, so the patriarchs added the keeping of 'dragons' to their duties."

"The patriarchs feared our power," Killock interjected, "and they feared each other misusing our power. The knights, because they are not a Family in the usual sense, were the only ones allowed to 'raise' us."

"Maybe they weren't wrong to be afraid," Hester said quietly, then flinched under her brother's sullen displeasure.

"You're both here, though," Devon said, gently sidestepping their feud, "so somewhere along the way, the Ravenscars must have ignored those orders and stopped sending children to the knights."

"Correct," Killock said, still scowling at his sister. He clearly did not like being disagreed with. "My predecessors chose to keep their *special* children, a decision that made our Family successful and wealthy. Over the decades, our numbers have grown significantly."

Which was the exact situation the patriarchs hadn't wanted, Devon thought. "And the knights just allowed this?" The bloody irony of it all.

"Not exactly. We had to pay them off to keep our secrets. And our children." Killock made a vague gesture. "Still, it was a broadly beneficial arrangement all around. Sometimes, they even offloaded their 'failed' dragons to our household. Those whose temperaments were unsuitable for dragon-training, that kind of thing."

"It was still oppression," Hester said softly. "We—the mind eaters of

Ravenscar—hoped for a future where there were no more knights at all. Where our Family could *openly* be a house for mind eaters." She sighed. "But building that future required gaining access to the secret of making Redemption—knowledge that the Ravenscar patriarchs passed down among themselves and never gave to us. Without that knowledge, we remained dispossessed."

Obvious in hindsight, Devon realized with silent chagrin. Killock could never be patriarch himself, not as a mind eater.

"Weston was both a book eater and a patriarch, making him unsympathetic to our issues and also set in his ways," Killock said, a note of old resentment in his voice. "He knew the cure, but he would not share it with me. *Set my people free,* I begged him, as Moses once begged the Pharaoh. And like Pharaoh, he only laughed. *Such secrets are not for your kind,* he said. To my face." Beads of sweat formed on Killock's upper lip; he wiped them away with his sleeve. "In his eyes, we were spoiled and lucky. He felt that what we asked for was an indulgence of extreme proportions."

Devon listened with growing alarm; she feared where this story was headed.

"Like you," Killock went on, "we found ourselves in a position where there was but one single person standing in the way of freedom: our patriarch." He leaned forward, breathing ragged. "When he would not give me the secret of Redemption, I *took* it from him. For the sake of our people, because it was God's will that we live freely!"

She should have guessed sooner. "You . . . ate your father's mind?"

"What?" Gray eyes dilated, pupils swallowing irises from within. "No, heavens no. I *communed* with him, Devon. *For my flesh is food indeed, and my blood is drink indeed. He who eats my flesh and drinks my blood abides in me, and I in him.* Thus it is written in the Bible, described as a sacred act of communion."

"Communion," she said, a little numbly. "Is that what you call mind eating? Is that how you . . . enshrine it?"

Hester wrapped her arms around herself, shoulders hunched.

Killock though, pointed like an auctioneer at a sale. "You are too literal, trapped in old ways of thinking. I thought as you did, once, and considered my actions the height of abomination, both my feeding and the changes enacted in me. But I know better these days." He was wild-eyed now. Nostrils red and flaring. "I have my father's spirit to thank for that. His soul lives on within me, teaching and guiding. We have forgiven each other and are at peace."

Devon bit the inside of her cheek. Adam and Eve had nothing on Killock and Cai. Apples were for amateurs. Sons eating fathers: *that* was a truly forbidden feast.

Bits of the Ravenscar puzzle clicked into place, weaving together threads of commonality between these siblings and herself. The complexity of it, unfolding into understanding of the Families that had crushed them, the shared trauma that bound them—her to Cai, Hester to Killock—and the unspeakable crimes that had finally, at such bitter cost, set them all free.

She picked her words carefully. "I can't pretend to know what you experience. If you call it communion, I won't contradict. Only you can know what that felt like."

"Quite." Killock twitched violently, shoulders hitching in repetition.

"What of me and Cai?" she asked, when he said nothing further. "How do you feel about us remaining?"

Another shudder. Then he shook his head, relaxed, and said, "Saints are we both, your son and I, and as one saint to another I say—he is welcome in this house, whether he takes Redemption, or takes communion. Though I hope, in time, he will embrace his nature, as I have learned to."

"I see." Devon shifted in her seat. Take communion and embrace his nature? Like fuck. Not if she could help it. "And if he ever leaves? What if he grows to adulthood and wants to choose another path entirely?"

Killock folded into a seat in the nearest library chair, fingers white with the tension of holding himself still. "Redemption is what saves us from sin. God gives Redemption to the faithful. No one else may have salvation." His grin came and went like a shark at sea. "There is no going or leaving, now that you know the location of our home. What if you went running back to the knights, eh? No, your son will have to stay."

And there it was, she thought; the hard line that lay beneath his flowery words and overcooked politeness. Killock kept everyone bound closely to him. His siblings, through a mix of love, loyalty, shared oppression, and their need of his drug. Her and Cai, through veiled threats.

She'd never had a choice anyway, not really; staying wasn't an option. But Killock's attitude made it a little easier on her conscience.

Devon held up her palms, as if surrendering. "It's no sacrifice at all to live among you. Far better than living with Matley."

"Good, good, I am glad to hear it," Killock said. "Do not think of Matley as being dead, by the way. Your husband lives on in your son, as my father lives on in me. Once you invite the Holy Spirit in—"

A bell began ringing from elsewhere in the house, startling all of them out of that moment.

"Is that an alarm?" Devon swiveled in her seat, deeply relieved for the distraction.

"Not at all!" Killock said, almost shouting. "Merely the signal for our Christmas service to begin."

"Christmas service? Like a church one?" She had so far assumed that his religious terminology was an affectation, not something literal. "Do you subscribe to human religions?" There was nothing in human beliefs about book eaters, and she could not fathom adopting that system herself.

"Come and see. Come and see!" His expression was inviting and polite, but as ever, his forceful tone underscored the words. This was a command, not a choice.

"Very kind." She glanced at Hester. The other woman was already standing, face hidden by a fall of curling hair. "What about my son?"

"We'll bring him along. It's a Family affair." He offered another absurd little bow. "Follow me, please. It would not do to be late for my own Christmas service."

23

REMEMBER THE SABBATH

PRESENT DAY

Father forgive me, for all my sins. For what I have done to you in the name of freedom and rightness, what I have done for love and brotherhood.

I hear you arguing with me as I try to sleep at night, the voice of you remaining in my head long after your life slipped away. How you hated me, still hate me, want me to die for what I am, but you don't understand that this is what must be done it is done IT IS FINISHED—

—Killock Ravenscar, private journal

The chapel had been beautiful once.

Devon craned her neck up, inspecting the smoke stains on the ceiling. Remnants of polished wooden pews and embroidered prayer cushions were piled toward the back of the room. Cheap folding chairs occupied that space, plastic ones with rusted hinge joints. A cracked altar, likely once worth a small fortune, lingered on miserably at the front, its white marbled surface plastered with melted candlesticks.

Next to the altar rested a large crate, covered in a once-white cloth to form a makeshift table. A Bible lay propped atop the covered crate, its pages stained and spattered with something unrecognizable.

Devon had eaten enough thrillers and horror novels over the years to recognize a bad setup when she saw one.

"What happened?" she whispered to Hester. "Was there a fire?"

"When we first moved in, yes. This building is ancient, and has been in poor repair for twenty years," Hester said. "Killock's been conducting work but it's slow going and things are still fragile. We don't use candles anymore, not worth the risk."

"Um. Sounds safe, I guess."

"Tell me about it, the whole building is practically dry kindling," Hester said, then dropped her voice to a lower volume. "Listen, we need to talk, if that's all right with you."

Devon gave her a sharp look. "Let me know where and when."

"After the service," Hester whispered, then added more loudly, "Since you're new, I'd like to introduce you to some of my siblings."

Devon spent the next fifteen minutes shaking hands with a series of Ravenscars, all Hester's brothers of varying ages. There was one other woman—another fraternal twin, like Hester, and so therefore also a mind eater.

Smile, nod, move to the next handshake. Between greetings, she spotted Mani lurking in a corner, nursing a plastic cup of tea. Hot steam fogged up his glasses.

The former journalist was still a mystery to her: one she felt the need to solve. How he had gotten here and why he continued to live among the Ravenscars felt crucial in some elusive way, but she didn't want to make a show of going over to seek him out.

Instead, Devon did a quick mental head count as she chatted her way around the room. About fifteen souls, discounting herself, Cai, Mani. The Ravenscar household had once held forty-odd members, so the rest must have died in the coup. The odds had surely been stacked against this lot for such an unfair fight.

Killock walked in. He'd changed from his plain gray slacks and shirt into an old-styled suit that was a few sizes too large. Devon would have put money on it belonging to Weston Ravenscar.

Without needing direction, the people of Traquair all found seats and fell into a quietude that bordered on reverential.

"Merry Christmas, my friends. God bless you on this sacred Sunday, and all the Lord has gifted. From the return of my sister, safe and well through the valley of death"—he jabbed a finger at Hester, who flinched—"to the advent of a new Son who has come among us." Dark eyes alighted possessively on Cai, in a way that Devon disliked. "Sinners all, we come seeking Redemption and salvation. And God gives. And God provides. God is here with us, my dear Sabbatarians."

Privately, Devon suspected God wouldn't be caught either crucified or alive within a mile of this place.

"On this day, when sons are born and fathers in Heaven rejoice, I find, dear friends, that my own father wishes to speak to us today. I have not heard from him in many months." Killock grabbed the Bible off the makeshift table, flipping it open. "Weston has this to say: *Then because of the dire straits to which you will be reduced when your enemy besieges you, you will eat your own children, the flesh of your sons and daughters whom the Lord has given you.* He quotes, you see, from Deuteronomy chapter twenty-eight, verse fifty-three."

Devon felt her toes curl. She recognized the start of an unhinged rambling when she heard one, and Killock did not disappoint. He perched on the burned-out altar, speaking alternately in the "voice" of his dead father, long consumed, and his own wavering, squeaky tones.

No church would have ordained such a speech; the vicar in Cai's head was probably tearing out his metaphorical hair. Killock had become a broken composite of two different men, his former patriarch acting as a kind of parasitic presence.

Again, Devon's gravest concern was that no one else seemed bothered. The other Traquair inhabitants listened to that religious word-salad with serious, thoughtful attention.

Well. Two people were bothered. Hester sat rigid, hands folded in her lap and lips pressed together. And on the far side of her, Mani was also unimpressed. He listened with nose wrinkled in distaste and struggling to control his discomfort.

She was missing crucial information. Devon could understand the siblings wanting autonomy from the other Families. What confused her was that none of this church madness squared with the original plans and intentions Killock had described.

"*But God provides!*" Killock said, so loudly that Devon, who had tuned him out, snapped back to attention. "From the old, He makes new. From the ashes, we rise. On the Sabbath we were delivered, the Father and the Son becoming the Holy Spirit." The strange shaking was back, and this time he did nothing to calm or quieten his body. "Remember the Sabbath, my Sabbatarians, and *keep it holy.*"

Ragged voices murmured en masse, "Remember the Sabbath."

"Divinity is within us." He clapped his hands loudly enough that Devon twitched from the echoing smack. "I will take the Chalice of salvation and call upon the name of the Lord!"

He strode over to the makeshift table and peeled away the white cloth.

The cloth had covered not a crate, but a large-size cage, the kind a mastiff might be kept in. Inside it crouched a terrified human figure. Adult man, stripped down to his boxers, hands bound and mouth gagged.

A bad feeling settled in Devon's belly. She forgot to breathe.

"Remember the Sabbath," Killock exclaimed again, "and keep it holy!" He leaned over the bound human, mouth wide and tongue unfurling.

Devon stopped watching, choosing instead to inspect the lines of her palms and fingers, the unevenness of her thumbnails. She found it unbearable to watch Cai feed, and that was a thing required for her son's survival. This, *this* was a wholly unnecessary consuming of an innocent, by a man who could absolutely choose Redemption as an alternative.

Cai himself would have given anything to never feed again. And Killock, the grotesque fool that he was, had no concept of the privilege he squandered. Killock had also squandered the chance to do something different. Instead of a haven, he'd created a coven of predatory monsters, squatting in an abandoned mansion. The Families would see it as definitive proof that mind eaters could not be left to their own devices.

The thought, rising up traitorously: What if they had a point?

She risked a glance at Cai. His cheeks were flushed, his gaze fixed on the floor in front of them. And on the other side, Hester had her eyes closed. Palms pressed together, either praying or trying not to be ill. Both utterly removed from the theater that played out in front of them.

No, Devon decided. The ideology that made Killock dangerous came from the Families. Killock's problem wasn't that he'd tried to do something different, but that he'd tried to do something too similar. The same system, the same manor house and patriarch and quivering obedience. And because the system was inherently cruel, it had only magnified the cruelty within Killock, rather than suppressing it.

Up on the stage, the victim's whimpering died away. The mind eaters cheered and clapped as Killock's display of so-called communion finally ended, and Devon fought her rising queasiness. A few chairs over, Mani had quietly removed his glasses, tucking them into his shirt pocket. A clever way to obscure his own vision.

"God bless you and keep you, brothers and sisters." Killock stood over the opened cage, where the huddled figure of a human now slumped lifeless. "Amen. Go in peace, to love and serve each other." Though his diction seemed unaffected, his accent had changed; he sounded Scottish now. Like the man he'd killed.

A murmur of soft conversation rose again as people chatted among themselves, some animated and some reserved. A natural ebb and flow of conversation, as if nothing extraordinary had happened.

Devon exchanged glances with Cai, who bore an adult's worried expression even as he squirmed with too much childish energy.

"Are you okay?" she whispered. A part of her wished he'd not been present for what they'd just seen, even while the logical side of her brain pointed out that he'd seen victims many times by now. Usually his own.

"I'm fine," he whispered back, then said, "Dev, why was he the only one who feeds? And if he's going to not bother taking Redemption, why do any of them take it?"

"Not now, love." Privately, Devon suspected that logistical issues prevented Killock from feeding as much as he would like, let alone allowing his followers to feed freely. They'd empty the town in a year, otherwise. "Ask me later."

Cai chewed his bottom lip and nodded in assent.

Hester caught her arm. "Well! What a lovely service. Dev, I've just remembered that I promised to take you shooting. I don't suppose you'd have time right now?"

"What about me?" Cai said, before Devon could ask.

"I'll look after the lad," Mani offered, surprising all of them. "I can show him around the house, and perhaps we can locate a suitable room for the pair of you to stay in."

"Sure," Cai said without missing a beat. For a boy who'd spent most of his waking hours away from other people or locked in small, damp flats, he'd adapted well to having company.

"I bear no grudges for our previous encounter—you may trust me," Mani said, seeing Devon's hesitation. "In any case, Ms. Fairweather, I suspect I have more to fear from your son than he has to fear from me." A sad, polite smile. "When you are done speaking to Hester, we could have a catch-up of our own, yes? Two Family survivors with a set of interesting tales."

Despite her curiosity about Mani, instinct also told her that a talk with Hester couldn't wait. And of all the people in this house, she felt Cai was perhaps safest in the company of an elderly human. Someone he could overpower, at any rate.

"Very well. I'm sure we won't be long," Devon said finally. Best not to dither, in case it looked conspiratorial. "Here, take this for me, if that's all right. I'd rather not carry it around." She handed Cai her rucksack, which she'd not had a chance to put down anywhere.

Her son took it grudgingly, slinging the too-long strap over his back.

They all stood up to go. As they left, Devon cast a last glance over her shoulder at Killock's lean figure. He was gazing down at the corpse of his victim with an expression that hovered between tender and reverential.

———————•———————

Hester led them out of the chapel and across to a storage room in the main building, stopping to collect a rifle and ammunition from a cupboard, then ventured through a north-side exit at the back of the house. The voices of other "congregation" members faded swiftly as they left the chapel behind. And still, Hester didn't speak.

On this side of Traquair's estate, the manicured lawns gave way to a sparse wood filled with extraordinarily ancient trees. Someone had set up a shooting range in a small clearing, and that was where Hester came to rest, rifle in hand, peering at a long row of milk bottles perched atop wooden posts. The sun was sinking but that didn't matter to either of them.

"We can talk here. It's quiet and far from the house." Hester sighed. "I'm sorry. I've lied to you from the first meeting, and for all of our journey. Killock is so afraid the Families will find out we are all mind eaters."

"Forget it. I've lied for less reason," Devon said uncomfortably. She was in no position to point fingers over lying. "Can we start from the beginning? I feel like my whole perspective on you and your Family has changed completely."

"I hardly know where to begin."

"How about with that display in there?" Devon said. "Is he *catching* people to eat? What the hell was that?"

"That, was a broken promise." Hester set down the gun and stood face-to-face with her in that ancient, war-steeped woodland, winter sunlight piercing through the oak leaves like arrows. And then she opened her mouth, wide as it would go.

A faint scar around the free edge was all that remained to indicate where the mass of flesh had once been long and tubular. What remained of the proboscis was skillfully severed, the fleshy muscle trimmed to a rounded point. If Devon hadn't been looking for a scar, hadn't had time to stare and examine, she would never have noticed.

The sight was oddly disquieting. Cai could always feed if he were at risk of starvation, but that wasn't an option for a mind eater who was maimed. No wonder Hester had been unsure about staying over at Alndyke Farm, particularly when she'd lost her supply of Redemption.

"So you *are* one of them," Devon said, with a calmness that felt disconnected from her own overwhelmed brain. "Did Killock promise to do the same?"

"He and I made a pact." Hester covered her mouth with a hand. "If we could get free of Weston, we'd set up a haven. The idea was that any mind eater would be welcome, providing they agreed to live off Redemption and have their tongues docked."

"Meaning, none of you could give in to temptation and feed," Devon said, working it out aloud, "and in turn, the other eaters could no longer claim your family were dangerous. Have I got that right?"

"That was my hope, and my plan, though I'm no longer sure my siblings ever shared it quite so passionately." She tucked a lock of wind-tossed hair behind one ear; it blew free again straightaway. "After Weston was dead, I kept my end of the promise. Had it done by someone here—one of my brothers has some medical knowledge."

"But Killock and the others didn't stick to it."

"A few followed my lead but not Killock, no," she said. "At first, he claimed there was too much going on. *It's not safe. The labs aren't up yet. Wait till spring.* Eventually, he started saying it didn't *feel right* anymore. At some point, I'm not sure when, he began venturing out and catching people in secret. Giving in to the hunger, seeking the rush of it." A shudder. "These days, mention tongue docking, and he'll flip his lid."

"That's a big change, to go from *give up feeding forever* to *feeding is divine communion*," Devon said slowly, leaning against the fence. "What turned him?"

"Consuming our patriarch altered his personality. The one variable we didn't foresee." Hester picked up the gun again and began loading it. "Killock has a strange way of talking about things. But he's not wrong in calling it communion. Consuming someone is—is so deeply *intimate*. You know them, you come to love them, and they become a part of you forever. It feels like merging souls. Their hopes and fears are yours, never coming to fruition but also never fully dying within you. It is the ultimate drug, Dev, and it's not for nothing that folks call it a craving. Mind eating goes far beyond hunger." She snorted. "Why do you think I smoke? Helps with the maddening hunger and gives me something else to be addicted to."

Devon watched the cartridges disappear into the stock. "This communion thing. Are you talking from experience, or is that what your brother has described?"

"Experience," Hester said curtly, and cocked the rifle. "After Weston refused to either let us leave, or to give us the secret of Redemption, violence was the only path left. We were outnumbered and lacking weapons, so we used our tongues. All of us ate at least one victim that night." Hester raised her gun and fired several times.

Glasses shattered as the bullets found their mark. In the distance, birds screamed; silence returned to the woods in the wake of that violent disruption.

"I told myself it worked out. That we were finally free, and that it would be worth the cost. I was naïve, and wrong." Hester tried a smile, let it collapse. "Anyway, now you know what I am. What my brother is. What we did, to get here. All the ways I've lied to you lately." She extended the rifle stock-first. "Want to take a shot? It's a good skill to learn."

"I mean, if you like," Devon said, thrown by the change of subject, "but—"

"Please. Humor me."

Devon grudgingly took the rifle, trying to fit it against her ungainly body.

"Let me help." Up close, the familiar scent of Hester's vanilla tobacco was unmissable. "Yes, like that . . . almost. Lift this elbow. Bit higher, you want a ninety-degree angle. Stock on your shoulder. That's it, barrel steady. How does that feel?"

"Lucky," Devon said, thinking of Clint Eastwood, and sighted down the barrel. "It feels lucky."

She fired. The noise rammed her eardrums.

"Incredible," Hester said, squinting at the distance. "You've missed by an absolute mile."

"No shit." Devon lifted the rifle again.

"You have to reload, by the way. That was the last cartridge."

". . . I knew that."

The echo of Hester's laughter carried across the green. Real laughter, shaking her petite frame.

And then it trailed off, that cheerfulness crumpling like a page tossed on the fire. "My brother is gone, Devon. Eating our patriarch was the unmaking of him, unlocking a terrible craving he's tried to ignore since childhood. I've watched him ebb away a little more every day for the past two years, as his violence escalates. When you spoke to him in the study . . . when you heard him preach . . . that wasn't Killock. It was some monstrous, amorphous collective of his victims, overlaid with Weston's personality."

The fresh cartridges weighed heavy in Devon's palm. "If I believe that about your brother, then I have to believe my son is gone."

"Not necessarily," Hester said, after a moment's consideration. "Cai is strongly himself, from the little I've seen. He must fight it. How, I don't know, only that he does. Was he close to Matley?"

"No," Devon said. "They barely saw each other."

"Maybe that makes a difference. Weston was an unusually powerful personality, and had a close, if twisted, relationship with Killock. That must complicate things, surely."

"What about you?" Devon said, carefully slotting the magazine back in. "Did you fight that influence? Did you change?"

"Yes and no. I mean, where did you think I learned to shoot?" She shrugged. "Girls don't get taught how to use guns. Not even mind eater ones. *Especially* not mind eater ones. That skill is only for men. Like the man I ate. He's a part of me now, as are other things about him."

Devon digested that information. "I hadn't wondered about the shooting till you mentioned it. Nor the smoking. I guess I assumed you got it all from a book."

"Nah. Eating a book on guns would give you technical knowledge of shooting, but it wouldn't give you muscle memory. Or instincts built on experience. Eating a person, though, is a whole new level of absorption."

"I see." Devon thought about that as she lifted the gun to her shoulder and fired, rather badly, at the targets. Her shots missed and she didn't care, was thinking about Cai doggedly playing the same video game through his feeds. The way he seemed to subsume himself after each victim and come "back" to her hours later, as if from a long journey. Had she risked losing him to another persona each and every time, the way Hester claimed Killock had been lost, the way Devon had always feared to lose him? A heart-stopping thought.

When the gun was empty again, she lowered it and said, "There's no reason to stay. You don't owe this man your life. Why not just grab some Redemption and leg it?"

"Why didn't you leave Cai?" Hester said. "If not for him you could be halfway around the planet by now. What price do *you* put on love, Devon Fairweather?"

She knew that answer by heart. "No price. There isn't one. Love doesn't have a cost. It's just a choice you make."

"Then you've answered your own question. I promised Lock I'd stay with him when we fled, that we would always be together. How can I renege? He destroyed himself trying to free me and my siblings." Hester took the rifle back, cleaning it out with expert speed. "I wish you could have met Lock when he was younger. He was lovely, sweet-natured, earnest. Never hurt a soul in his life, till that night."

"I'm sorry." She was, too.

"Everybody's sorry." Hester slammed the magazine into place and fired again, one shot after another until the gun was empty and every glass bottle broken.

Devon clapped both hands over her ears and waited till the thundercracks died down, ears ringing in the aftermath of each tinkling explosion.

Hester set down the rifle, lips quivering at the corners. "Sometimes I catch myself wishing he'd died. Is that awful? But I wish it all the same, because then I could be free of him without guilt or fear. Christ, listen to me!" Her face fell.

"You must think I'm a monster. There you are, doing everything possible to save your son, while the best I can manage is to pray my brother has a fucking heart attack in his sleep."

The familiarity of that sentiment wasn't lost on Devon. She couldn't not feel a twinge, a lurch, at the echo of words she'd so often said to herself.

"I don't think that at all," Devon said, and meant it. "I don't think less of anyone who just wants the misery to end. You're not a monster."

"That's kind," Hester said, bitter, "but you don't know me."

"Maybe not." Devon thought again of the vicar, and all the long line of Cai's victims who came before him, and it seemed she spoke to absolve herself as much as Hester. "But I *do* know we can only live by the light we're given, and some of us are given no light at all. What else can we do except learn to see in the dark?"

"Learn to see in the dark," Hester echoed, then added quietly, "I don't deserve that lie."

"It's the truth," Devon said, with more conviction than she felt.

". . . Thank you." Hester leaned forward and hugged her, the unexpectedness almost shocking Devon out of her skin.

And she shocked herself more by hugging back, though she had to lean down to do so, trying to remember when she'd last embraced another adult. Jarrow, before he'd left for London. Another woman, though—never, not since the aunts had said good-bye at her first wedding.

It was a small comfort against the wide world. She felt sorry for Hester, for herself, for entire generations of their ridiculous and twisted Families; for the lives they ruined and the misery they chose to inflict on each other, and on themselves. A grotesque mess.

And one she was probably about to make worse.

Devon said, breaking the fragile stillness between them, "Hes, I wasn't being honest, in Killock's study. I kept things back." A steadying breath. "There's something I need to tell you, too."

Hester pulled back, wiping at her eyes. "What is it?"

"The rest of the story," Devon said.

24

THE REST OF THE STORY

TWO YEARS AGO

When I used to read fairy tales, I fancied that kind of thing never happened,
and now here I am in the middle of one!
—Lewis Carroll, *Alice's Adventures in Wonderland*

Blood painted her mouth in bitterness. Devon gagged until she vomited up
chunks of flesh. She couldn't feel anything except dumbfounded amazement,
which seemed wrong to her. Surely you should feel something when you tore
out throats. Surely.

Cai was screaming. The noise punctured her numbness and she turned to
see him dragging himself across the carpet, banging his head against the wall.

Driven by some base functionality, she crawled over and tried to keep him
from hurting himself, wrapping her arms across his torso and smearing pu-
trefaction on him. Her protection only tainted him; how typical. Her breath
came shallow and she found it hard to think, but that was because Cai kept
screaming. Children shouldn't scream like that.

She was still there when Ramsey Knight arrived twenty minutes later to
find her covered in vomit and gore, kneeling on a floor soiled by the blood and
guts of two corpses while Cai thrashed and howled in her arms. Arterial spray
slathered the room in ropey strings of blood, more of it pooling and congealed.
Matley had lost bladder control and lay placid in his piss-stained trousers. Still
alive, somehow.

"Jesus-bloody-goddamn-fucking-Christ on a unicycle!" Ramsey glared
down at Matley's inert form as other knights filtered into the room, some of
them examining the scene and speaking in low voices. "Idiot Easterbrook.
What bullshit is this?" He gave Matley a hard kick in the ribs; no response.

Bullshit: noun, Devon thought dully. Stupid or untrue talk or writing; nonsense. Strange, that. She would never have described wanton death as bullshit.

"I'll get the lad." One of the knights bent over them.

Devon huddled into the wall. "You can't have my son." Her arms wound
tighter around the toddler, fingers seeking purchase in the slight mass of him.
"He's mine. He's mine and I'll keep him!"

She was snarling as she spoke, bookteeth bared. Even as the knight recoiled in disgust, it struck Devon that she could not quite remember *why* she wanted her son, other than she'd paid a terrible price to keep him and simply could not let that go to waste.

"You're something else," Ramsey breathed, scrutinizing her from top to toe. "Really, Dev, you are phenomenal in your way."

The other knight was already lifting his crossbow. "She's a lost cause."

Ramsey touched him on the shoulder. "Hold off a second, Ealand." He looked down at her over the curve of that proud, Roman-emperor nose. "I never did thank you, by the way. Getting me sent off to the knights was the best thing that ever happened to me."

She retched up another gob of human flesh, scarcely listening.

"I think we can still use them for the intended purpose." Ramsey pulled out a sleek mobile phone. "Don't separate them yet, and don't shoot her unless she attacks. I need to make a call to Kingsey. See if we can adapt the situation to our advantage." He stepped outside, phone in hand. The other knights exchanged glances but waited.

Situation. Purpose. Meaningless words drifting lazily through Devon's subconscious, nothing clicking together. Like a misaligned puzzle set. Matley had told her there were no more knights, yet knights were here, talking like they'd had a use for her. A plan. There were no plans. Mice and men. Was she the mouse, or the man? She tried to think but Cai was screaming and it overloaded her senses.

The room stank overpoweringly of viscera. She kept her son from rolling in anything too grotesque as he flailed in agony, her mind existing in a place that had long ago surpassed normal fear or worry. Cai was unwell, and she didn't understand; he'd fed, it was horrific, but he was a mind eater, and it had saved her, and why was he so unwell?

Ramsey came back in, tucking the mobile into a pocket. "Commander Kingsey says we should proceed. Is there anywhere else I can sit down? I need to debrief her, and I'd prefer not to do it while holding my nose the entire time."

Another knight said, "You think this can be salvaged?"

"She was useful before and is useful still," Ramsey said. "Take it up with the commander if you don't like it."

Silence descended. No one else argued.

"Your agreement is appreciated," Ramsey said. "Moving on. This is a working farm, aye? With trafficked illegals and other such labor?"

It was Ealand who answered. "Yes, sir."

"Excellent." Ramsey jerked a thumb. "Go to the building where the workers are housed and bring me back the youngest child you can find. We'll be in the adjoining room." He looked down at Devon. "Get up."

She looked up, Cai sobbing disconsolately against her chest. "What's going on?"

"If you want your son to survive," Ramsey said, "then come with me." When she hesitated, he added, "Or we can shoot you both now. Your choice, little sister."

She stood up, writhing child in arms. "What's wrong with my son?"

"His meal didn't agree with him. Matley always was a contrary bastard." Ramsey walked out, shoes leaving a trail of bloody prints on the hallway carpet. "I am already dealing with it. We have time to speak first."

"There's nothing to talk about." She thought about running for it since no other knights had followed them, but that was futile and stupid. They'd be on her in no time at all.

"That's where you're wrong. You are both more useful than you know." Ramsey led her a couple rooms down. "Potentially, anyway. If you cooperate." He shot her a cold smile and stepped inside. "Be Devon the Deferential, yes?"

She limped in, still dazed by the quick change of events and compulsively checking on Cai every few seconds. Still no improvement. She looked around reluctantly. They were in someone's private office. Filing cabinet, bland carpets. A desk. Some chairs.

"Sit." He gave her a push.

Devon sat, conscious of the dried blood and encrusted vomit that stained her front. Cai arched his back, wailing, and twisted out of her arms.

"Let him go," Ramsey said. "He'll be seeking dark corners, lower sensory input, to ease the pain he's in."

"What's wrong with him?" she said again, and gently set the boy down. As Ramsey had predicted, Cai crawled into the farthest corner and curled into a crying ball.

"Eating a book eater is not like eating a human. It can be done, but the sheer quantity of information is a struggle. We are vast repositories, closer to walking libraries than we are to humans. Your son"—he gestured at Cai—"is barely out of babyhood, and consuming Matley has overloaded him. I've seen something like this once before."

"What the hell does that mean!"

"Exactly what it sounds like." Ramsey took out a large leather wallet from his inside jacket pocket, unfolding it to reveal a set of syringes. "With your permission, I'll give him a short-lasting sedative while we wait for my colleague to return. In the meantime, you and I should talk." He cocked his head. "Can't say knights don't know how to manage dragons, eh?"

"With my permission," she echoed hollowly. "Like I have a choice."

"What can I say, I enjoy the ritual of politeness. Sometimes." Ramsey stooped over the toddler, needle easing carefully into a tiny arm. Devon could not look away. Part of her feared what was in that syringe, but if her brother wanted them dead, they already would be.

Within moments, Cai settled down. He now drifted in and out of consciousness, no longer screaming or crying but still twitching like a nervy rabbit, huddled into his little tangle of limbs.

"Don't get up," Ramsey said, when she tried to rise. "Sit down and stay in your seat. We talk first. Your son will come to no harm sleeping on the floor."

Slowly, Devon sank into her plastic chair. Cai wheezed, eyelids fluttering.

"Good girl." Ramsey slid into the opposite seat and gave her that familiar lopsided grin. "Do you know why I'm here?"

"No." Devon tried to concentrate. "Matley said you were disbanding. The knights are gone. No more space for Cai."

"There are some in the Families who would love that. But we're not gone, not quite yet." The grin widened. "Dev, do you know how my order control the mind eaters we have?"

"Redemption," she said. Then sat up, sharp with realization. "Wait, if there's any Redemption around—"

"That won't help him right now," he said impatiently, "it only takes away hunger and he's already in overload. *Forget your son* for a second, please, or this will take all evening."

She ground her teeth. "Fine. Everyone knows you control your dragons' hunger with Redemption." Just like they would have controlled Cai. "So what?"

"Redemption is produced by one manor—the Ravenscars," he said. "I'm told the Japanese might have something similar, but they don't deal with outsiders much. No one else on this continent can make that drug, and the Ravenscars themselves have always kept the process secret." Ramsey leaned forward, palms pressed to the table. "Which is a problem, because two months ago the entire brood disappeared."

"Matley already told me that." Devon forced herself to focus. "I don't understand how. Manors don't disappear overnight."

"They do when people burn them down," he said. "Some of the patriarch's adult children have—from what we can tell—staged some kind of rebellion and run off into the night. Ravenscar Manor has been razed." His gaze was hard and steady. "All Six Families . . . well, *Five* Families now . . . are without Redemption. Including my knights, and our dragons."

Devon sat silent, wrestling with the enormity of that. Startled into interest despite the awfulness of the night so far, despite her own consuming problems. No wonder Matley had said the knights were disbanding. Their power and influence were bound up in the dragons they controlled. If Ramsey were being truthful, their order was finished. Especially with fertility technology on the horizon, and the end of arranged marriages.

And with them went Cai's future, she thought. She'd wanted to save her son from life as a dragon. Not if it meant his death, though.

"That doesn't tell me why I'm here," she said. "What do you want with us?"

Before Ramsey could answer, Ealand came in again, carrying a sleepy baby. Only a few months old and feeble, its features wan from malnutrition.

"Perfect timing." Ramsey clapped his colleague on the shoulder and took the infant.

"The mother put up a fight, but I got it off her in the end," said the other man. "Want me to stick around?"

"Aye, wait outside, if you will, and then you can return it." Ramsey laughed as if sharing a secret joke.

"What's going on?" She hated being so ignorant, always five steps behind him.

"As I keep saying, your son is overloaded," Ramsey said, turning back toward her with the baby in arms. "His mental processes are suffering as he tries to process Matley's mind. Leave him untreated, and he'll slip into a coma within a day. The only thing that can help him right now is to overwrite his difficult feed with an easier one. Even then, there are no guarantees."

The baby began to cry.

"You're going to give that kid to my son?" she said, dumbfounded.

"Absolutely not." Ramsey jostled the whining infant, trying to shush it with the clumsiness of someone who'd never been around children. "*You* are going to give this child to your son."

Devon stared, still haggard, gore-drenched, and shell-shocked from the most violent night of her life. This was one of those moments, she thought, where love was very much *not* a good thing. It had become a flood sweeping her to darker and darker places while she burned and fried under its many hideous demands.

"You seem disbelieving, but trust me, it works." Ramsey gave up shushing and simply put a hand over the infant's mouth, muting its cries against his palm. "A blank little mind will flush his system clean and scrub out much of Matley's complex personality. It will save your son's sanity, and his life." He paused. "Or we can watch him die in agony. Up to you."

Devon sat perfectly still, hands resting lightly on her knees as she gathered all of her focus. The initial horror was fading, lost to an ongoing nightmare in which terror had become ordinary life.

Ramsey thought he presented her a pivotal choice, but there was no such thing as big decisions in life—only the sum total of many tiny ones across the span of her hours, where she was constantly assessing Cai's value to her, and how much she cared. If he cried, she chose to pick him up; if he was hurt, she chose to soothe. If he needed something, she chose his needs over hers.

A thousand different times a day in a thousand different kinds of ways she had chosen Cai, until the choosing of him had become like breathing. Mother, at all costs.

Devon stood up. "Give me the baby."

Ramsey passed her the squalling bundle of human, eyes alight with avaricious interest.

Innocent in arms, she knelt by her son and, with nudges and soft whispers, urged him to feed. He was dazed, barely conscious, and clearly in so much pain. She finally managed to pry his mouth open and place his unfurled tongue against his victim's ear. And instinct took over.

A moment of perverse beauty: one child holding another, with Cai's mouth on the baby's ear. Almost a kiss, almost a cuddle. It was love and it was death and Devon thought that, for her, those things had become inextricably yoked. Her children were fires who needed fueling; she would burn anything and everything to keep them going.

There was no other course she could ever take, no other path she could ever walk. Not anymore.

Devon sat with Cai as he fed, one of the only times she would ever do so. She watched his eyes widen at the sudden cessation of pain, replaced by that same milk-drunk expression she'd seen after he'd first fed on Matley. And this time, when he let go of the unprotesting baby, he drifted into a true and quiet sleep.

The infant lolled on the floor next to them. Incredibly, it was still alive, though only in a physical sense. She ignored its vacant stare, trying to shut out any memory of the tiny, squashed face.

"Phenomenal," Ramsey said. "But you were always special, even when we were kids."

Devon spat at him, then drew her son into her lap and slumped against the wall.

"It's not chance that I'm here. Matley's antics aside, I'd already arranged to come tonight because we both need the same thing. You need that Ravenscar cure for your son, or he'll suffer all of his days. I need that cure for my dragons, or the knights are finished."

"Are you *recruiting* me?" Her turn to be incredulous. "To . . . what . . . find these lost Ravenscars?"

"Naturally," he said as if it were the most obvious thing in the world. "Matley has complicated things by behaving like an idiot, but my plans can accommodate that hiccup. Make use of it, even."

"Are you insane? I can't just rock up to these Ravenscars, wherever the hell they are, and ask nicely for their secret drugs!"

"On the contrary, yes, you can." He stood up, stretching his legs. Looking down at her. "We'll discuss the details later. First, though, I want your agreement to come quietly, and to *listen,* because there is a helluva lot more that I need to explain." He caught a fistful of her hair, tilting her face up toward his. "It's very simple, Dev. Will you work with me, or not?"

She wet her lips. "What happens if I turn you down?"

"Then your story ends tonight, princess."

And for all that she was the one covered in other people's blood, tongue still tainted by her double murder, she could not help but shrink from her brother.

Sometimes, decisions really were a straightforward life-or-death question.

"I . . ." Devon squeezed her son tight. "What do you want me to do, exactly?"

25

CAMELOT, INC.

TWO YEARS AGO

Courage—and shuffle the cards.

—George MacDonald Fraser, *Flashman*

The night passed in a blur.

Three knights peeled off Devon's ruined clothes and stuffed them into a trash bag. Someone gave her a man's suit to wear, complete with boxers. The suit fit well, her height and build an advantage for once. She dressed in an embarrassed rush, only to find herself hustled back to the gore-strewn room from before.

Matley's safe had been broken open, presumably by one of the knights. The door hung from its hinges, rendered useless in its prime function.

She gawked at the stacked bills inside.

"Fit what cash you can into this." Ramsey handed her a messenger bag. "Should net you about twenty-odd grand, if you're efficient."

Understanding dawned. "You're making this look like I attacked him and robbed him, and then fled with the money."

"I'm not 'making this look like' anything of the kind. That is precisely what you *will* be doing."

She gripped the bag with bloody hands. "What did you do to Matley?"

"He bled out internally," Ramsey said flippantly, and she could not tell whether that was true, or whether it implied the knights had finished him off. "We moved the remains to his bedroom."

Every action she took was writing another word of her own death sentence. The Families would think it was her fault. She would take full blame for her husband's death; the full blame, too, for stealing his money and for killing his men. And it kind of was her fault, which made things even more complicated. Just not to the extent that Ramsey was implying.

But four knights were in the room and they were all armed, so Devon set down her son on the cleanest bit of carpet she could find and crammed bills into the messenger bag until it could barely zip shut. By the time she'd finished, her fingerprints were everywhere: mixed with blood and dirt and fuck-knew-what from the men she'd killed. More rope to hang herself.

"Perfect," Ramsey said with a winning smile, and took the bag off her.

Someone crammed a poorly fitting dragon-painted helmet on her head, and now she grasped finally why she'd been given a suit. The knights were removing her from the scene of the crime without drawing attention.

They walked through Easterbrook Manor. The household buzzed with activity, men and the few women talking in corridors or arguing in corners. No one recognized Devon in her suit and helmet; dragons had a kind of special invisibility in that way.

"What have you told them?" The helmet muffled her voice.

Ramsey glanced back. "As I promised earlier, they think you murdered Matley and fled with Cai. Under normal circumstances they might have enlisted the aid of knights to hunt you down, but apparently we're disbanding. I've told them we can't help." The last was said with savage venom.

Devon, inside the safety of her dragon apparel, hunched her shoulders and said nothing further as they wound through the house and out into the gentle darkness of the witching hour. The air smelled crisp, and the breeze brought welcome coolness.

"We have a long drive ahead," Ramsey said, settling on his bike. "You'll ride with me, your son will ride with someone else." He gestured for her to sit behind him, and reluctantly she did. Cai was being bundled up in a passenger's seat the next bike over, still unconscious.

"Where are we going?" Devon clasped on the seat belt.

"Oxford." He revved his bike into motion.

Devon left Winterfield Manor in the dead of night wearing a dragon's suit, bundled discreetly onto the back of Ramsey's motorcycle. The luggage he kept on it surrounded her tightly, and she fell into exhausted sleep.

Dawn was breaking when she woke, some four hours later. The knights had skirted the city center, keeping to side roads and winding through smaller villages before eventually rolling up to a lonely concrete building in the commercial district, surrounded by concrete walls and a barbed-wire fence. A large-lettered sign bore the words CAMELOT INCORPORATED.

"I can feel you laughing," Ramsey said. "Something funny?"

"Of course you'd live in Camelot," Devon said, almost wheezing. "I should have known. Not much of a castle, is it? Do you have a round table, at least?"

"Modern times don't accommodate such symbolism," he said, coasting to a stop in front of an enormous pair of electronic gates. "Much as we'd enjoy a drawbridge and moat, this is rather more secure than the Arthurian variety."

A pair of young, suited knights leaned out of a security booth, offering a greeting in Latin; she caught the word *Camelot* in there.

"How do you afford this?" she said as the knights approached their motorbike. "None of you take jobs."

Most book eaters worked in Family-run firms, or other labor that required only minimal interaction with the rest of human society. Some had illicit businesses, like the Easterbrooks, using humans who did not ask too many questions. The knights, so far as she knew, did none of that.

"Up until two months ago," Ramsey said, "every Family paid us a tithe to arrange and facilitate marriages. We also had a special arrangement with the Ravenscars, which is complicated, and nothing you need to know about." He gave a series of signals to inspecting guards. "During this period of transition, we are living off savings to pay the bills. You might say."

"They paid you a tithe because you are supposed to have no agenda of your own," she said. "This looks like you're just another manor. Just another Family."

"Nonsense." He revved the bike and drove through the gates, raising his voice so she could hear him above the grumble of engines. "A regular Family is bound by all sorts of rules, which we don't have to follow. The knights have far more freedom and power than any of the patriarchs."

"Stupid me," she muttered into his back. "Here I was thinking you existed to serve." No wonder the patriarchs were eager to shed the knights.

Ramsey and the other knights drove down a length of asphalt to an indoor garage, where they parked and dismounted. Cai was still fast asleep, bundled onto the back of someone's motorbike. Devon squashed her urge to dash over and check on him.

As he helped her off the bike, Ramsey said, "Protect, not serve."

"Pardon?" She had lost the thread of their discussion.

"You said we exist to serve. Not quite correct. We exist to *protect* the Families by ensuring their survival through the marriage system. Among other things. At the moment, losing the Ravenscars is our biggest threat, because we have lost the ability to control the dragons, and the knights will disintegrate if something isn't done."

"That threatens you, not them," she said. "The Families are in early stages of testing their own fertility treatments, so marriages will be less and less strict with every generation. We can *choose* to have girls, whole generations of them if we want. Even if we hadn't lost the Ravenscars and their Redemption, so what? Knights couldn't have lasted forever. This has just sped things up."

"Don't be so short-sighted. We have plenty of use still." He tucked a pair of bike gloves into one pocket. "Follow me, please. We are on a tight schedule and must cover a lot of ground."

She took half a step toward Cai, sleepy but stirring in the arms of another knight.

"We'll meet up with him again, at the end of your little tour." Ramsey stepped in front, cutting off her view. "The quicker we do this, the quicker you see him again."

The knight carrying Cai was already moving swiftly in the opposite direction. If he was not especially loving in his hold, he was at least competent and not unkind; head cradled, knees supported.

Devon clenched her fists, watching them disappear around a corner, then reluctantly followed Ramsey through another series of internal security gates and into the "castle" proper.

Family manors were all lush in one way or another. The Winterfields had lavish and stately decor; the Easterbrooks opted for contemporary yet expensive. Even the Fairweathers, old and debt-riddled as they were, had contained the remnants of extravagance in carpets and tapestries and chandeliers. Book eaters had a fondness for trappings. And books, naturally.

Nothing of that legacy showed in this compound. Concrete walls stood bare and gray; the tiled floor shone polished but plain. No lights, only darkness. No accommodations for human visitors or any nod toward human culture. Presumably they had books to eat, though none were on display. No unique bookscent, either. Devon wondered what grown-up knights consumed.

The hall branched into two directions. Devon was about to keep going straight when Ramsey caught her shoulder.

"Not that way."

She let herself be nudged down the other corridor. "What's down the other route?"

"Barracks and training. Nothing you need to see." He put a hand on the door. "We'll take a route through the dragon pens instead."

"Pens?"

"An in-joke."

In the corridor beyond were a series of cell doors, with viewing panels at head height. Some were open. Heart in throat, she stepped closer to peer through thick glass.

A solid white room, the walls and floors layered in white soundproofing. Not much space, eight feet on all sides. A white table with one white chair. Insanely bright white lights, which would be annoying even for a human, and was surely headache-inducing for an 'eater of any stripe. A youngish-looking dragon, eighteen or so, was dressed in all-white clothes and curled on an all-white bed, arms around his head.

"I don't get it." Devon stepped back, uneasy for reasons she couldn't quite pinpoint. Nothing in the room had been unusually cruel, per se, and yet the sight of that cell made her teeth hurt. "What's the point of this?"

"Extreme sensory deprivation." Ramsey came to stand at her shoulder. "Sometimes melodramatically referred to as 'white torture.' We use it as a form of depersonalization therapy, to keep the cravings at bay."

Something must have alerted the dragon inside. He raised his head and sat up, staring at them with wide, bloodshot eyes.

She grimaced. "How long do they spend in there?"

"In where? Their rooms?"

"That's his personal room? They all sleep in that kind of place?!"

"When not on duty, yes. Which, at present, is most of the time."

The dragon got up and padded over on bare feet, scrabbling anxiously at the viewing panel. He did not look at Ramsey at all, only Devon.

"That's awful!"

"Typical princess mentality." Ramsey rolled his eyes. "The lives they have now are strict, but it's still a striding improvement from seventy years ago, when they'd just be dead."

The dragon pressed his face to the viewing panel, tongue hanging flaccid. Saliva ran down the glass. He looked miserable, eyes red from frequent crying.

"This is cruel." Devon pressed a palm to her side of the glass, trying hard not to imagine Cai in such a place. "There must be a better way to treat them."

"Don't be stupid." Ramsey plucked her hand away and slammed the viewing panel shut, cutting off all sight of the dragon within. "Hunger is a powerful thing, especially when it is a hunger for dominance and violence. Few people can resist the temptation to abuse power."

"The fucking irony of *you* saying that," she snapped. "You don't care about Cai, and you're not talking to me out of kindness. Why are we here? Why were you coming to collect me yesterday?"

"Finally, some intelligent questions! Let's get out of this area first. I do have a round table of sorts, to show you. Since you asked earlier."

He shut the remaining viewing panels as they walked down. It didn't escape Devon's notice that most of the rooms were empty. Come to think of it, the whole building seemed a little empty. Hardly any other people walking around. Were knights leaving? Ramsey's innocuous decision to not walk her past the barracks took on a new interpretation. Maybe he felt the need to obfuscate how bad things were for them.

Another door, followed by a set of stairs. Devon walked after, glad to leave behind the white corridor with its horrible white cells.

The stairwell exited into a raised viewing gallery, encased in glass and overlooking an operating theater. Surgeons and nurses moved around an oval table, passing instruments back and forth as they worked on their unconscious patient. Not just any patient; a small, dark figure—

"Cai!" Devon slammed herself against the glass, thumping with both fists. "*Cai!*"

One of the surgeons looked up, squinted, and went back to work. The rest didn't appear to notice.

"I suggest you relax." Ramsey took his own advice, flinging himself into a viewing chair. "The procedure will be done in less than an hour. Quick and painless, and your boy will never remember."

She whirled, fists raised. "*What are you doing to him?*"

"Hit me and neither of you will live to find out."

Devon counted to twenty, willing herself to calm incrementally. Everything was tipped against her and she had to push it all aside, survive moment by moment. She allowed herself a shudder, tamping down on the roiling emotions.

"Sit," he said, as if she were a dog. "We talk like adults, aye?"

There was nothing else she could do. Sundered by impotent fury, Devon sat, not taking her eyes off the surgery below. Cai was half-buried beneath the medical equipment and gowns.

"Your son is being fitted with a surgically implanted explosive device, one that I can set off at a distance using satellite signals," he said, as if it were the most natural thing in the world. "A harsher version of an old technique we used to employ against particularly resistant brides, on rare occasions."

The air was missing from Devon's throat, as if her lungs had suddenly calcified. At what point had her brother lost himself so badly? The answer came welling up, unwelcome and foul: the moment she'd condemned him to a life among knights, when they were children.

"I thought we should get that out of the way," Ramsey went on. "Now you know why he's down there. Put a foot wrong, give me reason to doubt you, and the trigger gets pressed. Try to take it out yourself, and you'll set it off. No matter the distance, neither of you will be safe." He crossed long legs with casual indifference. "If you want Cai to live past today, or if you ever want that device removed safely, then listen."

"You haven't told me what you want yet!"

"I want my order back," he said. "Powerful, strong, protective. The way things are supposed to be. Through us, eaters have thrived in this country for the past century—"

"That's due to the Ravenscars," she retorted. "The knights had nothing to do with the drug being developed, you just benefited from it!"

He ignored her. "—and yet many of the patriarchs resent that. Even though we were the ones to enforce marriages, keep the species alive, and drag the older Families into modern times. They are not allowed to forget us so quickly. Do you understand?"

Devon certainly did understand. Ramsey was like a CEO trying to shore up a dying company, or a dictator refusing to surrender. It was always the same story, she thought tiredly. Just small, angry men, clinging to fading power. They feared living without privilege because they'd abused it against others, and were now terrified of suffering the same cruelty they'd routinely dealt out.

Personally, she didn't see how reclaiming Redemption or the use of dragons was going to save the knights in the long term. But that didn't matter to Ramsey and his ilk. He only cared how it affected him in the short term.

Aloud, Devon said, "None of that has anything to do with putting *an explosive device* in Cai's body."

"Can't you guess?" he said. "My commander and I have developed a little plan, rather straightforward, and it goes like this. We find out where the Ravenscars have gone, and we get someone to join them. Someone who they'll believe and feel sympathetic toward, who shares their values and whatnot. Then we use that person to track the Ravenscars to their hiding spot, and descend in the night. Capture them, take their drug supply, and wring the siblings for information on how to make it."

"That's fucking insane," Devon managed.

"Yet here you are, Dev, falling out of the sky like a pot o' gold with a rainbow attached. I could not have planned that fiasco with Matley if I'd tried!" He was laughing again; the whole world and its relentless cruelty was endlessly amusing to Ramsey. "Pretend to go on the run for Matley's murder, and we will pretend to pursue. The Ravenscars, should they find you, will believe you are a fugitive. Except none of it is quite pretend. Isn't this a wonderful bit of drama?"

"I . . ." Her head was reeling, her heart wrung with bewildered misery from the complexity of it all. "Why would they ever *want* to find me? How am I supposed to join a random group of dissidents I've never met?"

Ramsey held up a finger, poked it in his own ear, and then mimed an expression of dying that was somewhere between ridiculous and grotesque. Mocking Matley, she realized, and didn't know how to feel about that.

"Cai is guilty of patricide, as they are," he said. "I think they will find you both very tempting indeed. Birds of a feather, and all that. Must get lonely by themselves, eh?"

In the theater below, the procedure was wrapping up. Hands washed up, aprons crumpled and tossed away, gloves discarded neatly. Cai lay still and inert.

"I'm not a spy," she said. "I'm not even a knight. I'm just—"

"Authentic," he said, leaning toward her. "Desperate. Trapped. A good thinker on your feet. Occasionally imaginative, in a way that many of us are not. You are everything we need and more, Dev. Perfect for the role."

Cai was being wheeled away, out of her agonized and fretful sight.

"Lucky me," she said, watching until Cai's trolley was gone and the theater completely empty. "How about, you don't give me that rubbish? Because I've been playing roles all my life like a good little princess and now I've just watched my brother implant his nephew with a device that can kill him."

Ramsey's amusement faded. "Fine, allow me to rephrase. You're a core piece in the game, but you're not a player, or in a position to win. Only a position to be useful. Be useful, or get discarded." He rapped her forehead with a finger. "You're free to go anytime you like, but I don't think you will. Because that would mean abandoning Cai, and you'll never do it."

He was right. She hated that it was true, but hated the thought of leaving Cai even more. Wasn't that what it came down to, in the end? Every single time. She wasn't stupid, knew he'd "dispose" of her and Cai when done with them. The alternative was one or both of them dying even faster.

"I don't know how to survive out there," she said through clenched teeth. "I've never lived among humans or . . . or anything."

"We can prep you. It'll take a few months, but we'll need that time anyway to track down their human suppliers." Ramsey stood and stretched leisurely. "I'll go and make sure the procedure has gone smoothly. If it has, you may come see your boy. Wait here."

He strode out of sight, leaving her in the darkened viewing gallery. No one else was in sight, but she knew better than to run. This was a sealed compound, full of knights and dragons, and her son was still elsewhere in the building. Held hostage, now, with an explosive in his belly.

Devon curled up in the quiet emptiness.

If she disobeyed the knights, they'd either turn her over to the Families or kill Cai from a distance. If she refused to comply, neither of them would leave this building alive. Even if she could remove the device later, her son still needed the drugs—still needed the Ravenscars.

And yet if she obeyed the knights dutifully, she would end up in a shallow grave, scapegoated for their crimes while her children were fed like grist to a mill. She was too dangerous a loose end to leave hanging.

All her options ended in death and failure, her usefulness expired; she was a dead woman walking.

Devon smiled.

There had to be a moment, she thought, where you could pinpoint the tides of an ocean turning. A single specific flicker of time, recordable, measurable, where the waves stopped retreating and started advancing up the beach again. This, surely, was such a moment for her.

For the first time in years, her heart seemed to float within her chest, free and light and calm. Fear had been an anchor, dragging her down, and the certainty of death had finally cut that chain. If all this politicking were a card game, the knights believed they had stacked the deck against her, to cover every eventuality.

And if she could not win then she no longer had anything to lose. She would play with all she had because there was no other choice. In taking away her options, Ramsey had set her free.

All she had to do was figure out a plan of her own.

26

SOMETHING ROTTEN IN DENMARK

PRESENT DAY

They call it mind eating. *They look at me as a monstrous thing, a feaster of brains, something akin to the myriad flesh-eating and blood-drinking monsters of human legend. My own family saw me as heinous.*

But I know the truth, now. This is not eating. This is sharing, this is communion. What I do is the ultimate experience of divinity, the merging of two souls into a single body; the partaking and elevating of life into new, transcendent forms.

This is a miracle. I, am a miracle.

Bless me, Father, for I am divine.

—Killock Ravenscar, private journal

"Say something," Devon said into the silence that followed her story. The wind picked up, scattering leaves and twigs, rattling the trees. "Please."

"Say what?" Hester retorted, arms curled around herself. "That I feel angry? Of course I do! Everything was bullshit and you are here to *get us killed*! That fiasco on the train . . . losing my gun, my purse . . . that was fake, too, wasn't it? I can't believe you of all people would work with knights!"

"I'm not working with them through choice. Didn't you hear what I said? I'm exploiting them because I must. And I'm not trying to get everyone killed, I only need Redemption for Cai. The Ravenscars are free to leave before the knights descend. I would have given you warning!"

"Free to leave? Are you serious?" Hester's laughter sounded hysterical. "How generous of you to let us go on the run! When was this all going to come out, then? Did you think about our lives at all when you set out this plan?"

Above them, the sky was beginning to darken as clouds gathered. Another bout of snow or sleet waiting to drop.

"Did *you* think about the thirty-odd people *from your own family* who died in Killock's pointless coup?" Devon shot back, and the other woman recoiled as if slapped. "What is there to save? Look at this household. Weston hasn't been left behind. You've only transplanted him to a new body, a new house. Same bullshit, same bastard. Now with a fucking cult growing up around him."

"How does that justify the reasoning behind betraying us? You didn't know the situation here before making that decision."

"The Ravenscars are a Family like any other. I assumed you'd be just as bad as the book eaters I left behind," Devon said, shielding her eyes against the persistent winter wind. "When in fact, this is worse."

"Oh, piss off! Who gave you the right to pass judgment when you've known us for barely two days?"

"I'm not wrong, though, am I? Killock has created a gathering of monsters who steal locals to feed on for their twisted communion. Tell me that isn't worse than your average Family setup?" She took a step forward, dried foliage cracking beneath her still-bare feet. "Be real, Hes. It was only a matter of time before someone would have descended. If not me and the knights, if not the other Families, then human policemen. Killock was fucked the moment he ate his patriarch and lost himself to feeding. On some level, you must know this."

"Does that make your choice any more ethical?" Hester swung the empty gun up between them like a club. "What happens if I go to tell my brother? Will you stop me? Kill me, like you killed Matley? I should just hand you in!"

"You're too smart for that," Devon said with a calmness she didn't feel, and scraped windblown hair out of her eyes. "He'd kill all three of us. Me for my lies, you for bringing me here. By telling you this, I've made your situation impossible."

Hester gripped the gun so tightly that it seemed she might dent it. "Then why the hell did you bother talking to me?"

"Because you're trapped. As I was once trapped. And I want"—the truth unfolded, even as she said it out loud—"for you to come with me and Cai, when we go. We'll take all available Redemption, we'll flee, we'll get somewhere safe. Together."

"*What?*" Hester stared. "That's beyond absurd!"

"Why? Aren't you unhappy? Aren't you regretting the coup, wishing you could leave? All those things you told me earlier."

"It's absurd because it isn't possible," Hester hissed, furious—and Devon heard in that denial an echo of her own objections to Jarrow, so long ago. "I can't even . . . It's so . . . Godsakes!" She turned away and strode back toward the house through the woodland. Face stormy and dark like the sky above them, rifle held tight to her chest.

Devon jogged after, body angled awkwardly to face the other woman. "Hes, answer me this. Why do you think so few women run away? Why do you think nothing really changes for book eaters, century after century?"

"How should I bloody know!"

"We lack imagination," Devon said, relentless. "Even if we used Dicta-phones and scribes, we'd never be able to write books the way humans can. We struggle to innovate, are barely able to adapt, and end up stuck in our tra-ditions. Just eating the same books generation after generation, thinking along the same rigid lines. Creativity is our world and yet we aren't creative."

"I really don't care—"

"*Listen*," Devon shouted, stepping in front of her. "Just let me finish, all right? Our childhood books always ended in marriage and children. Women are taught not to envision life beyond those bounds, and men are taught to en-force those bounds. We grow up in a cultivated darkness and don't even realize we're blind."

Hester stood on that stretch of green, hands balled into fists and gaze averted. But she'd stopped trying to walk away, at least for now.

"I should have run sooner," Devon said, voice cracking a little. "But I didn't. Know what really stopped me? My lack of imagination, the same one that all 'eaters suffer from. *I could not imagine a better or different future*, Hes, and be-cause I could not imagine it, I assumed it didn't exist." Her throat was lumping up. "I was wrong. Life can be different. You're wrong, too. That's why I think you should consider coming with me, to try something different."

"I tried something different with Killock already, and look how that turned out," Hester retorted. "Isn't that what you were *just* lecturing me about? Our inability to be unlike other Families? What kind of bloody-minded arrogance makes you think you'd do any better than him?"

"Because I'm not a patriarch, and I don't want to set up a manor," Devon said. "Killock wanted the same things most 'eater men want: a household of his own to run. He didn't understand that the whole system doesn't work, that you have to leave it *all* behind and do things completely differently."

The sleet began to beat down; the storm had arrived. Both of them ignored it, immune to the chill and indifferent to the damp.

"There is no different way of life," Hester said sullenly. "The Families were right about mind eaters, anyway. We can't live without them."

"Bullshit," Devon said. "You conquered your hunger. Cai did too. Nei-ther of you ever went out feeding. Killock's sins are his own—the hunger is just his scapegoat. He wants you to believe his lies so that you'll excuse his behavior."

"That's—" Hester paused, face and clothes streaked by the half frozen rain. "Even if that's true, you're asking me to believe in a tomorrow that you tell me

I can't imagine. To work toward a future that I apparently cannot see, or afford the cost to earn. Please, just stop. I need space. I need you to go away."

Devon sighed, and stepped aside. "For what it's worth, I'm truly sorry."

"Everyone's always sorry," the other woman said again with renewed vehemence. She stalked toward the house, gun still cradled in her arms.

—————•—————

Devon waited a discreet amount of time for Hester to disappear into Traquair, allowing the thundering beat of her heart to calm down, then followed more slowly. She walked alone in the mid-afternoon sleet, minding neither the cold nor the wet. Forest at her back and manor growing larger in her field of vision. The white-painted exterior looked like glistening bone in this frozen rain.

Foolish, to talk to Hester as she'd done. Taking such a risk was highly unlike her usual self. Yet the alternative would have been to not involve Hester at all, to simply leave quietly with Cai. That in turn would mean leaving Hester to potentially get caught up in the knights' crossfire.

Not acceptable.

The strength of that reaction surprised her. At some point, Hester's survival had begun to factor in the continuous equations Devon ran inside her head for how to balance the needs of those around her.

Did that mean the connection between them was strong, or just an indictment of her loneliness? Grasping with wild desperation at the only semblance of friendship she'd encountered since Jarrow had left.

Too late to regret anything she'd said. The Ravenscar woman would either come with her, or not. In the meantime, more practical considerations weighed on her mind.

For a start, there was the question of Redemption, that Holy Grail for which she'd quested all these months and years. Gaining access to the actual recipe was likely off the table, given that the only person who'd apparently known it was now a specter inside of Killock's brain, and Killock himself seemed unlikely to cough it up.

Devon had already learned from her months with Ramsey that the Ravenscars made their drug according to the delivery schedule of chemical shipments. Materials arrived in summer, early production took place in fall, then finishing and storage in winter. Spring was a rest season.

That meant they tended to have stores of Redemption at any given time. Since they were still producing it, then it was a given they'd have supplies stored somewhere. Besides, Hester and a couple of her brothers still needed the stuff, and Killock presumably took it between his "ceremonial" victims.

The difficulty was finding where it was stored and being able to take any before Ramsey arrived. Her brother had not given her much time.

She skirted the maze and climbed the steps up to Traquair's north side, entering through the kitchen.

Mani, to her surprise, was waiting for her inside, seated alone at a cloth-draped dining table. He rose as she entered, bracing himself on chair and stick. "Afternoon, Ms. Fairweather. Good shooting session?"

"Turns out I'm a terrible shot," Devon said. "Where's my son?"

"Settled in his room. I gave him the tour and he picked a place to his liking." Mani offered a wary smile. "Thought I'd come and find you, to spare you the effort of searching up and down for us."

"That's very kind," Devon said, head still whirling. "Please do lead on."

Mani nodded. He got up and hobbled out of the kitchen and into the corridor. Then up a set of stairs she'd not yet seen, toward the "newer" wing of the house. New, in this case, meant it had been built in the 1700s, instead of the 1200s, like the rest of Traquair—a fact that Devon found amusing when Mani explained it to her. Fairweather Manor had seemed impossibly old when she was young, but this place had a good five hundred years of history on her childhood home.

"I'm glad I could catch you, by the way," Devon said, keeping a sharp eye out for other 'eaters. "I wanted to apologize again for how I screwed you over twenty-two years ago. I truly did think you were just an exciting guest."

His face fell, perhaps lost in unhappy memory. "And as I said before, don't be sorry. I can't hold a grudge against a child who knew no better, and who intended no malice. In any case, you've had your share of suffering, from what I've heard of your story."

"What about *your* story?" she prompted as they reached the second level. "How did you get here? What happened in between?"

A couple of mind eaters came around the corner, chatting in low voices. Mani gave them a respectful nod, and Devon did the same. Neither sibling took any notice of them, carrying on with their animated conversation.

When the brothers were gone, Mani said quietly, "I was sent north to Ravenscar Manor along with a small clutch of other humans, all shepherded by knights." He paused on the landing to rest for a moment, leaning hard on his stick, before reorienting himself down a long, lushly appointed hallway. "In those days, Weston still needed human subjects to help synthesize Redemption."

Devon stopped in her tracks. "Come again?"

"Ah. Has no one here told you yet?" Mani cocked his head, gaze shrewd behind the bottlecap glasses. "The patriarch who first developed Redemption worked out that mind eaters must be feeding on some component present in human brains. Because he was a rather clever fellow, he figured out how to isolate that component in chemical form, giving us the drug we have today."

"That's incredible," she said, utterly floored. "Also, absurdly simple. Why has no one else discovered it?"

"Probably because the other Families think like book eaters, while mind eaters have the benefit of a more *personal* angle on the problem," Mani said. "And it simply never occurred to any book eaters to just ask mind eaters. Your folk can be curiously blinkered in that way. No offense."

"None taken."

"All that to say, Weston kept me locked away for many years, brought me out only for blood draws and various extraction procedures on my brain." He gestured at his right leg. "Weston also had me hobbled, to make sure I couldn't run off."

"That's awful," she said, appalled. "Are humans still a part of the process? It sounds hellish."

"It was unpleasant," he said with the flat neutrality of someone who has become accustomed to trauma, "but it ended after four years, finally, when Weston cracked a fully artificial process for Redemption. Thank the gods! Every aspect of the drug is synthesized now, with no need for human input." Mani began walking again. "Mind you, that meant I no longer had a purpose."

Devon trotted after him, feet soundless on the emerald-hued carpets. "Why did he keep you alive? If that's not rude to ask."

"It's not. I was well educated, with a background in law and media. Weston preserved my life to use me as a proxy for anything that required writing. The one thing he couldn't do himself. I wouldn't say we became friends—that would be impossible, given the power dynamic and what he'd done to me already—but we understood each other. He was a cold man, yet truly brilliant in his way."

"That's not saying much. Intelligence is easy for book eaters."

"Rubbish," Mani said reproachfully. "Information is not intellect. Computers can contain entire books, too, but they're not considered intelligent yet. It is one thing to have a repository of data, and quite another to *use* it, let alone creatively. Weston could do both."

"I hadn't thought of it that way." It struck Devon that she did not see herself as particularly intelligent. Not when he phrased it like that.

"Anyway, I was Weston's scribe for sixteen years in total, and learned an enormous amount about your species in that time." A self-deprecating smile ghosted his lips. "I've been writing a book about the history of 'eaters, though God knows whether it will ever see the light of day. Even if Killock were inclined to let me publish, who would believe anything in it?"

"It's an incredible story," Devon said, with sincerity. "Did you have some kind of arrangement with Killock, after he took over?"

"After Killock removed Weston and the other book eaters, I was spared, providing I was willing to accept Killock's leadership." If Mani found such a tenuous existence stressful, it didn't show. Perhaps he had become adept at masking himself in a house of predators.

"Killock does seem to rely on you heavily."

"I remain useful . . . for now," Mani conceded, with an undertone that suggested this might change at any moment. "Like all mind eaters, Killock can write, but he still does not exist in a legal sense, nor does he have experience of the wider world. I, on the other hand, am an actual citizen of this country, able to make bank accounts and so forth, since I have personal documentation, which he lacks. I also help manage the Ravenscar finances, such as they are, and I oversee communications with their drug suppliers."

"Then you'll know the components that go into the drugs, and also where the finished drugs are kept," she said, glancing around; no one was about. This house could easily hold four times the Ravenscars' number and it was practically empty with only fifteen people in it. "Since Killock makes you do the grunt work and keep the records. Am I right?"

"Is that information of interest to you, Ms. Fairweather?" He slowed down again, coming closer. "Is there any particular reason you ask?"

"My son needs it to live. I'm interested in keeping him alive." She met his inquisitive gaze with her own hard-edged stare. "If I knew the ingredients going into it, perhaps I'd be able to make my own."

"That information is only needful if you don't plan to stay," Mani said, adjusting his glasses. "Are you perchance thinking of moving on from Traquair?"

"Aren't you?" she returned levelly. "I saw your face at chapel earlier. I can't begin to imagine what twenty-two years trapped among mind eaters is like for a human, but I doubt it's gotten easier or better since Killock's coup. Crikey, *I* don't want to stay here, and I'm practically one of them."

"It hasn't gotten easier. You are right on that account." A note of sourness crept into his voice. "But I am also sixty-five, arthritic, diabetic, and have been given a cruel injury that makes fast movement difficult. One must be realistic about these things."

Devon hooked her thumbs through her belt loops. "Well, I'm younger, healthy, fast as hell, and have certain resources at my disposal. Maybe we can help each other."

Mani took another step closer, almost shoulder to shoulder. "How so, Ms. Fairweather?"

"That depends. How much Redemption do you keep in store?"

He smiled. "How much do you need?"

"Enough for Cai to live the rest of his life, ideally, but I'll take whatever you can give me."

The ex-journalist folded his hands atop the cane, resting thoughtfully. "Fill a large suitcase and that's ten years' worth for a single person, I should think. The pills are only small. I can get even more, if you are able to wait a few weeks."

She couldn't. "Ten years' worth will be fine. I need it by tomorrow."

"Tomorrow?" His eyes bugged slightly, composure slipping. "Are you leaving so soon?"

"As soon as I've got Redemption." And had another chance to talk to Hester, she thought silently. "I need to be gone by tomorrow night. Can you help?"

"I believe so, yes." Mani shifted his weight, giving the tired leg a slight rest. "I will arrange to conduct an inventory of Redemption stores tomorrow. That will allow me to procure what you need without arousing suspicion."

"And any notes you can give me on the ingredients," she pressed. Ten years of medication would buy her plenty of time to figure out the cure, if she had the ingredients and processes in note form.

Mani was no fool, though. "Remind me what I'm getting out of it, again," he said. "So far I've yet to hear any counter-assurances from you, Ms. Fairweather."

"A car ride out of here, and an escorted ferry trip to Ireland. Safety and protection the entire way, provided by me."

"Ah-huh. Ireland . . . yes, a good choice. And will we be accompanied by anyone else?"

"Friends of mine, who I trust, and who will be picking us up," Devon said. "Maybe Hester. I'm not sure."

"Hester, eh? I did wonder if she'd . . . well." Mani considered a moment, still leaning on his cane. "Meet me at the brewery tomorrow evening," he said at last. "Seven P.M. sharp. I will aim to be punctual and expect you to do the same."

"I'll be there." She held out a hand.

Mani shook it briefly. "What a lovely reunion it has been," he said pleasantly, as if they'd been discussing the weather. "Come along, Ms. Fairweather. Your son is waiting."

27

THE PRINCESS SEEKS HER PRINCE

EIGHTEEN MONTHS AGO

Then the princess bound up her hair, put on her boots, and her coat of a thousand furs, and stepped out into the silent snowy darkness. She walked all night.

—Charlotte Huck, *Princess Furball*

Eight long months in Camelot, and Devon was finally "free" to leave.

Pitted asphalt rolled past her window, hemmed by pavements flush with pedestrians. A year ago, she'd have been thrilled by the sight. The idea now of living among them, indefinitely, made her want to crawl into the nearest sewer grate and never come out.

"We'll drop you at the station. You can make your way from there." Ramsey steered their Volkswagen people-carrier through lazy Oxford traffic; the first time she'd seen him drive anything other than a motorbike. "The amount of cash you're carrying will easily last years."

"Years?" In their months of training, he'd implied that it would only take a few weeks. "Are you really going to leave me out here for *years*?"

"It shouldn't take you that long. One year, at most."

That didn't reassure her at all.

"Co się dzieje?" Cai whispered from the seat next to her. "Gdzie jesteśmy?"

"I don't know what you're saying," she told him, for the third time since they'd got in the car.

His lower lip quivered, and she sighed. Cai had lived off the knights' dwindling Redemption supplies for eight months, his mind still that of an infant. There would be no more drugs now. Not till Devon found the Ravenscars. To make him travel ready, her son had been fed a human stranger, procured at Ramsey's request.

"Remember the rules," Ramsey said over one shoulder, as if he hadn't already given her a sheet of those rules to eat. "Call in every fourteen days, even if you have nothing to report. If you're more than twenty-four hours late to report, we detonate that device." He steered one-handed through an orange light, gesturing at the messenger bag heaped in Devon's lap. "Call sooner if you find the Ravenscars, or the plan changes. Your knight-issued phone and charger are in there—keep them safe. No contact with other Families, or human law enforcement. If you do attempt to speak to either, know that we'll withdraw all support and, again, I'll trigger Cai's explosive."

"Aren't you a model uncle." She supposed he'd learned well from Aike.

"Thanks, I try. Remember, if you see knights in the city, that's your cue to move to a new location. Any questions?"

"Aye, I've got a sodding question. My son doesn't speak English anymore. What am I supposed to do with that?"

Ramsey rolled his eyes. "Eat a Polish book, idiot. It's not exactly a difficult barrier for us."

"It's not about the language. He thinks he's another person!"

"That's very common." The Volkswagen turned sharply into the station, wheels bumping over potholes. "Welcome to the life of a mind eater who doesn't have Redemption. Consider yourself lucky that he doesn't think he's Matley."

"Lucky," she echoed darkly. "Sure."

"If it bothers you, then stop being so bloody squeamish, and find him a fresh feed once I drop you off," he said, irritable. "I recommend you give him small children, when you can. He's less likely to get overwhelmed, and it'll keep the accumulation of memories at bay a little longer. And, they're easier to catch, too."

Jesus, she thought, and felt ill. She wondered if Ramsey had purposefully given Cai an awkward feed, so that she'd be forced to hunt someone new. It wouldn't be out of character.

Her brother parked in a temporary space, switching the engine off. "Don't fuck up. You'll hear from me soon enough."

Devon unclipped her seat belt, popped the door, and stood slowly.

The world overwhelmed. Cars clustered like barnacles. The air reeked of car fumes and sweat. People streamed disparately to their various destinations in a choppy tangle. Lives and bodies remote from her own existence, yet so close and tangible.

In all of her life she'd never seen more than a handful of humans, mostly from a distance. Now they were everywhere, meaty and clunky and loud, stinking of the animals and plants they ate. So *many* people.

Cai clambered out, his hand slipping into hers, clinging to her side; she gave him a cautious squeeze. Perhaps he found this new environment as confusing and dirty as she did.

"Get going," Ramsey said, irritable and barely audible from within the Volkswagen. "I can't stay in this bay very long."

She gulped a lungful of pollution-tainted air. "I don't know how to live out here."

"Don't be bloody stupid. You've had months of training, you'll be fine." Ramsey leaned over, yanked the door shut, and started reversing. The last bastion of Family familiarity in retreat, however unpleasant that bastion had been.

In seconds, he was gone and they were alone: boy and woman on a patch of black asphalt, each inhuman and lost. Traffic roared to one side, trains lugged on the other. Every breath tasted of pollution.

Nothing Devon had read, eaten, or experienced had prepared her for any of this. Not even Ramsey's training, which had been little more than lectures and printed sheets of paper to while away the hours as his men had sought traces of the Ravenscars. Facts and details didn't comprise reality, and his instructions had left her no more prepared for this environment than her fairy tales had left her prepared for marriage.

"Boję się, Devon," Cai said, whimpering. He knew her name, at least.

"Don't you remember *any* English?" she asked, wishing for the millionth time she'd not let the knights take him out of her sight. "How about German? I've eaten some German fairy tales. Sprichst du Deutsch?"

"To nie jest moje ciało," he said, large dark eyes welling up. "Powiedz mi, dlaczego mam to ciało?"

So much for German, then. If only her fairy tale selection had been bigger and included a bit of Eastern European literature.

"It'll be reet," Devon lied, and brushed his tears away with a thumb. An aunt had said that on the day of her first wedding, and that had been a lie, too. "We're going to take a trip. A fun journey."

His tears didn't stop. He'd never been anywhere except Easterbrook Manor or the knights' compound, and his first feed had been hauntingly traumatic. Cai was terrified and hurting.

How did one soothe a mind eater child in distress? Not like she could buy him a lollipop. When he was a baby she would let him nurse to settle, but he was too old for that now, and her milk had dried up long ago.

It struck Devon with painful clarity that she did not know how to be a mother, not to Cai or to anyone else. She was supposed to have left her children already, the sacrosanct role of parenting transitioned over to an entire manor full of aunts. She sailed now in uncharted waters.

At the moment, she couldn't even get him to stop crying. Could she buy him a toy, or another distraction? Something to do, read, take his mind off whatever imbalance he was experiencing. Was that good parenting, or bad?

Devon decided that *good* and *bad* didn't matter in the face of necessity. She sat them both down on a bench outside Oxford station and rifled through her messenger bag for cash.

Sifting through the crumpled bills, she was startled to find not only the money Ramsey had forced her to take, but also her three fairy tale books and Jarrow's little Game Boy. Either the knights hadn't bothered to deprive her of those things, or else they felt it made her faux escape look more authentic.

"Hey," she said, taking out the Game Boy. "Want to give this a play? A friend of mine gave it to me."

Cai didn't even look at her. "Mały chłopiec zniknął." He wrapped both arms tight around his knees as he rocked back and forth on the bench. "Nie, nie. Jestem teraz małym chłopcem!"

Devon switched the console on, screen brightening. Mario cohered into existence as a series of pixels, accompanied by a fanfare of bleeping music. The landscape depicted a sketchy mimicry of nature.

Cai gave a shuddering hiccup, but his attention perked a little at the sight of the console. He seemed puzzled, and curious.

"Like this." Devon pressed buttons to make Mario move. "The princess has been kidnapped, and you're trying to rescue her. This is how you jump, and these things kill you. Look, I've died already on that mushroom." She couldn't keep the chagrin out of her voice. "But you come back when you die and you can keep trying, forever, until you win."

The ultimate fantasy, that. Games offered a dimension where one's mistakes had few, if any, permanent consequences. If only someone could reset the levels of her life, she thought. The changes she'd make. The princess she'd save.

Cai clutched the Game Boy awkwardly, fingers too short to hold it well. In biological terms he was a little young for such a game, but whichever poor soul he'd been fed was almost certainly older than three.

"Ciekawy," he mused, and began to play.

"Good lad." Devon scooped him up. Her son nestled in tight, playing *Mario* with utmost concentration, and she almost smiled.

For all that he spoke a language unknown to her, his memories blended with another soul she'd never met, he still smelled the same: warm, nutty skin and that faint sawdust scent to his dark curls. And for all that she had failed to comfort him with words, Devon reminded herself that he still clung to her, still hid himself against her shoulder. Some link between them lingered, despite the psychological confusion of his feeding. It was enough, for now.

Devon Fairweather walked into a train station for the first time in her twenty-seven years of life, messenger bag full of stolen cash on one shoulder and Cai monkeyed on her other hip. Her senses labored under fresh assault; the smell of moldy plastic and stale luggage. The chatter of people invading the spaces between her ears. A man yakking into his mobile phone walked straight into her, only to rebound in astonishment when she didn't budge. She ignored his swearing—couldn't he watch where he was going?—and kept moving.

Buying tickets felt like conducting a complex military operation. If the ticket counter gave her a raised eyebrow for paying with fifty-quid notes, so what. She didn't count the change because she didn't yet know how, and bumbled awkwardly around the station until she found the correct platform.

The train itself, at last. Collapsing into a pair of seats brought some relief. Fewer people were visible, the cushions were soft, Cai quiescent for the moment. He played on the Game Boy, muttering and exclaiming softly in Polish.

Outside her window the world slid by, the future drawing them down and southward. Toward her first contact on Ramsey's list. South was also where Jarrow was, she thought in a daze. Had to contact Jarrow, without the Family knowing. They would help each other. This was her best chance.

Possibilities eluded her when she tried to focus on them, and the train's repetitive motion was lulling her to drowsiness. Head against the cool glass of the window, Devon drifted into a tired sleep.

They arrived in Reading, a city Devon kept mistakenly pronouncing as *reeding*. She paid for a room in the first hotel they found, almost right across the street. Afterward, she curled up on a tiny, uncomfortable bed with Cai in her arms. Still tired despite all the sleep she'd had.

There was a lot Ramsey hadn't been able to teach her about the human world, probably because his own exposure was limited. Devon found she was physically superior, as she learned after her first disastrous handshake with a stranger, and she had a mental repository of books far higher than any human's.

Her book memory wasn't as useful as she'd hoped, though. She was culturally inadequate and spottily educated. Simple things like the process of buying items from shops, or how to take transport she understood. But other things eluded her. Major historical events and current affairs or politics were a bland list of bullet points in her head, divorced from emotional context or investment. The prime minister had done what? The queen snubbed who? Vague and convoluted, all of it.

After a whole entire week of being a stranger in a strange land, she finally worked out how to contact Jarrow.

Cash in hand, Cai sequestered safely in her room, Devon nipped down to a video game shop and picked up a copy of *Tomb Raider: The Last Revelation*. She paid the baffled cashier to write out her phone number as a string of Morse code on a bit of paper, watching carefully to make sure he got it right, then slipped the fragile scrap of contact inside the game's case and dipped into a post office.

"I'm so sorry, but could you write this address out for me? I've injured my hands and need to send this package to Jarrow Easterbrook, at Gladstone Manor in London. What? No, um, I don't know the post code, I'm afraid—"

The man behind the counter sucked his teeth sullenly. Not to be dissuaded, Devon simply repeated her request until he gave in, looked up the post code, and wrote it all out. She put on her best smile and walked slowly through the surging crowds back to her hotel room.

A video game was now carrying her phone number all the way to Jarrow. The Morse code would identify her as the sender, hopefully without tipping anyone else off, not that she expected anyone to go through Jarrow's mail. Better safe than sorry, of course. Then, if he were able, he'd call her, get in touch, reconnect. *Help* her as he'd promised. And maybe, just maybe, she'd be helping him, too.

Only—whispered a tiny voice in her head, as she eased through the revolving doors—it'd been more than three years since she'd seen him, shuffled away from her by angry Winterfields amidst the chaos that had followed Cai's birth and Matley's furious attack.

Since then, anything could have happened. Perhaps Jarrow had been sent elsewhere, or simply moved on. He had Vic now, after all; that might be enough for him. She believed he'd seek her out if she sent word, and hoped he would, but could not count on it or be certain of it. Devon decided to give it three months, then reassess.

In the meantime, she had some Ravenscars to find.

28

NYCTERIS FOLLOWS THE FIREFLY

TWELVE MONTHS AGO

Nycteris followed the firefly, which, like herself, was seeking the way out.
—George MacDonald, *The History of Photogen and Nycteris*

Seeking out the Ravenscars proved to be a brutal education.

Tracking down one of their former drug suppliers was straightforward enough with the address Ramsey had given her. She walked to their basement flat in the city, stinking of fumes and stagnant water. Four men were inside, faces matching the descriptions she'd been given.

She had never before spoken to humans who dealt in drugs or other illicit trade and assumed, wrongly, that they'd be willing to talk or trade. Instead, they saw her as an opportunity: a woman alone, naïve and uncertain, the perfect trafficking victim. When they finished laughing at her requests, they tried to capture her.

Her first punch broke a man's neck. Her first kick crushed another man's ribs. The other two went down moments later under her frenzied, terrified onslaught. She fled the premises, flustered by her accidental kills and also furious that they had even *dared*.

Later, limping back through gum-scabbed streets lined with faded brick buildings, it occurred to her that she should have approached with more tact. Strange, grim-faced women turning up at illicit warehouses and demanding addresses of secret clients wasn't anyone's idea of diplomacy. She lacked experience, in that regard.

At least there was a whole list of other names and places to try. But the first encounter had alarmed Devon badly. She dreaded trying again. Her phone still did not ring, Jarrow's silence another weight on her mind. She should have gone straight to the next town and yet, somehow, days slid into another week.

Meanwhile, she bought a Polish phrasebook to eat so she could talk to Cai, and bought glossy mags and TV guides and books on culture or politics so that she could talk to humans. Sometimes she ate them with ketchup as Jarrow had taught, to take the edge off that plastic taste.

In those days Cai wasn't perpetually weak from near-constant starvation, nor had she yet fallen into the routine of stalking the next victim. They spent many quiet hours walking in parks or woodlands, expanding the scope of their little world. Still lonely, but at least they weren't bored.

"Tęsknię za domem, ale to miejsce jest ładne," he said once, and she nodded in relief to hear his approval. This city *was* nice, in its way.

She thought about taking him to playgrounds, decided it was too risky; his tongue might show. He couldn't hide it well and lisped strongly when he spoke. To avoid problems, they often went out in the evening or early morning, when fewer humans were around.

And the humans themselves were a challenge to her preconceptions. Women in the wider world dressed differently than her aunts or herself. Her long linen skirts drew abundant stares in public. Someone asked her, once, if she were part of a historical reenactment. Devon said yes and made a fast exit, because it seemed the safest answer.

Sometimes, she would watch humans while out and about: this heaving mass of folk, so like and unlike her. Watched women wear jeans and hold hands in public, watched men get married to other men openly—not meeting discreetly like Family brothers did. The openness of their affection captured her curiosity. She bought sunglasses and wore them often, so that she could scrutinize strangers without anyone noticing.

She went to a charity shop and bought the strangest, most daring books she could find. Things she'd never have been allowed to consume while growing up. Then spent a week eating them.

Gender, sexuality, beliefs, and relationships branched out into endless layers of complexity, stunning her in their variety compared to the narrow sliver she'd experienced growing up. In books, in life, in the world around.

Soon after, she went back to the charity shop and bought new clothes. Jeans, dark slogan T-shirts, lace-up shoes made from dead cow. No idea yet what she liked, but she was going to find out. The linen skirts and long dresses she threw away. No one should have to wear them.

The same day, she bought scissors and, standing in front of the bathroom mirror, cut her braids off. The reflection staring back at her was no princess, but it was *her*. That gave her savage satisfaction. As if she'd shed a false skin.

Another week of that musing, meandering life and her phone rang. Devon's heart jumped, but it was only Ramsey. Filled with chagrin, she pressed to answer.

"You fucking idiot!" Somehow, he managed to snarl across electronic distance. "What are you doing? This isn't a goddamn bloody holiday!"

"I—"

"Human women do not wander around a city at two A.M. with their small children. You look conspicuous, you look odd, no Ravenscar would come within a mile of you, and I have had reports from a book eater who *sighted* you in the city. Do you know how difficult that's made my life?"

"How should I know what to do, I'm not one of them!" she bit back, finally getting a word in. "I'm learning, all right?"

"Well, learn faster! No more night walks, and clear out of Reading ASAP," he snapped. "You're supposed to be a fugitive. Start acting like it!"

He hung up.

Devon put her mobile down and looked at Cai, who was watching a black-and-white silent film on the television. He hadn't noticed her call, and anyway he still didn't know English.

"We need to leave," she said, speaking to him in dictionary-stilted Polish. "For a new city." There were plenty of places on her list.

Later that evening, Devon caught a bus in the pouring rain with a damp and grumpy Cai at her side. They sat near the front, because for reasons she couldn't fathom other humans seemed to prefer sitting in the back. Devon liked the wider view.

Reading slid away, its redbrick buildings and throngs of university students left behind in the growing gloom. Devon watched it through grotty windows with the mobile phone nestled in her lap.

"Głodny," Cai said, palm pressed to belly. "Głodny, Devon."

She winced. "I know, love. I'll get you something to eat. Very soon." She'd been dreading his hunger, unsure how to go about capturing someone for him. The idea gave her pangs of anxiety. Ramsey had suggested children; the idea made her sick. She resolved not to do that unless truly, truly desperate.

How, then, did one choose? Perhaps she could feed Cai the so-called "undesirable" humans: the killers, thieves, and rapists. Pretend she was a kind of vigilante people-cleaner, like the brooding heroes in Jarrow's graphic novels.

But eating each person had been hugely affecting for Cai, and Ramsey's offhand indication that *this is normal* had frightened her badly. She feared giving her son someone twisted or unkind to consume, and the mental corruption that would cause him. For Cai's sanity and mental well-being, she'd have to choose good people.

That in itself was a dilemma. Who was good, or even just good *enough*? What did goodness mean? How did she assess it? And what did that say about her, choosing the kindest and sweetest strangers she could find, all for her son's sake? If he became a "good" person from eating good people, would he not struggle with the morality of it all?

It would be the first of many such choices. She hated how hard it was; she dreaded that it would get easier.

Maybe "normal" strangers would do, ordinary people with ordinary lives. She tried to conjure up an idea of what an ordinary human was like, and could only think of peasants in fairy tales, or the servant staff in old English classics. And, more unnervingly, of the four drug dealers she'd killed.

The narrowness of her experience appalled her, this skewed intersection of sheltered privilege and lifelong abuse. Even after all the books she'd read and the new experiences she held, Family biases limited her parameters.

Like Nycteris, she thought, and cringed.

There was an old fairy tale called *The History of Photogen and Nycteris* that she still carried a copy of. The main character in it was a young woman who had been raised by a cruel witch, inside a cave beneath a castle. The girl had grown up knowing only darkness, which at the time hadn't seemed much of an issue to child-Devon.

But the general idea was that Nycteris's world was narrow: she thought the lamp in her cave was a sun, and that the universe was just a tiny series of rooms. She knew nothing of society and had very few books. A relatable situation, for a book eater woman.

One day, Nycteris escaped her cave by following a stray firefly. She ended up in the castle garden. But her reactions in the story were strange and unexpected. Upon espying the moon for the first time, Nycteris decided that it must be a giant lamp, akin to the one in her cave. She saw the sky, and likewise decided it must be another kind of roof. And when she looked at the horizon, she saw not a limitless world, but merely another room, albeit with distant walls.

The concept of *outside* didn't exist for one such as Nycteris, nor could it ever. Her upbringing had given her such a fixed perspective that, even when encountering something new, she could only process it along the lines already drawn for her.

The story's complexity had baffled Devon as a child, but she understood it well enough now. The truth was, Nycteris never really escaped. Oh, she got a prince and a castle and the cruel witch died at the end. But Nycteris could not ever leave the cave, because the cave was a place in her mind; it was the entire way she thought about reality.

Princesses like that couldn't be rescued.

Devon's last thought before falling asleep on the bus was to wonder if actually, she'd had it the wrong way around. Maybe *everyone* was living in a cave, and Nycteris was the only person smart enough to recognize it.

———•———

The bus arrived in Eastleigh, another town whose name Devon found confusing to pronounce. Her geographical knowledge was scatty, even with the maps she'd eaten.

"Głodny," Cai pleaded as they exited the station in near-torrential rain. "Głodny, głodny, głodny!"

"I'll get you food, very soon." Devon hugged him close, then yanked back in alarm when he nuzzled at her ear.

She should have found him someone sooner. Much sooner. Only, it filled her with horror, the idea of "hunting" a victim; she wasn't ready. She would never be ready.

But Cai was starving. She was running out of time.

They found another hotel—good God, why did everything cost so much? There had to be a cheaper solution—and left him alone, again, with just the Game Boy and the television. Time to feed her son. Somehow, she had to do it, manage it.

Through pure happenstance, Devon sourced her first victim before she'd hardly gone a block. An inebriated old man started swaying after her down the street, asking if she had a spare fiver for a drink and hey hey, where ya going, girl, on those big tall legs of yours?

Devon stopped, turning back to look at him. "Are you a good person?" And then, because that didn't seem specific enough, she added, "Are you kind?"

"Huh?" He squinted, eyes red from too much whiskey. "Will ya gimme a fiver if I say yes, tall girl?"

Over sixty years old, she reckoned, if he was a day. Long enough to have lived a full life.

"Sure, I'll take you back to my room and give you a fiver if you say yes." She regretted the offer almost instantly. He was sure to misinterpret what she meant and say whatever he thought she wished to hear.

But he surprised her by pausing and giving the question serious consideration. The rain came back in a depressed drizzle and still he stood, musing, a little sad, very drunk.

"I wanted to be good," he said eventually. "When I were younger. Me mam would've liked me to be a good bloke. But being good is hard, bloody hard. Life keeps grabbing ya by the collar, kicking you about."

"True that." Devon felt an unexpected heat behind her eyes. "Come on, I'll bring you out of the rain. I'm not offering you my bed, but I'll get you a drink and some cash, aye?"

So simply and easily was a life given away. If shame were an open wound, his handshake was a dose of salt and lemons.

Devon brought him upstairs to a starving Cai, then locked herself in the bathroom and cried into her fluffy hotel towels while her son fed to satiation outside. She kept fingers in her ears and the phone resting on her knees, always present, in case Jarrow called.

He didn't call. The mobile lay silent, inert and indifferent to her prayers like one of the humans' innumerable distant gods.

At last, all quiet in the room beyond.

Devon got up and exited her refuge. A messy scene greeted her, of sheets and blankets tumbled to the ground. A chair knocked over. Cai lay fast asleep on an unmade bed next to the old man's cooling body. Peace in the midst of that chaos.

These were the early days, before Devon had learned to be careful, or what the phrase *ongoing police investigation* might mean in relation to victims left behind. She simply carried the corpse to the bathroom and left him propped up against the toilet. He hadn't survived the feeding.

A problem for tomorrow. Grief rendered her exhausted and she needed sleep.

Later that night, crammed into the single bed, Cai talked to her while dozing on her arm.

"I never hurt anybody," he muttered. "Only a little. Only when she were getting on me nerves. Them fucking coppers, always taking the woman's side. God, I loved her, but I were no good to her. I coulda been a good man, if only I'd not loved." He twisted around. "My missus cried like you do. But I didn't do aught to you, only her. Why're you crying, tall girl?"

"It's too hard to be good," she said through clenched teeth. "Life keeps grabbing me by the collar, kicking me about."

"Ain't that the way of it," said her son, and for a horrible inside-out minute she felt as if it were Cai who'd died, his body inhabited by the spirit of the old man he'd absorbed. But then he said, with a crisper accent, "Good night, Devon. I'm so glad I know English again."

"Night, love," she managed, choking out the words from some withered memory of maternal comfort. "Sleep well."

Long after Cai, or whoever he was now, drifted to sleep, the weight of everything settled across her like a second skin, tightening until she could hardly breathe or move. It occurred to her that she could just leave. Get up, walk away. A few days from now, Ramsey would detonate that bomb and Cai would be no more. Meanwhile, she herself would be fleeing somewhere, fast, solo, off on adventures and cut loose at last—

The compass slid cold against her chest. Clarity doused her nerves like a bucket of water to the face. Leaving him was not an option. Courage, she told herself. Breathe in, breathe out; endure.

She squeezed the compass tight. The important thing was to focus on her goal. To not let Ramsey and Uncle Aike and Matley and all the rest win; to not fail Cai as she'd already failed Salem.

Focus.

Find Jarrow.

Lay out her plan, get him on-side.

Find the sodding Ravenscars.

Steal drugs for Cai.

And after that—

In the still darkness of her hotel room, the phone began to ring, rattling the bedside table with its vibrations. She scrambled for the mobile, flipping open the clamshell lid.

An unknown number, using an unfamiliar area code.

Her heart pounded a frantic rhythm. "Hello?"

"It's me." Ragged, tired, reedy and—unmistakably—Jarrow Easterbrook. "I got your package, but I can't talk long on here. How far are you from Brighton?"

ACT 5
HIGH
NOON

29

GRENDEL AND HIS MOTHER

PRESENT DAY

Maybe every monster is a miracle meant to change the world.
—Maria Dahvana Headley, *The Mere Wife*

The room Cai had chosen was a big, overdecorated space, reminiscent of the quarters Devon had occupied as a girl in Fairweather Manor. Teak shelves and faded paintings of frog-eyed humans jostled for space, overlooking a four-poster bed and scattered furniture. The fireplace was cold and once-lush wallpaper peeled and flaked, patches of it subtly mottled by rising damp.

Cai sat on the bed, legs crossed and back to her, bent over something. Devon assumed it was the Game Boy until she spotted the little console resting next to him atop the duvet.

"Hey." She crossed the oak-paneled floors on still-bare feet, filthy from miles of travel, and perched on the duvet next to her son. "What's up?"

Cai twisted around and glowered with such hostility that she stopped abruptly.

"Someone's been texting you," he said. And held out her phone, the one she'd left behind for her conversation with Killock and Hester.

New Message, the icon declared. Three of them, in fact, and all from Ramsey.

"That's mine," Devon said stupidly, and reached to take the mobile off him.

But Cai withdrew from her, holding the phone close. "I heard your phone beeping, so I checked it. Who are you texting? I thought you only used this to find the Ravenscars' suppliers."

Her voice had disappeared along with her courage, and she wished the ground could swallow her whole. This wasn't how she'd wanted her confession moment to go. All the danger Devon had faced in her life and yet, somehow, this was the most afraid she'd ever been.

"Why are you hiding things from me?" He was beginning to redden, a slow flush creeping up his neck. "I thought you were the one person I could trust, who's supposed to be on my side! Who is texting you?"

"It's a long and complex explanation," she said, sounding weak even to herself.

"Then explain it!" He glared at her from under a mop of dark curls. "You're lying to everyone about something and I'm tired of it. *Who is texting you?*"

"One of my brothers," she snapped, then clapped both hands over her mouth because she hadn't meant to shout at him. The strain of a long, conflict-laden day.

Cai's hostility melted into shock. "You have brothers?"

"Of course," she said wearily. "Everyone in a manor is related to each other, so all the Fairweather men are my brothers or uncles." Or father.

"But you never talk about them!"

"No, I don't." Devon exhaled through her nose. She'd never talked about childhood adventures with Ramsey, or the heather-grown moors full of rabbits and foxes. About breaking into forbidden library wings or scrambling on parapets. To Cai, the Families were simply a shadowy fear in perpetual pursuit of him. "You're right. I've been hiding things from you."

"No shit!"

"Hey! Watch your mouth."

"Watch *my* mouth? You're the bloody liar!"

Devon jammed both hands behind her back to keep from slapping him. "I'm your protector. Your mother. I do what I need to. Are you going to hear me out, or not?"

"Hear *what*?" he shouted, tearful with brimming emotions; still a child at heart. "I thought we left the Families behind and you're talking to them in secret!"

"I have no choice!" She caught him by the shoulders, gripping hard. "You're carrying a surgically implanted explosive in the peritoneal cavity of your abdomen, which the knights deliberately put there. Do you understand the words I'm saying?"

Cai hiccupped and choked at the same time, too startled to protest or twist away from her touch as he usually did.

"I don't know whether to be relieved or exasperated that you never asked about the scar on your belly, or the missing eight months of your life," she said. "Do you remember *anything* at all between eating Matley, and arriving at the Oxford train station?"

"Flashes," he said in a small voice. "Just bits."

"You asked me for the truth," she said. "Here's some truth. We didn't escape after killing Matley. The knights caught us and took us to their base just outside of Oxford. In exchange for not killing us, they charged me with hunting down the Ravenscars, who had disappeared, and finding their Redemption drug, which the knights want. And to make sure I stayed loyal, they fitted you with an implanted explosive."

Cai's mouth hung open; he looked stricken.

"I have to report in every two weeks, or you die." Devon let go of him to rake both hands through her hair. "I do everything they ask, or you die. I've found the Ravenscars like they wanted, and the drugs like they wanted, but once they arrive you'll still die at the press of a button. Unless I take some rather drastic action."

"Why didn't you tell me this?" He lifted the hem of his shirt with one hand, seeking the scar. Hovering a palm above it with newfound anxiety, as if touch alone might set the damn thing off.

"Because you have spent the last two years struggling not to starve to death. You didn't need any extra worry of some uncontrollable death threat hanging over your head." She gestured helplessly. "I would have told you when the time is right."

"When would that be?" He dropped his shirt, anger reasserting itself. "Right when we're trying to leave? After we put a foot wrong and I blow up, maybe? You always *do* this, Devon. Make decisions for me and drag me around. Why don't you trust me? Give me a say?"

She flinched. "You were so small when we left home. Barely out of babyhood. And now you're—"

"Twenty-five different adults," he said, the answer ready-fire. "I'm not like other kids. I should get a say in what we're doing, especially if it affects me. You had over a year to tell me. I deserved to know sooner. Not *the day of* whatever you're doing."

She groaned, holding up both hands. "Aye, I know. Truly, I'm sorry I didn't explain sooner. There just never seemed to be a right moment."

"And *this* is a right moment?"

"Well—"

"Seems like a late moment to me!"

"Look, I'm sorry, all right?"

"Don't say that," he huffed at her, lower lip sticking out. "*Sorry*s are just something you say to avoid doing anything different or better."

"Jesus fuck," she said, stung.

"I don't want your stupid grown-up apologies," he said. "I hate hearing you say you're sorry!"

She was still reeling from his first broadside. "What *do* you want, then? What can I say or do that will make a difference?"

"Give me the truth from now on. Always and every time." He scowled, small and fierce. "Promise me you won't lie again. At least, not to me. Little or small, I want all the truth, always."

She opened her mouth to tell him *I can't promise that* because how could she? Who knew what the future would require of her, what sacrifices or private decisions she'd have to make?

The sight of his pale, anxious face killed those excuses dead. In a life of endless chaos and uncertainty, she had become Cai's only constant. Her decisions had already damaged and taxed the trust between them; if she didn't draw a line right now, their relationship might break down completely.

Devon could not keep him safe if he didn't trust her.

"I promise," she said, sticking out a hand and trying not to sound reluctant. "Shake on it, aye? No more lies between us. Even if the truth is painful, and it will be at times." She yelped at his pincer grip, adding, "I can't promise that to other people, though. Only for me and you."

"Other people aren't family," he said, withdrawing his hand as if she were acidic to the touch. "We're family, *real* family, so we can't lie to each other."

Devon didn't know whether to laugh or cry. She settled for snorting and scrubbing her eyes to dry them.

"Truth, then," he said, stubborn as hell. Stubborn as her. "Why is your brother texting you?"

"My brother is a knight," she said. "His name is Ramsey Fairweather, and he implanted you with *that*."

She pointed at his scar and launched into the same explanation she'd given Hester. Family patriarchs who sought to phase out dragons, and rebellious knights who were alarmed by the ebbing of their power. Ravenscar twins who triggered the whole fallout by upending their manor. And herself, caught in the middle, teetering between factions. All while sweating from anxiety that someone would walk in on them, or that Cai would decide he'd heard enough and storm off.

But he didn't storm off. Her son sat perfectly still, forehead furrowed and eyes dancing back and forth sightlessly: the enormous intellectual power of twenty-five adults at his disposal.

"Neither Family nor knights will let you live, even if you do whatever it is they're asking," he said, when she had trailed into silence. "Agreeing to work for the knights has only bought a little more time, at best."

"Exactly." Devon brushed a stray hair out of his eyes, oddly pleased to be having a chat with someone who understood. What a relief to not just be wrestling with everything on her own, in silence. "Here's the thing: all you and I need is a cure for mind eating, and a solution for that explosive. The rest is peripheral to us, existing only as an obstacle. If we get those two things, we can just *walk away* and never look back."

He rested his chin on a fist. "The cure is here, if we can get it."

"We can, I think. I've been talking to Mani, the human man who does a lot of the grunt work for Killock. He's going to help us out, in exchange for coming with us."

"Oh yes, that man," Cai said. "Okay. What's the solution for this . . . thing inside me?" He was holding his abdomen again, fingers splayed against his shirt.

"A friend has been working on that."

"Since when do you have friends?"

She swatted at him. "A man called Jarrow, who is helping me escape. The Game Boy you own belonged to him. He gave it to me, and I to you."

"I see," he said, and she wondered if he really did. "Where is he?"

"Traveling up from London. I'm scheduled to meet him tomorrow morning in person. Before we escape."

"Will everyone here die, after we escape?" Cai actually squeezed her hand. "You'll tell me the truth, right? If you think lots of people will die, you won't lie?"

"No more lies between us. I promised." She squeezed back. "I don't know if everyone will die. If my plan works out, we'll have enough time to leave, and then give the Ravenscars some warning so they can clear off if they wish." If they believed her warning and could get organized in time.

"What about Hester?"

"I've told her the truth, before coming to see you," she said, embarrassed all over again that her son was the last person to find out. "She's thinking about it. I'm not sure she's convinced, though."

Cai pulled at his bottom lip. "All our options are dangerous and hurtful."

"I'm afraid so." She caught herself on the edge of apologizing.

"No matter what choice we take, someone will always suffer in some way," he said, a little sadly. "I gave a sermon on that once."

She couldn't let that slide. "Not you. The vicar did."

"Is there a difference? If you eat something and then go for a hike, do you say *my food hiked up a mountain today* or is it just a part of you?"

"You've lost me, love."

"Never mind." He sighed. "Is there really no other way, Devon?"

"If there is," she said, "then I've not thought of one, even after all these months."

"And now we're out of time," he said, looking at the clock, then at the sky visible through their bedroom window. "No more lies, but it's too late for me to make choices. The only way is your way now." He paused. "Do I even want to go with you, when you leave?"

The question hurt; she tried not to let it show. Tried to focus on the right words to say.

"No, Cai, you do not have to come with me. I'm going to help you escape from here, with enough Redemption to live on, but you're not a child the way other children are. If you wish to be free of me as well, then I won't stop you going, once I've got you out."

She would never keep him bound, the way the Family had kept her. Devon had strong feelings on that one.

He looked at her sidelong. "Wouldn't you hate me if I left you?"

"No. Never. No matter what you did."

"Really? Even if I betrayed you?" He was studying her intently now, scalpel-sharp. "Even if I ran and told Killock everything and then I lived here with him and we ate people together like brothers, for the rest of our lives?"

"I'd think you were making a mistake, but yes, even then."

He mulled that over, still fiddling with her phone, and she felt like a prisoner awaiting their sentence: resigned, almost at peace.

Into the breathy silence between them, Cai held out the phone to her and said, "I want to stay with you. Even though you lied about so many things."

She couldn't not ask. "Why?"

"Because you're a monster. Like that man said, the night I ate Matley." He scooted over and gave her a hug, thin arms circling her waist; a surprise. "A mean, tall, angry monster who looks out for me."

"Oh. Is that a compliment, then?" Devon said, a little faintly, and indulged herself by hugging him back.

"I know what Matley thought of me. Everyone is scared of me, even the other mind eaters here. You're not scared of me because you're an even bigger, meaner monster than me," Cai said, face muffled against the join of her shoulder. "You'd eat the whole world to help me out and I think I'd do that for you, too. You're my monster and I'm yours, and even though I'm sad you lied to me and I'm sorry that we have to hurt more people, we must go together because we are a monster family."

Only pride kept her tears at bay. "I'm glad," she said, trying and failing to not sound choked. "Understatement of the year, but—I'm glad."

"I do have one condition," said Cai, twisting his face up toward hers. "I want to come meet your friend, when you see him tomorrow. You know, Mr. Game Boy guy. Can you tell me more about him?"

30

HAPPILY NEVER AFTER

TEN MONTHS AGO

The prince heard a voice and thought it was familiar. He advanced toward it, and as he approached, Rapunzel recognized him, and crying, threw her arms around his neck.

—The Brothers Grimm, "Rapunzel"

It'd been so incredibly long since something had gone right.

Devon hummed happily all the way from Eastleigh to Southampton, was still humming when she caught a straightforward train to Brighton with Cai in tow. She endured a call from Ramsey at noon railing about "obvious victims" left in hotel bathrooms and police who sought a woman of her description. She promised to do better and shrugged it off. They were already on the move, what was the fuss?

"I don't like traveling." Cai had scarcely looked up from *Mario,* preferring to hide himself in the safety of the game, but he'd put the console down long enough to frown out the window. "Where are we going now?"

"To the seaside." Salem would have wanted to go to the seaside, she thought disconnectedly. Shells and sand. "You'll like it. Even better than where we were before."

He pulled a four-year-old's pout and said in an old man's voice, "Can I have a lager? I miss having a lager with me lunch."

"Um. No."

Less than an hour later, Brighton rolled into sight with its mix of souvenir shops and authentically archaic buildings. The tail end of February was not a popular time to visit, and the streets were eased of their burdensome tourists.

She paid an exorbitant amount of money for a hotel room, this time by the sea. And then, because neither she nor Cai had ever seen a beach before, let alone the ocean, they walked down to have a look. It was en route to the pier anyway.

Beaches in books were soft, friendly, sandy places, warm and deliciously tropical; Devon's fiction-fed imagination had prepared her with such imagery.

Brighton defied that utterly. Instead of sand, the shore was comprised of pebbles and rocks that bit Devon's feet, just small enough to get stuck between her toes while still large enough to dig deep. The sky was a smear of rotten gray, the ocean a cold soup of bitter salt that left a silty residue on her skin.

"Amazing," Devon murmured, and Cai nodded emphatically in agreement.

It was the most beautiful place they'd ever seen. Raw. Real. *Authentic.* Hard-edged, and unpretentious. In another life, she might have stayed here forever, lingering on that boundary between sea and earth. The kind of place you could get lost, and find yourself. If ever they made it anywhere safe, Devon hoped it would have a rocky beach to wander on.

Despite the unfriendly weather and lack of tourists, the boardwalk was populated with small carnival rides, each plagued by a handful of human children in coats and shoes. She and Cai wore only jeans and short-sleeved T-shirts, and Devon realized they stood out in a bad way. They'd need coats as the weather got colder, if they wished to fit in.

"Can we go on the rides tomorrow?" Cai said, awed and oblivious to her self-consciousness. Almost no trace of the old man when he was excited, a thing she found curious and hopeful.

"Aye, why not."

They walked along the waterline for a while, ambling slowly toward the Palace Pier. A handful of swimmers braved the sinking light and single-digit temperatures. Devon scanned every face that passed; none were her Easterbrook prince. Shouts and laughter from elsewhere on the seaside peppered her peripheral hearing. Groups coalesced and dispersed.

The tide washed low, leaving strips of pebbles for them to clamber on beneath the pier in wet shoes and spray-lashed jeans. Devon paused beneath the beams, inhaling the tangled scents of salt and wood-rot. Lapping water threw wet echoes around the pier's cavernous underside.

Somewhere in the city, a cathedral clock struck a late hour. No sign of Jarrow.

"I'm bored now," Cai said. "Can we go sleep? Or watch the telly." He had stopped asking to go home in recent weeks, having finally understood that Easterbrook Manor was lost to them forever.

"Yes," she said, "we'll go back to the hotel."

Devon pivoted, crunching up the rocky sand. If Jarrow did not show then she would simply manage on her own. Hadn't she always, in the end?

A glimpse of movement caught her eye, too fast and fleeting for a human, and she paused. Devon saw perfectly well in the dark, but here beneath the Palace Pier where the wooden beams rose like a branching forest, it was difficult to get a good line of sight.

"Why are we stopping?" Cai wheedled, tugging at her hand. His childish lisp was particularly strong just then. "*Corrie*'ll be on the telly soon. I like catching a bit of *Corrie*."

No, the old man liked *Corrie*. "You've never seen a single episode," she retorted, then regretted the careless words immediately when his eyes filled with tears. Not his fault; none of it was his fault. "Sorry, I didn't mean that. We'll head back so you can catch *Corrie*, aye?"

She wasn't even sure what this show *was*, just some kind of soap opera thing. But so what, she thought. It mattered to him. And it cost her nothing to indulge his interests, regardless of their source.

"Okay." He sniffed and wiped his nose on her sleeve, mollified for the moment.

They picked their way up the pathless gravel beach. This time, when that same flicker of movement tracked in the corner of her vision, she didn't stop or look sideways. Definitely not human.

In a handful of minutes she was off the shorefront, across the road, and bundling Cai up a set of stairs to their expensive-in-cost, but cheap-in-furnishings room. She turned on the television, helped him find his silly program while he sprawled on the bed.

"I need to go back out," she said, careful to sound casual. "I think I've dropped my phone on the beach. Will you be all right here?"

His gaze flickered briefly at the mini fridge. "I'll be fine."

Devon frowned. "For the last bloody time, you're barely four years old, you don't need—and cannot drink—any lager. Touch that fridge and I'm chucking out the Game Boy."

"Okay, okay." He scowled. "I won't have any."

"Good lad."

Back out to the promenade, the sweetly darkening streets speckled with lights and laughter. Brighton did not want to sleep.

The beach, however, had emptied of people. Humans had enough sense to retreat from a cold, dark ocean they couldn't safely swim in. Devon huddled into herself, a habit she'd acquired over recent weeks in a bid to look shorter, and slouched down to the shorefront beneath the Palace Pier. She stumbled across the rocks in her unnecessary human sandals, the hems of her jeans already damp from trailing over wet ground.

Jarrow was waiting.

No hiding or skulking this time; he simply stood at the water's edge, hands in pockets. Almost motionless. The hoodie was gone, replaced by a nondescript bomber jacket of an out-of-date style better suited to a man twice his age. His curls were shorn into a military buzz cut. The beard was new and unruly.

He also wasn't alone. Next to him stood a tallish woman, feet bare. Her dark hair was bound in a Victorian bun and she wore a crocheted shawl like a Jane Austen heroine, albeit with Mediterranean coloring.

This, surely, was Victoria, the invisible presence whose vivacious personality had been stamped all over the games room at Easterbrook Manor.

"Hey," Jarrow said, without turning around. "Been a while."

Devon opened her mouth to say something sensible, and burst into tears.

Nearly four years since that fraught bedside good-bye and she was again unable to speak, this time hiccup-crying into her sleeve. Everything circling back, cycling round. The months of planning and silence; her uncertainty over his commitment; mutual courage, shared resolve. The long separation.

And in that time, what had she become, seen, done? Did he still know who she was—did she still know who *he* was? Their relationship was so fractured and disparate that she hardly dared call it a friendship at all.

Pull it together, Devon told herself, and wiped her nose on an already-soggy sleeve. "Sorry. How are you? I'm really sorry."

"Dunno what you're sorry for." Jarrow scooped up a stone and skipped it badly across the uneven salt water. "We're just enjoying nature. A nice, peaceful chat. Aren't we, Vic?"

Victoria Easterbrook nodded. Her gaze looked out over the sea; she seemed perpetually lost in thought.

"This is my sister, by the way," he said. "I've told her about you, and she was happy to come."

"Pleased to meet you, Vic." Devon cleared her throat, composure regrowing second by second.

Dark brown eyes met her gaze, then flicked away. Victoria said, with obvious effort, "Evening."

"We have good days and bad days," Jarrow said. "But she's feeling better than she did a few years ago—that's what she says, anyway."

"I'm glad to hear you're feeling better," Devon said, addressing the other woman. Privately, she wondered whether today was good or bad, and what the reverse looked like. To Jarrow, she added, "How's exile, princeling?"

He groaned. "Boring and privileged. *Stifling.* I do IT stuff. They still let me play games. Mostly, though, I get to see Vic. That's the main thing."

"Eye-Tea? Is that some kind of drink?"

"What? No, IT stands for information technology. Computers and the Internet and shit. The Families are trying to *get hip* with voice-to-speech programs. It's a way of writing without writing, you know?"

Devon shrugged. She didn't know. "I'm glad you're here. The knights are intermittently watching. I hope you don't get in trouble."

"Me too." Jarrow bent and gathered a handful of too-sharp pebbles in both hands, rattling them absentmindedly. "Sorry I didn't call sooner. Got the package, didn't open it, forgot about it, finally looked in it. And then took me a while to work up the courage to call, once I found your message and realized you were the sender. Also took me time to find a phone." He sighed, tumbling the pebbles back to the beach.

Victoria, despite her silence, angled her shoulders in their direction, listening intently.

"It doesn't matter," Devon said, the agony of past months already washing out of her. "You're here now. I'm grateful."

"I promised I'd get in touch. Couldn't leave you hanging."

"Bullshit. You absolutely could have done, and no one would have faulted you for it. I'm your brother's killer, after all." The last bit she said with a wrench of bitterness.

A satisfied smile ghosted Victoria's face, though it faded quickly.

"I don't believe that rumor for a second," Jarrow said. "That said, if you feel like telling me what really went down, I wouldn't mind hearing it from the horse's mouth, so to speak."

She did mind, but he deserved the truth.

Reluctantly, she talked about that night in a voice so quiet that the outgoing tide almost drowned out her story. Basic facts, simply stated, nothing more. Around them, the ocean clattered rocks together in slow, angry surges; the air was so thick with salt and damp that Devon thought she might pickle. Victoria listened, too, edging closer to Devon—though she still kept Jarrow in front, like some kind of body shield.

When the story finished, Jarrow said, "Matley's death was announced a couple days after you left. The knights have gone AWOL, far as we know, and the Easterbrooks blame you for everything."

"Are you okay with what happened?" The brothers hadn't got on, she knew. Still, Family was Family.

"It's two years ago. I've made my peace since then. We weren't exactly close, in any case." Jarrow rubbed his nose with the heel of his hand. "Speaking of relatives. Where's your son? I saw you walking with him earlier. He's really grown."

"Back in the hotel," she said, adding, "It's not his fault, the stuff with Matley. Don't be angry with him."

"I'm not angry. Told you, I made my peace." Jarrow began to pace back and forth with noiseless steps. "But a sting operation? Going after the Ravenscars?" He shook his head. "It's like a low-budget action film."

"The Ravenscars are very real," she said, "and so is their cure, if they still have it. Or use it."

"Why would they even deal with you? Why would . . . Oh, forget all that." Jarrow caught her arm gently. "None of this matters, Dev. Let's just leave it all behind, and their rubbish politics."

She blinked, brushing windswept hair out of her vision. "Leave it behind? You mean run away?"

Confusion creased his features. "Isn't that what you called me down here for? To talk about how to run away?" He gestured at his sister. "Vic and I are ready to go tonight, if need be."

"Today? Right now?" She laughed, even though nothing was funny. "Oh, Jarrow. Where would we go?"

Victoria had gone very still, her face pensive.

"Ireland, like I suggested before," he said immediately. "Doesn't have many people, and the Family has no reach there yet—"

"That doesn't work," she said. "My son has been fitted with a surgically implanted explosive. If I don't check in regularly, Ramsey will kill him from a distance."

"Ah," he said, "shit."

"*Ah shit* indeed."

"We can get around that," Jarrow said, rallying with a speed that impressed her. "If you know what kind of device, we should be able to interfere with the signal. Faraday cage, or a transmission blocker."

Devon wanted to hug him for that. Instead, she said quietly, "I have no doubt you're correct. But in many ways, that device is the least of my problems. My son also needs feeding every month, soon every fortnight. Eventually, he'll need someone every week. Even if we block that signal permanently and go live somewhere remote, where will we find food for him? A person a week for the rest of his life is no small matter."

"All good points," Victoria said softly. Her brother gave her a surprised glance.

"Running away will get him killed," Devon said. "Remote areas don't feed my son. However, if I do what the knights ask, Ramsey will still not let me live. There's no way out of this trap. There's no happy ending for me or my children." She kicked at the beach, sending sand and pebbles flying. "Do you see the bind I'm in?"

"Then that leaves one alternative," Jarrow said. "You know what I'm going to suggest, don't you?"

A raw wind scoured the shore, scattering water droplets, and Devon said, "No. I won't abandon Cai."

"Why *not*?" He flung his arms wide, making his question as big as the world. "At least consider it! Living remote would be easy for you and me. No special considerations. No drugs. No human victims. We could be in Ireland by *tomorrow* if we left tonight!"

"I said *no*. I'm not going to Ireland without my son, or anywhere else for that matter. I'm not leaving this city without him. I'm not abandoning him to starvation, or taking him away just to watch him become a monster. Even if it kills me."

Jarrow stared. "How can one child be worth the loss of everything else? How can you justify this cost?"

Victoria drew her shawl tight around herself. Her gaze was focused, thoughtful; weighing the pair of them.

Devon sought her compass, fingers curling tight around it. "Love doesn't have a cost. It's just a choice you make, the way you choose to keep breathing or keep living. It's not about worth and it's not about price. Those concepts don't apply."

A space of two breaths passed—her tense, him coiled. Elsewhere in the city, the clock struck 10 P.M. On the Palace Pier above, lights were dimming, some going out completely; fun had ended for the evening.

"Then I can't help you." His temple throbbed, veins strained against skin by high blood pressure. "I kept my promise. I came to see you, never minding the risk to me and Vic. But you won't save yourself, and you *can't* save your children. There is nothing I can actually do, I don't know why you bloody got in touch!"

Victoria reached out and laid a hand on her brother's arm. "Jarrow . . . be calm."

"I *am* calm," he groused. "She's the one being ridiculous!"

"Is that it, then?" Devon's cheeks stung from the wind, but her eyes were dry as a library shelf. "You'll just go back to Family life? Live like a peon, shunted from manor to manor. Complicit in trafficking, forced marriage, crimes—"

"It's better than dying!" he railed, terribly loud on that barren beach. "It's better than watching *you* die on a quest you can't win, for a monster you can't save. I have Vic to look out for and you're . . . you're a lost cause. Do you hear me? I have a fucking limit!"

"I don't," Devon said. "The Family took my limits away. Or motherhood did, I'm not sure."

"Your defining trait," he retorted, and she'd never heard him sound so bitter, so calcified. "Being unwilling to abandon your kids is why you're here, and it's why you'll die. Ramsey knows you won't abandon them and he's bloody using it against you."

"On the contrary. I think I can win this."

"Jarrow," Victoria said again, louder. She sounded exasperated.

"Just a sec, Vic. Listen, Dev, for the love of fuck! This is not, and never will be, a game you can win!"

"So let's exit the game," Devon said. "Stop being a piece. Change the rules."

Jarrow threw up his hands. "You just said that was impossible."

"Unless," she said, "we do what Ramsey wants, to a point. Find the Ravenscars, like he wants. Cai needs them anyway. *Then* we build your signal blocker, or your Faraday cage, whatever you called it, and take off into the night. With drugs for my son."

"That's the most ridiculous plan I've ever heard!" He glared at her, dusky skin flushed with fury. "There are a million sodding variables that need to fall into place and I refuse to be—"

"*Jarrow*," Victoria said, almost shouting. "We must help her!" She let go of her shawl entirely to shake her brother's arm, indifferent as the crocheted drape fluttered off her shoulders, tumbling across the beach.

"What?" he said, astonished. "Vic, you can't be serious!"

"I am utterly serious," she said, emphatic and deliberate. "We must help your friend, because no one ever helped me."

Her words might as well have been a sucker punch. Jarrow seemed to deflate, looking suddenly much older than his years and very tired.

"I hear you." Victoria swiveled up toward Devon, hair fraying loose in the persistent wind. "*I hear you,* Devon Fairweather, and I know you are right. Love has no cost for our children. Living or dead, here or gone."

"No cost," Devon agreed, and extended her hand.

After a moment, Victoria took it. Her grip had strength.

"Gods and demons help us." Jarrow scooped up a razor-sharp shell, running his thumb along its shattered edge. "All right, Dev. I'm listening. How are we going to play this?"

"By taking one step at a time." Devon flicked the compass open, turning slowly till the needle faced north, the sea at her back with all its endless strength. "Talk to me about signal blockers."

31

NO MORE SECRETS

PRESENT DAY

Almost a year since that meeting on the beach, and Devon was again walking to a crossroads of water and earth in search of Jarrow.

She and Cai had slept well, despite the stress of the previous days, or perhaps because of it, and risen very late. She insisted on a shower for both of them, before going anywhere. The bath was well stocked with expensive, if very out-of-date, soaps and shampoos. She poured a few bottles into the water, sluicing days of embedded grime off her skin.

Bath done, emptied, and refilled for Cai, Devon went poking around the wardrobes. None of the jeans or trousers were cut to her size. Something to shop for, while in town. She made do with a tartan skirt—floor length on most women, but just below the knee on her. It looked ridiculous, something an American tourist might wear, and didn't have any pockets. But it was clean, and that was enough for now.

Morning was tipping towards noon by the time she had set out with Cai, the pair of them ambling hand in hand through the gates of Traquair and down the single main road toward the town of Innerleithen.

Winter still clung to the land in strips and patches, thin fingers of frost grasping at the barren fields and speckling the leafless branches with ice. It was abnormally warm, the sun eroding yesterday's sleet, yet the sky predicted more snow. Typical English weather.

As the River Tweed came into sight, Cai said, "What did you say to the Ravenscars about us coming out here unsupervised?"

"I told the truth. I'm going shopping in town." Devon checked her wrist-watch: a little past 11 A.M. "And we will go shopping, because we have some things to purchase for our escape tonight. We'll also happen to drop by the island and pay a visit to Jarrow first."

"What about Hester?"

"What about her? She knows where our room is," Devon said uncomfortably. "She could have come by all morning and didn't. I thought I'd leave her in peace and not be a nag."

The main road led them to the shores of the River Tweed. A low, wide bridge banded the rushing water, the road leading over and onward toward the town of Innerleithen proper.

"Over there?" Cai pointed at the bridge.

"No, we're going along the bank," Devon said.

"But there isn't a road by the shoreline," he said.

"We follow that bike trail. See where it leads to that field, ahead of us? We can follow it to those islands."

They left the bridge behind and trekked through high grass, steep hills to their right covered in a patchwork of trees, before finally reaching a chained-up fence. The bike trail splintered off into a fisherman's footpath, leading straight to a steep bank.

Devon stopped at the edge. Below them, the Tweed tumbled fast and frothy between tree-lined shores. Tricky for a human, but easily fordable for her and Cai.

Ahead, she could finally see the riverine islands. The smallest of them was little more than a soft, raised mound of sand around which the water diverted. The largest had a sandy shore, however, with a small wood of densely tangled trees and foliage.

"I don't see anyone." Cai shaded his eyes, standing as tall as his low stature would allow. "Aren't they supposed to be here already?"

"He'll be there." She offered a hand. "Up on my back, you're small for this river."

Her son obliged and Devon stepped off the bank into the water, which came up to her thighs. The current streamed against her legs as she forded across. Spray flecked and foamed.

But the islands, when she slogged wetly up their shores, were empty. No sign that anyone had been recently, much less stayed on site. They crisscrossed the tiny patches of wooded land, the whole area roughly the size of Traquair's downstairs floor space, sandwiched by rushing water on either side.

"Could it be a different trio of islands?" Cai scratched at the eczema on his elbow.

"It's definitely these islands. There's nothing else even *resembling* a trio in these parts." A trickle of doubt crept up on her. Could she have got it wrong? Normally she wouldn't have worried, but in this case the consequences for such a banal mistake were enormous.

"Then they left early?" Cai, trying to be helpful by loading her with more things to worry about. "Or they got caught up in London last minute, or—"

Crunch. Crackle. Against the rustle of trees and the rush of nearby water, those footsteps echoed loud to sensitive book eater ears. Somewhere off to the northwest of them.

Devon cupped her hands together. "Hello?"

"It's me." Jarrow Easterbrook pushed through the last set of brambles, coming into view as he picked his way toward them, with Victoria at his side. She gave a wave, and even a smile.

"Apologies for the tardiness." He grinned that same sheepish grin. "We stayed overnight at a local B and B, and overslept this morning."

Devon thought he looked a bit like a displaced sixties grunge singer on a budget holiday. He wore hiking shorts that did not suit him, and hiking boots that did. His beard had gotten out of control, and a trace of early gray marked his temples.

She was also wildly, deeply, unabashedly glad to see him, and couldn't stop smiling.

"Hello, Devon." Victoria seemed calmer and more confident since they'd last spoken. "It's been a long time."

"I'm so glad to see you both," Devon said, the words heartfelt. "And it *has* been a long time."

"Getting sentimental in your old age, eh?" Jarrow leaned in to hug her, and it was as awkward as it was unexpected, a kind of lopsided, stiff clasp to the chest. Devon laughed, and returned the gesture.

Victoria hung back. She was staring at Cai now, who squinted at her with frank wariness.

"Glad you could make it." Jarrow held her at arm's length in a swift inspection. "Interesting skirt. Never had you down as a tartan person."

"Oh, well. When in Rome, aye?"

"Right. Just so." Jarrow shifted that piercing gaze to her son. "Hey, kid. You've grown. Last time we met, you were this big." His hands spanned a roughly baby-sized length in the air. "Let me introduce you to my sister, Vic. She's your aunt, by marriage."

Victoria's lips moved soundlessly. She swallowed, tried again. "I have two sons . . . somewhere."

Cai was speechless, transfixed by their appearance. For all that the Easterbrook siblings had varied in temperament and nature, they shared many of the same features: darkly curling hair, dusky skin, and hints of a Mediterranean heritage.

It was a heritage that Cai now bore, to some degree. And if Devon had been a stranger, looking at the two of them, she might well have been forgiven for assuming Jarrow and Cai were father and son, instead of second cousins.

"I still have your Game Boy," Devon said, rescuing the boy from his tongue-tied state. "Or rather, Cai has it. He's very fond of *Mario*."

Her son turned bright red and mumbled something incomprehensible.

"Well, that's something," Jarrow said. "If the lad is here, then I suppose you must have finally come clean about . . . what's inside him."

"Yes, he knows everything now."

"Glad to hear it." Jarrow took a seat on the nearest flat rock, pulling out a crudely made black plastic rectangle, roughly the size of a large mobile phone. "All right, real talk. I've built you a signal blocker—you can thank me later for eating dry, nasty manuals about bombs and RFIDs."

Devon had to refrain from snatching it out of his hands. "And it definitely works?"

Cai said, simultaneously, "What if the batteries run out?"

"Smart lad!" Jarrow took out a second, near-identical black device, holding both out. "I've built you a spare, which your mother can carry on her person. Keep batteries on both of you, always have one on when you're replacing batteries on the other. The closer this gets to crunch, the more likely Ramsey is to use his trigger." To Devon he said, "Yes, it will work. I've tested and tested this signal blocker across the past six months. Swear on my grave, Dev. No satellite signal or mobile signal will get through that. Make sure he keeps it on his body or very close by, at all times."

He held out the blockers, one to each of them. Cai flicked the switch to On and inspected it closely. Devon did the same. She willed her hands to stop shaking and when that didn't work, she settled for squeezing the signal blocker tightly.

It was extremely unlikely that Ramsey would set the thing off within the next few hours, not unless he wanted to alert the Ravenscars that something was drastically wrong, but she felt miles better for having the blocker in place all the same.

"As for the other things we talked about, it took me almost eight months, but I've learned to drive and got a fake license, at excruciating cost. We can take off for Ireland. I couldn't get you one without a photo—"

"Aye, it's fine. I knew that was unlikely."

"—but it's easy enough to get you and Cai across to Ireland itself. Hide in the car and we'll take the big ferry from Cairnryan to Belfast. Only person they'll check at the border is me."

"This is incredible." She was welling up. "What you've done . . . I'll never be able to pay you back."

"Love doesn't have a cost," he said, and gave her a squeeze around the shoulders with one arm. "You taught me that, Dev. Nothing's owed. No debt. What's the phrase you Northerners say? Oh, I remember. It'll—"

"—be reet," she finished, and they both smiled.

"What is our schedule?" Victoria hovered with nervous energy.

"Sorry. Schedules, yes." Devon ran a hand through her short hair. "Ramsey will be here around eleven P.M."

"You're sure of that?"

"Aye. He texted to confirm time and location yesterday, and I've replied to him, with Cai's help." She tapped her mobile phone. "The Redemption for Cai will be ready at seven P.M., courtesy of a human assistant who works in that house."

"A human?" Jarrow raised a doubtful eyebrow. "Are you sure that's a good idea, to involve other people?"

"If he doesn't come through, I'll sort things myself, but I do believe he is motivated to assist us," Devon said. "It's a long story, that one, so you'll have to trust me."

"Take things on trust? From you? What else is new," Jarrow said wryly.

"Yeah, yeah. Anyway, I hope that we can all be leaving once we've picked up Redemption. If you could pick us up with your car at that bridge back there, I'd be grateful." She hesitated. "And if things go wrong, if we don't turn up, then don't wait, all right?"

"I'll hang around till dawn, or till I see some sign of knights," he said gently, "whichever comes first. No later than that. But I'll give you every chance if I can."

"You already have, Jarrow." She rose to her feet. "I'm sorry to leave, but I have some things I need to buy in town before our journey. We'll get going and see you tonight, if that's all right."

Jarrow stood, too. "See you tonight, my friend."

———•———

"Are you worried?" Cai said as they tronked along the road into Innerleithen, feet still wet from the river. "For real, I mean. I know you told Jarrow you weren't."

"Worrying is my way of life. It keeps me alive, and you, too. But we deal with one thing at a time, and right now I'm worried about buying all the things we need. I want to pick up books for the journey, clothes that don't make me look like an idiot, and *shoes,* for heaven's sake. Can't keep going everywhere barefoot." She clambered up the bank to increasingly dryer ground, angling a route across an unkempt playing field. "This way, love. Town's up to the east."

"Oh." Cai poked her side, needling at her ribs. "What about your girlfriend?"

"She isn't my girlfriend. I've only known her two days."

"I think we should buy her a card or something," he said doggedly. "You don't have a lot of friends. It's not smart to let them go so easily."

"Who raised you to be such a cheeky sod?"

"Just saying."

"Sure you are." She ruffled his hair in revenge to wind him up. "Maybe if I see something suitable."

The path evolved into a concrete sidewalk as they followed it into town, buildings springing up like weeds. Innerleithen's high street wasn't much of anything: a church, some stores, a few houses scattered between, and essential things like bigger shops or specialist services. It would do.

She bought shoes in the first place that sold them, ignoring the baffled expressions of the store staff. Good solid boots for that heavy, faux human tread. Just the way she liked them.

Clothes were easy enough. She raided the men's section of a charity shop for black jeans and a black shirt, putting them on in the changing room afterward. She was pleased to be rid of the tartan skirt.

For Cai, she also chose a small backpack, something to store his books and clothes and—now—his signal blocker. When that was done, they bought food. Magazines and sci-fi books for him, thrillers and gory crime for her. Commercial fiction had a kind of sugariness she always found addictive.

"What was that book you picked up?" Cai said. "*Carmilla,* or whatever it was called? It looked interesting."

"Um. It's just an old-fashioned Gothic story." Devon didn't feel like explaining to her son why she'd bought a novel about lesbian vampires. He'd never stop laughing. "You wouldn't like it, I'm sure."

Shopping done, they were making their way home when Devon walked past the Vintage Emporium.

And did a double take. Proudly displayed in the window, behind layers of thick glass and lots of security locks, was a vintage Chanel handbag in black crisscrossed leather with a gold chain strap.

Old-school but timeless, and also devastatingly expensive. Even a fringe social participant like Devon could tell from the make and brand that it was something quality.

She caught Cai by the shoulder. "Hold a sec. I need to buy that purse."

"That one in the window?" He gawked at the sleek black leather in confusion. "Why? You already have a messenger bag."

"Not for me, for Hester. She lost her handbag when we ran from the train, you know. I should get her something." In case it was the last time they saw each other, she added silently.

"Will that make it better?" he said, eyeing the handbag distrustfully.

"It won't make up for upending her life, no," Devon said. "Nothing can."

"Huh? Then why are you doing it?"

"Weren't you the one just saying I should do something nice for her?" she said, with casual lightness.

He scrunched his nose. "It's so *plain* looking."

"Sometimes, the nicest things are," she told him as they stepped inside.

And stepped out again fifteen minutes later, carrying a pinstripe box full of tissue-wrapped handbag.

"Wow!" He was goggling. "A thousand pounds? I don't think you've ever spent that much of your money on *me*!" He pouted. "And you didn't even want to give her a gift five minutes ago! It was *my* idea."

"Oi! Greedy lad! I think I've done my fair share for you, thanks." The purse was indeed a lot of money. Devon couldn't find it in herself to regret the purchase, though. It was only cash, she'd get more. "Besides, I decided you were right. I don't have enough friends to lose."

"I'm always right." He stuck his tongue out, puffed with pride.

———— • ————

They arrived back at Traquair House, both flushed and warm from a day of walking and shopping. Her watch suggested 3 P.M.; only a few hours left till their rendezvous with Mani. And a few hours after that till the knights arrived.

"Can I meet you upstairs in our room?" she said to her son. "I want to go looking for Hester first, if that's okay."

"Have fun talking to your girlfriend," he said, and darted away before she could flick his forehead.

Hester was in the downstairs drawing room, thankfully alone, and facing the window. A small pad of paper rested in her lap on which she sketched a view of Traquair's maze and gardens.

Her black-and-white drawing wasn't fully accurate to the scene outside. With no color to soften its tones, the shadows looked darker, and the highlights brighter. She had carefully depicted the iron gate at the maze's entrance, but omitted its exit; there was no path out of the thorns.

"That's really good," Devon said, edging over. "Are you self-taught?"

"It's *not* good." Hester pressed her pencil point hard into the pad; it broke off, tiny chunk of graphite skittering across paper. "I can only copy, not create. Because I'm not actually creative. I guess you were right about that much." She looked up, eyes red-rimmed. "What do you want?"

"To talk to you," Devon said, clutching the box tighter than necessary. "And although I'm probably the last person you want to see right now, I just wanted to pass along a gift. Before, you know, we run out of time."

A puzzled frown. "A gift for *me*?"

"For the bag you lost." Devon offered up the box in all its tissue-wrapped glory, feeling more embarrassed by the second. "I couldn't replace the gun but I could at least do this much."

Hester stared in bewilderment at the flouncy packaging. "What on earth did you buy? Did you get this from Vintage Emporium? That place is awfully expensive!"

"Never mind where I got it from," Devon said, a rare blush creeping into her face. "Look, I know this is probably the wrong time for this conversation"— Was there ever going to be a *right* time?—"but if you want to come with Cai and me, we'll be at the brewery by seven P.M. If you don't want to come, then please, *please* clear out before eleven. Promise me you won't hang about, aye? The knights mean business."

"I—" Hester began dazedly.

From the hallway came the sudden noise of people chattering; it sounded like Killock, and perhaps some of Hester's other siblings. They both started guiltily.

"Remember, seven P.M., at the brewery," Devon said, retreating to the opposite door. She added over one shoulder, "I do think the drawing is creative, you know. It's your vision. Your spin on it."

Hester stared at her, lips parted.

Devon darted out through a side door just as Killock and a few other men entered, then she headed up to her bedroom where Cai would be waiting. Both of them impatient for darkness to fall.

32

DARK HORSE

PRESENT DAY

Something of vengeance I had tasted for the first time; as aromatic wine
it seemed, on swallowing, warm and racy: its after-flavour, metallic and
corroding, gave me a sensation as if I had been poisoned.

—Charlotte Brontë, *Jane Eyre*

Evening settled over Traquair House like a freshly washed duvet, thick and
damp. Watching the darkness descend, it occurred to Devon that it was this
exact day two years ago when she'd tried to flee Matley.

The situation was different, at least. She actually had a plan this time, and
help. It would go better. Devon pushed aside her worries and cracked open her
bedroom window. She checked the time; 6:45 P.M.

Her son lounged on the window seat, slowly eating one of the *New Scientist*
magazines they'd bought in town. Jarrow's Game Boy lay next to him, inert.

"How does it taste?" she asked, enjoying that this was a question she could
put to him.

"Like stars and thunder," he said, stuffing another page into his mouth.
"Not salty and hot, the way *you know* tastes. I'm so glad I don't have to eat
anyone, ever ever ever again!" An uncertain pause and he added, "That's right,
isn't it? If we leave here, I don't have to, and Killock can't make me?"

"I swear by every computer game ever made, I will never again ask you to
eat someone," Devon told him, and was pleased to see his happy expression.
She meant it, too.

"I'm bringing the Game Boy, right?" Cai moved to perch on the edge of
the bed, legs swinging. "Oh, and my favorite shirt, the one with Doctor Who
on it."

"I'd no more leave your Game Boy behind than leave your fingers and toes
behind," she said. "Absolutely take the shirt, too. Leave nothing good behind."
Her own new clothes looked almost smart: black jeans, black shirt, denim
jacket. The joy of once again having trousers with pockets.

"What have you packed?" he said.

"All I'm taking is money"—she showed him a soft folding wallet full of cash—"and the clothes on my back, and Salem's compass."

"And Redemption."

"And Redemption. Once we collect it up from the brewery." She picked up his backpack, full of other magazines and some clothes, and the signal blocker. "Pop that Game Boy in here. We should get going."

He tossed in the handheld, slinging the backpack on. "Everything always seems to happen at night."

"That's how it is, with princesses. Shit goes down at the witching hour." She slung the bag over one shoulder. "Take my watch. You can be my timekeeper."

"Okay." He slipped the too-large band over one wrist, tightening it carefully.

"Is your signal blocker turned on?"

He nodded, showing her the black plastic box, switch flicked to the right setting for both of them.

"What's wrong?" she said. "You're giving me sad-orphan eyes."

"Nothing. Sort of. Actually, my stomach hurts." He made a face. "I hope we don't get caught and stuff. I hope things don't go wrong."

Devon didn't have an answer for that, so she kissed his forehead and said, "Are you ready?"

Five minutes to seven, and the house had quietened. The drawing room accrued tired folk, chatting lazily and playing card games; outside, nature seemed to have fallen into a lull. The wind had died down, creating a perfect absence of sound. Book eaters walked softly at the worst of times, and the carpets here were thick, so Devon drifted like a fluffy moth. A six-foot-tall, black-clad fluffy moth. Cai, meanwhile, was so light on his feet he seemed almost ethereal.

Hand in hand, they crossed in companionable quietude through the corridors, through the main entrance and the enormous iron-studded door that— mercifully—didn't creak on opening, and out into the night. White flakes drifted from the sky; another light snowfall.

The noise of someone clattering around came through a downstairs window as they crossed the courtyard. She yanked Cai to a standstill, holding him against her. Through the window came the sound of a toilet flushing, and a tap running. Evening trip to the loo, then. A door banged and she breathed a soft sigh. Cai stifled a giggle into his palm.

Up ahead, the brewery loomed silent as they crossed the empty drive on light feet. No sign of anyone else out here. And no sign of Hester, either. Disappointment nettled, subsiding into resignation. What else had she expected?

They'd met two days ago, and completed a single fraught trip together. Hardly the basis for absconding in the night as partners in crime.

All the same, it stung just a little.

"Seven exactly," Cai said softly as they ghosted toward the entrance. "Dev, this is so cool. I feel like a spy!" He pressed a hand to his belly. "But my stomach still hurts."

"We *are* spies, more or less," she said, then tested the handle. The door was unlocked.

They stepped inside.

The brewery did not look quite right. The distilleries and tanks and all the usual gear were there, but one side had been cleared away and laid out with tables, burners, chemistry kits, and a few small vats. Plastic, lidded bottles nestled tight in metal racks, packed with pills. Half-finished Redemption was piled on one of the work surfaces. The sweetish smell of yeast and hops clashed unhappily with the metallic, chemical stench of drug-making. Devon wrinkled her nose, confused by mixed sensations.

Amarinder Patel was seated at a desk in the far corner, casually dressed in winter trousers, shirt, and a puffy jacket.

He rose as she approached, with the slowness of someone who was no longer on friendly terms with their own joints. "Evening, Ms. Fairweather." A suitcase rested on the ground next to him; his glasses lay folded on the table. "Perfectly on time."

"I'm glad to see you," Devon said.

"The feeling is mutual. I'm keen to go."

"Aren't you concerned?" she said, genuinely curious. "I keep wondering when you're going to ask me what will happen to these people after we leave."

"I couldn't care less," the ex-journalist said bluntly. "I lost my career, my family, my whole way of living to spend twenty-two years in lonely anxiety, sometimes being tapped for my blood. Keeping a smile plastered on my face and making myself useful lest I get eaten. I want out." He added, almost thoughtfully, "And I should rather like to publish my book, which Killock would never allow. To hell with him, in any case."

"Fair enough. I won't question that again."

"Much appreciated."

"Do you have the Redemption?" she said.

"Everything bottled and finished is in that suitcase," he said. "The rest we'll have to leave as is."

"Seven ten," said Cai cheerfully.

"Go keep watch," she told him gently, "and there's a lad. We don't want anyone sneaking up on us."

He nodded smartly and zipped over to the window, peering out between the slatted blinds.

Turning back to Mani, Devon picked up the suitcase, put it on the table, and clicked it open. The entire thing was stuffed with pills, carefully packed. Treasure beyond value, for her and Cai. Her hands trembled a little. All these months of strife for this single item of luggage, and the pills it contained.

Devon zipped the case up again. "Looks good," she said. "What about the notes?"

"Two steps ahead of you." He fished out a leather-bound notebook and tossed it over; she caught it reflexively. "Killock's personal business diary. It lists components, quantities, shipments. Has a few notes on production. With time and perseverance, and samples of the drug itself, I'm certain you'd be able to crack the recipe." He smoothed his moustache with an agitated gesture. "Can I safely assume that you have plans in place to prevent Killock coming after us? He'll notice this book is missing by tomorrow, if not tonight."

"Killock is about to have bigger problems," Devon said. "The knights will be here in a few hours. They're likely already in Innerleithen, waiting to descend."

"I see." He blinked slowly and adjusted his glasses. "A dangerous game to be playing, Ms. Fairweather."

"It's not a game," Devon said, "not to me." She tucked the notebook into her messenger bag, with the other important things they owned. "All right, you can come with us, and I will protect and assist you in escaping the country while we travel together. However, once we reach Ireland, any agreement between us is finished. We'll part as allies, and peacefully go our separate ways. Agreed?"

"Suits me. I have no desire to live with 'eaters a moment longer than necessary. Again, no offense."

"Again, none taken," she said dryly.

Cai said suddenly, from his place at the window, "Dev, there are people outside."

"What? Which people?" Devon crossed to the window, peering between the gap of blinds.

Two figures had emerged from the house to stand on the gravel driveway. Their conversation was inaudible from here, but the gestures were exaggerated and angry.

Mani joined her at the window, squinting myopically into the darkness. "Is that—"

"Killock?" she said tersely. "Yes. And the person he's arguing with is Hester."

The disagreement escalated. Echoes of shouting carried across the driveway that even Devon, from this distance and inside the brewery, could catch a hint of.

"What are they doing? Why are they fighting?" Cai whispered.

"Were you expecting her to come?" Mani said. "What about Killock's presence?"

"I don't know," Devon said, "but I don't like this all the same. It could be trouble."

"Maybe we should make our exit, then," Mani said, straightening up and leaning away from the window.

Devon grimaced. Truthfully, it'd be easier and smarter to just depart, in case whatever was happening outside spilled over to them and interfered in the escape. One less person to worry about on the journey that followed.

"Dev?" Cai whispered. "What do we do?"

Except she couldn't just walk off. The idea of leaving her friend behind if there were any chance of traveling together filled Devon with such terrible misery. *You don't have many friends,* Cai had said, and it was true.

On the driveway outside, Killock wheeled away angrily from his sister and stormed off toward the chapel, fists visibly clenched. Hester, meanwhile, remained on the driveway, the cloud of her breath misting in that winter cold.

"I'm going to investigate," Devon said, making her mind up. "Maybe she was planning to join us, and he interrupted her."

"Is that wise?" Mani asked.

"I'd rather know what's happening and be able to deal with it." She turned and proffered the suitcase to Mani. "Take my son, take this Redemption, and exit through the brewery's west-side entrance. Circle round the maze, head north. I'll meet you at the observation tower on the north side of the estate. Won't be even fifteen minutes, I'm sure."

Mani caught her sleeve. "And what if you don't arrive? How long should we wait?"

"She will be there," Cai said.

Devon smiled. "It's all right, love, he's asked a fair question." To Mani, she said, "If I'm not there in fifteen minutes, then get to the rendezvous car. Cai knows where it is." Better if Mani didn't know the car's location, she thought; less chance of him panicking and leaving her son behind.

The ex-journalist nodded. "Understood, Ms. Fairweather."

"Good luck." Cai gave her a quick hug, and she could have kissed him for not arguing. "I'll be safe, don't worry."

"Be careful," Devon said. "All right, shoo, the pair of you."

33

INTO THE LABYRINTH

PRESENT DAY

I call death onto those who don't know a child when they see a child. Men who think they made the world out of clay and turned it into their safe place, men who think a woman wouldn't flip the universe over and flatten them beneath it.

I have enough bullets for all of them.

—Maria Dahvana Headley, *The Mere Wife*

Empty-handed and alone, Devon stepped out of the brewery and shut the door behind her. Snow still littered the gravel driveway. Killock was long gone to his chapel; she chose not to think about what he might be doing there.

Hester remained on the empty driveway, snowflakes settling on the shoulders of her green blouse, flecking her hair. She stood solitary and silent, faced away from the brewery.

Devon allowed herself to walk loudly across the crunching gravel, giving polite warning of her presence. "Hey," she called out, soft but clear.

"Dev!" Hester turned around. She was carrying the Chanel bag, held close to her chest. "I'm glad I caught you. I thought I might be too late."

"Too late? What for?"

"Everything and anything." Hester laughed; it turned into a sob. "You flipped my world inside out and there's no time to think or—" She pulled a handkerchief out of her new purse and dabbed her eyes, blew her nose. "Can we talk? Just for a minute or two?"

Elsewhere, knights were gathering to bear down on Traquair while Salem slept in a manor far away. Cai ran with Amarinder Patel toward a small observation tower and Jarrow waited with his sister in a dark car by a bridge. But here and now, on this sleepy estate beneath a moonless winter sky, she and Hester were the only two people who existed.

"Yes," Devon said, stifling the reflex to hand out another feeble apology. "I'm here, and listening."

"I'm angry at you for all the wrong reasons, and none of the right ones," Hester said, stuffing the handkerchief away. "I had this hope when we met—

ridiculous, I know—that bringing a stranger to this house would change things. That you'd come in like a magic solution and sort my life out. I don't even know what I thought would happen, only that something would." She shook her head. "Instead, you made everything more complicated, and demanded that I make an impossible choice."

"That's what fairy tales do to us," Devon said, rueful. "If we grow up thinking that we're princesses and someone else will rescue us, then we spend our lives waiting for that rescue and never trying to escape ourselves."

"Which is what the Families wanted, I suppose." Hester crossed her arms. "I still feel betrayed by what you did."

"So you should. It *was* a betrayal," she said. "I wish I'd trusted you sooner."

"I wish we both had."

A garbled cry came briefly from the chapel; they both glanced uneasily in that direction, as if expecting Killock to pop up in the window like a jack-in-the-box. But the shutters were drawn, and her brother did not emerge.

"I don't know how I feel about the future," Hester said, twisting away from the chapel again. "But I'm coming with you and Cai, if that offer is still open. For now, at least. Killock won't be pleased, but I can't help that."

"We'd love to have you," Devon said, too quickly by half.

"We?" The raised eyebrow, inquisitive and indignant.

"Me, then. *I* would love to have you with us." Again, that rising blush; a reaction so unlike her. "By the way, speaking of Killock, I saw him here just before I came out—"

Hester's face fell. "Yes, he was going to the chapel. He was—" She stopped.

"For 'communion'?"

"I really wish that he and I hadn't argued. This may be the last time I'll see him. But done is done." She sighed. "Where's Cai?"

Devon was about to answer when her phone buzzed, loud in the relative quiet. She plucked it out reflexively and flipped it open.

Incoming call, from Ramsey.

She stared at the small gray screen, adrenaline skittering through her. He had no reason to get in touch right now, unless something had gone wrong. Or else his plans had changed.

The phone buzzed louder, like an angry electronic insect.

"Aren't you going to answer that?" Hester said, making futile shushing motions at her. "Or turn it off, at least?"

Filled with sudden suspicion, Devon mashed the Reject button and listened, hard, in the silence that followed.

The quiet pace of a sleepy country night. Birds and insects. Winter wind in the trees.

No—not so quiet. In the distance, she could hear engines rumbling, low but distinct, and rapidly growing louder. Like a group of vehicles approaching.

"Shit." She dropped the phone, stomping on it with her heel; plastic and lithium cracked beneath her boots. "We have to go, right now."

"What's wrong?"

The engine rumblings grew louder. Vehicles were definitely approaching, more than one.

"Ramsey is here! Hours early!"

At the far end of the lawns, headlights gleamed as vehicles turned off the main road and on to the edge of Traquair's property. A *lot* of headlights. And here she was, still out in the relative open, still in plain sight.

"Go," Devon said frantically. "Back through the house, that's the fastest route!"

She broke into a sprint, Hester at her side.

Rubber tires burned grass as the knights' motorbikes ate up distance, veering across the green. In Traquair House, more lights were coming on and faces were appearing at windows. Folks inside Traquair were noticing the disturbance. Killock's face appeared at the chapel doorway, alarmed and wide-eyed.

"Where are we going?" Hester said in a hissed whisper.

"Observation tower. Mani and Cai are already there!" Devon crashed through the iron-studded front door and into the entrance hall, slid wildly on the slick tiles, and caught her balance against the rough-hewn walls.

From the front of the house, sounds of honking and engines roaring as the knights pulled up en masse.

"Hes?" A worried-looking Ravenscar man came running in. "What's going on? There are visitors on—"

He cut off into a yell as Devon shoved him aside, veering past the Blue Room toward the kitchen, where she knew there'd be a different exit. She shouldered open the kitchen door and sidestepped another pair of surprised mind eater siblings who were making inktea on the stove.

Devon burst out of the kitchen's back door, arm still linked with Hester's. A series of steps led down to yet more green space, dominated by the overgrown hedge maze. And beyond that, mostly covered from here by trees, the little white observation tower. Hopefully Cai and Mani were already there.

She sprinted down the stairs, Hester at her side. Glad that Cai was safely away from all this. The first scream rang from Traquair House behind them, followed by a gunshot and a crash. More soon followed, the knights' cover broken in a matter of seconds. There would be blood all over those walls in short order, if there wasn't already.

"There's no time for my brothers to run away." Hester sounded faint, looked fainter. "Everyone in that house is going to die and it's my fault for not warning them!"

A crossbow bolt split the air between them, narrowly missing Devon's nose. A lone knight emerged from the same door they'd just used. His crossbow was already reloaded, the beam swinging up and angling for another shot.

Hester pulled a battered revolver from her new handbag, fingers a blur of speed. Ravenscar and knight fired simultaneously. Her bullet blew his neck apart. His bolt skewered her shoulder with a meaty thud.

She staggered back from the force of impact with an un-Hester-like cry, catching herself on the railing. The knight folded to the ground, black blood pouring from his fingers as he tried to stem the bleeding.

Devon sprinted toward the fallen knight and stomped hard on his injured throat. His death scream came out garbled. She snatched up the discarded crossbow with its detachable quiver and turned back.

Hester hadn't moved. She was still clutching the railing, black blood soaking her blouse. Silk fabric pinned to a freckled shoulder.

"Are you okay?" Devon asked, then kicked herself for sounding so inane.

Hester laughed through gritted teeth, her forehead already running with sweat; she must have been in awful pain. "Peachy. Just, lovely." She tried to straighten and swore loudly.

"I'll get us out of here." Devon slid an arm back around her waist, bracing them both. Crossbow hanging off her shoulder by its strap. She started hobbling them down the stairs, as fast as she dared when the steps were so narrow and slick.

Hester laughed with an agonized wheeze. "Can't believe I had to get shot just to get you to touch me!"

"All you ever had to do was ask." Devon was surprised to discover the words came easily enough. "I liked you from the start. If we'd met any other way . . . well, never mind. We didn't."

Hester stared up at her, startled. "Why didn't you say so?"

"Why didn't you?" Devon countered.

Several gunshots echoed from Traquair House; the Ravenscars, fighting back. Followed by a smattering of screams.

"Good, I'm not the only one who's armed," Hester said. "They'll give the knights a proper fight."

Devon quickened her pace, torn between taking the steps four at a time and being careful with her friend's shoulder.

"Not that I'm complaining," she said, pausing to readjust the other woman's weight, "but how'd you get a new gun so quickly?"

"Picked it up from the gun cupboard on my way to see you," Hester said. "Thought I'd need one, if we were leaving."

They reached the foot of the external stairs. The maze lay directly ahead, surrounded by green fields on either side. At the edge of the fields were woods, where Hester's shooting range was located, and beyond *that* was the lone observation tower.

They could take the long route, going around the maze to reach the woods, and then the tower, as Cai and Mani had likely done. But that meant crossing a flat stretch of green lawn that would leave them exposed to anyone with ranged weapons, as the knights carried.

"Hes! Mani! *Anybody!*" Killock Ravenscar staggered out of the house from the same kitchen door they'd just come through, lanky silhouette framed by moonlight. His clothes were a wreck, the long red hair hung free. "Where is everyone?"

The words had barely left his mouth when Ramsey came striding out through the living room's French doors, flanked by two more knights and a trio of snarling dragons.

"Devon!" Ramsey called out, breaking that momentary spell. From his pocket he pulled out his signal transmitter. "Wherever you've hidden your son, you cannot protect him from this!"

He stabbed the button, and despite all her preparation, Devon winced.

Grand, satisfying *nothing*. No screams, no explosion of any kind within earshot. Killock stood momentarily frozen in confusion; he didn't and couldn't understand the layers of this confrontation.

"Good fucking luck with that!" Devon called out, more relieved than she dared show. "You can't touch Cai anymore!"

"I don't need Cai, anyway," Ramsey said, snarling, and pointed at Killock. "I've got *him*. Men, take the Ravenscar!"

"The hells you will!" Killock roared. "Sinners! Enemies! *Knights of Satan!* God be with me!"

The last Ravenscar patriarch charged with red hair streaming, straight at the knights. One man against three. Committed to his belief in self-divinity, even at the last.

Ramsey pulled out a pistol, the same one Hester had lost a day ago. He fired but missed—lacked practice, probably, and the patriarch was a fast-moving target.

Killock laughed wildly, closing the distance between them. He lunged for Ramsey's stolen gun and managed to knock it flying, even as hostile knights surged around him.

Hester made a sound in her throat. "Lock—"

Devon didn't stick around. Melodrama was for heroes, and people who had too much spare time. She picked up a wounded Hester in both arms, taking advantage of Killock's timely distraction, and ran headlong into the maze.

34

THE KNIGHT AND THE DRAGON

PRESENT DAY

*There was a pain now, burning through him. He had won everything, and
lost it all, and he was ashamed of himself to be weeping.*

—Cynthia Voigt, *The Wings of a Falcon*

Traquair's labyrinth had seen better days. The bushes rose seven feet on either
side, the pathways only two feet wide and badly overgrown. Left untended too
long, for too many years.

A couple twists and turns into that dark, prickly mess of a maze and Devon
set down a still-bleeding, still-dazed Hester. "Can you walk?" Her lungs burned
from the effort of sprinting, arms aching from carrying another's weight.

Hester clutched the Chanel bag as she sagged against the foliage. "If I must."
The bolt quivered in her freckled shoulder every time she moved and her blouse
had crusted over with drying black blood. "Oh my God. Killock! He—"

"Died defending his home and his sister," Devon said, as gently as she could
manage while still panting and sweating from her sprint. "Which is better than
continuing as a monster."

"I hope you're right."

"Me too," Devon said, then took hold of the bolt in Hester's shoulder. "I need
to snap this, or you'll catch it badly on something. Are you ready?"

The Ravenscar woman grimaced and made a gesture that Devon took for
acquiescence. She broke the shaft off, as quick as she could make it.

Hester yelped, stifling the cry with her sleeve.

"Done now," Devon said apologetically. She tossed the broken haft aside.

"Can you help me up?"

"Always." Devon assisted her to stand straight and, once Hester was steady,
they set off again, as quickly as the injury would allow.

"That knight," Hester said through teeth gritted from persistent pain. "The
one who called your name. Was he known to you?"

"Ramsey? Aye, he's my brother."

"I thought so. I remember you mentioning that feud in the library, and then
I forgot to ever chase it up."

"Ramsey Fairweather," Devon said, tasting the syllables grimly. "You'd have liked him when we were kids. Him and Killock might have been mates."

Hester's laugh was tortured in every sense. "Does anyone have family that grows up functional? At all, anywhere?"

"In books, sometimes. A few rare cases." Impatient with the winding pathways, Devon muscled through the hedge wall to their right. Thorns caught at their clothes as they struggled to squeeze through the knotty foliage. Branches whipped bare skin and snagged tears in fabric, tangling in hair. They stumbled into a different portion of the maze, both gasping.

In the distance, a faint roar of flames; the house was on fire. Devon could just about glimpse smoke rising from unexpected places in Traquair House. Either the knights were torching the place, or the Ravenscar brothers had enacted some kind of bizarre self-destruct. Both options were equally ridiculous, and equally plausible.

She turned round to say *Not far now* but the words died at the sight of her companion's face. "What's wrong?"

"Please tell me," Hester said raggedly, eyes on the spreading fire, "that I'm doing the right thing. I feel like I've committed the worst crime in the world, and all the reasons I thought could justify it seem so far away right now."

Devon put an arm around her shoulder and kissed her.

Hester tasted the way she smelled: sweet and bitter, vanilla and tobacco, clean skin and a film of cheap lip gloss. Far better than any stuffy old husband. And why not, why shouldn't they have this moment, so perfectly disastrous? The night was looking increasingly uncertain with every passing second. If she did die, it'd be one less regret to take to her grave.

Hester broke away first, hand pressed to her belly and head buried against Devon's shoulder. But she stayed close and didn't pull away.

Devon said, speaking into her hair, "Don't look back, Hes. Never look back. We make our choices and we keep going. Do you hear me?"

"I hear you," Hester said, low.

Another crossbow bolt punched through the foliage, skewing past them and shattering the moment.

"Shit." Devon scooped her up and launched into another stumbling run.

"Devon!" Ramsey shouted from somewhere in the maze behind them. No more singsong nicknames, he was too angry for that. "No bloody chance are you leaving this place alive!"

She didn't answer, too busy seeking ways to put layers of hedge between her and the knights. Branches snapped, feet scuffed. Even book eaters couldn't run silent here.

"I need line of sight, and then I can knock out a couple of them," Hester said against her ear. "How many are following?"

"No idea!" She darted through another archway and down a tunnel of briars that seemed no different than the one she'd just left. She *thought* it was the correct direction.

Hester dug out the revolver. "I think I can see one. I'm going to take a shot."

"Wait!" Devon was conscious of the gun resting on her shoulder, practically next to her ear. "Don't waste bullets—"

"No time to argue!" Hester twisted in Devon's arms, an action that must have cost her in pain, and fired.

The noise thronged inside Devon's skull, accompanied by the pop of her eardrum bursting. She swore and could barely hear herself swearing. All other sounds came back weak and soft, smothered by a ringing echo.

Someone yelled in outrage. Incredibly, Hester's shot had struck a body.

There was no returning shot, either. Ramsey must not have had time to search for the pistol that Killock had punted away. Small mercy, that.

"Stay back!" Hester called out, but she was already slumping. "Or you'll get a bullet between your eyes next time!"

Devon tightened her grip around her friend's huddled body and hustled faster. She caught a glimpse of woodland on the other side of the briars; the land beyond. No time to waste seeking the exit gate. She simply shoved through one final wall of hedge, branches raking her lips and eyes, Hester squashed tight against her chest, and burst out of the sodding labyrinth at last.

The observation tower was fifty meters farther into Traquair's little woods, nestled amid the ancient trees. It was small and made of limestone, encircled by an external spiral walkway. No more than ten or twelve feet high, with a low wall around the platform at the top. It'd been built for stargazing and bird-watching, though it looked like a toy castle for children.

And peering from that toy castle was a tangle-headed boy of five.

"We can't—" Hester began.

"—outrun the knights, I know. We'll have to stop there and fight." She fled through the woodland, arms aching from strain and mouth dry. Her clothes, which had been clean and newish not an hour ago, were near ruined with sweat, rips, and blood, mostly Hester's. The shouts of knights and dragons stuck in the maze receded some as she drew to the tower's base, surging up the spiral walkway with her remaining energy.

"Stay hidden!" Devon called out as she reached the top. "We have company!"

Cai dropped like a rock, instantly obscured by the low walls. "What happened?" he said as they half collapsed onto the platform. "You were *ages* and then we heard gunshots and, Devon, *look,* the house is on fire!"

"Hester, my girl!" Mani exclaimed simultaneously. He was already—very sensibly—crouched low, his arms wrapped tight around the luggage. Sweat plastered his thinning hair.

All of them were framed in a halo of orange light; flames infested Traquair, casting shadows and beams even at this distance. The house must truly have been in terrible shape for the fire to spread so quickly, or else the knights had set it alight in multiple places.

"Me, indeed," Hester answered thickly, as Devon set her down. She leaned against the journalist, clutching reflexively at the Chanel purse. Already, the expensive leather was grass-stained and crumpled.

"Where were you?" Cai dragged a scuffed sleeve across his nose. He'd found a pair of ancient, rusted hedge shears from God-knew-where and was waving them uncertainly. "I was so worried!"

"Told you I'd come back," she said, pleased that he'd thought to arm himself. "Keep down, men are following!"

"They're here," Mani said tightly.

Devon peered over the wall as two dragons emerged from the maze, through the hole she'd created by barreling through the dense shrubbery.

"Where are the knights?" she said. "Why are they on their own?"

"Worry about it later!" Hester levered herself upward, revolver tilting over the edge of the tower barricade.

Devon clapped her hands over Cai's ears. The gun went off twice. Her own ears rang louder than ever. One dragon fell but the second had ducked, crouching just out of sight. Hester fell back against the wall.

Devon let go of Cai and fumbled with the crossbow she'd stolen. "Christ, how do you load this thing?"

"Oh, for heaven's sake! Take my gun, and give that to me," Hester said. "All that time on Family estates and you never went hunting?"

"You're joking, right?"

"I have a weapon, too!" Cai waved his hedge shears. "Let me help!"

"Help by staying put," Mani said, resting a hand on the boy's shoulder. "Don't get in the way or distract your mother."

"Listen to the man, and *don't move.*" Devon snatched up Hester's revolver and fired, right as the second dragon tried to sprint from the hedge to the foot of the observation tower.

The shot went wild and she should have missed, except the dragon dodged sideways again—straight into the path of her misfire. Bullet met head and exploded his skull, patterning the hedge wall in brain matter.

"That," Devon said savagely, "is what luck feels like!" The revolver was out of bullets, there were more knights and dragons coming, and she was trapped in a toy castle with a critically injured friend. But it'd been a banging shot.

"Loaded up." Hester clutched the crossbow; her sleeve was streaked with dark blood. "I could do with a doctor, or something."

"Knights!" Cai shouted. "They've circled round through the woods—"

The dragons had only been a distraction. Knights had taken another route to circle through the trees. Devon spun as Ramsey and Ealand vaulted up and over the tower's railing from the north side.

Hester pulled the trigger of the crossbow. Her shot punched through Ealand's throat and knocked him backward over the wall.

"E!" Ramsey shouted, and then he was firing, too. He'd lost the gun, or maybe spent his bullets on Killock, and had reverted to a crossbow. His bolt skewered Hester's chest, pinning her to the stone like a collector's butterfly.

Hester made a noise like a hooked fish suffocating and Devon, blazing in fury, launched herself with fists flying. Let him see how well he used that stupid crossbow in hand-to-hand. She was vaguely aware of Cai shouting and Mani trying to hold her son back; the rest of her attention was for her brother.

She fell on him like an ocean wave.

Years ago, as young children, she'd fought with her brothers when they disagreed, or sometimes just for fun. A bunch of scrawny children scrapping in the dust.

This was a whole new level. He caught her in a grapple as she charged, and for a moment they teetered at the top of the spiral stairs, strength straining against strength, devastatingly matched.

She sank her bookteeth into his collarbone. The repulsive taste of blood filled her mouth and triggered unwelcome memories. Ramsey hollered and lost his footing. They tumbled backward down the tower steps in a struggling heap of limbs and anger. His fists rained blows on her back and she jammed her knee into every rib.

They bumped down all twenty-odd stone steps and landed on the ground beneath the observation platform, both swearing and sweating and bruised. Devon had lost the grip of her bite at some point, and before she could grab down again, her brother bunched his feet up under her belly and *kicked* her off.

Devon rolled away, retching. Ramsey scrabbled to his feet. The crossbow was hopelessly broken, reduced to little more than a wooden club with jagged edges.

"The hell are you doing?" Dark hair streaked his face, plastered down with sweat. "Because as far as I can tell, you're stabbing every fucking person in the back. Is there anyone or anything you're faithful to?"

Devon pulled herself upright into some semblance of a fighting stance, fists raised and feet apart. "I am perfectly faithful to my family. My *real* family. Not that you would know anything about that!"

"*Our* Family gave you everything. You were a princess!" He snatched up the broken crossbow and swung it at her; she ducked.

"I never asked for that!" She scooped up a broken brick and lugged it at his head; he ducked. "All I ever wanted was the tiny, narrow life you promised me—a happy ending with my children. All anyone ever had to do was return Salem and leave me alone!"

"Admit it, you've lost," he snarled. "I'll kill every single person in this fucking manor!"

"Lost?" Devon almost pitied him. Almost. "The knights are done, the Families have abandoned you, and my son is safe. I've *won,* whatever else you do!"

He halted, broken weapon still in hand, chest heaving with exertion. "No. I can salvage this." A glassy-eyed calm tightened Ramsey's features into a mask of cold fury. "I *will* salvage this!"

"Dev! Catch!" Cai leaned over the wall, throwing something large and shining.

A pair of hedge shears landed in the grass a few feet away. Blades stuck fast into the ground.

Devon dived for them. So did Ramsey, but she was closer. Her fingers closed on the handle and she pulled the tool from the soil, swinging it hard.

Flat blades slammed against skull. Ramsey yelped and went down in a heap, sounding far younger than his thirty-three years. He pressed a palm to his bleeding, swelling temple. Devon lurched atop him, this time angling the shears point-first in a stab toward his throat.

She was strong but he was quick. Up came the broken crossbow, the blow landing hard against her eye socket.

Agony radiated through her head, the surrounding skin already swelling shut. Somehow she was laughing and couldn't stop because there was a wild hysteria in them rolling around on the grass, each trying to stake the other, like a vampire film gone awry.

Ramsey didn't find it funny. He wrenched the garden shears from her weakened grip, whirled them round, and stabbed upward. Devon flung herself backward and away. Instantly he was up on his knees, forehead bleeding. This time it was him atop her with all his weight, as he bore down with the blades against her sternum.

Barely in time, she caught his wrists. He pressed down, weighty, ridiculously strong, and she strained to hold the deadly edge away from her chest.

Blood ran in a trickle from his forehead, dripped off his chin to her cheek. "You won't leave alive!"

In the corner of her one good eye, she caught a glimpse of movement as Cai crept down the spiral stairs. Sneaking up on them with his tongue flicking in warning.

Flicking in preparation to feed.

Even in the heat of her losing battle against Ramsey, she had to dissuade her son from doing the one thing that would destroy him. But if she called out, Ramsey would realize something was wrong, and turn on Cai; that couldn't be allowed to happen either.

Arms shaking with the strain of keeping her brother's weapon at bay, Devon said through gritted teeth, "Are you . . . a good . . . person? Are you . . . kind?"

In the gathering gloom Cai shook his head, and her heart sank at the sight. His choice. Not hers.

"The fuck are you on about?" Ramsey's weight pressed the metal point down and down, until it embedded in her skin. "Crazy sodding—"

Cai *sprang.*

Devon saw him; Ramsey didn't. Her son landed atop Ramsey's back, scrabbling for the older man's ear. His presence added more weight and Devon hissed as the shears veered sideways, slicing down across her chest and flaying the skin open.

Ramsey let go to twist around, trying to get his hands on Cai's throat.

Her child. In danger. Devon wrenched the shears from her ribs and lashed out.

She struck flesh. Tempered metal parted the muscle tissue of his upper leg. Ramsey howled. Inky blood soiled the muddy earth.

And Cai kissed him. Lips to ear, proboscis unfurling. Ramsey gasped, hands gripping the boy's shoulders with a strength that rapidly dwindled. He struggled to stand but the leg Devon had stabbed gave way, and he tipped forward.

Cai clung to his uncle's back, like a small cursed monkey. Ramsey shrieked with a terror that astonished her, his limbs jerking weakly as he tried to crawl away in panic.

Devon stared.

She'd hardly ever watched Cai feed, choosing instead the cowardice of hiding away while he feasted on his prey. He was used to this struggle, the movement of his victims. He'd learned to make himself small and mobile, folding around them like a humanoid leech.

Ramsey locked gazes with her. His eyes were wide with horror. She could *see* that very moment—as she'd once seen with Matley, long ago—when the knowingness of him became unknowing, when mind became merely brain.

Cogito, ergo sum. Ramsey Fairweather-Knight collapsed, no longer a man and merely an empty vessel.

The brother she'd grown up with was gone.

Devon fainted.

35

NO MORE FAIRY TALES

PRESENT DAY

Some day you will be old enough to start reading fairy tales again.
—C. S. Lewis, note to his goddaughter

She dreamed of Hell, as she had been in the habit of doing for many years.

In her dream she was a lone wolf lost in a labyrinth filled with the bodies of the people she'd killed. The brambles and briars rose in thick, prickly walls, heavy with fetid leaves and braced by toothy roots. Her weapons lay broken, her body ached with injuries, and the princess she'd tried to protect was dying in a white stone tower, slain by dark knights.

A drop of wetness stung her face. Then another, and another. Devon blinked. Not tears, only freezing December sleet. This wasn't a dream. This was reality and she was awake.

Painfully, she sat up.

The hedge shears had left a seven-inch slice down her ribs. Blood loss was making her light-headed again, and disoriented. Black streaks stained her already-filthy shirt, running in rivulets to mix with rain and dirt into a hideous, iron-scented mud.

She turned her head. Nearby, Ramsey sprawled in the grass. Dying or dead, not yet crumbled to paper.

Her son, meanwhile, lay snuggled against the man's inert form, drowsy and sedate despite the rain.

"Cai!" She crawled over and shook his shoulder. The memory of how overloaded he'd been the last time he'd eaten a book eater was gnawing at her, worse than any of her injuries. "Are you okay? Do you need anything, do you—"

He opened his eyes. "Devon the Destroyer," he slurred, tongue lolling awkwardly from his mouth. "You are . . . phenomenal, in your way."

Relief warred with abhorrence, and she laughed through her tears. She had succeeded wildly tonight, and still managed to fail her son in the final test. Because despite her promises and her murders and her fanatical commitment to protect him from the world, she hadn't been able to protect him from his own choices, his own crimes that were his to commit.

The sins he chose to bear, for love of her.

Love was sometimes a terrible thing, and he had discovered that just as she had. No words left so she opened her arms, terrified of his rejection but unsure what else to offer or do. He was still her son—wasn't he? She didn't know if that still meant anything or not.

Cai crawled into her embrace, folding his scrawny frame against her battered flesh and burying his face in her ruined shirt. She hugged him close.

Someday, Devon thought, her promises would have worth. Someday, she would have enough strength to *force* the world into the way it needed to be. She would be good, and so would Cai. Somehow, in a place far from here.

"Never again. Please. Never do it to yourself again. Not once we get free." Devon breathed him in. At least his scent was his own, unchanged from birth and unchanged despite the myriad souls inhabiting his mind.

"Okay," he said, then released her suddenly to look up with a worried expression. "Dev, what about Hester? She's very hurt. We've forgotten about her."

Guilt, so much guilt. "I haven't forgotten. But I had to check on you first." Devon peeled off her damp shirt and wrapped it tightly around her midriff. She wasn't sure how to compress a slice across the ribs, it wasn't like a limb where you could tie a tourniquet. "Sit here. I'll go have a look, if you're all right."

"I'm . . . all right," he said. "I'll be reet, Dev."

She nodded and wiped her eyes, a futile gesture in the increasingly heavy sleet, since her face was soon wet again. He wasn't sick, at least. Confused, certainly. Overloaded, probably. But not screaming, in pain, or at risk of stroke.

Ribs bound, tears all wrung out, she climbed agonizingly up the tower steps where only ten minutes ago she and Ramsey had tumbled down in a murderous fury. Her brother; Christ. No, don't think of him. Hester first.

Devon turned the final step, reaching the observation platform.

Alone on the platform, Mani crouched over Hester, who was still curled over. One crossbow bolt in her right shoulder, and a second protruding from just below the ribs. Black blood spattered the walls in Rorschach patterns.

Not good, Devon thought, nauseated with panic. A limb was one thing, but there were no good organs to hit in the torso. Why hadn't she ever eaten a first aid manual, all these years? Stupid oversight.

"She's fine," Mani said, shaken. "She's . . . Good God, what a night!"

Devon said, confused, "She is?"

"For a given value . . . of fine." Hester unfolded with a gasp. "I'll live. I think."

"How are you alive?" Devon said, dropping to her knees. More from tiredness than anything else. "That bolt should have . . ." She trailed off.

Ramsey's bolt had struck the black Chanel bag. A good half inch of quality leather had skewed the shot sideways. Little more than a shallow cut and a bad bruise along Hester's midriff, though that hadn't been possible to see until now.

"You," Devon said, awestruck, "are very lucky. I guess it's true that you get what you pay for with purses."

"Luck? I pulled it in front of me . . . perfect timing. Got to . . . make your own luck!"

"Clever girl," Devon said, grinning from relief, and scooped her up again. For the third time that night. "Hang in there, Hes. The nightmare is almost over." Surely that was true. This couldn't go on forever; nothing did.

"Yeah? Are you kidnapping me?"

"Nah. I'm rescuing you, princess."

"Much appreciated," Hester murmured. When Devon next looked down, the other woman had passed out.

She picked her way down the stairs, careful of the steps slick with sleet and her precious burden and her own spinning head that made her dizzy. Mani followed, slow and huffing, but uninjured. The suitcase full of Redemption thumped on every step, pills rattling in bottles.

Everything hurt, but Devon was used to that. Hurting meant you were still alive, at least for now. Driving sleet soaked her to the skin. Maybe it would put out that fire.

She arrived to find that Ramsey had quietly expired in the interim, his body only a sodden pile of pages in a ruined suit. She felt relieved not to have seen that transformation. As if she'd preserved some tiny, final scrap of dignity between them.

"My men will be after you," Cai said, standing up at her approach. "I brought every remaining knight and dragon in the house to clear out the Ravenscars, and at least some of them will have survived. Even with the fierce resistance we encountered." He paused, giving her an up-and-down critical look. "You don't know what you've done, Dev. When the Families find out about this, they might decide you're a threat after all."

He did not sound like her son and kept switching into what she thought of as Ramsey's voice. The thought chilled her.

"Who are you?" she said. "Am I still calling you Cai? Are you Ramsey, the vicar, the lawyer, the electrician? Some kind of collective?"

"There's no difference," he said serenely. "I am them, and they, me. Killock was right, in his way."

"Jesus," she groaned.

"Nah, I'm no god. I'm not omniscient." Cai tilted his head and Devon could have sworn, for a moment, that it was her brother's expression on his face. "I *can* tell you that it wasn't your fault, though. One small miracle."

"Um." She was still processing his change in demeanor. "What am I being absolved of, exactly?"

"No absolution," Cai said. "I can't take away your sins. Just wanted to explain that it wasn't your fault Ramsey got taken away. That was the adults. You and he did nothing wrong and Ramsey knew that, deep down. But he couldn't acknowledge it." He paused, considering. "Sometimes, when people hurt us, we can't be angry at them even when we should be. Sometimes, the scale of what's been done to us is so big and painful that acknowledging it is too overwhelming. There's nothing you can do about that kind of pain except to ignore it, shut it away. Or shovel it sideways onto someone else, like he did to you."

Devon blinked at him, dumbfounded.

"Harm was done to Ramsey," Cai said. "Things he never could admit to or think about, even in his own mind. Again, that wasn't your fault. None of it was." He looked embarrassed and uncertain, suddenly childish when before he'd seemed adult. "Anyway, I thought you should know."

"Thanks, I think," she said, a little doubtfully. And then, because she had nothing to lose for her honesty, "A part of me will miss him."

Cai nodded. "He knows. He's glad."

Maybe, Devon thought, that was the best anybody could hope for in life: to be missed when gone, however one had lived.

They walked through Traquair's ancient woodland where bears had once roamed, Devon limping as she carried an unconscious Hester, her own wounds still seeping blood through the ruin of her shirt. Cai walked at her side, helping a thoroughly silent Amarinder Patel pull their luggage full of Redemption.

In the distance, the song of police sirens rose and fell like a banshee wail. Someone must have finally noticed that raging fire, and gotten official organizations involved. The Families would hate that.

"Was it worth it?" Cai said, as they approached the river at last—and, a little farther along, the desolate bridge. "The death, the destruction, the sacrifice of your brother, and Hester's brother? Just for us to get away?"

Devon gazed down at her son, who looked like her and who now spoke with her brother's inflection. It was as if she looked upon the ghost of Ramsey's childhood, and the sight filled her with disquiet.

"It's not a question of worth, or cost," she said. The same answer she kept giving, because any alternative response had become unthinkable. "I have always done the best that I can for the people that I loved. There's nothing else that anyone can do."

He tugged at his lip. "What about Salem?"

What about Salem. A hell of a question. If Luton had been true to his word, then somewhere down to the south was a brokenhearted ten-year-old girl who would be seething from Devon's betrayal, hurt that her mother hadn't loved her enough to show up for her tenth birthday. And if Luton had lied, had never told Salem anything about her mother, then somewhere down to the south was a ten-year-old girl who barely knew Devon existed, and probably did not want to see her at all.

No good endings for that story, however she spun the yarn.

Devon said, at last, "I do think about Salem, and I haven't forgotten her. When you're safe and far from here, then I'll go back for your sister."

Every step she took led her farther and farther from her daughter, onward toward Ireland and freedom. Walking away was consigning Salem to the misery of book eater marriages, but rescuing Salem would require a far bolder effort than all she had enacted so far to liberate Cai.

Those were journeys and quests for another day, and all she had energy for right then was simply to put one foot in front of the other.

"I'll come with you, when you go back for Salem," he said. "Family should stay together."

"Sure, love." She was too tired to argue, and there would be time later for discussions.

They reached part of the main road. At long last. On the other side near the base of the bridge, a dark car was parked up on the hard shoulder. The headlights shone like Nycteris's lamp in a desolate cave, like a firefly leading the way to a vast garden: tiny brightness against the encroaching dark.

"There they are!" Cai flashed her a grin and set off running toward the car where Jarrow and Victoria waited—running toward a life neither of them could yet imagine, humming the theme song from *Mario*.

ACKNOWLEDGMENTS

———◦———

There would be no book eater novel without the tireless labor of the following champions, to whom I am ferociously grateful:

TEAM TOR
- Lindsey Hall, editor extraordinaire who whipped this story into a lean, mean, fighting machine
- Rachel Bass, the brilliant and ever-prompt assistant editor
- Deadly publicity ninjas Sarah Reidy and Giselle Gonzalez, working in tandem
- Renata Sweeney, marketing genius and Rachel Taylor, savvy social media manager
- Jamie Stafford-Hill, cover designer, who chopped up a book he owned just to make a cover mock-up
- Kaitlin Severini, for patiently enduring my inconsistent use of "bookeater" and "book eater"
- Rafal Gibek and Dakota Griffin, who run a tight ship on an even tighter schedule

(HARPER) VOYAGER VIGILANTES
- Vicky Leech, my passionate UK editor who floored me (in the best way!) with her vision for *The Book Eaters*
- Robyn Watts, the production controller whose relentless energy has shepherded this book through production
- Jaime Witcomb, a publicity powerhouse whose ways are mysterious and magical to me
- Fleur Clarke, who spearheaded marketing with deft precision

BOOKENDS BATTALION
- Naomi Davis, rock star literary agent and the greatest champion I could ever have for my work. They always kept the faith even when I'd genuinely lost it.
- Jessica Faust and the rest of the folks at BookEnds, who have lent their advice and expertise, particularly in the minefield of contracts and foreign rights

- The countless foreign agents, literary scouts, foreign acquiring editors, and foreign language test-readers who worked so incredibly hard to get this book sold and translated in other countries, even though they do not know me and we have never met. Truly, it takes an army to bring a book to life.

HEARTY HEROES

- Lee Muncaster, my awesomely geeky, trombone-wielding boyfriend, who met me at the lowest point in my life and didn't hold it against me, who took my writing seriously and insisted on calling it "work" even when I hadn't yet made a dime or sold anything, and who so often gave me coffee and hugs as I staggered towards the finish line of this manuscript. I could not ask for a more supportive partner.
- Su Blackwell, my marvelously talented cover artist. I am so honored to have her lovely creations on the front of this book.
- My real life friends who have all contributed words of wisdom or support at crucial moments (or childcare!). In alphabetical order; Allison Hargreaves, Eve Skelton, Laura Musgrove, Liska Piotrowska, Michelle White, and Simon Webb.

FAMILY FERALS

- My children, C and V, without whom this book would never have happened. Parenting has changed my whole approach to writing and pushed me to make a success of it for their sakes.
- My mother, who is also mentioned in the dedication and is a model of human resilience, and my father, who indoctrinated me into the Way of Science Fiction from a young age
- Lee's brilliant and quirky family—especially Hannah and Charlotte, his utterly fabulous daughters—who have been such a source of support and joy
- Gareth, for all his support and advice through the years

WRITING WARRIORS

- Essa Hansen, my first critique partner and one of the best humans I've ever known, from whom I've learned so much and with whom I've shared so much
- Darby Harn, for our 100,000 words of emails ruminating on life, the universe, and everything as we tackled the madness of writing
- Ravaena Hart, my oldest friend (it's okay, we're not old ladies yet) and frequent early reader
- Alan Deer, a better friend than I deserve and also a great early reader

- Gregory Janks, who perfectly balances brutal critique with endless optimism
- The whole gang at Writer Alliance, whom I adore and am cheering for! Special mention to Al Hess, for his fantastic family heraldry artwork and general friendship, and PK Torrens, who has been a determined supporter from afar.
- The wonderful Novelist gang at Leeds Writers Circle who read early bits of this novel, back when it was called *Paperflesh*. In alphabetical order by first name: Andrew Davies, Andy Armitage, David Cundall, Edward Easton, Kali Richmond, Peter J. Marcroft, Roz Kendall, and Sandy Hogarth.
- My super brilliant beta readers!! Also in alphabetical order: Amanda Steiger, Anne Perez, Eric Bourland, Jerry Lizaire, Nisha Tuli, and Wayne Santos. Thank you all so much.

And, of course, a final shout-out to my weird and wonderful friend, John O'Toole, whose name opened this book and whose name shall now conclude it.